Emma Stirling was born in Dalkeith, Scotland, and in her early childhood lived in India. With her husband and two young children, she went to live in what was then Southern Rhodesia and Nyasaland, where another two daughters were born. She has since returned to the United Kingdom and now lives in London. She started writing in 1974 and has had a number of romantic novels published under a pseudonym. She is also the author of *A Field of Bright Poppies*. Besides writing full time, she is kept busy with her family and three grandchildren.

The Cockleshell Girl

Emma Stirling

KNIGHT

First published in 1991
by HEADLINE BOOK PUBLISHING PLC

First published in paperback in 1991
by HEADLINE BOOK PUBLISHING PLC

This edition published 1999 by
Knight an imprint of Brockhampton Press

10 9 8 7 6 5 4 3 2 1

ISBN 184186 0271

Typeset in 10/12½ pt Times
by Colset Private Limited, Singapore

Printed and bound in Great Britain by
Mackays of Chatham PLC, Chatham, Kent

Brockhampton Press
20 Bloomsbury Street
London
WC1B 3QA

This is for my children
and their children.

Chapter One

Early one morning he saw her. She came riding across the sands, and although it was his first sight of her, it was like an exquisite photograph printed on his memory. The donkey on which she rode trod daintily, leaving small round footprints in the sand. Her hair, jet black, unrestrained, fell in a vibrant mass of thick curls and waves to a point halfway down her back. Her blouse was of thin cotton, loose and full, but still he could see the proud thrust of her breasts against the white stuff. The faded rose colour of the wide skirt ended halfway down her calves so that the slender white ankles and bare feet were clearly visible.

Over one arm she held a round wicker basket into which was heaped fresh shellfish. Cockles, he guessed, purchased only minutes ago from the fishermen he could hear further along the beach. Tied to her skirt, jangling with each step the little donkey took, was the tin pint pot with which she would measure her sales. The slim arm that held the basket against her hip had a fine sprinkling of freckles although there were none on her legs, his keen eye saw. Her toes were neat and straight, so white they looked as though they had been carved from alabaster.

The girl's free hand guided the donkey with gentle

sureness across the sandy ridges left by an out-going tide. He ached to paint her; to reach for a brand new canvas and palette and begin mixing paints into those mystical colours of which he alone knew the secret.

He would use ebony and carnation and jasper and yellow ochre. Peach and magenta and azure, with magnolia white for that incredible skin.

His artist's eye feasted on her, like a man who had been too long without water in the desert and suddenly finds it in a clear, sparkling pool. His eyes drank their fill of her slenderness and grace.

Finally, as though leaving the best to the last, they lifted to her face. There was a hint of wild rose colour on the high cheekbones, a deeper colour on the wide sensual mouth. Her eyes were dark as spring violets, fringed by a curtain of sooty eyelashes. The eyebrows swept like gulls' wings across the high forehead.

He sighed, feeling suddenly a hundred years old. Women he had painted in plenty, particularly ballerinas and circus bare-back riders in their pink tights and gauzy skirts. These canvasses had all been full of action, and had brought him great acclaim. Titled ladies too had sat for him, posing regally in ballrooms, tiaras glittering under crystal chandeliers. Some not quite so stiff, clad in soft muslins and thin silks in a rose garden or playing with a toy spaniel in a buttercup-filled meadow. In the summer of 1912 it was considered the done thing to be painted by Marcus Dillon.

Yet this girl, ingenuous, working-class, probably with an accent so rough it would sound like a saw grating on wood, this girl intrigued him.

He watched as in response to a soft clicking of her

tongue, a slight pressure of her bare foot on its soft brown side, the donkey came slowly between the sand-hills and stepped daintily on to the cobbled quay. The artist rose to his feet, watching beast and rider draw abreast. Then he stepped forward, one hand reaching for the bridle. The donkey faltered and came to a halt.

For a long silent moment he stood and gazed into the girl's face, noting the guarded, suspicious expression that crossed her features. He watched the violet eyes flicker nervously, the colour rise in her cheeks at his close scrutiny.

'I wasn't wrong,' he said casually. 'Close to, you are even more captivating.'

Alys Hughes looked askance at him. No customer, this! A gentleman, she thought, although from his care-less way of dressing, it was difficult to be sure. Her lips firmed into a hard, straight line. She'd had to battle with men like this since she was fourteen. Just because he spoke with a posh English accent, no doubt he felt he had every right to proposition her in broad daylight, even with the other fisherwomen looking on. For she was only too aware of the speculative glances thrown her way by the other street hawkers passing by.

Instinctively her hands tugged at the reins, causing the little donkey to skitter nervously on the smooth cobbles. To her surprise, the man murmured soft, soothing sounds, calming the animal.

'I think, if we're going to talk,' he said, 'you'd better dismount. We can sit over there,' nodding towards the ancient sea wall, green with moss. He smiled. 'Away from the inquisitive ears of your compatriots.'

'What makes you think I'm going to sit anywhere with

3

you?' Alys spoke stiffly, although in fact she was dying of curiosity. Men didn't usually choose a time or place as public as this to accost her. She regarded him quite openly, as interested in him as he was in her.

He was tall, taller than most men she knew, and even from her perch on the back of the donkey Alys had to tilt her head back to look past his broad chest to his face. His hair, made unruly by the stiff sea breeze, was the colour of chestnuts, his eyes a startling blue. A thin scar started in the middle of his right cheek and cut into the darkness of his beard.

She had to admit he was handsome, and appeared to be young though his beard made him look older. She felt herself staring and was forced to steady her voice as she said, 'I've a living to make, even if you haven't.' She tilted the basket to indicate the small shellfish, which she still had to pluck from their shells and soak in salt and vinegar. 'So if you'll please step aside . . . ?'

Again she made to urge the donkey forward, and again he stopped her. 'I appreciate that. But a few minutes of your time. Aren't you at all curious as to what I might be offering?'

Alys's small chin lifted in contempt. 'Not in the least. Now will you please let go of my donkey?'

'Not until you've heard me out. You don't even know what I'm going to ask you. A few extra shillings in your pocket for an hour or two of your time sounds reasonable enough to me. And you wouldn't even have to remove any of your clothing, just your shoes and stockings, exactly as you are now.'

He regarded her with amusement, knowing exactly what she was thinking, knowing he shouldn't tease

4

but unable to help himself. She looked so deliciously righteous! Alys flushed bright scarlet, such indignation taking hold of her it was a wonder she didn't hit him over the head with her basket. When she spoke, she actually stuttered. 'I think you'd better repeat that. I can't have heard you right.'

He sighed. 'I'm losing patience, girl. Will you stop behaving as though I've just threatened your maidenly virtue, and get down from that ridiculous animal so that we may talk?' Again the sigh. 'I'm not asking for your undying devotion, merely a few hours of your time.'

'And you can go on asking, for it'll get you nowhere!'

He answered easily, as though recognising the fact that he'd lost the battle but didn't really care, 'Oh, well, no doubt there are other girls who'd be willing to earn a pretty penny for doing nothing.'

He released the bridle and stepped away, giving her a mocking bow. He'd spoken of other girls, but in truth, among the scattering of women standing watching, there wasn't one who would be worth the effort. He was sorry if she'd misunderstood him, as she obviously had, but he wasn't one to waste time with arduous explanations, especially not to an ignorant street hawker who would probably spend the money she earned on gin or that strong ale they served in the taverns. He wasn't a man who gave up easily and this girl would find she had met her match in Marcus Dillon.

He turned once before he strode away, regarding her with narrowed eyes. Whys and wherefores had never worried him. If he saw something he wanted, he went out and got it. And this girl's face he wanted! That rose-flushed skin and wide pansy eyes gazing out from a canvas, captured for all time . . .

Alys watched suspiciously as he approached the groups of other women by the quayside. She shrugged, urging her mount forward, clutching the basket more securely to her hip. Many of the street hawkers used a clean white folded cloth as a pad for their heads on which to balance their baskets of fish. Others used handcarts, heavy and cumbersome. Alys scorned both methods, preferring her own unique way of selling cockles.

She could hear the high-pitched laughter of the other women following her. It sounded as though they were enjoying a joke. Alys hoped it wasn't at her expense. It was too lovely a morning to be bothering her head about a group of girls too silly for their own good, or a strange man who appeared from nowhere with offers that would have had her stepfather reaching for his belt. Ought to have threatened him with the police, so she ought!

She sighed for no reason that she could think of and urged the donkey on its way. Craven Bay in the spring was a paradise of daffodils that lay like a living carpet in sheltered hollows of the valley. Deep in the shadows where a small lake reflected the blue of the sky, thick-coated sheep grazed, moving restlessly from patch to patch of succulent grass. The patches of heather were still brown, not yet in blossom, the shadows of the clouds resting lazily on the countryside.

There was nowhere like the long stretches of golden sand merging into a turquoise sea and creamy surf. The headlands shimmered in a heat haze, their slopes veiled by a hundred shades of green. The very sight of all this beauty caught at her throat.

Yet she couldn't forget the other side of this small Welsh town, the gaunt features of industry that lay behind all that beauty; tall smoking chimneys and heaps of slag from the mines, ugly winding gear that stood at odds with the rest of the land. But without the mines Craven Bay would be a poor place for they gave work to the majority of men who lived here, and fortunes to the lucky few.

She watched a flock of seagulls as they squabbled over something washed up by the tide. She hoped sales this morning would be good so that she could finish early. She had promised Mary she would walk up to the big house and have a talk. Mary O'Malley was her best friend and they planned to go to the dance held in the church hall this coming Saturday.

Her first meeting with the little Irish girl had been the Sunday when they made their first Holy Communion. It was only as she grew older that Alys was able to appreciate how her mother must have scrimped and saved to provide her with the dress and veil all the little girls were expected to wear. Alys had gloried in the smooth, chill feel of the white silk against her legs, her hands fussing with the square of fine veiling Mam had produced from goodness knows where. The orange blossom wreath – made from wax and slightly yellow with age, picked up for a penny from old Jakob's pawn shop – perched slightly askew atop her mass of curls. She remembered how Mam had laughed, saying she looked like a slightly inebriated fairy. Alys didn't know what 'inebriated' meant but hoped it was something complimentary.

She thought she looked very nice. Mary O'Malley

7

looked even nicer, like one of the blessed saints on a pedestal, she thought, as the girls were informed in a low whisper by Sister Philomena that they were to proceed to the altar rail in twos.

'Like going into the ark!' whispered the pretty blonde girl who moved to stand beside her. Alys giggled and then clapped a hand over her mouth as she caught Sister Philomena's stern gaze.

After Communion the children gathered in the back garden of the priest's house and were served breakfast of boiled eggs and hot cross buns, for Easter was upon them. The eggs had been painted with water colours; a clear pale blue that looked so pretty Alys was loath to crack hers.

Watching her, Mary suddenly leaned over and gave the egg a sharp tap with the back of her teaspoon, shocking Alys to the core by saying, 'Jaysus, don't be scared! The thing'll not bite you.'

To the tap-tapping of the donkey's hooves, she let her thoughts drift through a shoal of memories rising inside her. She was back once again in the neat little fisherman's cottage along by the headlands. Built of sturdy Welsh stone to withstand the gales that battered that part of the coast, it had been in the Hughes family for generations, passing from father to son. She recalled the tempestuous night when word came that her father's fishing boat had gone down with all hands. The lifeboat had put to sea in a brave attempt by her father's friends who manned it. She remembered running after Mam to the beach, the wind shrieking in her ears, women screaming and calling to each other. Mam, with her shawl and a dark woollen scarf wrapped tightly about her head, became suddenly aware of the small girl running behind her. She'd turned to shout: 'Go home, Alys! This is no place for you, you'll catch your death of cold.'

Someone had lit a fire of driftwood on the sands and it cast shadows that danced crazily in the thick darkness, lighting up the cluster of women huddled there, waiting for news. The following day, when word finally came of bodies washed up on far beaches, Alys heard Mam's first despairing cry. Startled by the anguish in her mother's face, she flew to her, arms clutching as though to hold her where she would be forever safe. Alys cowered against Mam's skirts, one eye glaring at the bearer of the dreadful news.

At first the storm had reminded her of Mam's stories of her first meeting with Dad. The fishing trawler on which Jon Hughes worked had been blown off course in St George's Channel and had limped into Liverpool harbour, necessitating a forced stay in dry dock while repairs were carried out. Jon had got a room in the Sailor's Home on the docks, and on his first free night attended a dance in a local hall.

It was smoky and noisy and not really to his liking. He was on the point of leaving to go to a pub when he came face to face with the most wonderful creature he had ever seen. She was small and dainty, with the look of a timid fawn. She stood in a corner with her friend, a cloud of midnight hair framing her perfect face. Jon Hughes asked for a dance and took the delicate girl in his arms, amazed at her warm softness, the fresh scent of flowers emanating from her. From that moment he was lost. They arranged to meet again after the dance. She laughed at his Welsh accent, saying it was funny, and he joked about her Liverpool one. 'A scouse accent,' he said teasingly. 'Can't think of anything funnier than that.'

'Does everyone talk like you where you come from?' she wanted to know.

He straightened his shoulders. 'You wait till you hear the *real* Welsh tongue,' he swaggered. 'Best this side of heaven.'

She told him of her grandparents and their flight from the potato famine in Ireland many years ago. 'They came as ballast in a ship to Liverpool and just stayed here. They had no money, see, so weren't able to travel on. Besides, hundreds of their countrymen were settling all around them, and I suppose that helped in the beginning when they felt lost and bewildered. And the priests urged us to stay and build up a community.'

He gave her a doubtful glance. 'Catholic then, are you?'

Glynis nodded and he went on, 'Your name's not Irish.'

'Well, I *was* born here so I suppose me mam and dad thought that only right and proper.' She looked at him under her eyelashes. 'Don't you like it, then?'

'I think it's a lovely name that goes with a lovely lass,' he said softly. 'Will you marry me, sweet Glynis?'

She didn't even blink. 'What about our religions? Me mam'd skin me alive if she thought I wanted to marry a – what is it you are?'

'A nonconformist,' he said gruffly, and shrugged. 'It doesn't matter. Nothing matters as long as I can be with you. I'd never interfere in what you wanted to do or how you brought the children up. So please say yes, Glynis, and put a poor man out of his misery.'

They were married by special licence in the local

Catholic church, a fact that had many a shrewd glance turned her way, examining the slight figure in its white satin gown and veil. Mam took to her bed immediately after the young couple left for Jon's home in Craven Bay, declaring her daughter was lost to the faith forever.

A storm had brought them together, and now fate had turned full circle.

Sympathy for Glynis Hughes was strong in the small town where many families had suffered the loss of a breadwinner in similar circumstances. But it didn't soften the hearts of the fishing company that owned the row of cottages and although they gave Glynis time to find other accommodation, the struggle was long and hard.

For Glynis, going straight from her father's home to her husband's, there had always been a man to take care of the everyday responsibilities of life. Now she was alone and the home she had come to as a bride had been taken from her. She felt lost and on the verge of despair, conscious even more of how her grandparents must have felt on coming to this country. Her only mainstay was her daughter. Even at the tender age of twelve, Alys was a blessing, seeming to grow up overnight from a funny, shy little girl into a calm and dignified young person, keenly aware of her daughterly duties.

Men had eyed the comely face and figure of Glynis Hughes with interest, attracted by her dignified manner and pale beauty. When a year after Jon's death, Dan Radloff came into their lives, offering a home and protection, Alys was resentful. Dan was a big man, well over six feet tall, with thick black hair and good white teeth that seemed forever displayed in a smile. Standing in the kitchen of their small cottage, his powerful presence seemed to take up every inch of space.

His voice was loud and autocratic, and he had the kind of animal magnetism that appeals to certain women. Alys couldn't think what her mother saw in him. Chided by the priest that the Dear Lord works in mysterious ways and that she was to learn to accept the man as her stepfather and be glad that someone had lightened the burden from the young widow's shoulders, Alys still found it difficult to accept.

'Your mother,' the old priest had added, 'is a comely and warm-hearted woman, and is entitled to another chance in life. In this sad world every woman needs a man's protection. In a year or two, when you have flown the nest, she would be all alone should she not marry now. Would you, as her child, be happy with that thought?'

Alys knew she wouldn't. But marriage to Dan Radloff!

Brought up to respect the church's guidance, Alys pretended a happiness she did not feel. While talking to her one day as though Alys was grown up and so able to understand, Mam admitted how much she enjoyed Dan's company. She confessed she hadn't realised the extent of her own loneliness until she had walked down the street on his arm. 'Loneliness is a curse, my love,' she said, gazing into her daughter's wide, spring violet eyes, 'I pray you never have to experience it as I have.'

Within a year, Mam had died, giving birth to a stillborn son. Even though it had seemed the end of the world to the stricken girl, coming so soon, barely a couple of years after the death of her father, she was soon made to realise that life had to go on. Sitting and moping didn't help. And now she had her stepfather to look after.

Dan worked long hours in the coal mine, and thankfully she saw little of him. He expected his meal to be ready when he came in and his washing and ironing done, and kept a strict eye on her comings and goings, warning off many a lad who eyed Alys with a young man's appetite. Apart from that there was little contact. Sometimes she felt sorry for him, spending his time digging like a mole in the ground, seldom seeing the sunshine or the seagulls flying against a blue sky. Sometimes, when he'd made a particularly noisy scene about a young man who had come asking for her, she hated him.

Dan Radloff's parents had come from Poland. Weary of the troubles in their own country, the internal divisions between radicals and conservatives, the series of unsuccessful uprisings against the Russian Empire, the newly married Stefan Radloff decided he'd had enough. Buoyant with opimism and accompanied by his young wife, Jacoba, he made his way over the seas to England. It was a hazardous journey and the poor little wife hated every minute of it. Even the soft rolling green hills and valleys of the Welsh country where they finally settled did not relieve her constant homesickness for her own land.

It was only when her son was born that she came to accept her lot. Dan was a big baby, robust and noisy, demanding a lot of attention. The young Jacoba was intensely proud of him, and indeed was kept so busy that the nostalgia she had felt for her own country was soon a thing of the past. In the small town of Craven Bay, its smoking chimneys contrasting so poignantly with the wild lonely sweeps of the surrounding sands, Dan grew to manhood, constantly in trouble at school, eating his hard-working father out of house and home.

He went to work in the mines beside his father as soon as he left school. When he was in his thirties and still living at home, his father lost his life in a pit accident and his mother, who never fully recovered from the shock, passed on soon after.

He continued to live in the small two-up, two-down cottage belonging to the colliery. It was there after his marriage that he had brought his bride and young Alys.

With the passing years Alys's friend Mary had gone into service in the home of Thomas Jenkins on the headlands. She had tried to persuade Alys to join her, but she dreaded the thought of life spent within the four walls of someone else's house. She knew girls who sold shellfish from the quay for a living. The idea appealed to her far more than one spent in service.

In the evenings, walking barefoot across the sands with the sea far out, shimmering under a summer sun, her skirt hitched up at one side to her waist, affording her easier movement, Alys would hunt for a likely spot. Then, stooping, she would scoop up the wet sand in handfuls, sieving it through her spread fingers. The harvested cockles were then tipped into the bucket and Alys would repeat the procedure until her bucket was full.

Back in her kitchen, they would be tipped into a large bowl of cold water to which she would add a handful of salt, and left overnight. Before going to bed Alys would stir the shells about with her hands, ensuring that all the sand seeped out. Beneath the salted water, the shells would open and close, affording a glimpse of their bright orange flesh. In the morning she would again check for sand and then set them to boil on top of the stove, the shells crackling and bobbing up and down in the bubbling water. When they were cooked the water would be emptied out and after cooling Alys would wash them yet again and pick out the discarded shells.

When money was short, as it invariably was in the small household, Alys would make do with a saucer of cockles sprinkled with vinegar and slices of bread and butter for her supper, followed by a cup of strong black tea.

Presented with this, her stepfather had been known to throw the plate across the room, leaving a tight-lipped Alys staring mutinously at the yellow stain left on the wall. 'A hard day's work I put in,' he would roar. 'And I come home to a meal like this!' And he'd make for the front door, grabbing his cap on the way, and vanish in the direction of the corner tavern. Strange how there was always enough money to buy him his nightly drink, Alys thought, but never enough for food!

Sometimes, when the fishermen had had a good haul, they would insist on making her a gift of the shellfish, saving her the onerous task of finding them herself. They still remembered her father and many of them had a soft spot for young Alys. If they could make her burden easier, they would.

Somehow, she always felt close to her father while she could see the wide blue stretch of Craven Bay. Sometimes, walking, she thought she could see him out of the corner of her eye. She'd catch a shadow, a blur, and then it was gone. But something lingered – the echo of a laugh, Dad's voice teasing her about something. He was a great tease, was her dad . . .

Dragged rudely back to the present she only saw the group of women standing on the corner when a shrill voice broke the silence. 'All right for some!' Lizzie Grant tossed the words at Alys with scorn. The cockle sellers of Craven Bay were well known for their hardiness and rough sense of humour. Alys had never really fitted in with them, uncomfortable when they tried to draw her into their jokes and constant talk about men. Considering her 'uppish', they didn't know what to make of her most of the time and so, like people the world over with someone they don't understand, they tried to ridicule her.

'Who's the man, then? The one that was asking about you? A gent like that don't belong wi' a girl like you, Alys Hughes, that 'e don't.'

'Be a cold day in hell when someone asks about you, Lizzie Grant,' she shouted back.

A scream of laughter followed. Thereafter she decided to ignore them. It never paid to bandy words with that crowd. Mary, with her quick wit and fine flow of swear words, could handle them. Not Alys.

Chapter Two

Marcus walked quickly over the springy turf of the head-lands, coming at last to the white-walled cottage that he had rented for the summer. The road leading to Craven Bay's larger houses, homes of the wealthy pit owners, was rough and lined with grey boulders removed by the road workers years ago and left standing where they had fallen. Sheep moved lazily over the grass, cropping around the stones.

Small white daisies and glistening yellow buttercups struggled for existence in the rough grass. Marcus inhaled deeply of the many scents as he walked, refreshed already by this place. He sat down on a sun-warmed boulder and let his gaze wander over the panorama before him. Yellow gorse blazed in the sunlight and he could see where the heather would soon blossom into a pinky-mauve carpet. London was where he made his living, where his parents now lived, but this was where his heart dwelt.

Pity about that girl, he thought. But then, what would she know about beauty or art or anything that lifted a man to the stars? He had to admit to himself that he'd been surprised by her manner, especially by her way of talking. The lilting sing-song of the Welsh tongue was there, marking her at once for what she was, but there'd been nothing harsh about her voice. Rather, it was soothing to the ear, reminding him of his nanny when he was a boy, and of the spell-binding tales she told of dragons and magicians and fierce fighting Celts. Although born in the valleys, he'd gone away to finish his education, coming back for school holidays and fitting into the life there as though he had never been away. Now he had returned for a spell, wishing to recapture some of that earlier magic, and had found it in the black-haired witch who had spurned his idea without even hearing it. He'd known if he hadn't departed quickly he would have lost his temper, and that was one weakness he never permitted himself.

Scorning the pattern set by generations of Dillons, gentlemen farmers to a man, his own father had been determined to qualify as a solicitor. Gerard Dillon had gone on to succeed in local politics, dismaying his father by joining the Labour Party. The subsequent estrangement didn't bother Gerard. Driven by fierce ambition, his aim was to get on in life without the backing of his family. Young and dynamic, there was every evidence that he would.

On their journeys into town, the young Marcus would gaze at the long lines of once proud miners waiting outside the local Exchange Offices for their dole handouts. They would pass women and children scrabbling about on tips of waste coal, filling buckets and baths and anything they could carry with the slaggy coal. His father would shake his head and mutter below his breath. He told Marcus that it was as if a whole community had been thrown on to the scrap heap, for the incessant strikes had taken a human toll. The fourteen-year-old Marcus had gazed at the ragged women and the hollow-eyed children and asked why something couldn't be done. His father replied something was being done, but not nearly enough.

By then an elected Member of Parliament, his plan was to move to London and lobby the House each and every day for an improvement in the miners' lives.

One morning Marcus accompanied his father, watching the 'struggle or starve' march that wound through the town before setting out on its hopeless trek to nowhere. Violence broke out among the crowd, egged on by some of the hothead spectators. A stone was thrown. Marcus saw windows broken and felt a sharp pain, then warm blood pouring down his cheek on to his jersey. He cried out, fear mixing with the unbelievable thought that it was his own blood that stained the cobbles beneath his feet.

The scar, partly covered by the short beard he wore, would forever remind him of that day and the tragic history of that time.

Once the coal of South Wales had gone out to the world. Huge profits had been made, and coaling stations set up all over the globe. The seams were lucrative, although often difficult to work. Danger from fire damp was a constant threat but it did not stop the pit owners, and stories about disastrous explosions were rife. Marcus listened to his father talk about the clashes between owners and miners over methods of working and wages. He said the miners would never forget the terrible strike that had lasted three long years before they were forced back to work by hungry wives and children, under particularly humiliating terms.

Their skin blackened with coal dust, whites of their eyes

gleaming, at the end of the day the men trudged back to the pathetic cottages they called home, finding little satisfaction in being able to hand their wives the derisory amount of money the pit bosses felt fit payment for a week's hard, back-breaking work. Throwing down their food boxes and the speckled enamel cans that gave them the only hot drink they had throughout the day, they grumbled as they stripped and bathed in front of the kitchen fire. Their wives assisted while the children looked on, wide-eyed and silent for a change. After supper the men would make their way to the corner tavern and the rafters would ring with the sound of anger. Gerard had told his son of this many a time, for he felt it his duty to join his constituents in their own environment when he could and was respected for it.

The memory of his father's words was still vivid in Marcus's mind and he made it his duty to come back whenever he could.

Alys walked with the easy stride of the young. Her hair bounced on her shoulders with each stride, seemingly inbued with a life of its own. Around her the bright afternoon glowed like a benediction. The sun was warm on her head and shoulders – life-giving, comforting. She felt at peace, everything in her life neat and orderly. Drogo had been taken to his stable and given into the care of the retired coal miner who looked after him and sundry other donkeys from the mine workings.

The gates of Thomas Jenkins's fine mansion stood open. She walked round to the back, keeping an eye out for her friend.

'There you are, Alys Hughes!' Mary appeared on the

back doorstep. Dressed in a pale blue gown, with a white apron and cap trimmed with lace that looked more decorative than functional, Mary looked fresh and cool. At seventeen, she was even prettier than when Alys had first met her. Inclined to a plumpness that was pleasing, she was a favourite with the local boys and played a guessing game with them. But Alys knew she was in love with only one man and all the rest were a diversion. Straightforward and candid, almost to the point of rudeness, more than once Mary had confided in Alys about Jackie Rees.

'I'm saving meself for him. Although I might lark about with the others, it don't mean anything.' She spoke her mind, too, about the place of Dan Radloff in Alys's life. 'I don't know why you stay with that old eejit of a stepfather when you could be working up here with me. Old Jenkins likes his pound of flesh, so he does, but it's not hard work and at least you'd be away from the likes of Dan.'

Service with an upper-class family had given Mary status, and despite the blunt, occasionally harsh words of the wealthy pit-owner she enjoyed her job. She liked the comfort and elegance of the house, comparing it, without censure, to her own parents' small white cottage where her brothers ran wild and her father talked endlessly of what he would do when his 'ship came in'. Keven O'Malley liked to gamble and there would never be money enough to give his family a comfortable life while the fit was on him.

Mary loved her family; her small, blustering cockerel of a father, her warm-hearted mother, and the boys so noisy and full of life. But she also liked the good and plentiful food that went with her job, the pretty uniforms – one colour for the mornings, another for the afternoons – and her comfortable bed in the attic room high at the top of the house.

As always when Mary tried to recruit her, Alys smiled and shook her head. She kept Dan's two-up, two-down as spic and span as soap and water and good old-fashioned elbow-grease could achieve. True, the walls and ceiling badly needed painting, but those and the musty smell of the creaking old floorboards she had become used to. The things she could change, she changed. The things she couldn't, she tolerated.

One day, she promised herself, she would have a beautiful home with a garden front and back. She would plant tall pink hollyhocks in the garden and the path to the rose-covered front door would be lined with bright yellow wallflowers. She had seen such a house on her walks in the valley and the image stayed always in her mind. There were ruffled white curtains at the windows and the glass sparkled where the sun came flooding in. She imagined it lying like pools of melted butter on the tops of polished bookcases and small elegant tables.

Her day dreaming usually ended with the arrival of her stepfather, demanding food. She had difficulty in keeping from him the money she earned. Although Alys was not one for untruths, she had lied to Dan about her earnings. When he demanded all her money she gave him less than half, keeping the rest to buy a jar of strawberry jam or clover honey from the Co-op down the street, a satin ribbon to thread through the neck of her petticoat or a pretty slide for her hair. After Mam's death, Dan began visiting the pub every night and often Alys had to resort to going through his trouser pockets in order to pay the rent or buy foodstuffs. Wrinkling her nose in distaste at the stale smell that emanated from his heavy moleskin trousers, she would keep a wary eye on the prone figure snoring on the bed, gritting her teeth but continuing with her search until she had the two half-crowns that would keep them housed until next pay day.

Dan would remember only the good times and the singing as he made his stumbling way home, often with his arm draped around a pal's shoulders.

'Go and wait on our bench,' Mary told her friend. 'I'll be with you in a minute.'

Alys slipped through the back gardens, gazing in wonder at the vegetables laid out in neat rows – giant cauliflowers, tall string beans tied up on canes, peas and cabbages – all looking wholesome and healthy, too perfect to be real. Enough here to feed a whole army of children.

Glancing around to make sure no one watched, she bent and picked a handful of succulent green pods and then sat down on the seat she and Mary had come to think of as theirs, the handful of peas in her lap. Somehow, no one else's peas ever seemed as fresh or as delicious. Her small white teeth bit into their luscious juciness as she sat, completely relaxed, in the bright sunlight.

'Now!' Mary appeared, running along the path that lined the vegetable beds. 'Are you still goin' to that dance on Saturday? I hope you've not come to tell me you've changed your mind, me girl, for I've got me a new dress to wear. And sure, aren't I looking forward to dancing with that handsome divil of a man, Jackie Rees.'

She paused for breath then grabbed some peas from

Alys's lap, popping the green pods greedily. Alys smiled at her volatile friend. The two were a perfect foil for one other, one so dark yet with pale, creamy skin, the other fair with a skin kissed golden by the sun. They were of the same height but Mary, although she would die rather than admit it, was secretly jealous of the narrow eighteen inch waist that Alys boasted.

'You know I'm looking forward to it as much as you are.' Alys moved further along the bench to make room for her friend. 'Only I don't have a new frock to wear. Can't see any way of getting one, either.'

The dance to be held at the church hall this coming Saturday was a treat to which they had looked forward for weeks. The thought of her usual white shantung frock, with its ruched sash of brown and embroidery of a deeper shade across the bodice, was depressing to Alys. So old-fashioned and matronly, and hadn't everyone seen her in it so many times she could scream! But it was the only one she had. Although not of a jealous nature, the thought of Mary's new dress caused a small niggle of envy.

For a moment Alys's thoughts dwelled on the man who had accosted her that morning, and his talk of 'a few shillings in your pocket'. Had she been too hasty in not stopping to listen to what he had to say?

Mary was saying, 'You'll still enjoy yourself, love. Wear those long amber beads that belonged to your mam. They go lovely with that frock of yours, sure they do.' She smiled roguishly. 'Anyway, I'm determined to have fun and make that Jackie walk me home. He'll not get away so easily this time, that he won't.' She squeezed Alys's arm. 'I've got Sunday off and Jackie said he might be able to borrow the van for the day. He's going to drive me into the country and we'll take a picnic.'

Jackie Rees drove the green Co-op delivery van and because he possessed a driving licence was considered by some, Mary's mother especially, to be a cut above the other local lads. Even if he was a non-conformised or whatever the divil they called themselves!

'A picnic,' said Alys cheerfully, 'won't that be great?' She smiled. 'It'll be running wild you'll be accused of next, me girl. Your dad'll be after him for ruining your good name.'

Mary gave an unlady-like snort. 'As long as me dad's got his horses and dogs to gamble on, he doesn't bother his head about us young 'uns.'

Alys knew that wasn't quite true. Keven O'Malley thought a great deal of Mary's three young brothers and his vivacious daughter, forever boasting about the grand times he would give them when his luck changed. His hard-working wife took it all with a pinch of salt. Married to him for twenty years, she doubted that day would ever come.

Now, thinking of Mary's remark about Jackie's getting away from her, Alys said, 'I don't think he wants to get away.'

'Whether he does or not, he'd better not try it or he'll get the sharp end of me tongue, so he will.'

'They *do* say honey attracts better than vinegar,' commented Alys wryly.

'Well, we'll try both on him, see which works best,' laughed Mary. She stood up, smoothing down her apron. 'I'd better go, else I'll be gettin' me head bitten off by old Dean. Although she's only the cook she seems to think it's her money that runs the place, not Mister Jenkins's.'

Alys smiled. 'I'll see you on Saturday, then. About seven-thirty by the letter box outside the church hall?'

Mary nodded, the ribbons on her small cap floating behind her, already on her way back to the house. She called over her shoulder, 'Rightio! See you.'

Alys was coming round the end of the hedge that separated the gardens from the driveway when a sudden uproar brought her to a stumbling halt. Barking franically, two huge dogs rushed at her, almost sending her flying. They were terrifying, the biggest she'd ever seen, with rough greyish coats and large heads. They looked to her like an illustration she'd once seen in a book of old folk tales by the Brothers Grimm. A sharp command from the young man who accompanied them and they checked abruptly, sidling away and rolling their eyes sheepishly, as though ashamed of their own boisterousness.

'I'm sorry.' The young man bent to grasp a collar in each hand. 'They're quite harmless, really. Nothing to be afraid of in spite of their appearance.'

Alys brushed the dust from her skirt, eyeing the dogs with suspicion. 'I think I'll take your word for that. You really should keep better control over them, you know, and not let them rush madly around like that.'

The man smiled wryly. 'They *are* on private property, not in a public place,' he pointed out.

He was about her age or perhaps a little older, tall, with fair hair that fell artlessly over his forehead, giving him a boyish look. Dressed casually in baggy grey flannels and a white shirt, he seemed friendly and unassuming. She had heard of Thomas Jenkins's son but this was the first time she'd laid eyes on him. Mary had told her he wasn't a bit like his old man, who was unrelentingly strait-laced.

To Alys's surprise, the newcomer held out his hand in friendly fashion. 'I'm Evan Jenkins. You must be Mary's friend. I saw you talking together in the vegetable garden.'

Alys felt his fingers cool against her own and smiled. 'Yes, I'm Alys Hughes. I live in town. We were making plans for Saturday evening. There's a dance on in the church hall. Quite a novelty, really. Nothing much happens in Craven Bay.'

'I'd agree with you there. I've just come down from university and I'm finding home deadly dull.' Sudden interest showed in his eyes. 'A dance, eh? Is attendance limited to the town folk or can anyone join in?'

'It's in aid of the new organ fund for the church,' Alys told him, warming to his amiable manner. Dances were usually frowned on by the older members of the parish who complained that they were just an excuse for some-one's husband to put his arms around another woman. But, thank goodness, not all felt that way. 'They'll be glad to see anyone who shows up,' she said. 'But you have to pay sixpence to get in.'

Evan's fair brows rose and she got the impression that he was laughing at her. 'Sixpence, eh? I reckon I can just about afford that.'

Alys laughed out loud and cautiously made her way around the dogs who had collapsed on the ground, long tongues lolling. 'Have to get back,' she explained when he looked as though he might detain her with further chat. 'I've still got my stepfather's supper to see to.'

He gave her a wide smile. 'Might see you at the dance, then.' As he walked away, Alys saw a girl appear through the shrubbery and join him, laughing and linking her arm through his in a possessive way. Curiosity made her turn to look back one more time before she left the grounds. She saw that he was still watching her although the girl was laughing and tugging at his arm, and the dogs straining at their collars.

'You sly old thing, you! Chatting up one of the local girls already! You don't waste time,' she heard the girl say in a light, clear voice and at Evan's answering laugh a warm flush flooded Alys's cheeks. He'd been so casual, so friendly, that she couldn't help liking him. Good looking, too. A glow that had nothing to do with the sunlit day or the beautiful gardens lingered over her as she began walking away. He hadn't seemed to mind, or even notice, that she was not one of those spoiled, rich girls to whom he must be more accustomed. He'd acted as though they were on the same level, not a bit condescending or flirtatious. There had been few boys that she liked or that Dan had allowed into the house to call on her. She decided she liked this one though she wouldn't have to worry about his calling, for a young man of his station would be unlikely to appear in the part of town where she lived. She wondered if he would remember his promise – well, sort of promise – to see her at the dance, even five minutes after she had vanished through the front gates.

The firelight played a game of hide and seek, prying into the darkest corners and revealing the dim, dingy kitchen where Alys knelt before the fire, drying her hair. Her stepfather's dinner was cooking on the stove and permeated the air with its rich, appetising smell, concealing the fishy smell left by her preparation of the cockles. The only sound was the crackling of the fire in the hearth and the low murmur of the tune she hummed as she parted her hair with spread fingers, offering it to the heat.

When there was a knock on the door she uttered a soft exclamation under her breath. Then, puzzled, for callers didn't usually bother to knock but lifted the latch and walked straight in, Alys went to answer it.

The tall man who had tried to solicit her that morning stood on the step. Alys drew back a pace, one hand going to her curtain of damp hair in a self-conscious gesture. They stared at each other and at last she said, 'What do you want, coming sneaking up on me like this?' Even to herself her voice sounded shrill and not entirely controlled.

As though guessing that, he laughed. 'No need to panic! I haven't come to ravish you. Although,' contemplating the seductive tumble of silken hair about her shoulders, 'looking like that, you'd tempt a plaster saint off his pedestal.'

'I asked you what you wanted,' she repeated irritably, painfully aware of the gleam of amusement in his eyes and wondering just what he found so bloody funny. 'If you've come to play the kind of games you tried this morning, you can get lost. I haven't changed my mind. I'm not interested in your schemes, whatever they are.'

'Aren't you at least going to ask me in?' He glanced behind him at the windy night. 'You wouldn't keep a dog out on a night like this.'

She tried to think up a suitable answer, something

sarcastic and biting. Instinct warned her to refuse, to send him away with a flea in his ear. She made an attempt to close the door only to have him thrust a foot into the opening, stopping her with a jolt. 'Please!' he entreated, and saw her lips twitch on the beginnings of a smile.

'All right. Only don't think I've changed my mind, 'cause I haven't.'

Once inside he stood gazing about the small room for a moment, then rubbing his hands together he went over to the fireplace. 'You don't even know what I'm going to ask you.'

'I can guess.' It was said scornfully. 'Men like you, of your class, are only interested in one thing from girls like me . . .'

'Hold on – girls like you, men like me! You've been reading too many penny romances.' His eyes gleamed with amusement. 'Although I'd be mighty interested in hearing from you exactly what men like me could expect from girls like you!'

She turned her back on him, and reaching for the towel that was thrown over the back of the old leather sofa, began to rub her hair vigorously. A thought struck her. 'How'd you know where I lived?'

'Your friends on the quay gave me your address.'

She remembered the taunting laughter of Lizzie Grant. 'Humph! Well, my stepfather will be back soon. If he comes home and finds you here, there's no knowing what he might do. You'd better hurry up and tell me what it is you want, and then go.'

'Right. Although I'd like to point out I'd have told you this morning if you'd given me the chance.'

Firelight caught in her hair, giving it a dark, burnished

sheen, casting crimson shadows over her face. He felt his breath catch in his throat.

'You're very lovely,' he said, watching the way her eyes darkened as he spoke, the heavy lids coming down, thick lashes fanning her cheeks.

She gave an impatient gesture. 'I've been told *that* before.'

Was the sly minx flirting with him? he wondered. She would be expert at flirting, at leading men on. Boys had probably flocked around her since she was a little girl.

'Modest, too.' He smiled.

She flushed resentfully but before she could say anything else he hurried on, 'Then you won't be surprised when I tell you I want to capture that beauty on canvas.' Seeing her wary look, knowing she still didn't understand, he went on, 'I'm an artist. I paint people's portraits. I want you to sit for me.'

If he'd said he wanted her to fly to the moon she couldn't have been more surprised. 'In fact,' he pressed home his advantage, 'I'd be eternally grateful if you would consent. It wouldn't be for long.'

'Just once?'

'Oh, no, a good deal more often than just once. I'd have to see how it went.'

She thought of Mary's new dress. 'You said this morning there'd be a few shillings in it. I'd just have to sit still while you painted? Nothing else?'

'Very still. Even if you got cramp so badly you wanted to scream, you'd have to endure it until I said you could move.' Although his tone was solemn, his eyes teased.

Alys bridled. 'There's cheeky you are! For that, boyo, I'd expect more'n a few shillings. A guinea at least.' A

31

guinea! If she could keep it hidden from Dan's greedy grasp, it would buy her a new dress and maybe a pair of shoes for the dance . . .

She had a sudden image of herself, walking into the church hall in a new dress – pale primrose yellow, the one she'd admired in the Co-op's window, craving it so much it had become an obsession. Yellow went well with her colouring, and the dress had ecru cotton inserts in the bodice and three-quarter-length sleeves. Evan Jenkins would be begging her to save every dance for him . . . If, she thought ruefully, he turned up.

'If you pay me a whole guinea, I'll do it.'

'It's a deal.' He reached out and lifted a long shining strand of dark hair in his hand, smelling the fragrance of the sweet-smelling rinse she used. 'Now you'd better finish drying this before you catch cold. A red-nosed model is the last thing I need.'

At the front door, he turned. 'Be there early. Morning light is best for painting. Oh, and wear what you had on this morning, and come on the donkey.'

She could not repress her laughter despite the feeling of exasperation he provoked in her. 'You want to paint Drogo, too?'

'If Drogo's the donkey, yes, I do.' At the last moment he paused to say, 'The women on the quay called you Alys?'

She nodded. 'That's right. Alys Hughes.'

'And I'm Marcus Dillon. I'll expect you bright and early tomorrow, then. The white-painted cottage at the far end of the cliff path.'

Dan stared at her with suspicion when he came in a few moments later. 'Who was that I saw leave just now? No one I recognised, my girl. I'll not have you entertaining men in the house when I'm not around, hear?'

He threw down the sweat rag he used as a handkerchief and drew his shirt over his head, moving towards the sink. Alys averted her gaze from the pale fleshy body; the flabby breasts and gut that bulged over his moleskin trousers revolted her. Over the last few years he had put on weight and she wondered if her fastidious mother would still love him could she see him now.

Not answering, she grabbed a cloth to shift the heavy iron pot from the flames, ladling spoonfuls of the thick stew on to a plate and placing it on the table between the already set knife and fork.

The rich, appetising smell in the room grew even stronger. She poured boiling water from the old blackened kettle on to a spoonful of tea-leaves in the earthenware pot, and stood it to one side to brew.

When he had finished drying his face with the rough towel, Dan turned to stare at her. 'Well,' he demanded, 'who was he, then? That bloke I saw leaving as I came along the road?'

'None of your business.' Alys's retort was sharp and to the point. 'You're not my father.'

'I'm taking the place of your father, my girl, until you're old enough and wise enough to look after yourself.' He pulled a long-sleeved woollen vest over his head, leaving the three buttons at the throat undone so that tufts of matted grey hair showed through. She had no right to treat him with so little respect! He was her legal guardian, wasn't he? She should be grateful to him instead of subjecting him to so much impudence. Seating himself at the table, he reached for the thick chunk of bread Alys had just cut. 'So don't you go telling *me* it's none of my business or you'll be getting the back o' my hand, that you will.'

Knowing his hasty temper and how easily it was roused, Alys sat opposite at the table and began to tuck into her own meal. 'It was just someone who'd lost his way come to ask directions, that's all.'

Long ago she had decided that the best and least troublesome way to deal with her stepfather's probing questions was to lie, as she did about her earnings. She didn't consider it a sin, not even worth mentioning to Father Goodhew on a Friday night when she went to confession – although in her heart she doubted that the priest would view it in the same light.

The parish he administered was small and scattered, most families being of chapel-going stock. Perhaps because his flock *was* so small and few in number, Father Goodhew was extra punctilious in his shepherding.

On the night of her mother's death, Mary had come to sit beside her, one arm about her shivering friend. Together they rocked backwards and forwards, crouched on the cold doorstep. She had spent the night with the O'Malleys, sharing a bed with Mary. She remembered pulling back when summoned by the doctor the next morning, her whole being shrinking from the thought of having to go into that room where her mother had suffered such torment.

The priest was already there. The exhausted midwife and the elderly doctor took the opportunity to go down to the kitchen and partake of the hot, strong tea a distraught Dan had waiting for them, leaving her alone with Father Goodhew.

'God has taken them both to His bosom,' the old priest told her in a solemn voice. 'Your mother is at peace now, reunited with that fine man who was your father. Now we have to look to the living, as your mother would have wished.'

Alys knew he meant Dan Radloff and mentally she consigned her stepfather to hell. It had been his bestial lust that had killed her mother. If she hadn't married him, if she hadn't had the baby . . .!

A lot of 'ifs'. Somehow she managed to reply to Father Goodhew's well-meant advice. Bowing her head, she'd said between sobs, 'Yes, Father, I'll do my best . . .'

Perhaps the worst memory of all was when Mam lay in the front room, the coffin propped upon two chairs, the tiny still-born child laid across her breast. Somehow, that had terrified Alys more than anything else. The whole experience had been pushed into the furthest corners of her mind, too lacerating to dwell on . . .

Alys crumbled her own bread into bits, gazing down at her plate.

Dan grunted, 'Well, just you be careful who you open the door to, that's all I say.'

There was silence in the kitchen after that, except for the scrape of knife and fork against plate.

Chapter Three

The following morning, almost before the sun was up and over the valley, Dan set off for work. It would be a long and tiring day. Men here were used to hard work and took it in their stride, even though they might grumble a lot. Alys had his pack of sandwiches ready and filled the enamel mug with hot tea and milk and three spoonfuls of sugar. Dan safely got rid off, she tidied the cottage and went to fetch Drogo from the nearby stable.

Loving the silence of the seashore on a sunny day, glad that it was too early for many folk to be about, she urged the reluctant donkey over the damp grass. Drogo blinked sleepily and shied at the screaming sea birds in irritable manner until Alys laughed and told him good-naturedly, 'You lazy old good-for-nothing, you! You'd sleep all day if I let you, wouldn't you? Well, this is one morning you can't, for I'm about to earn the sort of money I don't get from selling cockles. You're to behave yourself, hear, while I go into that cottage and . . .'

Her voice trailed away as she thought of the risk she was taking, committing herself to being alone, in a strange house, with a man she didn't know, didn't particularly like, or even trust! She often confided in Drogo when she was riding and liked to think the little donkey understood and sympathised with her. Often he behaved as if he did, seeming to set his steps at a more gentle pace whenever she told him of things Dan had done or said, her voice husky with dejection. And when she was happy, when she'd made a good deal with the fishermen and the shellfish were plentiful and cheap, he would know and become quite skittish, like a young creature again, enjoying a day out in the sunshine with the promise of a good feed at the end of it.

Although Dan ignored Drogo's very existence – donkeys, to him, were for pulling the heavy loads of fuel the men cut from the coal face to the pit head, there to be loaded on trains for their journey to the docks or to another part of the country, and he thought Alys daft for even bothering her head about the old beast – to Alys, he was like one of the family. Better than one of the family, she thought at times, after one of her altercations with Dan. For Drogo didn't shout or bawl her out for refusing to take in washing from the local tavern owner's wife, scowling when she'd exclaimed heatedly that didn't he think she did enough work, foraging for cockles in the sand, or else up at dawn, down at the quayside to bargain with the fishermen, and then coming home to cook and tidy up after him!

The reins held loosely in her hands, her skirts riding up to reveal her bare knees, she gazed about her at the peaceful morning. Seagulls shrieked their defiance over her head, outraged at the presence of humans at such an early hour. The rising sun splashed the sea and sky with scarlet and gold ribbons as the little donkey trod placidly along the cliff path. Thinking back to the man, Marcus Dillon, she told herself she wasn't nervous. She had never been at a loss for crisp repartee, and would treat this like any other job.

All the same, when she stopped outside the front gate of the small white cottage, her heart began to beat a little more swiftly and the palms of her hands were damp. Her knock was answered at once and the artist stared down at her, giving Alys the impression that he'd been waiting for her eagerly.

'Good morning,' he said briskly, and stood back to allow her to enter. She had already tied Drogo to a sapling on the common in front of the cottage and hoped he wouldn't become too bored and try to uproot the young tree. There was plenty of grass for him to enjoy and he was usually patient when she tied him up like this, for it meant he could doze again, uninterrupted by her foot nudging him on his way.

Marcus did not ask her to sit and so she stood, hands folded across the faded pink cotton of her skirt, and stared at him unflinching. He grinned, thinking she was conducting herself like a grand duchess. There was no sign of servility and no indication of the self-seeking attitude he had expected.

'Glad you were able to come,' he told her.

Alys lifted a strand of black hair and tucked it into the neat chignon which she'd managed to achieve with the aid of innumerable hairpins and patience. 'I said I would.'

Once again he thrilled to the lilting sing-song quality of her voice, not at all like the harsher tones of her hawker cronies, not in the least as he'd expected. He looked at her thoughtfully, his head on one side. 'The first thing I need to do is get rid of these.' Suiting the action to the words he reached forward and unceremoniously began tugging the pins from her thick mass of hair.

He heard her gasp of indignation. 'What did you do that for? It took me ages . . .'

'I thought I made myself clear.' His tone brooked no argument. 'I want you looking exactly as you did when I first saw you, riding across the sands, not got up like some lah-de-dah society lady.'

Her cheeks flushed crimson and he strove to commit to memory the lovely colour as the blood swept beneath the delicate skin. He decided he would have to come up with a lot of insults if he was to get that tone right!

'Come on.' He took her hand and pulled her abruptly into a room that obviously did duty as his studio. Without speaking, her mistrustful gaze never leaving him, Alys watched as he adjusted a seat on a slightly raised platform before the large, uncurtained window.

'What about Drogo?' she asked him bluntly. 'I thought you were going to paint him, too?'

'You first. I need to sketch your head and shoulders this morning, get some idea of the composition. Drogo won't be neglected. I may be able to get a rough draft of him as well. Now,' brusquely he beckoned her to seat herself on the chair, 'do you mind? We're wasting time.'

He turned her shoulders, tilted her head, moved her arms until she felt as inhuman as a lump of clay. He showed as much emotion as though she was, too! she thought with brooding resentment. Finally satisfied, he warned her that on no account was she to move from the position he had achieved.

'For how long?' she demanded with a flash of her old spirit.

'Until I say you can.' He frowned. 'There, you've moved your head already!' With cool fingers he corrected her pose, arranging the long silken strands of hair to his liking. 'Talk if you want to.'

Puzzled, she stared at him. 'What about?'

'Anything. Most women can't sit still for more than two minutes without wanting to tell me all about their lovers or how their parents don't understand them.'

'I haven't got a lover. Or parents,' she said stiffly.

She didn't think he'd heard her for he made no reply, although she saw how his jaw tightened.

It wasn't as easy as it looked. The prize of a whole guinea for sitting still and letting someone paint her had been an inducement she couldn't resist. She couldn't have known about the muscles that after a while would cry out in agony, demanding to be eased and stretched. After two hours, with five minute rests when he could see she was tiring, Marcus told her she could relax. Standing, feeling the blood beginning to circulate again, Alys made an endeavour to peep at the work on the easel. With a sharp command, he stopped her.

'Why not?' she asked, puzzled. 'I only want to look.'

'You'll see it when it's ready – providing you can sit still long enough for me to finish it!'

She was hurt at the implication that she had been as fidgety as a child. Later, she sat in a wicker chair on the tiny white-railed verandah and watched as with lightning expertise he made rough sketches of the donkey, who by now seemed to have fallen into a doze.

'As long as you don't expect Drogo to stand still for

you as well,' she warned. 'He's got a mind of his own, has Drogo.'

Looking over his shoulder, he commented only that it might be a good idea if she made herself useful and put the kettle on. Implying, she thought, with a niggle of irritation, that he was not paying her a whole guinea to sit and watch him work.

She found the large airy kitchen and filled a kettle at the tap. The tea was brewing when Marcus came in. Seating himself at the table and propping his feet on a chair next to him, he drawled, 'You can be mother.'

She went to him every morning, sometimes riding Drogo, sometimes allowing the little donkey to stay dozing in his stall. She never knew what to expect from Marcus Dillon. Kindness and consideration one morning, abrasive sarcasm the next.

She was dying to see what he'd made of her on that square of canvas but he forbade her even a glimpse. One morning, the sunlight pouring in through the big window making it almost impossible to keep her eyes open, she jerked upright when he suddenly strode forward and took her by the shoulders, shaking her roughly.

'If you must spend half the night with your heavy-handed boyfriend, kindly make sure he allows you enough sleep to be able to function properly the next morning! You're worse than that blasted donkey, dozing off every few minutes.'

'I'm sorry.' A flush stained her cheeks, whether from anger or guilt he wasn't sure. He noticed she had not denied his accusations about not getting enough sleep and a sudden tremor of jealousy twisted inside him, startling him so that his hands tightened on her shoulders.

She winced and it was his turn to apologise, although it came out grudgingly. He turned back to his easel. 'All right. If you could bring yourself to stay awake long enough to complete this morning's session, I would appreciate it.'

She pulled a face behind his back, quickly resuming the pose when he turned and shot her a suspicious glance. She wondered what he would have said had he known she was thinking of Evan Jenkins and not some 'heavy-handed' boy from the town as he'd claimed.

But all the brooding resentment brought on by Marcus's brusque treatment was worth it, she decided, the day she stood and gazed at the yellow silk frock in the Co-op window. The Craven Bay Co-operative Stores was the grandest shop in town. In fact, the only shop where you could buy decent apparel. As a child, she'd been in with her mother, though not very often, and had gazed in awe at the solid dark wood counters and display cabinets and the funny arrangement of wires that ran like tram lines above them, carrying money to a cage-like office from where a clerk returned change. Superior sales assistants glared at you from lofty heights, or so it had seemed to the little girl. They all wore black skirts and crisp white cotton blouses and clearly wondered what the shabby woman and child could possibly be wanting here. There had been a smell of polish, of musty carpets and the faded scent of lavender drifting from the toiletry counter. Alys found it almost unchanged. The assistants seemed a little older, but no less superior.

Still, she wouldn't let them intimidate her. She had

made up her mind; she had the necessary money and she was going to enjoy spending it.

The showroom where the dresses were displayed was up a wide, polished staircase with a narrow strip of dark red carpet and a polished banister rail. On the landing above, small gilt chairs were placed at strategic intervals for the benefit of the ladies who found climbing the stairs difficult. Many would ask for a chair to be fetched while they discussed the fit or colour of a garment, and would sit in their elaborate hats looking, Alys would think with a stifled giggle, like feathered cartwheels while they considered the merits of a blue or a coffee-coloured gown for the next social gathering. In spite of her resolve to let nothing daunt her, Alys was aware of curious stares following her progress. Sales ladies paused in their arrangement of a skirt on a display model or a piece of lace, and turned to watch her as she passed.

She straightened her shoulders and lifted her chin, trying to look as though it was an everyday occurrence for her, this visit to Craven Bay's most fashionable store. The sales lady she approached looked doubtful when she explained that there was a frock in the window, a yellow silk frock, and she wanted to try it on. Although the girl was neatly dressed in a dark skirt and printed pink blouse, still the sales assistant hesitated before she went to check if they had the dress in Alys's size. It would be much simpler if they didn't, she caught herself thinking. This wasn't their usual kind of customer. But they had the size and so she guided Alys to a curtained enclosure at the back of the showroom and hovered uneasily outside.

At last Alys stepped out, and handing back the dress,

murmured. 'Thank you, it fits beautifully. I'll take it. Will you wrap it up, please?'

Counting out the money from her little hoard was the sweetest moment of her young life.

'To *paint* you!' Mary O'Malley's eyes opened so wide they seemed in danger of falling out. 'To *paint* you!'

Alys repressed the rude retort that rose to her lips at her friend's astounded stare. 'There's no need to sound as though I was some sort of a freak that no one could possibly want to look at! Marcus told me I had good bone structure and would still look young when I was an old, old woman.' Behind her back, Alys crossed her fingers. What he had actually said was that with bone structure like hers she would grow old gracefully and never really look her age. But she wasn't about to tell Mary O'Malley that. Her version sounded better.

Mary's eyes widened again. 'You call him Marcus?'

'He asked me to. He calls me Alys.'

'Jaysus! Weren't you nervous, going up to his place like that with no one with you? I mean, that cottage is in a pretty remote spot. What if it was just an excuse to get you alone? Some men will try anything.'

She nodded her blonde head knowingly. 'Mrs Dean tells stories that would make your hair curl. She knows the mother of a girl who was taken – well, they suspect she was taken – by white slave traders. Never saw hide nor hair of her again, so they didn't.'

'Mr Dillon is not a white slave trader. You're just being daft now. And I wasn't scared, not one iota.' Again the crossing of the fingers. She was giving the devil a good run for his money today, she thought ruefully.

45

She gazed at Mary speculatively. How come she knew, or thought she knew, so much about men? She was seventeen, the same age as Alys, and not so experienced with the opposite sex as to be an authority on their habits. Why, the only man Mary had looked at for years had been Jackie Rees, although he was playing hard to get, clearly reluctant to be snared. Still, Alys didn't give much for his chances once Mary really got to work on him.

The two girls were standing in the cloakroom of the church hall, fiddling with their hair in front of the spotted mirror. Alys leaned forward, wetting the tip of one finger and running it over the smooth wing of one eyebrow. She wore her hair tied back with a silk ribbon the same colour as the dress, the thick mass puffed out behind her head and falling in a tangle of thick curls down her back.

'You never know,' she said complacently, 'I might become famous, having my picture painted.'

Mary's lips twisted. 'More likely get pneumonia!'

'Oh no, it's not that kind of a painting.'

'I didn't think for one moment that it was. That really would have set the town on its heels, wouldn't it? There's enough talk going on as it is, all of it very suggestive.'

They both laughed. They had admired each other's frocks, Mary's a pale blue that went well with her corn-silk hair, Alys in the buttercup yellow. Mary had to admit she thought it very daring with its square neckline showing the swell of Alys's breasts. She said she felt like being daring, although if Mam were still alive she'd probably insist on pinning a scrap of lace across the top for modesty.

Mary nodded understandingly.

'Of course I wasn't afraid,' Alys said now, catching her friend's eye in the mirror.

'Well, you should have been,' Mary said decisively, moving out into the hall where the musicians were already beginning to tune up. Powdered chalk had been sprinkled on the floor and then rubbed into the hard-wood surface.

Alys still hadn't told Mary about her meeting with Evan Jenkins in the garden that day, or his half promise to see her at the dance. She'd have to wait to see if he turned up. If he didn't . . . she couldn't bear to think how she'd feel if he didn't.

Another thought struck her. What if he should bring that blonde girl she had seen joining him as she walked away? The thought was strangely disturbing.

And then she saw him and he was alone. He entered the hall and stood gazing about him, as though weighing up the chances of this being an evening to enjoy or merely a crushing bore.

He's forgotten, Alys thought with a feeling of desper-ation. His glance took in the white-washed walls and battered bentwood chairs that lined two sides of the hall. Two girls in summery frocks, practising in the centre of the floor, paused to smile invitingly at him.

When he was joined by Mrs Roberts, appointed by the church to keep an eye on these events, the two girls went back to their energetic dancing.

Alys felt Mary nudge her arm. 'Jaysus, there's that young Evan from the big house! Wonder what he's doing here? Wouldn't have thought he'd be interested in this sort of caper. Hardly his style, ya know,' putting on a posh accent.

'How do you know?' demanded Alys. 'How do you know what he likes or doesn't like?'

Mary's brows rose in bewilderment at her friend's sharp retort. 'No need to bite my head off,' she said reproachfully. 'One of the hoity-toity Jenkins slumming with the villagers . . . ?' She stopped, disconcerted by Alys's frown.

Mrs Roberts seemed to have taken root, standing and talking to Evan with animated gestures. Couples in their twenties or older began to fill the hall. The three-man band started with a quickstep. An infinite number of variations were introduced into the steps and the dancers smiled brilliantly at each other, as though sharing a rapturous experience.

Seated on chairs, knees and ankles primly together, Alys and Mary leaned back and watched the dancers, bright smiles on their faces.

How can I sit so still, thought Alys, knowing Evan's so close? That in a moment or two he might be asking me to dance! She watched him covertly as he talked easily with Mrs Roberts, and her heart pounded so loudly she wondered why no one appeared to hear. Her hands trembled as she tucked back a strand of hair.

There's silly you are, Alys Hughes! she scolded herself. He hasn't even looked at you yet. What makes you think he'll even remember you?

Whatever the topic of conversation, it seemed never ending and Alys began to despair. She heard Mary say, jubilantly, 'There's Jackie. Thought for a while he'd changed his mind, so I did. Hey, Jackie!'

The high-pitched call caused everyone to look their way, including Mrs Roberts and Evan. Jackie came meekly, a lamb to the slaughter. He flashed a wide, shy smile at Mary and she instantly rose to dance, pushing her handbag further under her chair with the toe of her shoe. Jackie went pink as he put his arm about her waist, holding her so tightly that Alys heard her say, 'All right, all right! Take it easy. I'll not run away.'

The breath tight in her chest, Alys began to wonder if Evan would ever notice her. Then she saw him give Mrs Roberts a small bow and walk away. Straight to where Alys sat.

'Hello.' It was all he said, then a firm hand was on her waist and an equally firm grasp on her right hand, leading her on to the floor.

'You didn't bring the young lady with you, then?' she asked, unable to stop herself.

'Young lady?'

'The one you were talking to in the garden the other day.'

'Oh, you mean Netta, my sister. No, she doesn't go in for this sort of thing at all.'

She couldn't help adding mischievously. 'Or the dogs?'

He grinned down at her. 'That would have caused an uproar, wouldn't it?' Neither spoke again as they circled the floor. After a moment or two Alys relaxed, allowing Evan to draw her closer. He moved so gracefully, smelled so nicely of soap and some slightly fragrant pomade, not at all like some of the other boys she had danced with. She closed her eyes and allowed the music to take her . . .

'Did you think I'd forgotten you?' he asked, his lips only inches from her hair.

'I haven't really given it much thought,' she answered, deliberately cool.

'Liar!' he breathed, and twirled her into a simple variation of the dance. 'A girl like you, sweet Alys, would be impossible to forget.'

Just in time she stopped herself from punching his arm and saying with a giggle, as she would to Mary, 'Go on!'

When the dance ended and they were seated once more, he remarked, 'Your friend seems to have got herself an admirer.'

Alys smiled, glancing across to where Mary and Jackie were standing, deep in conversation. 'Doesn't she!'

'How about a lemonade?'

'I'd love one, thank you.'

As soon as Evan walked away a gawky young man with a nervously bobbing Adam's apple was beside her, asking her with pink embarrassment if she cared to dance. She folded her hands in her lap and smiled politely. 'I'm waiting for my partner, but thank you all the same.' The boy pulled a wry face and almost fell over his feet as Evan hurried back, carrying two glasses. He handed Alys one and she sipped the cool lemonade appreciatively.

They danced a slow foxtrot and then, very daringly, a tango, the concertina player showing his versatility with many swoops and twists. The dramatic dance had Alys giggling and falling over Evan's feet. 'Shut up!' he hissed. 'This is supposed to be a very serious dance.' She laughed again at the fierce, forbidding expression Evan claimed the dance demanded, and said that all he needed now was a rose between his teeth.

She saw Mary between dances when she went into the cloakroom to tidy her hair. Busy applying bright red lipstick, Mary caught Alys's frown in the mirror and said defensively, 'Don't worry, I'll rub it off before I get home.'

'You'd better! Your mam'd scalp you if she saw you wearing that stuff.'

Satisfied at last, Mary turned to Alys as she thrust the lipstick back into her handbag. 'How're you doing with young Evan, then? I didn't realise you knew him.'

The cloakroom was crowded with other girls. Not wanting to gossip in front of them, though goodness knows she was already at the receiving end of some good old-fashioned looks from Mrs Roberts, Alys said she'd tell her later. 'Doing all right, aren't we?' Mary preened in front of the mirror, patting her hair, admiring the glossy red cupid's bow mouth she had suddenly acquired. 'Do you remember how we both planned to become nuns when we grew up? What a joke, eh?'

Evan danced with Alys until the end of the evening, oblivious to anyone else, and she glowed when he laughed at the funny things she said and wondered at the pure nerve of her, little Alys Hughes, talking to him as though they were equals. At first, conscious of her accent, she'd spoken too quickly, but as the evening wore on she began to relax, feeling more confident in his presence. Although born and bred in Wales, the fine schools to which he had been sent had eradicated all trace of the lilting Welsh tongue from Evan's own voice.

After the last dance, with the band playing 'Goodnight, Ladies', they made their way out of the smoke-filled hall to where Mary was waiting with Jackie. The girl's face was flushed, alive with excitement. As they approached through the darkness, Evan said politely, ' 'Evening, Miss O'Malley. Did you enjoy yourself?'

'Lovely, so it were, Master Evan.' Mary linked Jackie's arm with hers. Her shrewd glance fell on Alys's flushed cheeks and shining eyes. 'You, too?'

'Perfect.' Evan smiled down at Alys, making her cheeks flush even more.

'Jackie's going to see me home, Alys.' Mary gave her a look of triumph. 'Will you be all right?'

'She'll be fine,' said Evan in a voice that brooked no argument. Mary smiled and waved, and clutched Jackie's arm tightly as they began to walk away, her laughter ringing in the night air.

'Come on, then,' said Evan, and took Alys's arm. She said she didn't think he should, suddenly very conscious of the fact that he was the son of the town's wealthiest man. She knew what people would be saying about her if she was seen walking home with him. She'd been aware of the whispering in the hall as he had devoted the whole of the evening to her alone, ignoring all her half-hearted efforts to get him to ask other girls to dance. She'd said, smiling, 'Even if it's only Mrs Roberts. Look how everyone's glaring at me.'

'Let them,' he's scoffed. 'You're worth looking at.'

Now, smiling down at her in the darkness, he said, 'Are you ashamed to be seen with me, then?'

She hung her head and looked down at the cobbles. 'Of course not.'

'Besides, after dancing with me for most of the evening, if people are already talking, why not give them something to talk about? As you remarked when we first met, Craven Bay can be deadly boring. A nice juicy bit of gossip will make the days less dreary. Or don't you agree with me there?'

She thought of Dan and what might happen if the

gossip ever reached *his* ear, hearing Evan say, as though to clinch his argument, 'And, in any case, who cares? I certainly don't.'

Lightly he took her by the elbow and they began to walk. 'I've seen Mary's young man driving the Co-op van, haven't I? Good-looking chap. I bet there's many a girl about here that falls for those looks.'

It was on the tip of Alys's tongue to tell him that Mary had been after Jackie since they were children and in the same class at school, but she remembered who he was and said instead, 'He's nice but very shy. He doesn't seem to bother much with girls. He's a great sportsman, though, plays every weekend when the weather's good.'

'Football?'

'Rugby, mostly. He's what you might call a local hero over his rugby playing.'

'Good for him! I like Mary. We often have a joke if we meet in the garden when she goes out to pick peas or beans for Mrs Dean.' They talked companionably and Alys felt herself afloat in happiness. She didn't want to think of tomorrow, there was just here and now, and she wouldn't have accepted a king's ransom in exchange for the company of this man who walked so proudly beside her. It was as though she had known him for years.

Moonlight softened the harsh streets. It made Alys's pansy eyes glow and set her dark hair glimmering.

Evan was thoroughly taken with her and wondered how he was going to persuade her to continue this very promising friendship. It was a change to be with a girl who was honest and free of ostentation, with no artifice about her. He had enjoyed the evening, even if by his standards the music was atrocious, the laughter of the village women painful to the ear, and the hall had seen better days.

At her door she stopped. She glanced up at him and he stepped back a pace, fearing that any advance he made might be rejected. 'I like you, Alys. I'm sorry if I made it too obvious.'

'I like you, too.'

When she smiled, he bent his head and kissed her, a long, lingering kiss that she wanted never to stop. Feelings too wild and wonderful to bear raced through her body, leaving her breathless. When he let her go, he looked down at her as though he had just discovered the most wonderful thing in the world. Tracing the line of her jaw with one finger, he said, 'You'd better go. It's late and I think I can hear that stepfather of yours moving around in there. Or,' grinning wickedly, 'is he used to you bidding your men friends goodnight at the door?'

This time she did punch his arm.

Chapter Four

'You didn't even tell me you knew him!' Mary's voice was so full of resentment Alys had to smile.

'You didn't ask me.'

'But I'm your best friend. We tell each other everything.'

Alys laughed, the happiness bubbling up inside her. 'Of course we do, *cariad*.' She hadn't wanted to talk about it, fearing that to bring those sudden and quite inexplicable feelings out into the open would be tempting fate.

The two girls sat on their usual seat in the vegetable garden, the sun warm on their heads. Through the archway of neatly clipped yew, Alys could see the more formal garden. White butterflies hovered over the orderly beds of flowers: tall foxgloves by the wall, the bright scarlet of geraniums, the vivid blue of lobelia, yellow and pink snapdragons. Out of sight, obscured by the hedge, a small fountain sparkled in the sunlight like a bridal veil.

Turning to grasp Mary's hands in her own, she began to describe her first encounter with Evan. 'I should be everlastingly grateful to those dogs,' she laughed, 'for without them he might just have passed me by without speaking!'

'Are you seeing him again?'

Alys nodded. 'I don't know when, though.'

'You sly old thing, you!' Clearly Mary was impressed. 'Well, it won't be for a while, love, for he's had to go off on business for his father.'

Her heart sank. The disappointment must have shown on her face for Mary laughed and said, 'Just a few days, though, Mrs Dean mentioned. A week, no more.'

A whole week! Alys wondered how she would endure it. In a week he could have forgotten her.

'He's a nice man, Master Evan,' Mary went on thoughtfully. 'Much nicer than that sister of his.'

'Is she pretty?' Alys remembered only the blonde hair, hanging loose about her shoulders.

'In a frozen pudding kind of way. But Master Evan, now, he's always polite, the perfect gentleman. He's never bothered much with girls, although his father is forever inviting new ones to the house – thrusting them under his nose, so to speak.'

Alys's mouth twisted. 'Society girls, you mean?'

'That's the only kind men from his background know, love.' Mary patted her friend's hand. 'Don't let it bother you. Young Evan's got his head screwed on right. He'll know what to do. It's just that . . .'

She paused and Alys looked stricken, fear taking hold of her. Was Mary about to tell her of a previous engagement? Someone he'd perhaps known all his lifetime? She mustn't show dismay if this was so. Not even to Mary. She lifted her chin proudly and met the other girl's eyes.

'What?'

'It's just that, sometimes, this sort of thing doesn't work out too well. People from different backgrounds . . . I'd hate to see my best friend get hurt.'

'I won't get hurt. You don't have to worry about

that. I've yet to meet the man who can hurt me.'

In spite of her brave words, though, Mary could see the anxiety in Alys's eyes. She thought she was so grown-up, so able to deal with all that life threw at her. She'd been doing that for years, hadn't she? Ever since her mother died. So what had changed?

They heard a voice calling from the direction of the house and Mary said, 'There's old Dean shouting for me. I'd better go, else she'll be out here giving me a clip about the ear.' She peered into Alys's face. 'All right, are you? You're not going to go off and do something silly, like?'

'I'm all right, and I'm not going to go off and do something silly, so stop your worrying. I know what I'm about.'

The sun still shone but for Alys its warmth seemed to have diminished as she walked back down the hill to the town. A whole week of long, dismal days faced her until Evan's return and she wondered why it should affect her so. Daft thing! she told herself. Love at first sight is a myth, don't you know that? Then why should she feel only his smile would make her happy again?

Since her early teenage days, boys had been attracted to her and she'd enjoyed their admiration, although none had ever taken her fancy as this man from the big house on the headlands had done. Was it because he was different, his behaviour more courteous, his whole manner more easy and relaxed? She knew it was all those things, but most of all the sureness with which he seemed to know exactly what to do and say, how not to treat her with that disdainful arrogance that had distinguished so many of his class in the few dealings she had had with them. He'd told her he liked her, and she believed him. Which was really all that mattered . . .

She burned her stepfather's supper and almost let the fire go out so there was not enough hot water for his bath. 'What's wrong wi' you, girl?' He straightened from washing at the sink, the faint blue lines of the coal dust still ingrained in his skin. No amount of washing or hot water would eradicate them; they would be there until the day he died. 'You're as distracted as Jones the farmer's cow let loose in a field of clover.'

Rubbing his forearms dry with the rough towel, Dan gave her a sidelong glance. 'Up in the cottage at the cliffs again, were you? Hear he's a painter, Gareth Dillon's son, who used to live here in the valley before they moved up to London. Giving you money for posing for him, is it? Not that I've seen a brass farthing of it yet.' His eyes gleamed as he dragged the chair from the kitchen table and seated himself, ready for his meal. 'Well, we all know what these artists are like, there's enough talk already about that, so just you make sure it's cockles you're selling, my girl, and nothin' else.'

'Shut up!' Shaken from her reverie, Alys turned on him in a fury. 'Just shut up! You know nothing about it, so don't go passing judgement until you do. Mr Dillon is a gentleman – but then you wouldn't know about that, would you? I sit for him, and that's all.'

'I've every right to ask, my girl. I'm your stepfather and I gave a promise to your dear mother on her death bed.' And here he lifted his eyes heavenwards in a way that made her want to hit him. 'I vowed that I would take care of you, and aren't I doing my best to keep that promise?'

Bloody old hypocrite! she thought. I'd as soon push him over the sea wall as give him the money I earned. She didn't bother to ask how he knew about it. Gossip thrived in these mean streets and it wasn't hard to imagine the sniggers and sly remarks that were being bandied about.

Without saying another word she grabbed her shawl, and wrapping it tightly about her shoulders, went out, walking the streets where the Co-op and other shops were still ablaze with lights. She gave the pubs in the narrow lanes behind the quay a wide berth so as to avoid the drunks weaving their way from one to another.

The darkness brought back thoughts of Evan and that niggle of doubt returned. Had he really liked her, or just said it to round off the evening? Was she, perhaps, taking his light flirtatious talk too seriously, reading into it things that weren't there? He had admitted he wanted to see her again, that their friendship must not stop once he had said goodnight on her doorstep. And he'd kissed her . . . Even so, oughtn't she to take everything he said with a pinch of salt? Why was she letting it upset her so? Why had her stepfather's churlishness touched her more than usual? She was used to it by now and usually shrugged it off like an ill-fitting garment. A particularly old and smelly one! Water off a duck's back.

She sighed, holding the shawl more tightly about her. When all was said and done, Evan would soon be back. A week, Mary had said. Until then, she had her morning visits to the white cottage, with Drogo dozing peacefully outside in the sunshine and the polite conversation of Marcus Dillon washing over her while he re-created the colours of a Welsh seashore.

* * *

Mary was having trouble of her own. In the warmth of the kitchen of her parents' house that Sunday morning, they had been discussing Jackie Rees. Mr O'Malley's face was flushed a bright red. More than ever he resembled a little bantam cock against the calm plumpness of his wife. His long upper lip curled in derision as he blurted out, 'There'll be no heathen nonconformists in our family, my girl, so just you think on. Next time he calls, you leave him to me.'

Mary drew herself up to her full height. At five feet four she was taller than the blustering little eejit who was her father. 'I will not!' she said with spirit. 'I'll see who I like. It has nothing to do with you.'

'It has everything to do with me, young lady. Don't you go taking that attitude with me or you'll feel the back of me 'and, that you will.'

'I'll go out with Jackie if I want to.' She thrust an angry face close to her father's. 'Aye, and *marry* him if I take a notion.'

'Over my dead body!'

Mrs O'Malley gasped and made a hurried sign of the cross, watching her irate daughter and husband glare at each other like fighters in opposite corners of the ring.

'Holy Mother!' she breathed under her breath. 'Let's get this lot to Mass before they kill each other.' Her husband, for all that she loved him, was a heavy cross to bear.

If anyone had asked her, which they never did, she would have unhesitatingly stood up for Jackie Rees. Although not of their own faith, he seemed a clean-living young man, well set-up, and always with a pleasant word when they met. Her two eldest sons, Kenny and Dennis, thought the world of him and couldn't wait for their sister and he to marry so that he could become one of their family. Jackie's father, along with a dozen other men, had been killed in a colliery disaster when Jackie was still a young lad. Unable to take the hardship that a woman alone would face, his mother had run off with a passing insurance salesman shortly afterwards, leaving Jackie in the care of her late husband's widowed sister-in-law.

A big-hearted woman who had never been blessed with children of her own, Ellen Rees had taken the little boy without a qualm and seemed not to have regretted it for one moment. Jackie was a good boy, she was fond of telling her friend, Mrs O'Malley; thoughtful and sensitive to her every need. Arthritis had set in, making her more dependent on Jackie than ever as he grew up, and she never tired of boasting to her neighbours how he had told her that after all these years it was now *his* turn to look after *her*.

It had been no secret that Mary O'Malley fancied him and people said that although the O'Malleys were considered a wild bunch, that father of theirs and the two older boys, anyway, the mother was a hardworking woman, always neat and tidy in her blue print pinny, and Ellen Rees should be thankful that Mary showed every indication of taking after her and not her feckless father.

On Sunday mornings, the irrepressible O'Malley clan turned out in force, Mary's two brothers racing through the churchyard after the service followed by young Billy, the baby, on sturdy if somewhat unsure legs. Freedom seemed very precious after the enforced hour of standing and kneeling and the incomprehensible Latin phrases. Their mother shuffled her feet uncomfortably as she paused on the steps on her way out to shake the hand of Father Goodhew and receive his blessing, only too aware of his fierce blue gaze resting on her noisy children.

'They have sound lungs and a robust constitution, Mrs O'Malley,' he remarked dryly.

'Aye, that they have, Father.'

'Trumpets will not be needed at the gates of Saint Peter to herald their approach,' the old priest added as a particularly strident yell assailed their ears and those of everyone of the congregation who had stopped to greet the priest.

Mrs O'Malley flushed. 'I'll get them home, Father. It's just that they like to let off steam, so to speak, and sometimes forget where they are.'

The smallest of the boys, young Billy, had been sent flying. Mrs O'Malley dragged him ignominiously to his feet, then bent down and gave him a sharp slap on the seat of his pants, more out of habit than anger, causing the weeping child to shriek even louder.

Alys was keeping an eye out for Mary, acutely eager to speak to her, wondering if the Irish girl had any news of Evan. She glowed when Mary said he was back from Cardiff, hugging the knowledge to her. 'Well, smile then,' teased Mary, giving her a poke on the arm. 'I'd have thought you'd be pleased. I was dying for Mass to end so's I could tell you.'

'I *am* pleased. Thanks, Mary.'

How could her friend know that her whole being had hung suspended in a state of waiting until she could meet him again? That her heart thudded at the very thought of him. She wondered if Mary felt the same way about Jackie Rees. Mary glanced over to where her parents were gathering the boys together. 'I have to go, Alys. Oh, by the way,' almost as an afterthought, 'I was to tell you that if you happened – just *happened*, mind you – to be walking on the west beach this afternoon, you might find someone else walking there, too.'

Alys flushed with pleasure, although she couldn't help the note of resentment as she answered, 'You might have told me before!'

'Well, I'm telling you now. I love to see the usually cool and collected Miss Alys Hughes looking as though she is sitting on pins and needles. And would you look at her blushing! You wouldn't see redder than that on a monkey's backside.'

Rudely, Alys put out her tongue, then laughed as Mary parodied her action, their laughter fading as Father Goodhew looked their way. Alys grimaced and Mary hurried to join the rest of the family.

Although he was not a churchgoer, Dan had never tried to prevent Alys's own attendance. Sometimes it was the only place she could talk to Mary who was allowed time off for church every Sunday morning.

Today she could hardly wait for Dan to finish his midday meal before setting off for her walk. In the park, a noisy game of rugby was in progress, watched by men who stood in groups, hands in trouser pockets, white silk scarves about their throats. As Alys walked by, wolf whistles mingled with the shouts of encouragement for the players. A number of the younger men called out, 'Hey, Alys, looking for a bit o' company, then?' Used to this, she ignored them, thinking only of her rendezvous with Evan Jenkins.

The day had turned windy, strong gusts sweeping in from the sea, beading her hair and eyelashes with salty spray. She hurried down the steep path cut into the headland, to the beach below. It was a wondrous sight: a multitude of greens cloaking the high cliffs, silver-white beaches, and a sea that varied from pale blueish grey to deep sapphire further out. Today the wind teased the water into white horses and the usually gentle waves surged noisily on to the sand. She skipped the rest of the way down the path and jumped the last few feet, the black patent leather shoes with the small cuban heels she had bought for the dance landing half buried in the soft sand.

The tributary of the river ran fast here, flooding across the narrow isthmus on its way to the sea. Its narrowest point was crossed by a line of roughly placed stepping stones.

Holding up her skirt with one hand, slipping off her shoes and carrying them by their straps in the other, she jumped lightly over the white stones. Concentrating on where she put each foot, she didn't hear the man who came up behind her until two arms were about her waist and she was lifted and carried the rest of the way. Dumped on dry sand, she turned with an angry exclamation to find herself looking straight into the eyes of Evan Jenkins. He was grinning from ear to ear, thoroughly enjoying the trick he had played on her.

'Evan!' Her greeting was so joyful, his grin widened. He placed a hand on either side of her small waist, steadying her, as her feet sank into the sand. 'There now,' he said, still smiling. 'There really is no need for you to throw yourself at my feet to show how pleased you are to see me.'

Playfully, she attempted to punch him and felt her hand captured and lifted to his lips where he kissed her fingers one by one, grimacing at the grains of sand upon them.

'You nearly frightened the life out of me,' she chided. 'Coming on me like that. Didn't even hear you, so I didn't.'

'But you're glad to see me, aren't you?' He stood back, holding her at arm's length while his eyes examined her carefully. 'You look even more adorable than when I saw you at the dance a week ago.' The wind had teased her hair until it seemed a wild confusion of silky black filaments about her head, tendrils clinging to her mouth and cheeks.

Evan felt his heart lift and turn over, just gazing at her. 'Your hair's beautiful,' he murmured, lifting his hand to touch it, smoothing it back from her face.

Alys wrinkled her nose. 'Rats' tails!'

'Beautiful rats' tails.'

Young and full of life, like no other girl he had ever met, Evan gloried in her looks and quick wit. He knew that between them, given the chance, there could be something sweet even if it proved not to be lasting. He'd known her for such a short time and already she was threatening to lay claim to his heart; had inadvertently been the cause of his father's exasperation with him on his return from Cardiff without the signed agreement which had been the sole purpose of his visit. The boy had to learn, was Thomas's theme these days, constantly drumming it into him, reminding him he wasn't on this earth to exist only for pleasure but also to work. More particularly, to work in the family business . . .

Evan sometimes wondered if he could ever live up to the old man's hopes. 'If I didn't know better,' his father had exclaimed, peevishly, in his hearing, 'I'd say the young fool was in love.'

The thought of seeing Alys again had kept the hot blood coursing through his veins and for once he hadn't quailed under his father's frown.

Alys tugged at her hand and he released it reluctantly, liking the feel of the small, warm fingers, the rather rough touch of the palm. She made an endeavour to brush the sand from her skirt, but the wind took the full material and tugged at it so impudently it was a losing battle. Today being Sunday, she had on a green cotton dress with a round neck and wide sleeves that came to just below her elbows. A narrow ruching of a darker green trimmed the modest neckline and edged the sleeves. The matching green ribbon that had confined her hair was long gone, snatched by the wind.

Straightening from the futile battle with her skirt, she gazed up at him from under her eyelashes. Fishing for confirmation, she said lightly, 'So you've got nothing better to do on a Sunday than walk on the sands, eh?'

'As you see,' he said, confirming nothing. They walked to the edge of the water, disturbing a plundering flock of sea birds, and had a competition, skimming flat stones, seeing who could throw them the furthest. She guessed Evan let her win, although he steadfastly denied it. In the distance, above the sound of the wind, they could hear the cries of sheep on the headland. They walked the length of the beach, Alys bare-footed, carrying her shoes.

After church she had removed her stockings, the only decent pair she possessed, knowing the sand would be wet from the out-going tide. She couldn't afford to risk them on the rocks and rough places over which she had to walk before reaching the beach. Evan dodged the creamy waves as they washed over her feet, grimacing, pretending to shiver, asking if the water wasn't icy.

'I'm used to it,' she told him. 'It doesn't bother me.'

'One day,' he said, 'I'm going to walk along a beach where the sea is warm and you can just lie and bake in the sun and do nothing else. There'd be palm trees to shelter under if the heat became too much, but I can't imagining that happening.' He looked at her. 'Would you come with me if I asked nicely?'

She went along with what she decided was his teasing. 'I might.'

'I'm a stubborn man,' he told her. 'I could very well keep pestering you until you say yes.'

She bent down and gathered a handful of damp sand, letting it trickle back through her fingers. Didn't that just sound grand? If only life would go the way one wished it! The skies had darkened while they walked, unnoticed by the young couple, purple-black clouds like bruises forming far out to sea. Now a flurry of wind showered rain over their faces and Alys caught his hand and cried, 'Come on, I know a cave. We used to play hide and seek in there when we were children. Otherwise we're going to get soaked.'

Hand in hand they ran, her bare feet barely leaving an imprint in the sand. Evan's went deeper, slowly filling with water as they passed. He could see a dark opening in the base of the cliff face and she pulled his hand, making for that. It was narrow and quite a squeeze. She remarked wryly that it had never seemed that difficult when she was a little girl. 'We used to slip in and out like fishes.'

Inside the air was chill and damp, smelling strongly of seaweed. She could tell by Evan's face that he wasn't impressed. Still, when suddenly the sun came out, finding a chink through the moving clouds, it was with new eyes that he viewed the sandy floor and glistening rock walls.

When he turned to take her in his arms, Alys took a deep breath that became lodged in her throat, then released it with a shuddering sigh. Giving him a little push, she said, 'Don't, Evan. Don't spoil it.' She could not explain the instinctive restraint, that feeling as though, somewhere in the back of her mind, a warning bell was sounding.

There was damp sand clinging to the point of her chin and he raised his hand, brushing it away, saying, 'There, that's better.'

The hand stayed there, cupping the curve of her jaw, his fingers splayed over her throat. 'If we stay here long enough,' he said softly, 'we can forget the world we know exists and make up one of our own.'

'But it does exist. No getting away from that, no matter how long we hide away. And our two worlds are so different they might not even be on the same planet.'

'We can still pretend.'

She did not reply, could not put into words her sense of unease, the tightening of her stomach at the touch of his hand, the knowledge that she had got herself into a situation that she did not know how to handle. Fear stirred in her, heightening the tension. She told herself she should never have suggested taking shelter in this place, that it was too lonely, too isolated. And then, lifting her gaze to his face, that handsome face with the bright fair hair falling over his forehead, wildly teased by the wind, she was swept away by the feelings that had earlier gladdened her. She told herself she was being foolish. That this man would never hurt her. That she, Alys Hughes, who could hold her own with most men, easily bandying jests with the crew of some newly arrived fishing boat, could be at a loss for words was inconceivable.

'What's the matter?' said Evan. 'You're as tense as a strand of wire.'

Defensively, she said, 'What should I be tense about?'

He leered down at her in true music hall cad's manner. 'Ah, my pretty maiden, that remains to be seen. Who knows what schemes I might have for you, tucked up my sleeve.'

She couldn't help but laugh and immediately felt better.

'You're an eejit, as Mary would say.'

'An idiot, maybe, but a nice one. And a very good-looking one, you have to admit.' The ball of his thumb moved lightly over her cheek, his eyes smiling down into hers.

'There's vanity for you,' she said, lightly. 'Is it inherited or all your own?'

'Oh, all my own, of course. Although my sister is a very beautiful woman, if one can overlook the spoiled wilfulness of her nature, mine is a very special self-regard, only divulged to people who mean a lot to me.'

'I should have thought that was a part of your character that you'd have preferred to conceal.'

'Self-regard?' Was he still teasing, she wondered, or could she detect a serious note creeping into his voice? There couldn't be, of course. Hadn't she already decided he was perfect! A man she could happily spend the rest of her days with if he so wished. There was a sudden burst of wind, sweeping in the icy rain, and the sun of a few minutes ago scuttled back beneath the dark clouds, like a thief in the night. The light was so bad that she could barely make out Evan's face. She put her hands up to his chest and gave a little push. 'We ought to be off. There's going to be an almighty storm . . .'

His thumb, stroking her cheek, was suddenly still. 'You don't really mean that,' he said, gazing down at her with those blue, blue eyes. He bent his head and his lips found hers, at first experimentally and then growing more daring as his mouth moved gently, caressingly, forcing her to respond. It was having disastrous effects on her, causing an uprush of emotions that she had never felt before. A red-hot flame that she was powerless to extinguish licked at her nerve ends.

It was spring and she was seventeen and there was no way she could deny those tumultuous feelings that over-ruled her natural caution. Instinctively, her hands went up behind his head, fingers locking in the longish fair hair. She could almost hear Father Goodhew holding forth on the subject of lust and other deadly sins of the flesh and a deep flush crept up her throat and over her cheeks.

Timeless sensations swirled through her, heating her flesh with age-old needs. He groaned and his roaming hands moulded her closely to his body, holding her tightly. 'Alys, Alys!' he whispered.

Her legs felt as though they were made of rubber and she was glad to lower herself to the sandy floor of the cave, feeling him settle beside her. Nothing existed, neither time nor place. All that Alys knew was that she was enclosed in the warmth of Evan's arms. Little beads of perspiration were forming on his upper lip and when he looked down at her face he seemed to be warring within himself.

An instinct as old as time warned her that she had enticed him as far as she dared go. It wasn't fair to provoke him further. For hadn't Mary told her about men, cautioning her that you came to a point where you had to cry halt!

Gently, she pushed him away, then twisted to lie with her head on his shoulder, her back against him. She could hear the solid beat of his heart, feel the enfolding strength of his arms. Her body still tingled with pleasure from his kisses and she sighed softly when his lips nuzzled the hair along the back of her neck.

'Alys, sweet Alys,' he murmured. 'I've never felt like this about anyone before. It fills me with panic.'

She turned her head and kissed his throat where the white shirt opened at the collar. 'I know. I feel the same. But what sweet panic!'

'You've disturbed me since the day we first met,' he confessed, softly, 'when those blasted dogs sent you nearly flying in the garden.' Before she could answer he turned her towards him, framing her face with his hands and tilting it upwards. His burning kiss seared her lips, leaving little doubt that all he said was true. Or so it seemed to the captivated Alys . . .

'I love you.'

She sighed, too confused to think straight. 'You hardly know me.'

'It doesn't matter. Time has nothing to do with it. I shall never feel this way about anybody else.'

His touch played havoc with her strength of mind. When he bent his head to kiss her again, it was an effort to turn away at the last moment. His mouth grazed her cheek. 'I think we should go,' she said, the caution she had long denied finally overcoming the spell of his kisses. Suddenly she felt shy.

'It's early yet,' he reasoned. 'This place is so quiet and peaceful. Why do you have to rush home?'

The light outside the cave had dimmed as the rain continued and the sun stayed behind the clouds. It must be later than she thought.

'There's a tempter you are, Evan Jenkins,' she teased, in control of herself again. 'My stepfather doesn't like to be kept waiting for his supper, and tonight the pubs aren't open so he'll be sitting at home working up a fine old sweat.'

'Humph!' He rose to his feet, brushing off the grains of damp sand clinging to his clothes, and held out his hands to pull her after him. She allowed him to walk her part of the way home, his arm about her waist until they came in sight of the town, then insisted that they part. Reluctantly he agreed, reminding her of their plans for further meetings. Her step was light as she walked the rest of the way despite the thin rain and her damp clothing. She would be seeing Evan again, and nothing else mattered.

Surprisingly there was no sight of Dan, although the kettle was singing on the hob and the fire threw out a good heat. She changed her frock for her usual attire of skirt and blouse and hung the damp green garment over the back of a chair before the fire. In these dark little cottages, fires were seldom allowed to go out for no matter what the weather outside, indoors it was always cold and damp.

Without wasting time she began to prepare the supper, heating up the big bowl of cawl, a nourishing soup that was almost a meal in itself, and buttering slices of bara brith, a fruit loaf she had baked herself. She brewed the tea and let it stand on the hob to keep hot.

Although her hands were occupied her thoughts were with Evan, striding home, whistling a jaunty air. It was wonderful to know that he loved her, for gazing into those good-looking features or remembering the cultured voice, she wondered what on earth he could see in her, a common street hawker who sold cockles for a living from the back of a donkey.

What would become of them? The gap between their two backgrounds was so wide, difficult to bridge. Would the love they felt for each other be strong enough to overcome it?

Since the death of her parents, love had been a stranger to Alys Hughes, the nearest she had come to it being the friendship offered by Mary. And a woman needed more than that kind of love. She had been forced to grow up without a soul to offer her advice, no one to stretch out warm arms to still the anguish of having seen her beloved mother laid to rest in the churchyard, in a grave like a bleak, open wound in the grass. No one to assuage the shock she'd felt when she first noticed Mam's wedding ring was missing from her finger. She'd faced the neighbour who had come to lay Mam out, steeling herself to ask about the ring.

The woman gave Alys a pitying look. ''Spect your da took it for safe keeping, *cariad*.'

'It was Mam's ring, not his. I want it to stay with her.'

She had faced Dan with her accusation when he came home, screaming that he'd stolen Mam's ring, that he was to give it back or else . . .

She remembered the mighty surge of anger that had overcome her when he'd guffawed, and echoed mockingly, 'Or else what? The ring's somewhere, girl. Don't worry, it'll turn up.'

But it hadn't and Alys was haunted by the vision of Dan sliding it from Mam's cold finger and taking it into old Jakob's shop to pawn. She'd persuaded Mary to come with her and inquire of the elderly Jewish man who owned the shop. Daringly they had pushed open the glass door, hearing the jangling tinkle of the bell and waiting in trepidation for Jakob to appear.

The air reeked with the smell of stale perspiration and moth balls from the clothes stored there. The two girls started violently, clutching at each other, as a sudden draught of air caught the rows of dark suits and overcoats that hung in a line from the ceiling, causing them to flutter alarmingly.

Digging her fingers into her friend's arm, Mary had whispered, 'Me mam'd skin me alive if she knew I'd bin here.'

The ancient pawnbroker himself smelled almost as bad as the contents of his shop. Setting the broken gold-rimmed glasses more firmly on the end of his nose, he listened with ill-contained impatience to their story. Alys had glimpsed no pity in those dark, unrelenting eyes. It was well known in Craven Bay that pity was not Jakob's strong point, and even before she had finished talking he was telling her that he had so many wedding rings waiting to be reclaimed – trays and trays of 'em – that unless Alys could identify her mother's ring, he really could not help. Not without a pawn ticket.

He spread his hands and shrugged. Tears shimmered in Alys's eyes as she watched him return to the huge leatherbound ledgers behind the iron grille that protected the counter and the cash till.

The missing ring never turned up and Alys never did forgive her stepfather, although she never again accused him to his face.

Chapter Five

The sky was black and glowering. It looked as though a thousand storms were about to break over Craven Bay, although further along the headland, Marcus Dillon could see a fugitive burst of sunlight catching the tops of the trees.

Over the town, it was already raining; a dark, smudgy curtain that fell from sky to earth, making shoppers run for cover. He wondered if the girl would come today. He'd explained that this would probably be the last sitting. The painting was finished all but a few touches. Those he could do from memory. Still, the thought that she might not come troubled him deeply. He admitted to himself that he'd allowed himself to become obsessed by her, her freshness and beauty, and the thought of a morning when she didn't arrive at his gate with that ridiculous donkey made him feel dull and out of sorts. He despised himself for letting his emotions get the upper hand but he had no control over his heart, nor the way it thudded whenever she came close.

His mother had been ill and as a dutiful son he should return home. And he would, just as soon as he'd finished this bloody painting. A painting, he kept telling himself, he should never have started in the first place. A girl riding a donkey over the sands on a wild stretch of Welsh coast! Whoever heard of anything so ridiculous?

His father would think he'd lost his senses, and his mother wipe a tear from the corner of her eye and murmur reproachfully that, really, he seemed to prefer being anywhere to being home.

He'd been wrong about Alys in so many ways. First he'd been wrong in thinking her a common street hawker, interested only in spending the money she earned on strong gin or ale. She had a natural grace and dignity that belied her rough background. Marcus was a man who was strongly attracted to women. There had been many in his life, though none more than a passing fancy, women he could look back upon with a smile, thinking of the pleasure they had given each other. Only one had been a constant and she was not interested in marriage. Not yet, anyway. Fleetingly, he compared Joanna Ambrey to Alys. Poles apart, how could he even class them together? Alys as prickly as a young hedgehog, and the elegant Joanna who for a short time had taken Paris by its heels, loftily ignoring the whispers about her own free-thinking lifestyle.

He saw the curtain of rain drift slowly aside and then, plodding purposefully over the wet grass, the little donkey, head bent, long ears drooping in dejection at the gloomy weather. Alys walked beside it, the sturdy boots she wore today covered in mud. About her was wrapped the plaid shawl that appeared to be her only outer garment. The dampness of the air seemed to make her mass of dark hair even more rebellious. It sprang about her small face, made rosy by the rain, like a dark silken cloud.

He gave himself a shake. No use standing here when there was work to be done. He thought what he could say to her about her stepfather's visit the evening before. He'd been cleaning his paint brushes with an old rag kept for the purpose when a shadow in the open doorway darkened the room. Looking up, he'd seen a man, tall and broad-shouldered, with cropped grey hair. He was dressed in a dark jacket and trousers, a white silk scarf knotted loosely about his neck. His cloth cap was in his hand and he twisted it nervously as he stood gazing at Marcus. Even from where he stood, he could smell the drink on the newcomer's breath.

Before he could speak, the man had said, 'Mr Dillon, is it? The one who's painting my Alys?' Everything about him warned Marcus that this wasn't a friendly visit. He waited.

'Well, I'm the lass's stepfather and guardian, and I've come to tell you I want no hanky-panky, hear? Alys is a good girl, never given me any trouble except for a bit o' lip now and then. I don't want no gentleman from London coming down 'ere and corrupting her.' One eyelid had been lowered in a crafty wink and he added, in a man-to-man tone, 'Of course, she's a pretty lass and should you feel inclined . . . well, who knows the ways of wimmin? Alys likes the nice things in life. A proper gentlewoman her mother was, a lovely girl, and money's tight at the moment. But then,' with another wink that made Marcus's fist ache to reach out and strike him, 'it allus is wi' the likes of us.'

He got no further. 'You'd better go,' said Marcus ominously, 'before I break your neck.'

Dan's expression had turned sour, although he took a

step back at the same time. His tone was querulous as he said, 'No need to take that tone wi' me, sir. There's men who'd give their right arm to get my Alys.'

'And you'd sell her to the highest bidder!' Marcus's own voice had been tinged with scorn. He strode forward and caught the man by the front of his jacket, saying in a low voice, 'You're lucky I'm just asking you to go, and not kicking your backside down the garden path. But if I see you hanging around here again, I'll tear the head from your shoulders. Understand?'

He pushed the other man away. Dan staggered, clutching at the doorframe for support. Reproachfully, he'd said, 'Don't tell me you haven't already thought of it? Up here all alone wi' my lass all this time, and not one . . . ?' And Marcus felt his temper rise. 'I warn you,' and he emphasised each word, 'I want no more of your thinly veiled blackmail hints or your disgusting verbal innuendoes against your stepdaughter. So, are you going or do I have to . . . ?'

He took a threatening step forward and Dan retreated hastily the way he had come. Marcus watched as the thick-set figure wove its way back along the path over the headlands. He felt strangely let down, as though Alys had betrayed him in some way. Could she have known about her stepfather's visit? He didn't think so. Surely she would never have condoned such a thing? And yet with these people, as Dan had said, money was always tight, and Alys was a young and attractive girl . . .

The memory of the man's crafty face had disturbed Marcus's sleep. When Alys finally tied an extremely bad-tempered donkey to his usual tree and entered the cottage, she sensed straight away that something was wrong. This morning Marcus didn't seem in any hurry but seemed to want to talk. As she removed her muddied boots, putting them on a newspaper, careful not to stain any part of the floor, she watched him pour himself a drink. Her lips curled. This early in the morning? Whatever ailed him, it must be bad!

He faced her as she straightened up, slipping the wet shawl from her shoulders and draping it on the back of a chair close to the stove, her bare feet pink and chill-looking. 'You're a very pretty girl,' he began without preamble, 'but then, I've already told you that, haven't I? And you, in all modesty, agreed.'

She didn't know what to answer and so said nothing. He was watching her as though they shared some secret and he was waiting for her to acknowledge the fact.

But Alys knew she shared no secret with this man. She was grateful for the money he gave to her. Apart from that, she didn't give him a second thought.

'I wonder,' he began easily, 'who it was that suggested your stepfather should pay me a visit? Did you discuss it together or was it his own idea?'

'Why should my stepfather visit you?' she demanded, surprised at his tone.

'You didn't know he had? You're sure about that?'

'I didn't know you had even met my stepfather. *And* I haven't the faintest idea what you're talking about.'

His eyes narrowed. 'You put on a good act, I must say. Very artless and innocent. Is it a special technique of yours?'

Anger heightened her colour. 'If you insist on talking in riddles, how am I supposed to understand you?' she said hotly. 'And I very much resent your tone.'

He smiled thinly. 'Don't give me that. You know damn well what I mean.' He wasn't even pretending to be polite any longer. His blue eyes moved over her in glittering appraisal. 'You know very well about that visit from the man who calls himself your stepfather. Did you arrange it between you, or was it his idea?'

She stood very still, her back straight and proud. She was so angry it was difficult not to march straight out of the door and back down the hill, dragging poor Drogo behind her.

When she didn't answer he tossed off the remainder of his drink and put the empty glass down sharply. 'All right, if you insist on playing the innocent, I'll spell it out – although I would have thought you'd appreciate a bit more subtlety. Your stepfather came here last night, with insinuations that made me very angry indeed. I think you can guess what they were. Suffice it to say he didn't believe that I was paying you just for sitting still.'

Alys was appalled. 'There's a thing!' she breathed, still not completely understanding. 'And why should he feel that?'

He sighed. 'You really are a glutton for punishment, Alys Hughes. As an attractive girl, I imagine men have propositioned you before now. Do I really need to go on?'

She gasped. 'You mean—' the words came out brokenly, 'that he accused you of . . . that my stepfather said . . . ?'

He gazed up at the ceiling in exasperation. 'Good God, why do women exaggerate so? You sound quite melodramatic. I am not interested in deals of that nature. I find women more than willing to, shall we say, accommodate me, without resorting to such measures.'

The shock of his words made her feel suddenly sick. 'I don't believe you! Even my stepfather wouldn't be that – that inhuman.'

But he would, a small voice told her. Hadn't he spoken of it only the other night, warning her crudely to mind that it was only cockles she was selling?

Marcus was gazing at her searchingly. 'Are you really telling me you knew nothing about this? That you never discussed it with your stepfather?'

'Of course I knew nothing about it,' she snapped. 'Don't you think I'd have stopped him if I had?'

She had to get away from this arrogant man who seemed to take such delight in taunting her. She turned to go, making for the front door, and felt his hand on her arm, pulling her back. For a moment she almost lost control, thinking he was forcing her, but heard him say quietly, 'Just a minute! Haven't you forgotten something?'

She turned to glare at him. 'What?'

'The last touches to the painting. And the money I still owe you. You've worked for it, you might as well have it.'

His blue eyes glittered with amusement now. 'Frankly, I find it difficult to believe in a stepfather who would offer someone he loves for monetary gain, and the girl quite unaware of it. But we'll play it your way. The game has a certain astringent quality that makes it appealing. And I never did care for things, or women, that came too easily.'

As soon as the words were uttered, he would have given anything to have withdrawn them. Why was he talking this way to Alys?

She flared into resentment. He was twisting everything she said to suit himself. 'All right,' she hissed, 'I'll stay until you've finished the bloody painting. But I warn you, I won't listen to another word of this.'

She followed him quietly into the studio and sat stiffly while he made the finishing touches. Then, standing back, he said, 'All right, you may look at it now.'

It was sheer magic. The colours of the sea in the background merging with the pale sky, the turquoise shimmer of the waves, and in the foreground herself, perched on the back of the nut-brown donkey, her hair swirling about her head as though tossed by a thousand teasing winds.

Unbelievable that such an appearance of life could be produced by nothing more than a cunning mixture of paint on canvas.

'It's beautiful!' she breathed in wonder. 'You're very good. What are you going to do with it?'

With the passing of the rain the sun had risen and now bathed the wide-windowed room in a watery glow, heightening the shiny waxed leaves of a plant standing in a china pot on the windowsill. The tentative singing of a bird outside in the garden was the only sound.

Not for the first time she was caught up in the sheer unreality of being here alone with this good-looking, maddeningly arrogant man who made her more enraged than anyone had ever done before.

'Exhibit it at a show in London,' he told her, taking her arm and leading her towards the kitchen. Strangely, the touch of his fingers made her pulses race and she thought it wasn't just the painting that was magic around here! A girl could all too easily fall under his spell and not realise it until it was too late.

'You never know,' he went on, 'you might end up

famous, your name on everyone's lips. The girl with the cockleshells.' He stopped suddenly and clicked his finger and thumb together. 'That's it! I'll call it "The Cockle-shell Girl".'

She was reminded of her own words to Mary at the church hall dance – 'I might become famous!' and Mary's flippant reply. She smiled as he turned to ask her: 'What do you think? Do you approve of the title?'

'I'm sure whatever I say won't make a scrap of differ-ence, so why bother asking?'

He shrugged and went to fill the kettle, putting it on the stove to boil. 'You're quite right, of course. Why *should* I ask you? I don't usually ask my models for their advice.'

'Then why me?' she said frostily, something in her rebelling at his classing her with his other models. He studied her in silence for a long moment, then went over to the kitchen table where cups and saucers were set. 'Have a cup of tea before you go. The painting's fin-ished. You won't have to put up with my objectionable presence a minute longer after today.'

It was the first time he had shown her any real con-sideration. She could quite see how some women might find him enormously attractive. Later, pouring the tea, he sat down opposite her and she said, 'Look, we've got to get this straight before I go. About my stepfather – because I can't have you thinking I'm on the market for something – like that.'

Their eyes met and locked and she felt herself quite unable to look away. His gaze moved slowly down and fastened on her mouth and the breath seemed to leave her body. Then he moved, reaching behind him to a high shelf and taking something down. 'Here. I thought you might like this as a memento.'

It was a sketch of her in coloured chalks; a few rapid strokes and there she was on paper, glorious mass of dark hair, eyes wide and as purple as wood violets, delicately shaped lips. 'I've signed it,' he said, 'so if you hold on to it long enough, it might just be worth a bob or two one day.' He grinned. 'As for your stepfather's behaviour, forget it. I already have.'

Brushing aside her thanks, he took the empty cup from her hand. 'Come on, I'll walk you and Drogo part of the way home.'

He watched her struggling with the still wet boots. At last, the laces tied securely, she stood up and picked up her shawl. That, too, was still damp and he tut-tutted, making her promise that she would dry it properly just as soon as she got home. Remembering the warmth of her kitchen, he added, 'An open fire's best. If I could be bothered, I'd make one here.'

'It's summer,' she reminded him. 'We shouldn't really need a fire.'

His glance took in the soaking wet countryside, the trees dripping with moisture, the path that led to the roadway slick with mud. Even though a watery sun shone down, it was still a desolate scene. 'Summer?' he queried. 'I don't remember it raining as frequently as this when I was a child.'

She looked surprised, suddenly reminded of what Dan had said, that his father had at one time been MP for Craven Bay and Marcus had grown up here. 'It's difficult to imagine,' she told him. 'You as a little boy here – playing on the beach, building sandcastles, and raiding apples.'

He laughed. 'Sounds wonderful, but my childhood was nothing like that. I had a nanny . . . oh, a wonderful woman, proud of her heritage and determined that I would grow up a credit to her training. No stolen apples or running barefoot on the sand for me! I was an only child, you see, and my father, what with his work as a solicitor before he became a Member of Parliament, and then his official duties, had little time for me. The thing I remember most clearly is accompanying him on the walks he would take into town. We'd watch the men queue for their handouts. It used to upset him terribly. I remember particularly one day when we came across some men marching to Westminster, to demand better pay and conditions. Of course,' he grinned at her stare of astonishment, 'they never got there, although I admire their guts for trying. It's a long way, Westminster, from the Welsh valleys.'

She nodded, marvelling at the side of his character revealed by his description. Under all that arrogance and severity was a man who, given time, she might even have come to like.

But she had other considerations now. Evan had become a major part of her life, and she intended to devote every scrap of her attention to him and the way their friendship was heading without letting herself be distracted by other things.

Marcus didn't speak again, it was as if the earlier confidences had never been given, and Alys walked along, not seeing the green countryside all about her, simply putting one foot in front of the other, her hand clasping Drogo's reins. The little donkey did not relish the wet mud all over his feet and fussed and skittered about, bad-temperedly tossing his head and snorting at the shrill noise of the seagulls as they came out after the rain, ever on the look-out for scraps of food. At the junction of the road leading to town, Marcus asked her: 'I won't see you again, then?'

Did she imagine it or did he sound a little dispirited? She turned to rub the donkey's velvety nose. 'No.'

'Pity!' She *had* imagined it. He was definitely laughing at her now. 'I've enjoyed our little war of words.' Just before she walked away, after thanking him once again for the sketch, which thanks he brushed aside negligently, he said, 'Don't I get a goodbye kiss?'

She didn't even look back. 'I'd as soon kiss Drogo,' she told him, and heard his laughter as she hurried away, dragging the disgruntled animal behind her.

That night, as soon as he came in, Alys was ready for her stepfather. She turned from the stove where she had been stirring the stew, long wooden spoon in her hand. Like a weapon, thought Dan, uneasily, noting the flushed cheeks and fierce glare.

Without preamble, she began, 'What did you think you were doing, eh? Going up to Mr Dillon's house and pestering him like that. I could hardly believe it, even of you.'

Then, before he could say a word in his own defence, 'I'm surprised you even dare show your face after pulling a stunt like that! Have you no shame?'

Dan gave a sickly smile and began to edge round the table, careful to steer well clear of the brandished spoon. 'Now, girl, you've got it all wrong. The man's mistaken my words. It was just a friendly visit, that's all. The sort of visit any father who cared for the safety and welfare of his daughter would make.'

He cupped his hands under the running tap and scooped water over his face. He reached for the towel, his voice strident in his own defence. 'What sort of a father would I be if I didn't think to check up on the man an innocent young girl like you was spending so much time with?'

'Humph!' She threw down the spoon in disgust, spattering the thick mutton stew over the hot stove, making it sizzle. 'A fat lot you care, so long as I bring home a bit of money at the end of the day! I didn't know where to put my face when Mr Dillon told me what you'd said . . .'

'Aw, Alys, girl, don't go on so! I'm starving for me supper.'

'Don't you "Aw, Alys" me, you old sod! It'd serve you right if I tipped the whole bloody pot of supper over your head, so it would.'

Leaving him speechless, she grabbed her shawl and rushed outside, slamming the front door behind her so hard the small house shook. She had knotted the money Marcus had given her in one corner of her shawl. She fingered it now, wondering how far it would go if she had to fend for herself. Her stepfather was fast driving her to it . . .

Why should she stay with a man who made her life a misery? But what alternatives were there? She could always join Mary in service – there were constantly staff vacancies in the big houses along the coast. But she'd decided against that years ago. More and more she felt she was caught between the devil and the deep, blue sea.

This evening, when she desperately needed to see

Evan, hear his good-natured, 'Don't worry about it, worse things happen at sea', he had said he'd be busy. His father had invited friends and expected him to help entertain them. She tried not to think of the number of times that had happened lately. 'I won't be able to see you this evening,' he'd say. 'I'm sorry, Alys, but I have to . . .' and there would follow a long explanation as to why he couldn't meet her. She made excuses for him; a man from his background would of course be kept busy with social duties. Hadn't Mary told her about the dinner parties old Jenkins gave, how people would come from as far as Cardiff. 'Business friends,' explained Mary. 'The old man expects Evan to do his part.'

Alys had put her arms around his waist, standing close to him. 'I'll miss you.'

'And I'll miss you. You don't suppose I want to sit at a dinner table with a lot of stuffy old men who can talk about nothing but business, do you?' He'd pulled her closer, dropping a kiss on her forehead. 'And next time I see you, I'll show you just how much I've missed you. Have no doubts about that.'

Netta Jenkins was considered by most a nice enough young woman, but with a rebellious streak that didn't sit well in an age of lingering Victorian values. Mrs Dean called it 'Flamin' pig-headedness'. Netta's father, while strict and unrelenting with Evan, had spoiled her, creating a wilful and headstrong woman who liked her own way and let everyone feel her displeasure if she didn't get it. While Evan had been away at university, she had had things her own way pretty well.

Those big blue eyes, and the soft fair hair that curled

about her face in pleasing disorder, fooled most people into believing her soft and malleable. It did not take them long to find out they were mistaken. Netta would go to any lengths to get her own way, or something she wanted very badly. It was rumoured that two men had once fought a duel over her, risking the strictures of the courts, but in Craven Bay that sort of rumour took a bit of believing. Even so, women would sniff and say disparagingly, 'I shouldn't be at all surprised! Some men are just fools.' Men thought of the fall of blonde hair, the eyes that seemed to conceal so much and yet promise everything with their hint of lasciviousness.

Netta was twenty-four and worried that if she remained single for much longer, she would be left on the shelf. The more malicious of her female acquaintances whispered this already. There had been offers aplenty for her hand but none that Netta had cared to accept. The men her father invited to the house she considered poor, dull creatures, interested only in business. The talk over the dinner table would be of coal fields, recently discovered seams, and the quickest if least safe method of getting coal to the surface. How she longed to be free of the petty restrictions imposed upon her by this lifestyle. She didn't see why women should have to behave any differently to men. Men were free to do exactly as they liked. She admired the dancer, Isadora Duncan, envious of her flamboyant existence.

This morning, bored and restless, she strolled the gardens, oblivious to the riot of colours and scents wafting from the flower beds. Between her fingers, a yellow rose lost its petals, fretfully shredded and dropped to the ground. She was weary of her life and its lack of opportunities for excitement. She visualised a future spent pandering to a husband, cold and unimaginative in their marriage bed, having no thoughts for her pleasure, only his own. She would hardly ever see him, for he'd be at his office all day and yet expect her to be waiting for him when he came home in the evening. The future stretched ahead, empty and cheerless, although there would be children – probably lots of children, for sons and daughters were ammunition, to be used in future deals for the joining of dynasties.

Savagely, she plucked another rose, tearing it from its stem and using a word she'd heard a stable boy utter one morning when a horse had kicked out at him. A spot of bright blood sprang up on her finger and she wound the dainty lace-edged handkerchief she had in her pocket round the tiny wound and made a clumsy knot. The second rose, too, was pulled apart. It seemed to give her some sort of satisfaction, seeing the lovely blossom mutilated. She opened her hand and let the wind take the bruised petals from her palm. And at that moment, as though in answer to her prayers, a dark green van appeared from the direction of the road, the legend 'Craven Bay Cooperative Stores' stencilled in gold upon its sides. She'd thought, a moment before its arrival, of the message she had for Mrs Dean regarding the extra place that would be needed at that night's dinner. Perhaps that would be just the excuse she needed for arriving in the kitchen at the same time as the visitor.

Netta slackened her pace now, watching as the van came to a stop outside the kitchen door and a man jumped lightly down from the driver's seat and went round to open the doors. The most beautiful man she had ever set eyes on! He was like a young Adonis, although dark instead of fair, with thick curly black hair that clustered in disordered curls over his forehead. He had eyelashes, she noted as she drew closer, that a woman would give her very soul for. Thick and inky black, they cast a shadow across his flushed cheeks where the angle of the sun caught them.

Netta had seen him before, of course; making deliveries to the house, crossing the stable yard with his arms full of packages. Occasionally, she had heard Mrs Dean's pithy remarks about him and gathered that he was Mary O'Malley's boyfriend, and that Mrs Dean hoped Mary didn't intend to set him visiting the kitchen for that was something the elderly cook would never contemplate.

Netta had heard Mary's reply, spoken in a huffy voice, 'I haven't before, Mrs Dean, so I don't see why I should now.'

Suddenly, the young man realised that he was being watched and with a sheepish grin raised one finger to his forehead. 'Sorry, Miss, didn't see you standing there.'

His air of indifference intrigued her, provoking her to say, sharply, 'You really should be careful how you drive that thing,' nodding her head towards the parked van. 'Had I been closer to the driveway, you would have knocked me down.' There had been no danger of that and he knew it.

Still, for a moment he looked flustered, giving her a momentary feeling of gratification. Then: 'I'm sorry, Miss,' he mumbled, and looked at her with such a hangdog expression that the sense of power she experienced was delirious. She almost laughed aloud and said in a haughty voice, looking down her nose at him, 'As well you might be. You do know who I am, don't you?'

He shuffled his feet in embarrassment. 'Yes, Miss. You're Mr Jenkins's daughter.'

'Miss Natalie Jenkins.'

'Yes, Miss.'

'And you are Jackie, Mary's boyfriend?'

At the mention of Mary, his face lit up. Eagerly, he said, 'I am that, Miss.'

She began to cross the cobbled yard with barely concealed impatience, inexplicably annoyed at the way his face had glowed with pleasure at the mention of Mary's name. Would any man ever look like that for her? she wondered. It wasn't fair, or just, that a common girl like Mary O'Malley should be the cause of such a look.

Her hands were shaking as she swept through the kitchen, quite forgetting her message for Mrs Dean. Her resentment was such that when she saw Mary throw down the small knife with which she had been paring apples and run to greet him, Netta deliberately let the door slam in his face as he followed closely behind her, his arms full of parcels.

So inattentive was she at dinner that night, that a young man seated next to her at the table prattled away without her taking in a word he said.

Chapter Six

The news travelled faster than Drogo of an evening when he smelled the fresh hay of his warm stable. Different versions abounded, one being that Alys had been seen posing for that artist bloke, wearing not a stitch to cover her goose pimples. Another version had her lying on a bed of roses, equally nude. But most agreed that was unlikely. 'Just think of all those thorns! Even Alys Hughes wouldn't be daft enough for that!'

Even so, there was no getting over the fact that Alys had been seen riding Drogo up to the white cottage Marcus Dillon was known to have rented on the headlands. The story spread from house to house, pub to pub. Suddenly boys were looking at her with speculative expressions, wondering how much of the gossip was true. No one was really surprised for Alys had always had a reputation for doing exactly as she liked and divil take the hindmost. 'His dad was Gerard Dillon, you know,' they said, 'a nice enough bloke, all for the workers in spite of being upper class. Did a lot o' good, he did. 'Member when he led that march, saying if necessary he'd walk wi' 'em all the way to Westminster?'

'Aye, and then stones were thrown and the men

started fighting and police had to be called in.'

A sigh went through the group of shawled women as they recalled their menfolk coming home with bloody noses and black eyes. Really, you couldn't leave a man alone for more'n a minute before he was getting into trouble!

'Left soon after that to live in London, didn't he?' recalled one woman. 'That boy o' his don't really know these parts, although he comes back here often enough. Still,' she grimaced, 'an artist! Whoever thought he'd turn out to be one of those!'

Hard on the heels of that rumour came the new one of Alys's meetings with young Evan Jenkins. Gossips buying their fish from the market stalls predicted that no good would come of it. Class didn't mix wi' class. And they thought of the young, good-looking Jenkins boy, with his nice manners and hair that looked like yellow silk, and compared him to their own rough and ready spouses, and sighed.

Funny how she missed that morning ride to the cottage, thought Alys; even the long, boring hours of sitting still and the cup of tea they shared afterwards. The only bright spots in her days now were her meetings with Evan. She would watch eagerly from Drogo's back as the small donkey picked its way daintily over the cobbles, her eyes searching the headlands and adjacent beaches for that tall, lithe figure in baggy flannels and a white shirt.

When they met up, she would gaze into the eyes so near her own, burning to feel his mouth on hers, his arms holding her tightly, secure from all harm. It was a dangerous madness, there in the bright sunlight with dear knows who looking on. She knew of the gossip that had begun its insidious rounds. They were often seen together; sometimes there on the sands, Alys with her basket of fresh cockles tilted against her hip, sometimes walking on the headlands, outlined against a bright blue sky. Shyly, she had suggested the cave as an ideal meeting place but to her surprise Evan had wavered.

'It would make it seem all so furtive, darling Alys,' he told her. 'Besides, I don't know that I could trust myself, alone with you like that.'

This sudden reversal of roles touched her. Men were usually all too keen to get her to themselves. She prayed for some secret place where they alone might go, where they could turn the key and lock out the rest of the world. Would they ever share such closeness? How long could they go on meeting like this, snatching what happiness they were able, the eyes of the town upon them, gossip making an ugly thing of something so beautiful?

How he wished, Evan said, that he could take her out properly, as she was entitled. One day he would, he promised, flouting all the conventions and panicking her into saying, 'I know, love, I know. But for the moment I'm happy with what we have. Don't tempt fate by being too greedy. Your father . . .'

'Damn my father! You're the most important person in my life.'

She gazed at him in troubled silence. But there were times, too, when they talked about themselves, about their backgrounds, so vastly different it was unbelievable that they could find anything in common. Was love enough? she wondered. Would it be enough for the rest of their lives?

They talked about her childhood, of those happy times before her mother died. 'My father was such a big, happy man,' she said. 'When he came home from fishing trips, he'd always bring us something, just some little thing he'd seen and thought my mother or I would like. I would watch from the gate for him to come striding over the cliff path and rush out like a crazy person, calling his name and throwing my arms about him. He'd swing me up high and his laughter would boom out, making the seagulls shriek.' She sighed and he watched her face take on a sadness that touched his heart. She was such a naive, trustful little thing. Not for the world did he want to hurt her . . .

And yet, what future could there be for them together? His father would never accept her, and without Thomas Jenkins's money, Evan would be penniless. Not exactly a good catch for any girl. On reflection, Alys would probably do better with one of her own sort, even if the thought of it appalled him.

'Your father sounds like a brave man,' commented Evan, feeling that he had to contribute something, however trite, to her recollections of a happy childhood. There was nothing in his own that he recalled with any particular joy. 'Men who brave the sea to harvest the deep are all brave.'

'Oh, he was. I had a wonderful childhood.' She grasped Evan's arm, linking it with her own, pressing herself against him like a contented little cat. 'But our life will be happy, too, won't it, Evan? No one can make it any different, not as long as we're together.'

She's really too happy, he thought. When she talks, she laughs; when she walks, she dances. She displays her happiness to all who watch her. Hasn't that old skinflint she lives with noticed it yet? he wondered. Difficult not to. But then, he was probably the kind of man who noticed very little unless it touched him in some way. As long as she was there, getting his supper when he came in, he'd ignore anything else.

Alys shivered in the chilly night wind. Along the streets the gas lamps seemed to march for dismal miles, revealing the dingy, litter-covered lane in which they strolled. The wind had risen from the sea and smoke from the rows of chimneys threw long ribbons of grey across the darkening sky. Out beyond the harbour wall, a brilliantly lit ship moved slowly coastwards.

Gazing around their cheerless surroundings, Evan said, 'You know, you're much too beautiful to be wasted on this. It's difficult to believe that you're forced to sell fish for a living and live in a place like this, when you should be surrounded by luxury and beautiful things.'

His arm tightened about her slender waist, his lips tasted the sweetness of her skin. He smiled as she said pertly; 'A body's got to live somewhere. We can't all live in big houses with sweeping gravel drives and grand gardens. Any more than all our fathers can be wealthy pit owners.'

'I know, dearest Alys, and I cringe when I think of the conditions you have to go back to. Of that sot of a stepfather swilling down ale at the dockside taverns while you do your best to make a meal out of scraps. I swear, my heart turns over just thinking of it.'

She wrinkled her nose. 'It's not *that* bad! Don't think

of it if it upsets you so. Think of this instead.' And she reached up and took his face in her hands, pulling his head down so that their lips met and clung. A groan, deep and helpless, was wrenched from him. She could feel his body, hard and demanding; smell the clean, soapy smell of him. She trembled to think he'd chosen her above all the other girls he had been raised with.

'My stepfather won't be home yet,' she said, lowering her eyes in a demure way that didn't fool him for a minute. 'And it's going to rain! Why don't you walk me home? I could make you a cup of cocoa.'

Evan Jenkins, who hadn't been offered a cup of cocoa since he'd left the nursery, found it difficult not to laugh. So serious she sounded, with that petal-soft face raised to his, those bewitching eyes thickly fringed with dark lashes casting seductive shadows against her cheeks. The sight filled him with sensations no other girl could rouse in him.

Although he wanted to shout from the rooftops that he loved her and one day would make her his wife, he knew only too well it would take a miracle for his father to agree to it. He said only, 'Cocoa! Couldn't you come up with something a little more exciting than that?'

She knew he was teasing and cocked her head to one side, eyes twinkling. 'Champagne, is it, you'd be preferring? Dan was to see his wine merchant this morning, but with his working late I don't expect he had time.'

As she spoke the rain began to fall in earnest; huge drops that spattered against the cobbles, making Alys mutter beneath her breath and pull the thick woollen shawl closer about her. From the harbour came the plaintive hooting of a tug-boat and suddenly she wanted to be out of the chill night and the rain, safe in the arms of this man who loved her.

She felt Evan's hand grasp her elbow, propelling her along the narrow dark street. By the dim light of the gas lamp her shawl looked purple and he found himself speculating about the cotton blouse and full skirt she wore underneath. His pulses quickened. But then, she'd always had this effect on him, right from the day he'd first seen her, sitting talking in the garden with Mary O'Malley.

His stride lengthened and she was forced to break into a run to keep up with him. 'Come on,' he urged. 'You're going to get soaked.'

His arm slipped about her waist, holding her tightly as they hurried. The rain beat against her face, beading her eyelashes so that the night seemed to be bathed in a glow of misted sequins.

Evan's fair hair was wringing wet, hanging down over his eyes like a sheepdog's. Alys laughed aloud, revelling in the thought that soon they would be alone, with no spiteful or envious eyes to watch and spread gossip. They came to the street of shabby cottages where Alys lived. All down the street curtains were drawn, like blind eyes, the front doors tightly closed against the wet night. Alys led the way to her own front door and pushed it open. The musty smell of the floorboards left uncovered by the thread-bare carpet runner mingled with the stale smell of cooking. The light was too dim to see much of the dingy interior but what Evan could see was depressing.

A poor apology for a fire smouldered in the hearth. With a brisk: 'Soon have it blazing away,' Alys slipped from his arm and hurried across the kitchen, tossing aside the wet shawl to lie on the back of the old rocking chair.

The young man entered hesitantly, glancing nervously about him as though he expected her stepfather to emerge from the shadows. Even though he knew full well that as long as the taverns were open Dan Radloff would be there, drinking with the best of them.

It amused her to think Evan should behave this way, ready to jump at the slightest sound, starting visibly when a coal fell from the fire on to the stone surround. Deftly she bent and scooped it up with the tongs, then, hands on hips, faced him in the firelight.

'Well, what's it to be, cocoa or tea?'

She couldn't, he thought, know how tempting she looked, that wild mass of hair sprinkled with raindrops, the sweet swell of her breasts and hips clearly outlined by the firelight behind her. He crossed the room in one stride, taking her in his arms, brushing the tangled hair from her cheeks. 'You know that was only an excuse to get me here,' he laughed. 'You're enough to drive a man out of his senses.'

'So,' she murmured, with lowered eyes, 'be tempted!'

He gave a hasty glance towards the door. 'Is it safe? What if your stepfather should decide to come home earlier than usual?'

'He won't,' she said with a sureness that had him fumbling clumsily with the tiny buttons at the front of her blouse, his breath coming fast.

For one brief moment Alys felt a tremor of fear, for what did she know of love-making or the demands of a man's body? The only male body she had seen unclothed was her stepfather's when she poured the kettles of hot water into the zinc bath on a Friday night, averting her eyes with distaste from the overfleshed chest with its covering of matted grey hair. The rest she didn't want to see as he sat, waist deep in the steaming water, knees raised to his chest while a frothy scum floated between his mottled thighs.

Once when she had protested, saying she was a child no longer and getting too old to perform this task on bath nights, he had taken his belt to her. She remembered how he had slipped the wide black band from his trousers, lips parted to show discoloured teeth, eyes glittering with anger at what he considered her insolence. Although the thick petticoat she wore had been some protection she still bore the red welts on her thighs for days afterwards. She had curled up in a foetal position, her crossed arms shielding her head and face. Afterwards, he'd growled, 'That's just a warning, girl. Take care you don't cross me again for there's plenty more where that came from.'

It was the first of a number of beatings, some for trivial things, when the drink was strong inside him, some to punish her for answering back.

She thrust the unpleasant memories from her mind, overcome by the exquisite sensations that were overtaking her as Evan took her face between his hands. His lips teased hers, blotting out the dingy room. The dim glow of the fire threw flickering, mysterious shadows on the wall concealing its grime. This was everything she had ever longed for.

Mind and body conspired against Alys and soon there was no resistance left in her. She wrapped her arms about Evan in total surrender, a languor like warm honey flowing through her veins. He sensed this, gathered her up into his arms and carried her across to the ancient sofa that stood against the far wall.

He feasted his eyes on her slender unclothed body for many moments. 'Oh, Alys!' It was almost a sob. 'To think I might never have known you! That all this beauty could have been wasted on some thick-fingered wretch who could never have loved you as I do.'

'Don't speak,' she whispered, pulling him closer. 'Just hold me. That's all I want, for you to hold me.'

A stream of pure sensuality ran through her like liquid fire and she clung to him, knowing instinctively that her plea was impossible. Their emotions, running high, and their eager young bodies had carried them too far for mere embraces. She loved him so much she could not bear to deny him. He came to her slowly, anxious not to frighten her. She was like a spirited young filly, waiting to be coaxed, to be shown what to do.

He showed her and she didn't believe it was possible to love a man so much, that he could rouse in her such passion. The strength and the tenderness of him filled her with such abandonment that she yielded joyfully, not caring about the soft moaning sounds coming from her own throat, spurring him on. And then, when she was sure she couldn't take any more, had reached the pinnacle of desire, the real ecstasy began, with the weight of him warm and heavy above her, murmuring her name.

This was the love, the closeness which she had been seeking ever since her mother died, leaving her in the far from tender care of Dan Radloff. She remembered with sadness her mother's slowly dimming eyes, her pleas: 'Look after each other, you and Dan. He's all you have left, now.'

'I will, Mam, I will,' she had promised. 'Don't talk, sleep. You'll feel better after a little sleep . . .'

Funny how memory plays tricks on us, she thought, that she should be thinking of it at this time.

But now she was part of Evan and he of her as she arched, meeting him in a joyous response. She lay quite still, feeling as though her very bones were made of wax, melting in the flame of his passion. Evan was gripping her very tightly, his mouth covering hers. She could feel his teeth cutting into her lips. But she didn't mind. He loved her. After tonight he would be hers forever. She didn't stop to ask herself how, or see that nothing had changed.

'Alys, dearest Alys,' he murmured against her lips, hardly knowing what he was saying. 'I'll never leave you now, never . . .'

Outside, the rain had stopped. The gas lamps threw incandescent circles about their globes and the landlord of The Black Prince called for last orders. Dan Radloff banged his tankard on the scarred top of the mahogany bar. The landlord allowed him one last pint, though God knew he owed enough already and the landlord could see no way the debt would ever be paid off.

The buzz of conversation in the pub made it sound like a hive with the bees about to swarm. Three young sailors in naval uniforms sat at a table by the window. Like Dan they had been there since opening time and it was clear the landlord was going to have trouble with them when he finally did close. They lolled in their chairs, arms around each other's shoulders, singing bawdily.

Old Lilith, who plied her trade along the narrow streets and alleyways behind the docks, glanced over at them and gave one an encouraging smile. It was now that she recruited her clients, when they'd had too much to drink and were on their way home. Round, navy blue hats perched on the backs of their heads, they bellowed obscenities across the room, making lewd gestures with their hands. Lilith smiled and waited. She knew she had them. Sailors on shore leave were usually flush with money. That was, if they hadn't already drunk it away. The state they were in, she doubted it would take more than a few minutes to attend to all three of them.

She looked out of the corner of her eye at Dan Radloff seated a little way away from her. Now, there was a man! She'd always admired Dan Radloff although she didn't much like his young madam of a stepdaughter. Cheeky little bugger who thought she was a cut above everyone else! At one time, after his wife died, when Lilith was much younger, she had had ideas about encouraging his affections with a view to marriage. He'd used her services many times and she found him virile and strong, a bull when the mood took him.

She sighed, her eyes resting on him again, hoping he'd look her way. Maybe she could walk with him after the sailors had had their fill.

Customers began to drift away, the gaudily lettered glass doors swinging behind them. At last, on the pavement, Lilith gave the sailors an encouraging smile. 'Aye, lads, ready for a bit o' fun, then?'

Dan watched as they accompanied her down one of the dark alleyways. Then, his head spinning in the fresh, rain-drenched air, wended his way home.

Alys stirred and lifted one hand to smooth the thick fair hair from Evan's forehead. He rose and stretched, arms muscular and pale above his head. 'It's late,' he said. 'I'd better go.'

'Yes?' she teased, and smiled; that slow, sleepy smile that set his pulses leaping afresh although he doubted very much if he had the strength to do anything about it right now. He buttoned his shirt as he looked down at her, sprawled like a wanton on the old sofa. Whoever would have believed that small, slender body capable of such passion? He shrugged on his jacket.

'How do you feel?' he wanted to know, coming to sit beside her on the sofa.

'Wonderful! As though a million candles have been lit inside me.'

He grinned, bending to kiss the tip of her nose. 'Sounds painful!'

She made a fist and punched him on the shoulder. 'You know what I mean. Oh, Evan, I'm so happy! Why do married people have to be so nasty to each other when love can be so wonderful?' She threw her arms wide, stretching like a contented cat.

Teasingly, he answered, 'Only married people are expected to feel that, you mean?' Her talk of marriage had made him uneasy.

Now she said, 'But what can we do, Evan? Your father would never . . .'

His voice was harsher than he intended when he

replied, 'Damn my father! You're the most important person in my life,' unconsciously repeating the words he had used earlier.

'You do love me?' Suddenly she was shy, unable to meet his eyes. 'What if he should stop you seeing me? You'd have to obey him, he's still your father . . .'

He silenced her with his lips. 'Leave him to me, my dove. He has been known to change his mind before now.'

She gazed up at him doubtfully. 'Then he does know about us?'

'I suspect there's very little that happens in Craven Bay that my father does not know about.' Still, the thought filled him with misgivings. Old Thomas had been giving him some very old-fashioned looks lately, although he'd said nothing. Carelessly, Evan added, 'We'll just have to appeal to his better nature.'

'You really think he might agree to our . . .' She blushed, hating him to think she was pressurizing him. But when he spoke like that, so sure of himself, how could she doubt him?

He cast his eyes ceilingwards. 'Heaven protect me from a doubting woman!'

But as he walked home through the cool, damp evening, that tiny niggle of doubt stayed in his mind. Could he persuade his father that Alys would be a suitable match? Was he mad to have gone this far with what had started out so innocently? Acting recklessly had been a temptation in itself. He knew his father had plans for his future and had never gone against his wishes before. Lately, there had been numerous mentions of girls his father considered suitable material for a future

Mrs Evan Jenkins. Evan liked none as much as he liked Alys.

He corrected himself: loved. He *loved* Alys, not just liked her. Hadn't he convinced her of that?

Now all he had to do was to convince his father . . .

As Alys, gazing from the front-room window, watched him walk away into the night, neither of the two young people suspected that it would be many months before they saw each other again.

Chapter Seven

Thomas Jenkins was angry, and when he was in a rage his face became flushed like a turkey cock's and his voice rose in a bellow that could be heard all over the house. It wasn't enough that his son and heir was the talk of Craven Bay. Now he was saying he wanted to marry the girl!

Marry her? Hell would freeze over before Thomas allowed that. His bellow penetrated the green baize door that separated the kitchen quarters from the house proper, causing Mrs Dean to mutter, with a shake of her head, 'Ah, that's Master Evan, that's who it'll be, you mark my words. He's the only one I know that can make the old man shout like that.'

Mary, a large white apron tied carefully over her neat lavender-striped gown, pursed her lips and looked up from chopping the parsley. 'What's he on about then?'

Mrs Dean gave her an admonishing stare. 'Never you mind what he's on about, my girl. Just you mind you don't chop your fingers off wi' that knife. Got enough to worry about, I have, without someone losing their fingers.'

Mary managed a sweet smile and a soft 'Yes, Mrs Dean,' although the hot Irish temper that was never far

111

beneath the surface bubbled up inside her. Whatever the master was on about, he was certainly in a right old tantrum. As the sound of Thomas Jenkins's voice rose, Netta strained to listen up in her room.

Netta put down her piece of sewing and ran downstairs, into the room where Evan and their father were having it out. As she came through the doorway, she heard her brother's voice, full of scorn: 'Come out of the Ark, Father. All I'm trying to say is that this is the twentieth century. You're out of step.'

'Don't you talk to me like that, you insolent young pup!' Her father's voice rose again. 'I'd rather be out of step and know I've done the best for my children than be *in* step and let them ruin their lives.'

At Netta's entrance they turned flushed faces towards her. Her father grunted and with no word of greeting strode past her, out of the room. Hands in pockets, his back turned towards her, Evan stared out of the window. She came forward slowly and placed a hand on his arm. 'Evan?'

'All I asked was that he let me bring Alys here to meet him. He went off like a rocket on bonfire night. It's not fair!' And his sister was reminded of a petulant little boy denied his favourite toy. His face was filled with passion as he turned to face her. 'The more he forbids me to see her, the more I want to go against him.'

Netta's lips quirked. 'If you ask me that's a sure way of making him worse.'

Evan grimaced. 'I think I stirred things up when I tried to reason with him. He's got his own antiquated way of viewing things and nothing's going to change that.'

Netta pressed his arm gently. 'Be careful, Evan. You

know Father. I think this is what you could call the calm before the storm.'

'He just refuses to believe me when I tell him I'm in love with Alys.'

'You're not. You only think you are. It's a romantic notion, made even more romantic by the fact that girls like her are usually unobtainable. To the likes of you, anyway, dear brother.' She gazed at him, frowning thoughtfully. 'And why on earth would you want to become serious with *her*? A common fisher girl! She's probably had a dozen boys all sniffing at her skirts at the same time, and I bet some of them got around to doing a great deal more than sniffing, too!' The distaste in her voice was plain.

Her brother gave her a pitying look. 'I thought better of you, Netta, than to make a remark like that.'

She ignored his defence of Alys. 'She's a tart, Evan. A common little tart who's managed to pull the wool over your eyes. And you're fool enough to let her!'

He tried again, his words of justification causing Netta to give him a woeful look. 'You don't know her. She's not like that . . .'

'Don't you know what's going on between her and that artist? Remember Marcus Dillon? His old man got elected to Parliament and they moved to London. He comes back sometimes to paint. But where he used to paint the coastline or fishing vessels, this time he's taken to painting that girl. At least,' said with a smirk, 'I imagine he's painting her. That's the story, anyway, although she seems to have spent an inordinately long time in that oh, so deserted cottage with him.'

It was a long speech for Netta and in it she'd included

everything she thought Evan should know. He was, after all, the future of the Jenkins holdings, and thus of her own financial security.

His lips firmed, his jaw thrust out in a stubborn gesture. 'It won't be easy,' he agreed, 'I know that. And I don't want to listen to any more of your gossip, Netta.'

In the words of the old song, 'Love conquers all', their love for each other, his and Alys's, was strong enough to stand against a whole tribe of Jenkinses, all doing their best to drive them apart. Well, they wouldn't succeed . . .

Netta scrutinised him quietly as he went on, 'Alys is a delightful girl. She has a bearing and manners to match, or even excel, any of the women in our circle.'

'You haven't known her long enough,' Netta sighed. 'It will be all on the surface, a sprat to catch a mackerel, sort of thing.'

Trying to make Evan see reason was proving more difficult than she'd anticipated. 'I mean, look at Mary O'Malley. She's a nice enough girl, although I've suffered cheek from her in the past. Even insolence that she doesn't bother to hide. But would you marry her?'

'That's different.' Evan's voice came out sulky now, acknowledging he was losing the battle. Netta's arguments made sense, and in any case, did he really expect his father to bless a union with a fisher girl? Abruptly changing the subject, he surprised Netta by saying, 'This Marcus Dillon? Have we ever met him?'

He realised that he'd been in fact more shocked then jealous over Netta's revelations about Alys posing for the visiting artist. Sly minx? She hadn't said a word about it to him. Perhaps there was some truth in his sister's warnings after all.

'I seem to remember meeting him a couple of times at birthday parties when we were little. They left to live in London, or just outside, when Marcus was fourteen.'

'Can't say I remember him. What was he like?'

'Not bad looking, although he had a nasty scar on his cheek, running down to his chin. He's grown a beard since.' She smiled, reminiscently. 'Rather attractive, really. I shouldn't imagine there's many women could resist him.'

'And you can toe the line, my boy, or out goes Dan Radloff and that stepdaughter of his.' Thomas Jenkins was pulling no punches as he laid down the law to his son. 'Want that on your conscience, do you?' he demanded savagely. 'Would it please you to think of the old man and the girl walking the streets after I throw him out of his job? It's a tied house, remember, that place they live in. No job, no house. He with his drinking problem ending up in the gutter, and that floozy having to sell herself in order to survive. Because let's get this straight, son – if you persist in this foolishness, neither Dan Radloff nor that girl will work in this town again. I'll make sure of that. And as there'll be no money coming your way, for I'll see to that also, I somehow don't think you'll enjoy the prospect of having them both to support.'

Evan believed him. His father was a powerful man with a great deal of influence in the county and Evan knew he would carry out his threats without turning a hair. The prospect of being without a job didn't particularly bother him. He'd visualised his future as being comfortable and carefree, putting in the hours his father expected but no more, just enough to keep the old man happy. Not exactly looking upon it as a job. Certainly he'd never expected actually to *work*. And now his father was threatening to withhold everything that was to make life easy, his for the taking, because he'd fallen in love with the wrong woman.

He cursed himself for being such a weak fool, for making no attempt to stand up to his father. But nonetheless when Thomas thrust the sheet of writing paper and pen at him, Evan accepted them numbly.

'Now you sit down and get that letter off your chest, and don't mince matters,' said Thomas. 'Tell her exactly what I've told you, that the whole thing's impossible. And,' with one last fierce glance at his son, 'you can also say that if I see her hanging around here at any time, I'll set the dogs on her. And I'm not joking!'

The effort of writing the letter to Alys drained Evan, leaving him feeling that life was no longer worth living. Why had he persisted with the friendship when all along he had known what was likely to happen? Should have known anyway, even if Alys had not. How could he ever face her again, thinking of the things he had promised, the sweet sacrifice she had made of herself that evening in the shabby kitchen?

When he'd finished the letter he showed it to his father. It was brief and formal, the sort of letter a gentleman might send when trying to get out of an invitation he considered a waste of his time. Thomas squeezed his shoulder, looking pleased. At last the boy was showing some sense! 'That'll do, but I trust you realise what a young fool you've been. By all means have your bit o' fun with pretty girls, and in spite of everything I can see how you would be attracted to her – she's a very pretty girl. But a man's a dunderhead if he promises anything more permanent.'

Evan sighed, making one last effort. 'Father, my intentions were strictly honourable . . .'

The old man snorted. 'Honourable, indeed! Girls of that sort are two a penny. They don't know anything about being honourable, or even what it means. You'd best put the whole thing out of your mind and concentrate on getting ready for the job I'm sending you on.'

Alone Evan tore the letter into tiny pieces and burned them in the fire. Then he wrote another one, knowing it was useless to promise anything or to raise Alys's hopes but on the other hand wanting to let her down as gently as he could. Netta had been right, of course, and his father, even though he hated to have to admit it.

He told her he was being sent by his father on an important job that would entail his being away for some time. He was going to give his attention to the recently acquired gold and diamond mines that the rich soil of Africa was yielding to hordes of men there, willing to break their backs, and their hearts, some of them, to make a fortune.

He would give the letter to Mary, he decided, when at last he folded the single sheet of paper and sealed it in its envelope. He knew she would hand it on to her friend the first chance she got. He dreaded having to face Alys himself, even though he cursed himself for his cowardice. No, better to let someone else handle it. Let the letter speak for him.

In the kitchen, Mrs Dean informed him that Mary was on her day off. Eyeing the white envelope in his hand, she murmured, 'Was it something important, Master Evan? If it is, I can always get one of those lazy, good-for-nothing lads from the stable to run down with it for you.'

Evan looked relieved. 'Would you, Mrs Dean? Although I've written the name of another young lady on the envelope, I think if you could arrange for it to be delivered to Mary, at her mother's house, it would be a better idea.'

Mrs Dean held out her hand. 'Very well, sir. I'll see to it right away.' After Evan had left the kitchen she held the envelope up to the light streaming through the window, squinting her eyes in an effort to make out at least some of the words. Why would Mr Evan be wanting to write to that Mary's friend? No better than she ought to be, from what Mrs Dean had heard tell. Going to that lonely cottage on the headlands and letting that artist from London paint her picture! Even if he had come from the valley in the first place, his family had moved to London and Mrs Dean didn't trust people who lived in London. The folded page inside the envelope and the thick bonded paper prevented her from making out even a single word.

Maybe after the young master had gone, things would calm down. She thrust the envelope into her apron pocket. She would take her time over finding a boy to deliver it to the town. Evan would be gone in no time and the house regain its normal, peaceful atmosphere. She had enough to put up with, with Miss Netta's little peccadillos, without looking for further trouble.

'Is he ill, Mary, confined to his bed so that he can't get out to meet me?' Alys looked stricken at the thought of Evan suffering without her being able to lift a finger to help him. 'Oh, if there was only something I could do!'

She watched as Mary bent and snatched at her youngest brother as he poked his stubby little fingers through the mesh of the firescreen, suddenly captivated by the orange flames. The two girls sat in the O'Malleys' kitchen. Mary had promised to keep an eye on eighteen-month-old Billy while her mother was down the street visiting. The child had been sitting quite quietly on the hearthrug, pushing a brightly painted wooden train across the floor, making soft 'choo-chooing' sounds with his pink cherubic mouth, until the urge to investigate the leaping flames had claimed him. 'No, Billy, it'll burn,' Mary warned. 'Not to touch.'

The good-natured little boy plonked himself down on to the hearthrug again, where, not in the slightest vexed by Mary's intrusion on his game, he began trying to pull the wheels off the little red wooden engine. Mary sighed and said, 'It's a full-time job just keeping the scalpeen away from harm.' She felt in the pocket of her skirt and brought out an envelope, handing it to Alys with the words, 'Here, you'd better read this before you say anything else. It's been burning a hole in my pocket since that young scallywag of a Jimmy brought it this mornin'. I've been dreading giving it to you, but – well, it *is* addressed to you, so whatever it is you'd better know.' She sighed again, knowing in her heart that something calamitous was about to happen. Mary had tried to warn her friend, but Alys was listening to nothing but her own heart with that inherent stubbornness that had caused her own mother to marry a man she hardly knew and go off with him, far from her own people.

Alys stared at the envelope doubtfully. 'What is it?'

'Hadn't you better open it and see, love? It's not going to leap out of the envelope at you, now, is it?' Her heart contracted with pity for her vulnerable young friend as Alys tore open the letter with a trembling hand.

She read the single sheet of paper, tears blurring her eyes so that she could hardly make out the words. She blinked rapidly and tried again. After a brief explanation as to the reason for his absence, Evan had written:

> I'll never forget you, Alys. You were the greatest thing ever to come into my life. You are a young and lovely woman. Please don't waste your time waiting for me. I fear I shall be away for a long time, and the distance between us will be great, too far to bridge with memories. The moments we shared, however, will stay forever in my heart. God bless and think of me kindly.

He'd signed the one word: 'Evan'. He hadn't even sent his love, she thought numbly. And such a bland few words to describe all the things she thought she had meant to him! She raised her head and caught Mary's eye. Drawing a deep, steadying breath, she said, 'He sent Jimmy all this way to give this to you, instead of coming to tell me himself?'

'It was while I was on my day off. This morning, in fact. He must have given it to old Mrs Dean and she got one of the stable boys to bring it down.'

'But why you? Why didn't he just slip it under our front door if he couldn't face me?'

'Didn't want old Dan to find it, I expect. There'd have

been hell to pay if he'd come across it before you, and well you know it.'

Alys nodded, unable to find the words to express what she was feeling. A great emptiness, as though she had suddenly lost a limb. Wouldn't it have been better if Dan *had* found that letter first and taken his wrath out on her? If he'd killed her even? At least then she wouldn't be feeling this awful pain . . .

'I didn't think anything could hurt so much,' she said, sharing her thoughts with Mary as she so often did. 'And I know it's a pain you can't take anything for . . .'

She felt Mary's arm about her, offering understanding. 'You've no idea what he had to go through, these last few days,' she said. 'It was plain bloody unbearable. His father ranting and raving, Miss Netta adding to the shemozzle with advice nobody wanted to hear. Bloody little busybody, that one, always interfering in someone else's affairs! Thinks whatever she says or does is approved by God himself, hypocritical little cow!'

In spite of herself, Alys had to laugh. That's better, thought Mary. She's hurting now but she'll get over it. People of our class can't afford to waste time on the luxury of regrets. Maybe, in time, she'll confess the whole thing to Father Goodhew, and after a suitably humble act of attrition, fortified by her faith, she'll be able to face the life that fate has decreed for her.

She gave Alys a squeeze now and said softly, 'I hate to have to say it, love, but I did warn you.'

'I really did believe he loved me, Mary.'

She squeezed harder, feeling the fragile bones under the firm flesh of her friend's shoulder. 'You were both so young – and forbidden fruit's always the sweetest.'

This time, Mary's words brought no comfort, though. Alys felt sick, the pain of rejection so fierce it was like a physical blow. Later, as the warm friendliness of the small kitchen seeped into her, strengthened by a cup of Mary's strong tea and a piece of shortbread biscuit, the colour began to come back into her cheeks.

Mary smiled and said, 'There, see. You're feeling better already, girl.'

The back door burst open and two young boys erupted into the room, fighting and squabbling. Mary regarded her brothers with a frown. Their shirt tails were coming adrift from their trousers and their faces and hands hadn't seen soap or water since early morning.

'Just in time to stay and mind wee Billy for me,' she told them. 'I'm walking Alys back to her house, so you two monkey dials can just think on and see he doesn't get too close to that fire guard. I won't be long.'

Kenny made a face at Dennis and they groaned in unison. 'We was just going to . . .'

'Never mind what you was just goin' to,' said Mary firmly. 'Whatever it was, it'll keep.'

At Alys's house, Mary stirred up the fire and made another pot of tea. The two girls were grateful that Dan wasn't yet home. Alys did not think she could bear his probing questions tonight of all nights. She knew the episode with Marcus Dillon still rankled with him, although nothing else had been said about it. She thought that if he came in tonight, boasting and bragging and making those salacious remarks, she would probably go for him.

At last, standing back and giving one last critical

glance about the kitchen she had helped tidy, Mary said, 'Well, love, if there's nothing else I can do, I'd better be on my way. I don't trust those two savages alone with the baby for too long. No telling what they'd get up to!

'I promised Jackie I'd go with him to the picture house in Market Street tonight. They're showing a new comedy. It's a good laugh – exactly what you need now, young Alys. Why don't you come with us? Jackie won't mind, you know how easy-going he is, and I don't like leaving you alone just now.'

'Why, because a man's seen fit to ditch me?' Alys smiled. 'Jackie Rees won't want me along, no matter what you say. Thanks, Mary, but I think I'll stay quietly home and do some mending.' She pointed towards a work basket on a chair in one corner, piled with her own woollen stockings and Dan's socks. 'That should keep my mind occupied for the rest of the evening!'

'A good laugh would do you more good than mending.'

'Perhaps. I won't argue with you there. But another time, *cariad*.'

Alys didn't feel like being in a crowd of people, all laughing and enjoying a night out with their sweethearts. She would get over it, of course she would. She had too much self-esteem to let it get her down for long. But it would take time – and time was something she had plenty of.

She stood up and stretched, reaching high with her arms, straightening the kinks. She had been suffering a lot from backache lately. She wondered if it was all that sitting still, posing for Marcus. Well, that was another thing that was over. The artist had already returned to his home in London. Another episode of her life ended . . .

She had fitted the sketch he had done of her into an old wooden frame and hung it in her bedroom. She had found the frame in the backyard, abandoned years ago after it had fallen from the wall. She remembered Mam's small shriek of dismay and quick signing of the cross for Mam was a firm believer in the old saying that a picture falling from a wall was a sure indication of a death in the family. The original contents had been a sepia copy of her mother's first wedding photo. The frame had never been repaired, for it was the time Mam was carrying the baby and feeling unwell. Dan had shrugged, and despite Mam's protests had chucked the whole thing into the yard. Alys later retrieved the faded wedding photo, wrapping it carefully in tissue paper and stowing it away in her bottom drawer.

Dan had made many snide remarks about the truly lovely sketch Marcus had done of her, but Alys ignored him and he soon lost interest and left her alone.

She sat now and looked at the stockings she had been about to darn, crushed with an overwhelming sense of despair. She cried, the tears flowing freely in an emotional release. After a while she pressed her eyes with thumb and forefinger, willing herself to stop crying. She threw the stockings on to a chair and climbed the stairs to bed. It was cold and dank in her room. Fully clothed, she climbed beneath the blankets and huddled there, knees drawn up to her stomach.

God was punishing her for not having saved herself for her husband. She'd not even cared. She'd savoured every moment with Evan and suspected there was something terribly wrong with her for enjoying the act of love as she did.

Surely only girls who came from bad families, and fallen women, liked it? Her stepfather would kill her if he got to know, after tracking down Evan and killing him first . . .

She fell asleep, only to dream of Evan, and woke later with fresh tears on her cheeks.

Chapter Eight

In the back seat of the cinema, Jackie's arm warm and comfortable about her shoulders, Mary tried to enjoy the film but was finding concentration difficult. Her thoughts kept returning to Alys, all alone in that house with her misery.

Jackie turned his head and nuzzled her cheek. 'What's wrong, my lovely? Not enjoying the flick?'

How she loved him, with his unruly thatch of hair, smiling dark eyes, and the shoulders on him the width of two men's. But tonight his shy attempts at affection only served to annoy her. She clicked her tongue in irritation, saying in a low voice, 'Stop it, Jackie! I thought we'd come to watch the film.'

'We have, *cariad*, but that doesn't mean to say we've got to sit all prim and proper, like an old married couple, and not even hold hands.' But when he tried to take hers, she shook it away as abruptly as though some troublesome insect had landed there.

From the flickering screen, an ancient taxi cab blew its horn. It made a rude and impudent noise, the sort of noise which, at any other time, would have made them laugh. Now she sat straight-faced and stiff, unable to relax. Beside her, she heard Jackie say, 'Mary, what's wrong? I know something is. Don't you want to tell me about it?'

'No, I don't. In any case, it's nothing to do with you.'

'Sometimes sharing a trouble helps.' In the semi-darkness of the cinema he smiled. 'One of my Aunt Ellen's favourite sayings. "A trouble shared is a trouble halved." '

At that moment, Mary couldn't have cared less what his Aunt Ellen said. She sniffed. 'Your aunt obviously didn't have many troubles then, for it doesn't always work like that.'

'God knows, she's had her share.' Blind to everything but her own concern for Alys, Mary ignored the hurt in his voice. 'She's had a good living, that one. A nice home, no kids to bother her, only a small boy who was so good he'd lick the mud off her shoes if she asked him.'

Jackie rounded on her in unexpected anger. 'Shut up, Mary O'Malley! Don't you dare say a word against my aunt. Not one single solitary word, do you hear?'

After that he did not speak again, removing his arm from her shoulders and staring fixedly at the screen. And when he continued to stay silent, his very withdrawal was sudden anathema to Mary. Without a word she rose, ignoring the affronted glares from the row of couples seated beside her as she caused them to rise on tip-tilted seats for her to brush her way past. Jackie didn't ask her where she was going, or even turn his head to look back at her. She stumbled along the aisle and up a flight of steps and found the Ladies, which was none too clean and badly lit and smelled of careless use.

The pale face that peered back at her from the discoloured mirror over the tiny hand basin and tap did nothing to cheer her spirits either. She tucked strands of hair behind her ears and washed her hands and face in the cold water, wishing that she had some of that red lipstick she had used for the local dances, and all the time she was thinking of Alys and the misery through which she was going.

Men! Not worth the time or effort we put into trying to keep them happy, she thought. She patted her wet cheeks and the backs of her hands with a handkerchief she carried in her handbag, taking her time, not hurrying. Let Jackie wonder, and perhaps worry about where she'd gone. She was so sure of him, knew he would sit quietly waiting until she returned. Asking no questions, only giving her a fond smile and a soft: 'All right?'

But when she came back, she saw that his seat was empty. He'd never done this before, walked out on her. She was shocked. Feeling the curious gazes of people who obviously wondered if she was going to disturb them again, she turned on her heel and left the cinema.

It was raining and she held her coat more tightly about her, pulling her soft felt hat down over her forehead. Her day off ended at ten o'clock and Mrs Dean liked her back on time. She reminded herself she still had to walk the distance over the headlands. Jackie usually walked her back. Tonight she felt drained, too exhausted even to think about it. Mam would fuss and insist that Kenny and Dennis accompany her, and ask questions about Jackie's absence. Questions were the last thing she wanted to be bombarded with, especially about Jackie Rees.

At home, Mam was back from her visit, young Billy tucked up safe and sound and out of harm's way in his cot, and Dad, his dark hair glistening with raindrops, showing that he had arrived home not long before, sat in his big chair reading one of the boys' comics. Mam, standing in front of the warmth of the fire, waiting for the kettle to come to the boil, looked round as Mary came through the front door. 'Over early tonight, isn't it, the pictures?'

Mary shook the rain from her coat and hung it over the back of a chair. 'We didn't stay to the end.'

Mam raised her eyebrows, peering through the front passageway, expecting to see Jackie come in behind her. Things had been sorted out between him and Mary's father and he was a welcome visitor at the house these days. When there was no sign of him, she glanced over at her husband, her brows still raised. Seeing that something was up, however, she turned back to her task of making them all a nice cup of tea, although she did say, trying not to sound too curious, 'Jackie not with you, then?'

Mary shook her head. 'No.' It was a bald statement, made in a tone that showed she was not prepared to discuss things further. Mrs O'Malley sighed and lifted the heavy kettle, watching the steam rise from the boiling water as it flowed into the old brown pot.

'The boys had better walk you back, then,' she said, placing the pot on its stand on the table.

'It's raining, Mam.' Mary looked at her brothers, settled comfortably in their usual place under the table in that mysterious seclusion that the long chenille tablecloth offered. She'd done the same when she was a child, concealed from parental eyes while all about her soft voices flowed, gently discussing events of the day. 'Don't disturb them.'

Mam shot her a worried glance. 'You can't walk all that way on your own, lass.'

'I've done it before. I'm used to it.'

'Oh, stop mithering, the two of you,' exclaimed Dad, reaching for the cup of tea his wife had just poured. 'I'll take the lass. The walk'll do me good, clear some of the cobwebs from this old head of mine.'

His wife grunted. It wasn't cobwebs that he had in his head but too much drink. Still, he was her man and she loved him, and he was a good, if somewhat feckless, father to the children. And if that Jackie Rees was going to give our Mary trouble – although she'd be surprised, Jackie being the nice, polite boy he was – then Mary was the one to deal with it, no one else.

Jackie Rees loved the green Co-op van, the game of rugby he played every weekend, the pint of beer he enjoyed afterwards while he and his mates dissected the game, and last but not least, Mary O'Malley.

Women terrified him. Most women, anyway. But not Mary, although at times even she bewildered him. He had never quite known what was expected of him as a suitor and so had allowed Mary in all her moods to take the initiative, following blindly. His mates laughed at him, saying he'd got all the makings of a hen-pecked husband. Although he joined in their laughter, he resented it, not seeing himself in that role at all.

They had teased: 'Never had anyone else, have you, boyo? Bad, that! Ought to try a few before you buy. Plenty more fish in the sea. Your Mary's a fine girl, but she's one hell of a temper.'

That was something he'd never once considered.

Taking an interest in another girl. Although, after the way
Mary had acted the other evening, walking out on him in
the pictures, it would serve her right if he did. He had to
agree with his mates that a rare old temper she had an' all,
but was he a man or a mouse that he should let her take
whatever was bothering her out on him? There were girls
who were soft and comfortable to be with and *they* had not
been reluctant to show an interest in him, either, although
not for the life of him had he done anything about it.

So when the manager of the Co-operative Stores told
him on Monday morning that he was to drive up to the big
house to deliver goods to Miss Jenkins, suddenly all he
could think of was the large, brooding eyes of Evan's sister
and the fine corn-silk hair, so soft and springy it seemed to
have a life of its own.

The parcels consisted of half a dozen flat boxes, the kind
the Ladies Department used to pack dresses and other
items of apparel. Even entering the department with its
displays of frills and furbelows made him blush. It was
always so quiet there, you were almost afraid to set one
foot in front of the other. The fashionable women of
Craven Bay came here to be fitted with the new models:
long narrow skirts with a hint of a train at the back, for
evening; tightly fitted sleeves and bodices for day wear.
Jackie paused at the top of the wide staircase, looking
around him as though seeking help. One of the more pert
assistants, who always had an eye for a likely young man,
saw him and called out, 'Over here, Jackie.'

He avoided her gaze as she handed him the boxes and
her drawled 'Got some real eye-openers here, Jackie boy,
so you be careful how you handle them', made his blush
deepen.

Quickly, he made his escape into the back yard of the shop where his van was parked. He drove slowly over the headland, careful because the road was narrow and dusty; despite annual promises made by the council, it had never been tarred and deteriorated more each year. Concentrating on his driving, Jackie braked just in time to avoid the sleek chestnut filly that skimmed the ditch beside him and in a graceful glide came to rest bang in front of the bonnet.

The harsh words of protest died on his lips when he saw the rider was Netta Jenkins; a slim figure in hunter-green velvet with a lacy cravat at her throat and her unbound hair falling down her back, the colour of new pennies in the sunlight.

Although his lips set in irritation at the foolish risk she had taken, to herself and her mount as well as the van, he knew he couldn't put his anger into words. He jumped to the ground, grasping the bridle of the horse as it backed nervously away.

Netta smiled down at him from the saddle, then with the small riding crop she carried reached down and touched his cheek, slowly moving the leather tip across his mouth and down to the opening of his white shirt, unbuttoned at the neck beneath the fancy Fair Isle pullover he wore.

An involuntary shudder ran through him, as though she had touched him herself. 'Miss Netta!'

'Startled you, did I?' she murmured, showing perfect teeth in a smile that made his heart lurch in his breast. He felt the first nudgings of panic. This was unfamiliar country and he didn't know what sort of reaction she expected. Indeed, he was shocked that she could act so intimately. 'You did, a little,' he admitted, feeling a fool in the triteness of his answer.

'Poor Jackie! I suppose I should apologise. I startled you at our first meeting too, didn't I?' Her speech was lazy, the words long drawn out. She saw the way his gaze lingered on her hair and face, coming to rest on her mouth.

Netta felt the first run of excitement, the stimulus of success and again its accompanying sense of power. It was a wonderful aphrodisiac.

Giving him no warning she leaned down in the saddle and Jackie felt her mouth press briefly against his. 'There, better now,' she said, straightening up. Then with a flick of the whip, she urged her horse forward in a startled gallop, leaving Jackie staring after her, his mouth foolishly agape.

Slowly and very carefully, he drove the rest of the way. Turning into the yard, he stopped outside the open back door. At the same moment Netta came hurrying from the stables, throwing instructions over her shoulder in a haughty voice. Jackie heard a man answer, then she was crossing the cobbles to the back door, pausing briefly to say to Mary who had appeared at the opening, 'The Co-op man has brought some parcels for me. See that he brings them straight up to my room.'

'At once, Miss Netta.'

Netta looked deliberately into his eyes as she passed, then abruptly away, her expression set and disdainful. Once she was out of earshot, Mary, who had been studying Jackie with a closeness that made him feel suddenly uncomfortable, said, 'In one of her moods, is she? Closes up like a prodded winkle when she's in one o' them. Never know when they're going to appear, that we don't.'

She smiled then, putting her arms about his waist, standing on tiptoe to plant a kiss somewhere in the region of his left ear. 'Got time to spare for a cup of tea? Mrs Dean's out for the moment and I'm all by meself.'

She was acting so naturally, thought Jackie, that the other evening might never have happened. To Mary's surprise, and not a little vexation, he drew away, leaving her to hurry round to the rear of the van. Opening the double doors, he lifted out the flat boxes. 'You heard what Miss Netta said. That I was to take these straight up to her room. So, Mary O'Malley, you'd better not delay me, had you?'

She looked flabbergasted. She had wanted so badly to show him that things had not changed, to say she was sorry for her behaviour the other night. Now, with a toss of her head that sent the fair hair bouncing on her shoulders and her cap ribbons flying, she flounced back into the kitchen.

Jackie climbed the stairs slowly, his arms full of parcels. On the landing he paused, uncertain of his way, until from an open door to his left, where the landing swept in a graceful curve of highly polished banister rail, a soft voice called: 'Here, boy. Don't dawdle, now. I'm a busy woman.'

His heart thudding, feeling decidedly panicky, Jackie followed his instructions. That was what he was paid for, wasn't it? His not to reason why . . .

The room he entered was like nothing he had ever seen before, not even in his dreams. A symphony in shades of blue, with a cream carpet and curtains, it took his breath away. What his Aunt Ellen would have given, he thought, to be able to greet each new day in a room like this!

There were roses everywhere; pink, white, red, arranged beautifully in white ceramic vases. Netta stood by the window, a background of blue sky and rolling clouds high-lighting the windswept tumble of her hair. As he hesitated at the open doorway, half in, half out, she motioned that he should place the boxes he carried on the table in the bay window beside her. With a hasty look at his boots to make sure there were no traces of mud, for the stable yard had been newly hosed down and puddles lay in the hollows of the cobble stones, he crossed the pale carpet, taking as much care as if there'd been eggs beneath his feet.

Netta smiled. Relieved of the parcels, he caught her eye as he stepped back. Again she smiled. 'Don't go!' It was an order. Then, before he was aware of her intentions, she'd slipped the lid off one of the boxes and laid it aside. She lifted out a silky white garment that looked, to the startled Jackie, almighty like a nightgown. But nothing like the nightgowns worn by his Aunt Ellen, which he'd seen in all their full, high-necked glory flapping on the washing line in the back garden on wash day. No, this nightdress, if such was the garment, was an eyeful of fine lace and satin, long and flowing, and to Jackie's astonished eyes seemed to have no top at all. Not what you could call a top, anyway, with only those pipe-cleaner thin straps to keep it up.

His thoughts revolved wildly around a fantasy of Netta in that gown. He would have been horrified had he known she was reading his face like a book. Holding the white satin garment in front of her, she twirled around the room, coming to rest in front of him. Her voice was low, deliberately husky and teasing. She was enjoying the effect she was having on this young boy. What fun to take a man like this and mould him to the way she wanted him, seeing exactly how far she could go!

The society men she knew were boring. She couldn't drum up one ounce of interest in any of them, whereas innocent Jackie Rees was a challenge . . .

'Well?' she challenged when he didn't answer her teasing. 'Like it?' She gave another twirl. 'Or would you rather I showed you some of the other things I ordered?' And she giggled, frantically opening boxes and pulling out silks and laces and shining satins in delicately tinted pastel shades of lilac and pale coffee and turquoise, until the polished rosewood table was strewn with them. He took a deep breath and managed a shaky, 'Miss Netta, I'd better go. I have other deliveries to do . . .'

'Oh, poof!' Netta pouted like a spoiled child. She gathered the items of lingerie in her arms and came and stood in front of him. 'Well, if you must. There are other things I need, anyway. I shall be in the shop in a day or two, and we can see each other again.'

She lifted her eyes and looked him full in the face. 'That's a promise.'

When he came downstairs Mary didn't even look up from her task of polishing the silver soup tureen. Jackie's jaw hardened for a moment, the sudden and inexplicable feelings for Miss Netta still clouding his mind, then without a word he passed through the kitchen and out the back door. A moment later Mary heard the van start up and then the crunch of its wheels on the gravel drive.

As Jackie drove back over the headland, he thought of the things his friends had said about other women. Over the years, Mary's treatment of him had been casually friendly, so sure of him that he'd been like putty in her hands. Until, that is, Miss Netta had indicated the interest she felt for him. Nothing casual about that one! Indeed, hadn't she made it plain that she found him attractive? It boosted his confidence, and goodness knows after the way Mary was treating him these days, anything that did was welcome. Not for him to wonder what ulterior motives there might be behind the attentions of such a wealthy young woman. She was lovely and spirited, the complete opposite to anyone he'd met or spoken to before, apart from Mary. Although he'd seen enough of her sort in the shop, lording it over the sales girls, their voices loud and autocratic, used to being indulged the moment they spoke, not one of them had actually spoken to him as an equal, as Miss Netta did.

He wasn't as naive as some people seemed to think. He had not failed to notice the interested glances some of the younger women directed his way. He wouldn't have been a man if he hadn't.

Miss Netta might be far above him but under her fancy words and frocks she was just a woman – and Jackie had decided it was time he followed his friend's advice. Mary might assume she was the only woman for him.

Jackie was no longer sure.

The fog that had drifted in from the sea hung low, the globes of the street lamps luminescent in the white haze. Alys shivered, chilled to the bone. Sleep had brought nothing but nightmares and she kept waking up, sweating, going over and over in her mind the time she had spent that evening in the kitchen with Evan. Wearily she set about poking the fire into a semblance of life, scattering the fine grey ash until there was a little pile of it on the hearth. She carried firewood already chopped from the coal shed in the yard, holding a corner of her shawl about her mouth and nose in order to avoid breathing in the acid taste of the fog.

'It'll be better in the morning!' The words came suddenly to her mind. How often had she heard her mother say that after she had come home crying from some childish disaster? 'Better in the morning.'

But this was one morning which would bring nothing but memories she wanted to forget. In his brief letter of farewell, Evan had said she must forget him, even though he would never forget her. Easy to say, when everything in that shabby kitchen reminded her so vividly of that sweet time together. He had shown her what love was, had made her into a woman.

But there was nothing to be gained from dwelling on what might have been. She mustn't waste time on it. He had let her down badly so she would put Evan Jenkins completely out of her mind, and concentrate only on the future. She hadn't the heart to go out, so she sat huddled over the fire for most of the day.

Dan came in and silently she placed the plate of mutton stew which had only had to be warmed up in front of him, ladling out potatoes and vegetables. After stuffing his mouth, he swallowed hard and said, 'I've been hearing stories about you and that Jenkins boy from the big house. Seems if I'd come home a little earlier some nights, I would 'ave caught you together in my house.'

Avoiding his fierce stare, Alys turned towards the fire.

'Is it true, then?' he demanded, tearing off a chunk of fresh bread and thrusting it into his mouth. 'I hear he's gone off somewhere. On another job for Daddy, is it? Or to get out of your way?'

Dan's words were so close to the truth that she began to laugh. It seemed so funny that she couldn't stop laughing for several minutes. Then, as abruptly as she'd started, she stopped and very quietly said, 'You don't have to worry any more, Dan. I know my place, and it's certainly not with someone like Evan Jenkins.'

For a long time Alys had refused to acknowledge what was happening to her, knowing only that her breasts seemed fuller and painful to the touch, the nipples glowing a deeper pink. Blue veins showed against the creamy white skin, and that which should have happened had not. Aware that all was not right, that the rhythms of her body had somehow betrayed her, she felt confused and irritable, something completely foreign to her usually ebullient nature.

She nagged Dan, fully aware she was being unfair but unable to help herself. Even Mary had been on the receiving end of her sharp tongue, and had exclaimed peevishly, 'What's wrong wi' you, girl? You're up and down like a fiddler's elbow.'

And it was Mary, with her earthy shrewdness, who finally put her fears into words.

'You're in trouble, aren't you?'

Alys flushed scarlet, looking away. 'I don't know what you mean. What kind of trouble?'

Mary snorted. 'What kind of trouble do girls like us

'sually get into?' Her voice softened. 'Come on, love, you know there isn't anything you can't tell me. You're pregnant, aren't you? Jaysus, it was that Evan Jenkins!' Gazing into the girl's stricken eyes she held her close, one hand patting her back as though she were a baby. 'You little fool! Oh, you stupid little fool!'

Mary's words, blunt as they were, brought things out into the open.

Suddenly, Alys remembered her own mother and was terrified. Mam had had a terrible time right from the beginning: sickness that lasted for most of the day, not just the morning; splitting headaches that laid her low, causing her to spend long hours lying on her bed in a darkened room.

She recalled with harrowing clarity the screams that had gradually died to low moans as the doctor and midwife fought to save the baby, and then Mam's life. She was twelve years old and her mother was bearing a child in terrible agony. To Alys it was a nightmare she would never forget.

Almost as though she knew what was going through Alys's mind, Mary said gently, 'You mustn't think about what happened to your mam, love. Mine's brought four healthy children into the world without having to take to her bed for more'n a few hours.'

Compassion overwhelmed her at the terrified look on Alys's face. She wiped her friend's eyes with a corner of her pinny. 'Come on now, you mustn't let it upset you too much. We've got to think, decide what's best. This isn't something you can stick into your handbag like a mothball and just forget.' She gave Alys a little shake. 'It's not good for the baby to get too upset.'

'There'll be no baby!' Suddenly Alys knew what she had to do. She met Mary's shocked expression defiantly.

'Jayus, Alys, what are you saying?'

'You know what I'm saying. I'm not going to have the baby.' She took her friend's hands in hers, holding them tight. 'And you're going to help me.'

'Holy Mother!' Mary's face turned a shade whiter, if that were possible, the freckles standing out sharply across her nose and cheekbones. 'I don't know about things like that. And neither do you, Alys Hughes, so you'd better put the whole thing out of your mind and face facts. I'll not jeopardise our mortal souls for a deed like that.'

Alys put both hands to her cheeks and turned away, unable to meet the accusation in the other girl's eyes. When she didn't speak, Mary went on tentatively, 'There must be something we can do. Go to the doctor, or even Willis the chemist.'

'The doctor would charge two and six and I haven't got two and six to spare, and even if I had he wouldn't do anything to help me. He's not allowed. Oh, Mary, what are we going to do? How can I bring an illegitimate child into the world, knowing the kind of future that awaits it? Don't you remember Nancy Griffiths and the child she had, and how they drove her out of the village?' Her breath broke on a shuddering sob. 'I'd rather it died first!'

Mary crossed herself quickly. When Our Lady didn't appear to upbraid her and God didn't strike them both dead, her heartbeat returned to its normal tempo and she recalled the unfortunate Nancy with a shudder, remembering how she had been forced to take shelter in a barn and how her baby's feet had been eaten away by rats one night, and how on their way to school the next morning they had witnessed the pitiful sight of Nancy running down Market Street, her screams echoing on the quiet air, the bloody bundle that was her baby clutched in her arms.

She wouldn't wish that on her worst enemy. An illegitimate baby in this small community was unthinkable. The disgrace would be terrible. She didn't object to Alys's use of the word 'we' either, for hadn't they always faced things together, right from the first day they had met? They would face this together, too. But there had to be a way other than the one Alys was proposing. Hugging the frightened girl to her, Mary said gently, 'Let's not be too hasty, *cariad*. We've got to think it out, properly and safely, and do what's best for everyone.'

Alys gave a harsh laugh. 'Best for everyone? There's only one thing I can think of that would be best for everyone, and that would be to put the bloody clock back!'

Mary nodded. 'But it did happen, and there's no getting away from it.' She paused, her gaze thoughtful as it rested on her friend. 'Did no one ever warn you about such things? Heaven knows, it was drummed into us often enough by the nuns.' Hopefully, she added, 'Perhaps he forced you?'

Alys laughed, shaking her head. 'No, Mary, he didn't force me, I didn't need any forcing.'

Mary looked shocked. 'Alys!'

'I know. I know what you're thinking and you're right. Your mother would call me a shameless hussy, fit only to join the ranks of Lilith and her cronies. But, oh,

Mary, if you knew how I felt . . .' She shook her head. 'There was no need for forcing, believe me.'

Mary tut-tutted like an old woman and then said, 'Well, we've just got to put our heads together and think about this. Let's leave it a day or two, eh, when you're a little more clear in your mind,' adding, coaxingly, 'perhaps something will still happen.'

Alys looked glum. 'I don't think so. I'm pretty sure by now.'

She sighed, catching Mary's glance of entreaty. 'Well, a few days. Then I'll have to decide . . .'

But there was really no other course than the one she'd already decided upon. Intuition warned her that it might be dangerous to leave it too long.

As the days went by and nothing happened, she became pale and lost weight and dark rings circled her eyes. 'What the hell's wrong wi' you, girl?' Dan yelled at her, coming in one day to find no food waiting for him and Alys slouched in a chair with her feet on an old footstool. 'You look like something the cat dragged in.'

Shocking him into silence, she burst into tears, running from the room and up the stairs where he heard her bedroom door slam.

Mildly for him, Dan scratched his head and said, 'Well, I'll be blowed! What's got into her, then?' Muttering at the inexplicable behaviour of women, he set about getting his own supper, even going so far as to call up to her, 'Want some, do you? It's ready if you do.'

Alys buried her face in her pillow and didn't reply.

She'd made a complete fool of herself, she thought. She couldn't go on like this. Something had to be done.

Dan was no fool and if he should begin to suspect . . . she shuddered.

The next time Mary visited, casting her mind back wildly to scraps of conversation overheard between her mother and other women when they were gathered with cups of tea about the fire and she not supposed to be listening, she said, 'They say carbolic soap, the hard, red kind with the strong smell . . .'

Alys stared at her in fascinated horror. 'Carbolic soap? How on earth would you use it?'

'I think you make a kind of frothy paste and shove it up . . .'

She stopped as Alys made a gagging sound and rushed to the corner sink, her stomach emptying itself of its contents at Mary's graphic description.

The church was a quiet place where she sought refuge. She was in tears as she knelt before the altar. 'I know I've done wrong and should be punished,' she whispered to the serene face above her, 'but I'm not sorry. Not really. Oh, Holy Mother, if you could only know the joy of it . . .' She caught her breath at her irreverence. 'Forgive me, Holy Mother, I shouldn't have spoken like that in front of you.'

But the serene face didn't offer any advice and after a while Alys crept from the church, tears dimming her eyes while the blue-robed Madonna stood in her niche and watched.

Chapter Nine

In the corner tavern, the air was blue with tobacco smoke and the conversation lively. Gusts of shrill laughter came from the corner where a cluster of women sat, drinking gin. Dan saw that Lilith was among them, her laughter louder and more raucous than the rest. She waved to him as he came in, calling a greeting.

A heavily built man entered the glass swing doors and stood looking about him, as though searching for someone in the crowded bar. His silvery white hair did nothing to soften the pugnacious red of his face, and his well-cut suit and shining soft leather boots set him apart from the roughly dressed miners and fishermen.

'Evening, Mr Jenkins,' the barman called, as though expecting him. 'Would you like to come through to the back? Got a nice warm fire in there, and it's quiet and comfortable. We can discuss our business in peace.'

Gesturing to the fuzzy-haired barmaid to take over serving, the barman led Thomas Jenkins across the room. Hearing the name, Dan looked up from the serious bout of drinking which as usual engaged most of his evening. His eyes focused blearily on the silver-haired man and he thought: Aye, this is him. The man whose son has buggered around with Alys and then gone off

God knows where, leaving her jumpy and fractious as a wet hen.

With a roar, he slammed the jug of ale down on the bar counter, spilling half. Then with the speed of an angry buffalo, he snatched the elderly man's jacket and heaved him back, flinging him to the sawdust-littered floor, adding insult to injury by placing the toe of his boot in the man's fat buttocks.

'I'll not forget the way your boy's treated my girl. I should wipe the floor wi' you. In fact,' his huge fists closing threateningly, 'I might just do that now I've got the chance.'

Thomas Jenkins lumbered painfully to his feet. When he had recovered, he turned to look back at Dan Radloff, his face contorted with hatred. His closed fists came up in a classic fighter's stance and Dan grinned as he all but spat: 'I'll teach you to lay a finger on me, my man. As for your girl – if you can't keep her away from her betters, then you'll just have to put up with the consequences.'

Dan's temper was up now. Slowly swinging his arms, he advanced on the older man, who in spite of his fighting words backed away.

'You shut your bleeding gob,' Dan hissed. 'I'll learn you and your kin to interfere with respectable women, so I will.'

Men were on their feet, watching; women giggled nervously for although Dan was in a merry state of drunkenness he was still a force to be reckoned with. His fist shot out and nearly lifted Jenkins off his feet with the force of the punch to the point of his jaw. The other man staggered, turned for help to the open-mouthed barman, and collapsed with spread arms on the bar top.

Dan brushed imaginary dust off the sleeves of his jacket. Grinning to the room at large, he announced, 'I think he got the message, don't you, mates?'

The customers resumed their seats, talking loudly about how you couldn't even go into a public house any more for a quiet drink without some form of violence happening.

The barman, sustained by a stiff brandy, came forward after seeing Thomas Jenkins safely into the back room. 'If you're not out of here in two minutes I'll call the cops, d'you understand? This is a respectable house.'

Dan lifted his almost empty mug and tossed the contents back with one swallow. 'I wouldn't stay in 'ere if you paid me, boyo. Not wi' the likes of 'im under the same roof.' He nodded towards the back room.

'On your way, then.'

'Be glad to.' Dan smiled through the comfortable mist in which he was floating, wiped his nose on the back of his hand and walked through the swing doors of the tavern. The wind had risen, bringing with it a white mist from the sea. The shops were long closed, although many still had lights in their windows. The whole street seemed deserted, except for him and the shadow that followed him into the darkness.

He stopped by a lamp post, making out the dumpy figure behind him wrapped closely in a shawl. 'Lilith, is it?' he hazarded slowly.

'If it's not me then it's me ghost,' she said cheerfully. She came closer and slipped her arm through his, peering up into his face. 'There, isn't that cosy now? 'ow about you an' me goin' for a little walk down by the quayside?'

He thought of the few coins that remained in his pocket, money which he had had every intention of giving to Alys. But the adrenalin was still flowing after his encounter with Jenkins and the thought of tamely going home to a lonely bed was mortifying. The warmth emanating from the woman beside him was strangely comforting and her voice whispered agreeable things in his ear. He grinned. Why not? Alys expected him when she saw him. She wouldn't wait up for him. Arms linked, they began their stumbling way down the steps to the deeply shadowed privacy of the quay.

'I'll be yer sweetheart, if you will be mine . . .' Dan sang, and Lilith joined in with her shrill voice. There wasn't a movement anywhere except for the watchman's light on a ship out at sea, rising and dipping on the slight swell of the water.

They paused by the low wall which separated them from the dock below and Dan began fumbling at her skirts. Lilith giggled like a young girl and rested one foot on the wall, the skirts riding above her knees. 'There, that better, boyo?'

'It's lovely, you are, girl. Come 'ere and make an old man happy.'

Lilith did her best to make him happy, leaning back so far over the low wall that he lost his footing and the last she saw of him were his legs, jerking frantically as they disappeared over the parapet and into the oily black water below.

That night when Dan didn't return home and the loud knock came on the door, Alys was ready. The constable was red-faced, clearly embarrassed, but the sympathy in his eyes was plain to see. 'I'm afraid I've got bad news for you, girl.'

She'd expected a night locked up in the cells at the police station for disorderly behaviour, but not this. She could not believe her stepfather was dead. That large, noisy man who had been so full of life! The constable hadn't the heart to tell her of the circumstances of the tragedy or of the wild-eyed Lilith who had come banging on the door of his cottage, screaming something about Dan Radloff falling over the wall of the old quay.

All Alys knew was that her stepfather's body had been found floating in the harbour, caught up in a tangle of nets left hanging over the side of an anchored ship.

She felt a stab of pain; she still couldn't believe Dan was dead. It was as though time had moved backwards and she was again on that dark, windswept beach, waiting with Mam for news of her father. Even though her feelings towards Dan hadn't always been the friendliest, she could not help but grieve for the man he had once been; the man her mother had married, who in the brief year they were together had made Mam laugh, her face taking on an animated glow as she walked by his side, the envy of her neighbours.

'Shall I get someone to come and sit wi' you, girl? You can't be alone at this time.' The elderly constable was worried by the calmness of her manner, more used to hysterics at the breaking of such news.

She shook her head. 'No, thank you. I'll be all right.'

After the funeral, alone again in her own kitchen with Mary gone back to work, Alys shivered. She tried not to think of the future, but it was there, a threatening spectre wherever she turned.

The silence of the house became a miasma which oozed out of the walls and wound itself around her. She huddled shivering in front of the fire, wondering what she had done to deserve such a fate.

She had bitterly resented her stepfather, blaming him for her mother's death; resented the way he had undertaken his paternal duties, even using the strap on her when he saw fit. Even so, she knew she would miss him.

She thought of the time he had gone up to the cottage on the headlands, to confront Marcus Dillon with those outrageous suggestions. She allowed herself a few moments to dwell on the good-looking, enigmatic features of the painter, wondering where he was now. Would the portrait of her and Drogo really hang in a posh gallery in London, with society ladies and gentlemen gazing at it, curious as to the model's identity?

Would Marcus describe their first meeting, relating the way he'd watched as she came riding across the sands and her reaction to his first proposal. She imagined the teasing, the wry comments, and felt her cheeks flush. Well, she wouldn't be seeing him again so why should it concern her what was happening all those hundreds of miles away? With Dan gone, she had her own future to think of, and unless she soon took things into her own hands, the future of her unborn child.

But, oh, decisions were so hard to make, and almost impossible when you were all alone . . .

When she got a visit from Lilith, Alys was shocked. She knew of the woman's reputation, although it had taken a while for her to understand. 'For money!' she had exclaimed to an amused Mary. 'You mean she does it for money! People pay her for it?' She couldn't remember feeling so revolted in all her life.

Mary shrugged. 'Not people – men! Men who don't know any better.' Now, opening the door to the hesitant knock, Alys eyed the new black woollen shawl and dark skirt the woman wore, unaware of the scowl of disapproval on her own face. She drew back from the smell of gin on Lilith's breath. 'Well?' she challenged. 'What do you want? If my stepfather owed you anything, you're not getting it out of me.'

Lilith looked aggrieved. 'Who said I wanted anything? Dan Radloff was good to me. We 'ad a – a special relationship, like.'

Alys's lip curled. 'I bet!'

Lilith ignored her animosity. The words that followed shocked Alys even more. ' 'ow you off for money?' her visitor asked.

Alys was flabbergasted. She stared open-mouthed at the once pretty face and dyed red hair. 'No, really,' Lilith went on. She opened the shabby old-fashioned reticule she carried on her wrist. 'Please, you must be at your wits' end – please let me 'elp . . .'

She thrust a handful of coins at the scandalised girl, and when Alys drew back with an affronted gasp looked genuinely hurt. 'What's the matter? My money not good enough for you? Well, let me tell you, young lady, I worked 'ard for it, even though the way I got it might not be your idea of working. But the men seem to like it, and while there's men around they'll continue to pay me what I want.'

There was a burst of laughter from the dark roadway, a clatter of footsteps, and a small group of women returning from a church meeting gazed with open curiosity at the tableau framed in the light from the small cottage kitchen. Their voices fell to shocked whispers as they passed. Alys saw one look back over her shoulder and the others giggle.

Her temper rising, she stepped back and began to close the door. 'Leave me alone! I can't be seen talking to you.'

For long moments Lilith stood gazing at the closed door, then with a shrug of indifference, she raised two fingers to the backs of the retreating women and shrieked after them, 'And a piss in the wind to all of you, me beauties!'

She teetered off down the road, wondering if she should nip into the church to say a prayer and light a candle for the repose of Dan's soul. The last time she had entered those sacred precincts Father Goodhew had frowned a reprimand although he had not said anything. As she crossed the High Street the delicious aroma of fish and chips drifted her way and people with newspaper-wrapped parcels passed her. Lilith closed her eyes. With the money Alys had scorned she had enough to treat herself to a slap-up meal. Her mouth watered, her stomach rumbled, and with a smile on her face she hurried across to the fish and chip shop.

Alys spent a sleepless night, tossing and turning, agonising over the decision she must make. The Church would call it murder, but surely, with so short a time elapsed, it couldn't be that? She must put the thought completely out of her head otherwise she would never be able to go through with her plans.

On the one hand, it was Evan's baby and she dearly loved him. On the other, she might never see him again and there was no reason why he should ever know about the child.

But a concoction of red carbolic soap!

She shuddered, pulling the corners of the pillow about her face, stifling her cries. If Mary was here she could talk to her. But she had accompanied Netta Jenkins to Cardiff, acting as maid since Netta's own woman had been taken ill, and they wouldn't be back until the weekend.

And then it seemed as though the devil – for surely it could not have been our Blessed Lord – was listening to her pleas, for the very next morning as the other street hawkers clustered around the returning fishing boats, pushing to be first served, two women next to Alys began talking.

In hushed voices but still loud enough for her to hear every word, one said, 'There's worried I am, goin' to have to ask Willis the chemist for those tablets. I daren't wait any longer, me old man's getting suspicious.'

Her friend gave her an old-fashioned look. 'Not 'is, then, is it?'

A grunt of disgust. ''Course not! Bin away, ain't 'e? Only got back last week and bin too drunk to touch me since, celebrating wi' 'is mates.'

A shout from the boats had the crowd of women surging forward, elbowing Alys aside. 'Come on, girl! 'aven't got all day, mind.'

So there *were* things you could buy! A deep steadying breath had Alys turning on her heel, causing the women behind her to step aside hastily, pulling their shawls tightly about them at sight of the white-faced girl with the haunted eyes.

Willis the chemist would know what she meant. Discreet, he was. Had a name for it.

She hung around the chemist's shop for so long that finally the pharmacist's daughter, a tall thin girl with protruding teeth and glasses, came over and asked in a disagreeable voice, 'Want somethin', do you?'

Alys stared at her, the well-rehearsed words dying on her tongue. How could she bring herself to ask this unsympathetic girl for the pills the woman had spoken about? Would she even know what Alys was talking about?

Seeing the girl's eyes sharpen behind the spectacles, desperately Alys asked for carbolic soap. The girl said 'Humph!' and turned away to reach up to a high shelf to take down a bar of the flaky dark red soap. 'One bar?'

Would that be enough? Alys hesitated, sure that the keen eyes behind those spectacles could read her mind. 'Two, please,' she said, and walked up to the counter to pay the tuppence demanded by the girl.

She hid the white paper-wrapped package with its pink string and sealing wax under her shawl. Hurrying down the street, feeling like a criminal, she was sure that every eye was upon her, knowing what she was about and judging her.

She slipped quietly through her front door, hoping none of the neighbours would see her and come and inquire if she was all right. Some of them had remarked on her pallor and the pinched look about her face, asking if she was eating properly. They put it down to her stepfather's death and knew full well she was too proud to ask help of any of them.

She reached into the dark recess under the stone sink of the wash house, her searching fingers finally finding the large receptacle her mother had used for mixing the blue bag for the sheets and pillow cases. She had no idea how she was going to carry out her distasteful task or even if it would work.

That thought she pushed to the back of her mind. All she must think about now was how she would feel in the morning, when all was back to rights . . .

Chapter Ten

Cardiff was a lovely place to visit, Mary decided, but she couldn't wait to get back to the peace and quiet of Craven Bay. The streets were a nightmare of rushing people and carriages and the occasional automobile sounding its horn and frightening a body out of its wits.

'Jaysus!' she muttered as a bright yellow vehicle appeared as if from nowhere, causing her to jump hurriedly back on to the pavement. 'A body'd have to have eyes in the back of their heads to live in this town, sure they would.'

Rudely she stuck her tongue out at the elderly driver of the canary-yellow car who promptly flushed a bright, turkey red and almost didn't make the next corner. She struggled with parcels Miss Netta had purchased, her arms aching as her mistress walked ahead, turning an imperious head to warn Mary to keep up.

Back at the hotel, it was: 'Be careful, Mary, that happens to be an exclusive model you are handling so carelessly.' And 'Oh, why did Emily have to be sick just now, leaving me surrounded by fools?' And 'Hurry up, girl, why must you be such a slowcoach?'

Really, Netta thought, the girl was hopeless. If she could have done without a lady's maid on this trip she would have, but the gowns these days with their rows of tiny buttons were virtually impossible to get into without assistance. Besides, if Mary was with her she couldn't be with Jackie and the thought of that pleased Netta immensely.

She had been invited to a picnic by her Aunt Lucy and Uncle William. The day was warm and humid, without the fresh breeze that would be cooling Craven Bay, floating in from the sea. Aunt Lucy had decided at the last minute not to attend, saying she felt one of her migraines coming on; but the two girls must go, Netta and her cousin Clarissa, accompanied by Mary as a chaperone. Aunt Lucy charged them to pay strict attention to their manners and behaviour.

The afternoon had drawn on when Netta noticed an air of excitement come over the usually placid Clarissa and she remarked idly, 'Your cheeks are flushed most prettily, dearest cousin. Are you expecting someone special?'

Clarissa simpered. 'I suppose you could say he was special. To me, at least. You must remember him, Netta, from when we were children? Idris Dixon? He has been away at university but is now back to join his father's business.'

Netta pursed her lips. Idris? She brought to mind a tall youth with a multitude of pimples across his chin and lower cheeks. Not attractive. Not in the least attractive. So why should her cousin be acting this way, all mincing blushes as though he promised to be God's gift to women? She was equally perplexed when he was pointed out to her by a rapturous Clarissa. In place of the pimples there was now a smooth, ruddy skin, glowing with health and wellbeing. So much wellbeing in fact that the cheeks in a few years would be overly plump; the eyes, now small and pale blue, sunk into a morass of fat.

Idris Dixon leaned negligently against the trunk of the ancient oak tree that sheltered the picnic party, stifling a yawn. Whyever had he promised his mother he would come to an event that promised to be too tedious for words? His eyes were glazed, partly from boredom, partly from the heat, and he gazed with little interest across the smooth green lawns over which Clarissa and a young woman who seemed vaguely familiar were crossing towards him. Since university he had led a wild life, or as wild as a fellow could get in a town like Cardiff, keeping his taste for lively horses and livelier women and gaming tables from his father's ears. Make the most of your freedom now, his friends had told him, for one day soon you will have to marry and give up your foolish pranks.

Idris did not see any reason why he should give up his pranks, even when married. Provided he chose the right woman, who was to stop him? He stood politely to attention as the two girls came nearer, his gaze focused on Netta. They stood before him like two exotic butterflies, the calf-length skirts of their summery frocks, the colour of sweet peas, floating in the slight breeze.

He heard Clarissa's voice, light and high, a trifle stilted, saying of course he must remember Netta Jenkins, her country cousin? Idris remembered the crush he had had on her years ago, in his early teens and in a constant state of arousal at the sight of a pretty girl, and how Netta had not exactly discouraged it. But it was Clarissa who claimed him now, taking his arm in a possessive gesture and prattling on about showing him the new swans on the lake. 'Netta will excuse us, I know. There are dozens of young men dying to talk to her, and it's the first time I've managed to get you alone since you came home.'

As they walked away, Idris glanced once over his shoulder, chagrined by the careless way Netta accepted the attentions of the three young men who hurried at once to her side. She glanced over at Idris, smiled, and linked arms with two of her followers. The third scuttled close behind like an obedient puppy at her heels. Idris heard her laugh as they walked away.

Mary sat and watched from the shade of a tree, glad to take the weight off her feet. She'd had enough of Miss Netta to last her a lifetime, and had a sneaking suspicion that Netta felt the same about her.

She had never forgiven Jackie Rees for showing such an interest in the master's daughter, or Netta for encouraging him. She'd seen how Netta looked at him when Jackie delivered goods from the Co-op, these days more frequently than ever. The Jenkinses must be the Co-op's best customers, thought Mary, wryly.

He would enter the kitchen, eyes eager and watchful, a look of frank admiration coming over his expressive features when Netta appeared. Mary's lips twisted. These days, Netta had taken to hanging about the kitchen and stable yard like a bad smell, always popping in when least expected. Since the episode in the pictures, Jackie had avoided Mary, and thinking back on the way he had rejected her offer that morning when he'd been delivering all those boxes to Miss Netta – well, Mary was not too keen on speaking to him either. Let him get on with it! See if she cared! Best that she find out now that he could be attracted to other women so easily. Even so, in a way she felt sorry for him. Naive and innocent creature that he was, how was he to know that Netta liked her bit of fun and then it was on to the next one, good-bye Charlie. Or, in this case, Jackie.

She cast her mind back to the last time he had called at the house, brazenly going through to the front hall as Netta called from the upper landing; how the girl had run part of the way down the wide staircase and slid the rest, balanced childishly on the polished banister rail. She'd landed at Jackie's feet and from her position in the open doorway Mary had seen how with cool deliberation she had allowed herself to fall forward, pretending to stagger, forcing a bemused Jackie to catch her in his arms and steady her.

The brazen hussy had gazed up into his eyes, and Mrs Dean, watching from Mary's side, had hurriedly removed the small sharp knife with which the maid had been chopping parsley. 'Just as well the Master isn't around when this sort of thing 'appens. Be in for a right telling off, the two of them, followed by a word in Mr Kimble's ear.' She shook her head. 'Young people these days . . .' Mr Kimble was the manager of the Co-operative Stores and would do more than frown at the lack of seemliness of it all. Jackie could even lose his job.

Oh, decidedly, that Miss Netta had caused a lot of bother, thought Mary. She thrust aside her own hurt that Jackie could even look at another woman when she had thought he was hers. The sooner they were back in Craven Bay, the better Mary would like it.

Some of her fractiousness must have rubbed off on Netta, for to everyone's surprise, the next morning she expressed a sudden desire to return home sooner than planned.

The previous night, Clarissa had come to her bedroom, babbling on about Idris and what a wonderful man he'd turned out to be, how handsome and gallant. Netta almost laughed aloud when she said artlessly, 'I'm almost sure he's in love with me, Netta. What do you think? Did it look to you as if he was?'

Netta couldn't have cared less, one way or the other. Her thoughts were entirely at home with Jackie Rees. She thought of his thickly lashed eyes, the rich melting brown of them, and compared him with the young men she had met at her cousin's house. Not one of them could hold a candle to Jackie. She felt a tingling sensation run all the way through her just thinking of him.

'But you have two whole days left!' Clarissa pointed out when Netta announced her return. 'Why the sudden change of heart? I thought you were enjoying yourself.'

'I am,' Netta assured her. 'I have. I suppose I'm just exhausted with all this excitement after the quietness of Craven Bay.'

'Oh, well, if you feel like that . . .'

The train journey back was long and tiring, but still the first thing Mary did when she was allowed a few hours' freedom was to walk over to Alys's cottage. The kitchen was cold and empty, the fire in the grate grey ashes with no spark of life. Mary stood on the bottom stair of the narrow staircase, craning her neck to look upwards.

'Alys? Are you there, girl?'

A low groan answered her and Mary paled, understanding at once what had happened. 'By the Holy Saints!' she breathed. What has the little eejit been up to?

The small bedroom reeked of sickness. With just a glance at the figure on the bed, Mary's suspicions were confirmed. Alys's face was a sickly grey, with huge dark circles under her eyes. The girl's body was racked with pain and in her half-conscious state she thrashed about, whimpering pitifully. Mary groaned in sympathy. For a long moment, as terror gripped her, she stood gazing down helplessly. Then, gritting her teeth, she reached out and gently pulled back the bed coverings.

Alys was lying in a pool of blood. It took all of Mary's strength and courage not to turn and run back down the stairs, calling for help. Forcing herself to remain calm, she managed to get Alys out of the soiled petticoat and into a clean nightgown. She changed the sheets and folded a towel and placed it between the girl's legs.

Alys's eyes were open, wild with pain and confusion. She whispered in a hoarse voice, 'What are you doing here? I thought you'd gone to Cardiff.'

Mary's own voice cracked with emotion. 'I should have stayed, found some excuse not to go with Miss Netta, for didn't I know what you would be up to as soon as I turned me back? Oh, *macushla*, what if I hadn't come? Did you not stop to think of the consequences, doing this alone, with no one here to help you?'

'I had to . . . it wouldn't wait . . . oh, don't scold! I feel so awful . . .' She clasped Mary's hand and her own was icy. The huge pansy eyes gazed up beseechingly. 'Do you think God will be angry with me?'

Mary knew of course that what she wanted was reassurance, for Mary to tell her that she had done the right, the only, thing. But how could she tell Alys that when she didn't believe it herself? To Mary, the act her friend had committed had been a mortal sin.

With an effort, Mary bent over the bed, brushing the tangled hair from the white face. 'When I was a little girl, I was frightened of God,' she said softly. 'God and black beetles. No, love, I don't think He'll be angry. I'm sure He will understand.'

Alys's fingers tightened. 'Stay with me, Mary. I'm so frightened.'

'Of course.' Mary sank to the floor beside the bed, her skirts billowing about her. Alys clung to her hand as though she would never let go.

Dusk was falling and outside in the street the gas lamps were being lit. Mary was chilled to the bone with fear, in spite of the hot drinks she kept running downstairs to make, forcing them sip by sip between Alys's pale lips.

However, when she heard the church bell chiming the hour, Mary knew she had to go. Miss Netta had warned her that there would be plenty to do on her return to the house, unpacking and hanging the new dresses she had bought. 'And,' she added, crossly, 'they'll need pressing. Seven o'clock, mind,' she cautioned. 'Not a minute later.'

By the time she'd walked the mile and a half to the big house it would be well past that hour, thought Mary. And the rain had started . . .

She bent over the bed, relieved to see that a faint tinge of colour had returned to Alys's lips and hovered over the high cheekbones.

'Alys, I have to go, love. I'll call in on my mam and get her to come and stay with you for a while.'

Her head twisted on the pillow. 'No! I don't want anyone to know – no-one must know . . .'

'But my mam! You don't have to worry about her, and I can't leave you all alone like this.'

Still the dark head moved on the pillow. 'Please don't.'

Torn asunder by feelings of guilt that she couldn't stay and comfort her friend, Mary almost wept. 'All right, *macushla*, don't upset yourself. Try and sleep. I'll leave the kettle on the fire – it's nice and warm downstairs now, and before I go I'll bring up some hot milk, all right?'

Alys closed her eyes, nodding. 'Thanks, Mary.'

Then there was only silence and the sound of rain lashing against the windows. She thought: Mary'll get soaked, going out in this. Somehow it seemed terribly important that she shouldn't go. Alys opened her eyes, wanting to call her friend back, and stared at the grey outline of the window.

When Mary walked into the O'Malleys' warm kitchen, with the fire cheerful in the grate and Mam busy ironing at the big square table and asking how Alys was getting on, for sure they hadn't seen nearly enough of her, it was a relief to blurt out the whole thing in a whisper.

Mrs O'Malley almost dropped the flat iron on the head of her youngest son where he played on the rug at her feet, safely tied to the leg of the table.

She performed the unfailing ritual against evil and crossed herself. 'Holy Mother!' she exclaimed, sure she had misheard Mary's words. 'Alys Hughes! I don't believe it.'

Mary shot a warning glance towards her father, sitting on the opposite side of the fireplace, reading the racing reports in the newspaper. 'I've got to get back, Mam. Miss Netta'll be madder than a wet hen as it is. But if you could just take a look at Alys – say I told you she was in bed with that influenza, right? Don't let on I told you the truth.'

Mam was already reaching for her thick shawl. 'Don't worry, girl. I'll be the soul of discretion.'

'Oh, and, Mam, there's some stained sheets . . .'

Mam nodded. 'Leave it wi' me, girl. I'll leave 'em soaking overnight in the wash house and give 'em a good scrubbing in the morning.'

Impulsively, Mary hugged her. 'Who else in the whole wide world has a mam like ours, eh?'

Mam blushed like a schoolgirl. 'Enough of your blarney! Be off wi' you, and careful how you go, now. It's dark already.'

Life has a habit of going on. No matter how much Alys wanted to stay in her bed, hiding from the world, she soon found there was nothing you could do but face it. Mrs O'Malley had been a tower of strength, coming in and fussing like a hen with one chick, bringing bowls of steaming beef broth, mouth-watering in its goodness.

Alys would gaze out of the window at a sun-filled morning, to where the sea sparkled beyond the headlands and birds sang, and experience a sense of joy just to be alive and one with all this beauty. And just as quickly a dark shadow would descend at the thought of the tiny life she had extinguished, as casually as a flame from a candle.

Her arms wrapped about her, as though too late she would protect the tiny life that was no longer there, she would creep back into bed, hiding under the blankets and giving Mrs O'Malley an excuse to scold even more and threaten to send for Dr Parry.

That was one thing she must not do, Alys decided. The briefest of examinations would betray her secret, and besides there was no money to pay him.

Chapter Eleven

Evan Jenkins was discovering, too, that life did not come to a halt because of heart-sickness. Today as he leaned on the ship's rail and gazed at the white-topped waves rolling into Table Bay, he could sense a definite improvement in his spirits, a new awareness of the beauty of the day. He drew deep breaths of the dusty, sun-warmed scents of land that came rushing over the narrow strip of water towards them.

The grey and purple wall of Table Mountain seemed to rise out of a pure blue sea, the white houses of the town clustered at its feet. He could see the golden glow of the beaches, the green of the trees, all bathed in the radiance of an African sun. Beside him a light voice said: 'I always love this view on my return from England.'

Evan turned to smile at the young girl who had come to stand beside him. The long, tedious voyage had been made bearable only by the presence of Lavinia Dolman, whose small hand now rested lightly on his cuff, as though to steady herself as the ship rolled against the slight swell.

Suddenly, she lost her balance completely and tottered against him. He slipped his arm about her waist, inquiring solicitously, 'All right, my dear? The sea is rough today.'

She smiled provocatively from under thick golden-tipped lashes, deliberately allowing herself to stay against him. For long, breathless moments they stood close together by the rail.

'And how many times have you had this experience?' he teased, turning to smile at her. 'I mean, of course, the return journey from England?'

'Not often enough. I love it here, and it's Daddy's life, but I do miss dear old London and the shops and the West End shows.'

She was, in the parlance of the day, quite a catch. The only child of Joseph Dolman, the financier who, years ago, had ploughed vast sums of money into the gold fields up north and, it was claimed, was now reaping the rewards faster than he could count. Other young and eligible males on board had regarded Evan with a certain degree of animosity. Word had spread that the Welsh were a pushy lot, anyway, so what could you expect?

Lavinia's eyes were dark and twinkling, her hair the colour of burned almonds, and she showed a clear preference for Evan's company above all others. At the beginning of the voyage all he had thought about was Alys and their last meeting, anguished by a sense of his own betrayal that had caused him sleepless nights, tossing and turning on his bunk. But as the ship neared the tropics and the weather became increasingly more pleasant, Evan thought less of Alys and more of the spritely young woman who had become his constant companion.

Days were spent lounging on deckchairs in the warm sun, cosseted with long cool drinks served by white-coated stewards; nights dancing on a moonlit deck to the sound of music filtering softly from the saloon, where a small band entertained the passengers with excerpts from popular London shows. Above them the midnight blue sky shimmered with a million diamond bright stars. And that moon! That moon had a lot to answer for, thought Evan wryly. Last night, with Lavinia floating in his arms, humming the refrain played by the band— 'A garden of Eden, just meant for two, with nothing to mar our joy' – she had breathed, 'Wouldn't it be wonderful? Just like the song.'

She was wearing a new evening gown with a high waist and draped skirt, and sleeves and bodice cut in one – the fish silhouette as it was known. She leaned back in the circle of his arms and, her voice faintly petulant, said, 'You're not going to go away after we arrive so that I'll never see you again, are you?' Without waiting for his answer, she went on, 'I shall ask Daddy to give you a job in his head office so that we may see each other every day.'

Evan laughed. 'My dear girl, I already have a job waiting for me in my father's office in Johannesburg. So, much as I'd like to fall in with your wishes, I'm afraid I shall have to turn down your kind offer.'

'Oh, you!'

She pouted. 'Johannesburg is *so* far away, I'm sure I shall never see you.'

'I'm sure you will,' he assured her lightly, amused by her attitude. And Lavinia read something in his answer that was never intended, and suddenly she was breathless.

Alys made up her bed with the sheets Mrs O'Malley had washed, blue-bagged to pristine whiteness and smelling of sunlight and salt air from their blowing in the garden. She heated water on the stove and managed somehow to lift the huge kettle and pour hot water into the zinc bath which she had dragged from its place in the yard.

The hot water soothed her and she sat there for longer than usual, knees drawn up to her chest, her mind a blank. Realising suddenly that she was cold, she stepped out on to the folded towel and dried herself quickly. The draught coming in from under the back door caused goose pimples to spring up on her legs and arms, and a sudden attack of dizziness made her sit down for a moment. After a while it retreated and she was able to continue dressing. Her sleep was troubled and she woke in the night burning with fever.

One of the O'Malley boys, nine-year-old Dennis, came in the morning to say his mother couldn't call as they had had a message that their granny, who lived further along the valley, had had a fall and Mam was to go to her.

'She'll come when she can,' he explained, drawing a step back at the sight of Alys's white face and burning eyes.

She nodded and the boy turned to go, then looked back uncertainly. 'Are you all right, Alys? Don't want me to run any messages for you?'

She managed a sickly smile and nodded again. 'Thanks, Dennis, but I'll manage. I'll stay in bed for a while.'

It was his turn to nod and with a sagacity that amused her, he said, 'Aye, that's the best thing. A few days in bed'll work wonders.'

Somehow, she dragged herself up the stairs to her bedroom, pulling on the handrail like an old woman. Her skin burned, and although the day was chilly after the fine spell of sunshine, she pushed the bedclothes from her, gratified by the stream of cool air coming from the open window.

Something warned her she was being foolish. Inherited memory scolded: A sure way to catch cold, girl! Don't be silly, now. Keep warm.

She knew that everything was not right. She had thought her young body had overcome its terrible punishment. Now, it seemed, fate was striking back at her. There was nothing for it, she would just have to seek help for she couldn't expect Mary's mam to leave the side of her own mother and return to nurse her.

Dr Parry it would have to be. Shivering uncontrollably, she tipped the meagre contents of her purse on to the bed and counted the pitiful number of coins there – a couple of farthings, a penny, an Irish shilling that was no good to anyone – and felt her stomach contract with fear.

What was she to do? Without money she was helpless, for although Dr Parry was a kind man who had seen her through the usual childish ailments, she couldn't bring herself to ask for the kind of help she so desperately needed. If she'd been able to face his kind old eyes she would have gone to him in the beginning. But she'd felt by doing that, she would somehow be violating the memory of her parents. And Dr Parry's cleaning woman, who sometimes answered the telephone as well as the front door, was a renowned gossip and loved nothing more than newsmongering about his patients.

No, Alys knew of a place where she would not be refused help, where they charged nothing but an hour of your time. Even though the thought of it chilled her, she knew that she had no choice.

Resolutely she fetched the heavy plaid shawl that had once belonged to Mam, wrapping it about her tightly. She was still burning with fever and the cobbles under her feet seemed to tilt as she walked, forcing her to place a steadying hand against a wall as she made her way to the Mission Hall. She joined the straggling line of women and children already waiting on the pavement outside. The doors were still firmly closed and they sighed with resignation, knowing there could be a long wait. Well used to the capriciousness of those in authority, they stood with barely a murmur. A baby, sickly-looking, with a lard-white skin and scabby head thinly covered with fair hair, wailed weakly to be hushed irritably by its mother.

The children were ill-clothed, dressed mainly in cast-offs given to them by their betters. There were a number of gypsies with gold ear-rings and black oily hair, looking strangely exotic among the despondent group of local people. They eyed the rest of the crowd arrogantly, speaking in a tongue of their own.

Alys stood at the back of the queue, shawl covering the lower part of her face, eyes downcast. She prayed it wouldn't be long before the doors of the building opened, for she knew if she had to stand much more her courage would fail and she'd be forced to run home, forfeiting any help the Mission Clinic might offer.

That she would have to join in the service first was a pre-requisite of treatment by the mission group. Hymns and prayers came first, followed by a lengthy harangue full of fire and brimstone, warning the poor souls standing to attention in the cold, draughty hall that they must promise to mend their ways before an ounce of medical attention could be given.

At last the doors were thrown open and the people shuffled slowly in. Alys chose a seat near the back and the woman with the sickly-looking baby came and sat next to her. Alys couldn't bear the child's constant wailing or the streams of heavy yellow mucus that hung down from its nose. The mother ignored both the wailing and the mucus with apathetic resignation that sickened the watching girl.

The voice of the soberly attired gentleman at the front of the hall strengthened as he got into his stride, and people shuffled their feet restlessly. The gold chain of his watch, stretched across a well-fed stomach, caught the overhead lights and it seemed to Alys as though it shone directly into her eyes, blinding her, the sound of his voice drowning out a noise in her ears like the washing of the sea.

'Fellow sinners.' The voice became a bellow. 'Fellow sinners aye, for we are all sinners. Is there one amongst you who can stand up and say he is not—?'

Alys gave a little groan. Blackness rushed over her in a tide and she was aware of the stone floor rising to meet her . . .

She came to in hospital, in a high, white, chipped enamel bed close to others down each side of the long ward. Narrow windows high above gave little daylight, making the whole, dreary aspect of the place even worse. All about her was the smell of sickness and death. Alys was terrified, discovering that she had been put into a bed at the far end of the ward so as not to 'contaminate' other patients.

'Contaminate?' She barely understood the word,

knowing only that it had to do with people who had scarlet fever and diphtheria and that sort of thing. Girls from her class at school had had to go to special hospitals, far away from their family and friends, for fear that they would contaminate others.

'Yes, contaminate.' The thin nurse whose dark hair was drawn back so tightly into a bun that it pulled the flesh at the side of her temples, giving her a slant-eyed look, came to stand at the foot of the bed and frowned down at her. 'You, young lady, are what is known as a "dirty abortion" case, and so must be kept separate from the other women. We can't take the risk of one of them getting infected.'

Alys paled, the terrible words ringing in her ears. So shocked was she that she could hardly speak. She lay back and turned her face to the wall, away from the woman's accusing stare.

God in heaven, what had she got herself into? Tears ran scaldingly down her cheeks and she was reprimanded for wetting the pillow which was promptly whipped from beneath her head, leaving her to lie on the hard, striped mattress with its rough covering.

She cried that something that had begun so beautifully could end so shabbily. She cried for her mother and for things she could never put into words. The nurses on duty gazed at her with disgust. 'Oh, do try and pull yourself together,' she was told, without a flicker of compassion. 'After what you've done, I'm surprised you can shed tears at all. We don't want to have you here any more than you want to be here. We didn't have to treat you, or even admit you. The only reason we did was because Dr Parry requested it.'

They must have sent for him from the Mission Hall, she decided, after she'd fainted. How terrible! The whole town must know about it by now.

She cried on and off for the rest of the afternoon, stopping only when a hard-faced nurse came to tell her there was someone asking to see her.

Relief filled her heart. Mary! Oh, pray God, it was Mary! She would take her away from here, away from these cold-hearted, awful nurses who showed only too plainly the contempt they had for her. Alys sat up, clutching the thin scarlet hospital blanket to her chest, a look of anticipation on her face. To her utter confusion it wasn't Mary but Alys's parish priest.

He came down the ward with carefully averted eyes. He stopped by her bed and she met his gaze, which was cold and full of recrimination. He stood gazing at her silently for a moment or two, until Alys said hesitantly, 'Father Goodhew?'

He inclined his head, showing no flicker of compassion for her. 'My child.' He paused, as though uncertain which words to choose, and she cowered beneath those accusing eyes. 'I heard from Dr Parry, just a short time ago, that you had been taken ill and admitted here. And, speaking to the nurse as I waited to see you, I learned the reason why.' He drew a deep breath, as though seeking the strength to carry on. 'I must confess I was dismayed. Indeed, to put it more strongly, horrified. Think of the shame you bring on the name of your family. Did it not occur to you that you were risking your soul to eternal damnation by your reckless act?'

He didn't seem to care that the other women in the ward were listening, relishing the little scene. Alys wished he would lower his voice, but used to thumping out sermons from the pulpit on a Sunday, Father Goodhew didn't seem to mind who heard him. She sank even lower in the bed, wishing she had the pillow to bury her face in, using a corner of the blanket instead.

The priest shook his white head. 'Why did you not come to me before resorting to such a decision? And after committing a mortal sin against your own innocent babe, you would add to it by attending a church service not of your own faith.'

Suddenly, she sat up straight, the blanket falling back and revealing the high-necked rough cotton nightdress the hospital had reluctantly provided. Fists clenched on top of the bedclothes, she said in a low voice, 'I had no choice. I was ill. I badly needed help and there was no money to pay for a doctor. I know how strongly you feel about other beliefs, but surely our Dear Lord would understand this time?'

At least He would do a better job of understanding than you are doing, she thought bitterly. The old priest was set in his ways, he just didn't want to understand. She would remember that frown and the look of merciless recrimination to the end of her days. She wondered which was the greater sin in his eyes, the abortion or her setting foot in a rival church.

His thin lips twisted at her defensive words. 'You offer a poor excuse, Alys Hughes. There are still questions, important questions, to be answered. I am waiting.'

She plucked at the blanket with fingers that trembled, ready tears threatening to spill down her cheeks yet again. Finally, she blurted out, 'You know what would have happened, Father, if I'd sought help from anybody? I'd have been sent packing to the workhouse, to the place where they hide unmarried mothers or fallen women, as I believe they call them. I'd have been cast out by the whole valley, my baby branded a bastard.'

She heard the shocked intake of breath, not just from the priest but from the women nearby, listening to every word. Ignoring them, she continued with a determination that was unwavering: 'Nothing anybody could say or do would persuade me to choose such a future for myself or my child. No one coerced me or assisted me in any way, Father. I decided alone.' A sob shook her voice. 'And I beg no one's forgiveness for what I've done.'

Rigidly he drew himself to attention, looking at her with his unfeeling gaze. 'Perhaps, when you're feeling better and are again in full possession of your sense of shame, you will come to confession and we will talk about the thing you have done. Even now, it may not be too late to save your immortal soul.' Without a word of farewell he turned and strode away, his long black cassock flying.

Alys watched him go and became aware that she, in turn, was being watched. Faces from the other end of the ward were turned in her direction, examining her with ghoulish interest. She wondered what they would have done if she put out her tongue to them, decided it wasn't worth the effort, and turned her face to the wall.

Chapter Twelve

Today was the first chance Netta had had to be alone with him, for after her shopping spree in Cardiff there had been no excuse for her to purchase new dresses, therefore no excuse for Jackie to come to the house.

Today, her eyes bright and eager, she watched for the dark green van as it made its way from the village. Today she was waiting on the headlands, against a wide stretch of heath and the vast blue sky. She smiled and rose from the boulder where she had been sitting and went to stand in the middle of the road, seeing the dust from the van appearing on the horizon. Hurriedly, Jackie braked. He seemed surprised but pleased to see her, if a little shy. She liked that. Shyness in a man was something she didn't often encounter, all part of his attraction.

She stood by the open window of the cab, looking in. 'Hello!'

'Good mornin', Miss Netta.' He pulled out a handkerchief and wiped the beads of sweat from his top lip, for it was a warm day and the interior of the van stuffy in spite of the open window. Watching him, Netta said, 'It's very close, isn't it? Why don't you step out of there and take a breath of fresh air?' She turned her head lazily to survey the unfrequented stretch of headlands. 'There's no one to see or tell on you.'

'All right.'

She stepped back as he opened the cab door then walked to a secluded spot she knew, overlooking the sea. She knew he followed, knew he was hooked, knew that she only had to lift her little finger and he'd come running. She produced a packet of cigarettes from the pocket of her long skirt. 'Want one?'

She held the packet out to him, ignoring the look of surprise on his face. In the world Jackie frequented, women did not smoke. Nice women, anyway, and certainly not in public. She produced a box of matches from the same pocket and leaned across so that he took them from her and lit both cigarettes with the match. Jackie didn't often smoke, his sport would suffer with too much of that, and Aunt Ellen didn't like it in her small spotless living room. But he wasn't going to upset Miss Netta by refusing now. She said, 'I've been sitting here all morning, waiting for you to show up.'

Daringly, he asked, 'How did you know I would?'

She smiled again. 'Because I asked my father to order some things for the house while he was in town, with the express wish that they be delivered at once.'

Her eyes studied him intently while the smoke from her cigarette rose lazily in the still air, curling about her fair head, making her narrow her eyes slightly. 'You were wearing that Fair Isle pullover the last time you came. It's very colourful. Did your sweetheart knit it for you?'

'No.' His lips quirked at the thought of Mary coping with the elaborate pattern of different coloured wools.

'My aunty – my Aunt Ellen – got it at a jumble sale.'

He saw her smile and called himself an empty-headed fool. What must she think, blathering on like that about his aunt and jumble sales!

She leaned closer and the delicate flower scent of her perfume made him feel slightly dizzy. That and the nearness of her lips, and he felt something move inside him as her full breast, as though by accident, pressed against his arm. 'I'm glad,' she said softly, 'otherwise it would have been bothering me all day, the thought she had knitted it for you.'

The pressure against his arm increased slightly as she went on, 'These last few days have been pretty bad, you know.'

'Why?' His voice shook.

'I was lonely for you. And Cardiff bored me.' When he didn't reply, disconcerted by her frankness, she added softly, 'Jackie, what were you thinking?'

He shook his head. 'I don't think I was thinking of anything. I was – just content, I guess.'

'And I don't know when *I've* been this content, Jackie. You're sure you weren't thinking about Mary O'Malley?'

He was surprised enough to laugh. 'Good God, no!'

'Then why are you smiling like that?'

He felt his scalp prickle as she stared at him with those wide blue eyes, and what she saw in his face made her shudder deliciously. The same wonderful feeling of power she had experienced that morning in the yard filled her again.

'I wasn't thinking of Mary,' he repeated, and there was a defensive note in his voice. 'What's she got to do with all this?'

Netta ignored his question, asking instead, 'You don't work on Sundays, do you?'

Used by now to her quicksilver changes of mood, his mouth went dry, knowing what she hinted at. 'No.'

'Then meet me on the headlands, here, on Sunday afternoon.'

He didn't answer at once and she took one of his hands in hers and lifted it to her lips. 'Please, it's such a little thing I ask.' When still he didn't answer, not knowing what to say, she murmured softly, 'Do you know what a fatalist is, Jackie?'

'I think I do.'

'I believe that what is to be will be.'

'I suppose I believe that too.'

'Then that's all right.'

He watched her walk away, one hand holding up the skirt of her frock, showing slim ankles and pale silk stockings and the delicate leather shoes with their cuban heels and narrow straps. He felt as though he had been put through a mangle.

And so Mary and Jackie went on hurting each other, not knowing why they did it and unable to see the root cause of it all. All Mary knew was that these days he seemed to prefer Miss Netta's presence to her own. Oh, she was beautiful and poised, all the things that Mary was not, but she was also a coquette, used to leading men astray, and for some reason had set her sights on Jackie. Seeing how far she could tempt the naive young local would no doubt amuse her.

Mrs Dean had once said that Miss Netta was too knowing for her age, that in a working-class setting she would be called a name the like of which the cook wouldn't dream of uttering. 'The gentry have a different set of values to the likes of us,' she'd told Mary. 'And from being a little girl, ever since her poor, dear mother passed away – God rest her soul! – she's got her own way. Her father would refuse her nothing.'

'That still doesn't give her the right to go after my Jackie,' Mary had answered bitterly. 'Flirting with him, that's what she's doing. It's disgusting! And he can't see it.'

'Miss Netta has half the young men in town running after her, Mary. She's not likely to choose someone like Jackie Rees to become serious with. It's all a little game with her. You mustn't let it worry you.' Mrs Dean bent to open the oven door, peered in then slammed it again, satisfied that the roast was doing nicely. 'I've seen it all so many times; before you know it, she'll have set her sights on some other poor bugger and it'll start all over again. As I say, just a game with her.' She smiled at Mary in a reassuring way. 'And then Jackie'll come back to you, looking for sympathy.'

Mary sniffed. 'I'm not sure that I'll want him back.'

'Oh, don't you be a silly girl, now. The way you two young 'uns would look at each other, before Miss Netta started to get up to her tricks . . .' Mrs Dean shifted the pans standing on top of the stove, already filled with cold salted water and waiting for the fresh vegetables that would accompany the leg of lamb and roast potatoes. 'Of course you'll want him back. Jackie's a good man – a little too much on the placid side perhaps, certainly so for Miss Netta. I can't for the life of me think what she sees in him – no offence meant, of course,

Mary. But then, they do say opposites attract, don't they? And no two people could be more opposite than your Jackie and Miss Netta. And look at Master Evan and that friend of yours, that Hughes girl! Talk of the town, those two.' She eyed the girl narrowly, hoping for some response, but when Mary continued silent, went on, 'All men are tempted by the things they're not supposed to have, and your Jackie's no different from anyone else.'

Mrs Dean spoke as though a long life in the service of others had made her an expert on the subject of male behaviour. Instinctively, although she would never admit it, Mary knew the homespun philosophies of the older woman were right. But they did nothing to soothe her hurt feelings.

'Now, young Mary,' having said her piece, Mrs Dean turned back to the task in hand, 'if you'll just nip out to the garden and pick me some of those peas. The fat ones, please, not the ones that are still skinny. Then I can get on with this meal. The old man'll be in shortly and you know what he's like if it ain't ready.'

Reaching for the yellow enamel colander, Mary went outside, making for the vegetable garden at the back where once, in the days before all this trouble started, she would meet Alys. What a joy it had been to sit and talk in the sunshine, moments snatched away from her work, discussing the local Saturday night dance and whether she could persuade Jackie to go. He'd always go into long explanations about the rugby match that would be played that afternoon and how if he could get away early from the boys, especially difficult if they had scored a victory over the other team, then he would try and see her there. Mary accepted this, not minding too much that she had a rival in the game and the other members of his team. That was something she could handle. Miss Netta's philandering was not.

Although Jackie was no dancer he would come, she knew, just to please her. Scrubbed and shining, his face pink with good health, sometimes a little foolish with the beer he'd consumed with his mates in the bar after the match, he would appear on the dance floor and for Mary the rest of the dancers didn't exist.

She sighed and tears shimmered in her eyes as her slim fingers plucked the fat ripe pods from the rows of peas. She thought of what Mrs Dean had said, that of course Mary would want him back, and knew the woman had been right. No matter what Jackie did, what transgressions he got up to behind her back, he would always be her man. Just now he was resentful of the way she had treated him and so she should really blame herself for his recalcitrant attitude. For a moment some of the tranquillity of the peaceful garden seeped into her and she smiled.

She took so long gathering the peas that Mrs Dean greeted her sourly when she came back but Mary just smiled and tipped the green peas over the scrubbed wooden kitchen table. Seating herself on the old wooden chair, she began to shell them.

Much to Alys's relief and, she was sure, that of the nurses, after a short period she was allowed to leave hospital. Stepping through the arched doorway, she shivered. A cold wind had picked up from the sea. It had been cloudy all morning and now she glanced apprehensively at the sky. The wind stung against her cheeks, whispering of rain.

Her legs trembled and her knees threatened to give way so that her progress down the street was at a snail's pace. As she rounded the corner she passed women standing in groups. They turned their backs on her and whispered. Alys held her head high and walked on. Their voices followed as she passed, calling after her, 'Don't want the likes o' you in our street, so we don't.'

'You'd better find somewhere else to live, you baby killer,' cried a second.

Alys hunched her shoulders as if to defend herself from their hatred and had crossed the street when she saw another group of women waiting outside the fish market with baskets on their arms. Seeing her approach, nudging each other, they too turned and began to whisper. She gave them a frosty stare.

'Two gents she's 'ad,' yelled one woman. 'Not satisfied wi' one, 'as to 'ave two.' A burst of laughter followed and Lizzie Grant, her old antagonist, pushed her way to the front of her cronies to shout, 'And we all know where that gets you, don't we, girls?' Lizzie's shrewd eyes roamed over her figure and Alys prayed for the pavement to open up and swallow her. 'Got rid o' the bun in the oven pretty damn quick, though, didn't she?' Lizzie came to stand in front of her, hands on her ample hips, mouth pursed tightly. 'Whose was it then, that painter bloke's or the young master from the big house?'

Alys escaped their taunts as fast as she could, breaking into a stumbling run as she neared her own doorway. Her hand was on the latch when a man came out of the shadows and stepped behind her. He'd been drinking.

She could smell it on his breath. 'Want some company?' he rasped.

'No, thank you.' A pulse fluttered in her throat. She tried to edge away from him.

'It's the Hughes girl, ain't it?' He leered at her from the dim light of the narrow roadway, his grin widening as she seemed to draw into herself, shrinking away from him. 'Well, now, I 'ear you're not reluctant to a bit o' male company. Quite the opposite. And now that you're all alone . . .'

Alys felt her heart pounding. Weak from the events of the past few days, she felt degraded by his hints. Not so long ago she would have sent him packing with scorched ears. Now his very presence behind her was sending her into a panic, leaving her panting, trying to quell the rising tide of terror that threatened to escalate into hysteria.

Somehow, she never knew how, she managed to get the door open and slipped inside, closing it behind her with a slam. Quickly she shot the bolts, top and bottom, then stood frozen just inside, hardly daring to breathe, as though the very drawing of breath would nudge him into action. She could hear him moving about outside, his voice close to the door panels. 'C'on, girl, I only want to welcome you 'ome, that's all. 'ear you 'ad a bit o' bad luck.'

She recalled the other women in the ward whispering to their visitors, casting furtive looks her way, and realised the speed with which the news would travel through the town. Breath still held, she felt a recurrence of the old dizziness and her hand fumbled behind her for the back of a chair. Collapsing on to its seat, she huddled in the darkness for what seemed an eternity until all was silent outside, although she didn't dare open the door to see if he was really gone. What if he was standing there, waiting for her to do just that? When, a long time later, there came a sharp knock at the door and the handle rattled, she stifled a scream.

It was Mary, and drawing the rusty bolts Alys all but threw herself into her arms, crying and babbling like a baby.

And it was Mary who picked up the folded piece of paper that lay on the doormat, telling Alys that she must vacate the premises by the end of next week or be evicted.

Mary took her in her arms, her own face white as a sheet.

'Oh, my dear! I came, you know, to the hospital, but they wouldn't let me in. Mam was so upset when she heard, I've never seen her like that. She would have come, but she just couldn't leave Gran alone . . .'

'Don't blame your mam, Mary.' Some of Alys's strength was beginning to creep back and Mary marvelled at the smile that flooded her face. 'I didn't expect her to fuss over me when she had to be with her own family. I decided, all of a sudden, to go to the Mission Clinic. They say they never turn anyone away.' Her lips twisted. 'What I didn't reckon on was fainting like a silly schoolgirl. They sent for Dr Parry and he got me into the hospital.' She said nothing about the nurses' heartlessness, determined to put that whole episode out of her mind. 'When he came later to visit me, he brushed aside the fact that I had no money. But I'll pay him, Mary. One day I'll pay him what I owe.'

'I know you will, love, I know. Now,' holding the printed form up to the light, 'what are we going to do about this?'

'It'll be that Thomas Jenkins.' Alys didn't know how

true her guess was. 'Makes you wonder how a man like that can live with himself, doesn't it?'

Mary nodded. 'Or produce a son like . . .' She caught her breath, one hand going to her mouth in dismay. 'Sorry, love. I didn't mean to . . .'

'I didn't hear a word. I'm far more bothered about this notice now. Old Jenkins would just love to see me thrown out on to the street.' Recalling Mary's accounts of the rages and outbursts that had erupted over Evan's brief period of friendship with her, Alys knew she'd never spoken a truer word.

'Don't be daft! As though we'd let him do that. You can always come and live with us. Mam'll find room for you somewhere.'

Alys thought of the already cramped conditions of the O'Malley household and was touched. 'Thanks, but you mustn't worry about me. I'm strong, I can face anything now.' After the terrible thing I did to my baby, she thought, what could possibly happen that would be more terrible? 'I'm sorry,' she went on, smiling at Mary. 'I haven't even asked you how your grandmother is.'

'She's fine, moaning like mad about being bedridden. But she's a tough old girl. Take more'n a fall to quieten her.'

Marcus made his way from the station through the gloomy wet day, not noticing that the gutters were over-flowing or that his boots or his trouser cuffs were soaked.

His mother had said she would never understand him and from his actions he would have to agree with her. He didn't understand himself sometimes. Yesterday at the opening of the new gallery in Mayfair, with Joanna Ambrey by his side, he had felt jumpy and tense, so ready to take offence that his friends had tactfully avoided him. Unintentionally, he had cut Lady Jersey dead and had received some very icy looks from his hostess. In a foul mood, Marcus had left early although Joanna in her diplomatic way had tried to smooth things over, without much success. He had thought he'd put behind him all thoughts of the black-haired witch and her endearing donkey but as soon as he'd looked on the painting of 'The Cockleshell Girl' again, he had known she was still very much in his thoughts.

Recognising his black mood when his son visited them that weekend, his father had growled, 'For God's sake, my boy, go down and get on with another blasted painting if it means so much to you. Although why you can't use a local model I'll never know. What has this girl got that you can't find in London?'

Marcus refused to be drawn. He accepted the cup offered to him by his mother and stood, back to the fire, stirring his tea thoughtfully. 'You've seen "The Cockleshell Girl", Dad. Are you so blind that you can't appreciate the freshness there, the look that no other girl has been able to give me?'

Gerard Dillon looked baffled. 'Oh, she's pretty enough, I'll grant you that, but then there's something about a Welsh girl that no other race produces.'

Martha Dillon pulled the lacy shawl about her shoulders for in spite of the fire the summer day was, to her, chilly. She murmured, 'Why must you do another painting of the sea anyway, and with that particular girl in it? Why is it so important?'

Marcus wished he knew. The girl haunted him. He ached to feel a brush in his hand, capturing again those lovely features, the purple of the long-lashed pansy eyes, the clear white skin. He could hear the whisper of the sea, see the full peasant skirt she was wearing flutter in the breeze, outlining the long slim legs, the small feet half buried in the wet sand. See the way the wind tossed her hair, black silken strands that streamed behind her like a satin banner.

He sighed, turning to place the tea cup with its delicate pattern of roses and ivy leaf on the high mantelpiece behind him. Avoiding his mother's faintly accusing gaze, he said, 'It's important, Mother. Leave it at that.'

So important that he had to make everyone around him suffer for his black moods! he thought. It was like the time when he was a small boy, shopping with his mother one Christmas in Regent Street. He remembered catching sight of a window display of toy soldiers arranged about a fort, their lead bodies painted in the scarlet jackets of the British Army. How he'd wanted those soldiers and the very realistic fort, refusing to be fobbed off with anything else. He'd wanted it so badly that he hadn't been able to rest until it belonged to him. How he'd treasured that fort and its brave defenders, reliving the pleasure while the rain slid down the nursery window panes, the day too miserable to venture out to climb trees or kick a ball about with the gardener's boy.

The fort was still somewhere in the house, stowed away in an attic that was full of childhood mementoes; his stamp collection, cases of butterflies, books, cricket bats, and an ancient and much beloved teddy bear.

Now he had his heart set on this new portrait and knew

he would not rest until it was completed. The busy High Street hummed about him. He saw the dark green van driven by that young Rees fellow flash its lights before turning into the alleyway beside the Co-op Stores. He watched a cockle woman, walking straight-backed, basket balanced on her head, come towards him, and at that same moment a hand pulled on his sleeve from behind and a voice said, 'Mr Dillon?'

He turned, seeing a pretty fair-haired girl blinking at him.

'I wasn't sure whether it was you or not – we've never met, although from the description I thought it must be you.'

He raised an eyebrow. 'Description?'

'Yes, sir, Alys's description. I'm sorry, I'm Mary O'Malley, Alys's friend. She told me about you, about your . . .' She paused, confused, her gaze resting on the silky growth of beard. He smiled, understanding. 'Ah, yes. But do go on, Miss O'Malley. Is something wrong with Alys?'

He felt a quickening of his heartbeat as he said it, praying that the answer would be no. Mary made up her mind, liking him immediately, his well-set-up figure and casual air of authority. 'She's all right now – although she wasn't a few days ago . . .' She glanced about them at the busy street. 'Look, can we go somewhere and talk? I don't know the purpose of your visit, Mr Dillon, and I don't want to keep you from your business, but there are things you should know.'

He nodded, and taking her arm guided her across the pavement and through the glass doors of the plush Victorian hotel. He chose a secluded table by a large potted palm and ordered tea and hot toasted muffins from the smartly dressed waitress who bustled over.

Enjoying the fragrant hot tea, stopping frequently to lick her fingers free of melting butter from the muffins, Mary told him everything. When she got to the abortion, Marcus let out his breath and sagged against the table, shaking his head in disbelief. Although he made no comment, Mary could see a tic at the side of his jaw.

'Are you sure she's all right now?' he said at last. Mary nodded. 'Much better. She's – what's the word? – resilient, is Alys.'

He grunted. He hadn't thought her such a fool, to be so easily led. What concern was it of his if she'd been stupid enough to let herself get pregnant? Again he shook his head, as though trying to clear it. What Alys had done was nothing to do with him; she was responsible for her own fate, a grown woman, and he certainly had no right to interfere . . .

'Are you here for long?' he heard Mary ask, and replied, 'Just a few days.' Beckoning to the hovering waitress he held out his hand for the bill. 'Is Alys at home now?'

'I left her about an hour ago. I don't think she was going anywhere.'

'Right!' Mary was heartened by his decisive tone. 'I'm off to talk to her. I'm extremely grateful for your concern, Miss O'Malley. Alys must find you a valued friend.' He smiled. 'I shall be staying at this hotel until Wednesday, then I must return to London.' He met her gaze, his own steady. 'I shall be asking Alys to come with me.'

Mary could only nod. 'That might be the best thing

that could happen to her, Mr Dillon. She's just been given notice to quit her cottage.'

The muscles at the side of his jaw twitched again. 'Indeed! Then I'd better be on my way.'

He thought of her stepfather who had come up to the cottage that morning, insinuating that any man with red blood in his veins would have been tempted . . . It wasn't often in his free and easy life Marcus was shocked, but he had been shocked that day. After he'd sent the man packing, he'd stood by the window, gazing out at the white-capped sea.

It had been Alys's purity that had first attracted him; her fresh, flower-like face, glossy hair, and those deep, pansy eyes. He wouldn't have touched her if they were trapped together in a snow-bound log cabin with no other woman in sight. Yet women liked him and usually he had no qualms about taking them to his bed. While he was wrapped up in his work, it was they who usually instigated the affair. Joanna had told him once that he gave the impression that he was doing them a favour by allowing himself to be captured!

When Alys opened the door to his knock, her first thought was how like a drowned rat he seemed. She said so with her usual frankness, stifling a giggle. Somehow, after the miserable events of the last few days, the sight of Marcus standing in the doorway, begging to be allowed in out of the rain, cheered her immensely. She opened the door wider. 'You can come in as long as you don't drip all over my carpet.'

He looked down at the wooden floorboards covered with bits of ill-matched carpet and grunted. The kettle was singing on the hob and within minutes she had built up the fire and had a pot of tea brewing.

Steam rising from his damp clothing, Marcus stood before the hearth.

'So?' Alys settled herself in the old rocking chair and folded her hands in her lap, looking up at him from beneath those incredibly long lashes. He knew she was waiting for his explanation and deliberately delayed answering. Instead he asked her about her work, saying how he'd met Mary and how disturbed he was to hear about her stepfather's untimely end. She lowered her head at his words of sympathy, unable to stop the sudden surge of tears in her eyes at the mention of Dan. She had never thought that she would, but she missed the old scoundrel.

There was a moment's long silence while the fire crackled in the hearth and the rain assailed the window panes. Marcus asked, 'And what are your plans now?'

He noted how her fingers twisted in her lap, how her eyes avoided his. 'I haven't any. I'll just go on with my life, probably somewhere else, in another valley.'

He nodded, as though agreeing with her words. 'Where will you live? Mary mentioned something about your having to leave the cottage.'

She looked down at her hands, the silken black hair falling forward with the movement, shadowing her face. 'Until I have decided what to do with myself, Mary said I could stay with her family.'

'And money?' Like a dog with a bone, he was not going to leave it alone. 'What will you do for money?'

Resenting the nature of his questions, she flushed and answered stiffly, 'I've got my work. I can do that any-where, on any part of the coast. People eat shellfish wherever you go.' Her chin rose in that indomitable gesture he was beginning to know so well. 'I'll just get on with what I know.'

His own gaze was unreadable. 'So you're going to sell cockles for the rest of your life, is that what you're saying?'

Bewildered by the sudden anger in his voice, Alys pushed back her hair with an impatient gesture. 'I don't have to justify myself to you, Marcus Dillon.'

'That wasn't the impression I got.'

Suddenly, she was aware of a tension between them, almost tangible. Abruptly she rose to her feet, conscious of the sight she must look with her hair unbound and about her shoulders in a tumble of waves and curls. Irritably she blurted out, 'Anyway, who are you, and what gives you the right to come here and tell me what I should do with my life? You've got a nerve, you have . . .'

Cutting into her arguments, surprising himself, he said in a rough voice, 'Come back with me.'

She blinked and stared at him open-mouthed. 'What?'

Marcus knew suddenly that all it would take to release him from the black mood that had plagued him for so long would be the simple presence of this girl. Having her near him while he wrought his magic of paint and canvas, capturing her dark beauty for all time, for all to gaze upon and wonder . . .

He sighed. 'There are times when I could get very angry with you but I haven't the heart to show it. Come back with me to London, and if you are very good I will take you to see "The Cockleshell Girl". It hangs in a very exclusive gallery in Mayfair and is greatly admired.'

Alys sniffed. 'Can't be much good if it hasn't sold yet.'

Her scornful comment made him smile. 'Oh, no problem there. I could have sold it over and over again, and at a very handsome fee, too. But I don't intend to sell. Not yet, anyway. Not until I have another portrait of that girl hanging where I can see it daily.'

His eyes mocked. 'In short, I want to paint you again. Why else do you suppose I should be asking you to accompany me to London?'

Alys stared at him, unsure of whether he was being serious or not. It was always hard to tell with this man . . . Finally, she managed, 'To paint me again? Wouldn't you need to be here in Craven Bay to do that, if it's to be that same kind of picture?'

'Not really. There are many places on the English coastline where I could find a suitable background.'

She took a deep breath and stared into the flames of the coal fire. Outside the rain continued to beat down in a steady pattern. So engrossed were they, it was doubtful if either of the two people in the dingy kitchen were aware of it. Then: 'I couldn't take Drogo,' she warned, making him smile. 'Not all the way to London. He hates being uprooted. Did you know he was a pit pony but that Dan managed to get him for me? He'd become too weak to pull the coal trucks any more.' Her eyes grew vacant, remembering the day one of the miners had brought the small bad-tempered donkey along the road, leading him by a rope, the children of the neighbourhood skipping along beside them. Mean and evil tempered to others, for Drogo had always been treated with scant respect or even kindness by the miners, all too busy earning a living to bother about the welfare of the poor beasts that spent their lives in the darkness of the mine tunnels, he had soon shown a patience with Alys that had dumbfounded onlookers. Although Dan was no animal lover, he yielded to Alys's pleas of 'adopting' Drogo, as long as it didn't cost him anything!

She laughed, remembering. 'He would try to bite the other children if they got too close to him, and they used to tease him. He was skinny and ill-kempt when I first got him but in the fresh air and sunlight he soon became bright-eyed and cheeky again.'

As she spoke of the little donkey, she felt a touch of guilt. Over the past few weeks she had neglected Drogo, if unavoidably. For sure, he'd been well looked after by old Lear who never minded waiting for the small fee she paid him for the donkey's keep. If she went to London, the animal would grow fat and lazy, eating his head off and dozing in his warm stall, with no long walks over the headlands to keep him sleek and trim. If she went to London she'd miss him. Miss a lot of things in Craven Bay: Mary and her mother and her small naughty brothers.

She bit her lip. 'Did Mary – did she tell you about . . . ?' She couldn't bring herself to finish but in an agony of desolation whispered, so softly that he could hardly make out the words, 'They said it was a dirty abortion. They put me all alone at the very end of the ward and wouldn't let me near the other women. It was cruel . . .'

Marcus felt as though a giant hand had taken hold of his heart and squeezed. He held out his arms and pulled her gently to him, murmuring soft sounds. She came to him like a small child seeking shelter from the dark. She felt the silky softness of his beard against her cheek, breathed in the fresh scent of an expensive cologne. 'Shh,' he murmured. 'Shh . . .'

Would she ever get over it? she wondered. Would there ever come a night when she would sleep without that awful, empty feeling, or wake in the morning as she once had, eager to face a new day?

Minutes later she fumbled for her handkerchief and heard him say, 'So you will come with me!' It was a statement, spoken softly, not a question, and suddenly conscious of his nearness she stepped back, pushing away. 'I haven't said I would.' Again she bit her lip, wanting to fall in with his wishes but not too readily, ashamed of giving way to her grief in his presence. She'd thought she was made of sterner stuff than that . . . Even so, why should she let him think he'd scored an easy victory? Lifting her head to gaze into his face, she saw his confidence and it irked her. To gain time, she queried, 'What sort of arrangements would I be going to?'

Still shaken by her show of grief, nevertheless he managed a nonchalant: 'Arrangements?' His brows rose comically. 'What do you mean?'

'Where would I be living? Not with you, I hope.'

He grinned lopsidedly. 'And here I was, under the mistaken impression that you were actually beginning to like me!' He shook his head. 'No, that wouldn't do at all. Although a number of my artist friends, the more Bohemian ones, do live quite openly with their models.'

Her cheeks flushed and she tossed her head. 'There's a thing! Well, this is one model who won't be following their free and easy ways. All my mistakes are behind me and they're going to stay that way. I won't be enticed into anything, as you'll soon find out.'

He grinned. 'There's the courageous Welsh spirit coming out! I was expecting it so I shouldn't be surprised. No, you'll be quite safe with me, I assure you. You'll find my studio quite comfortable and it will be easy for you to get around. There are buses and those new London taxi cabs to take you anywhere you want to go, so you'll have no trouble getting out to visit the cafés and see the sights.'

She gazed at him with pursed lips, a slight frown marring her brow. It all sounded so plausible, as if he'd planned everything down to the last detail. And, she had to admit, exciting too. Still, she wasn't entirely satisfied. 'And where will you be living?'

'I have my own bedroom on the floor below yours.' Seeing her undecided air, he grinned, lifting his hands as though in surrender. 'Your own room would be sacrosanct, my dear. So, does my proposition appeal to you, Alys Hughes, or would the thought of leaving your birthplace be too unbearable to contemplate? I must ask for a firm yes or no, for there will be things to arrange and I don't have much time.'

'I can't give you my answer just like that, now can I? I'll have to think about it.'

'Well, don't think too long. Hanging about is not one of my strong points and if I can't paint you, then I shall have to look elsewhere. You should know by now, young lady, that I'm not a patient man. If you do decide to come with me, you'll have to learn to make up your mind quickly.'

He gave her until Tuesday afternoon to make up her mind but she knew already what her answer would be.

Chapter Thirteen

Stifled with heat and dust, Lavinia leaned her head against the begrimed window and stared at the veldt stretching away into the distance. Mrs Harvey dozed in the seat opposite, her lips making soft 'put-putting' sounds as she snored. The train moved slowly, never seeming to reach that horizon where white smoke warned of raging bush fires or the even more distant purple-shaded mountains.

Lavinia wished she could sleep like her companions but the rattling of the train and its stuffiness, for to open the windows would invite all manner of flying, stinging insects, made it impossible. Even at night the iron monster kept her awake with its constant noise and vibration.

In spite of her excitement at the thought of seeing Evan again, Lavinia was showing signs of fatigue. Cape Town without Evan had quickly lost its charm and even the constant sunshine and glittering ocean did not compensate for his absence.

The weeks before he left to continue his journey up country had been heaven. They had gone riding on the lower slopes of Table Mountain and picnicked in the secluded bays. Spreading a blanket on the golden sand, Lavinia would explore the depths of the wicker basket like an excited little girl, producing a bottle of wine and cold roast chicken and cheese and so many different kinds of exotic fruit he didn't know which to try first.

Joseph had insisted that Evan stay with them in the palatial house on its green slope overlooking the town. Evan felt that no matter how long he lived there, he would never get used to the beautiful white house with its canopy of crimson bougainvillea, the pleasantly mannered servants and air of sybaritic enjoyment.

Prompted by her, Lavinia's father invited the young of the town to dances. To the music of popular songs played on a wind-up gramophone, the dancers spilled like colourful beads from a broken necklace, off the verandah and on to the smooth green lawns, dancing the night away. The moon washed the garden with silver-edged brilliance. The grass on which a couple of dozen young people danced took on a greyish-silver hue, the stark white of the house was veiled in dusty purple shadows. Trampled unheedingly by careless feet, the once neat flower beds showed a confusion over which tomorrow the gardeners would shake their heads sadly before doggedly beginning a programme of replanting.

Lavinia had never thought of herself as a girl who did things on impulse. And yet the past few weeks seemed to have been full of snap decisions.

From the moment she had seen Evan Jenkins seated opposite her at dinner that first night aboard ship, events had crowded in thick and fast. She was surprised at the urgency of her emotions.

Gazing at her by the light of the full African moon, Evan seemed to sense some of her feelings. He wasn't in love with her, he told himself, of course he wasn't. What he felt in this moon-kissed garden with his arms about Lavinia as they danced, was merely a primitive, purely physical reaction to a girl who was not only beautiful but also wise in the ways of men. His allegiance was to Alys. He must never forget that. Yet Craven Bay and Alys were so far away and the delicious Lavinia so near. And you really couldn't blame a chap for grasping at happiness . . .

But inevitably there came the day when Evan must leave and travel north, to the rich, wild lands of the gold and diamond fields where his father's business awaited his attention. It was a simple matter for Lavinia to convince her father that she, too, was dying to see the place where fortunes were being made at the turn of a shovel.

'It's all so exciting,' she enthused, assuming the wide-eyed little-girl look her father could never resist. And why should he? Lavinia was all he had left now. 'Mrs Harvey is travelling up to join her husband and she has agreed to act as chaperone to me if only you will give your consent.'

'Got it all worked out, haven't you, you little minx!' Joseph Dolman grinned, thinking how like her dear mother the child was. Stubborn, and bent on getting her own way. And, God knows, her mother had led him a pretty dance!

Lavinia had arrived late in her parents' lives, an unexpected gift. Her mother had died when she was ten and since then her father had indulged her in everything her heart desired.

'All right,' he finally agreed, as Lavinia knew he would. 'As long as you keep out of mischief.'

Her blue eyes widened. 'Dear Papa, what mischief

could I possibly get into under Mrs Harvey's watchful eye?'

Her father smiled and patted her shoulder and went about his business, knowing his daughter better than she thought he did. The Jenkins boy was a presentable enough young fellow, he supposed. Lavinia could have chosen worse. A wedding in the family might be just the thing . . .

As the journey continued, grinding slowly through vast, tawny plains the colour of a lion's coat, a young girl travelling with her mother excitedly pointed at moving dots that turned out to be bucks feeding on the lush grasses. They moved in enormous herds; buff-coloured kudu, eland with their beautiful spiral horns, delicate-looking steenbok and fawn springbok, arching their backs in fantastic leaps. Game by the thousand.

The girl squeaked with excitement, jumping up and down on the hard leather seat made gritty by dust and the residue from the thick black smoke that issued from the giant engine pulling the train.

Lavinia regarded her scornfully. Such effervescence! And in this heat. Used to the cooling winds of Cape Town, this blazing, dry climate was already proving a curse to her. Flapping a languid hand in front of her face, brushing away the flies that, no matter how tightly the carriage windows were closed, still managed to find an entry, she concentrated all her thoughts on Evan. That way the dreadful ennui of the journey was made bearable. But only just.

Their first sight of the town was through a pall of red dust. A carriage waited, pulled by two nervous, high-stepping horses which showed their teeth and the whites of their eyes as the small party approached. Mrs Harvey's husband had arranged this and appeared now, smiling in greeting, his face red and perspiring heavily for the temperature was somewhere up in the nineties. Mr Harvey represented the railways in this part of the country, his wife had told Lavinia, and took his responsibility very seriously.

On the drive to the house they passed buildings that looked like stables but they were told by Mr Harvey were shops. 'They sell everything,' he said. 'Felt hats, shoes and boots, pickaxes and shovels, as well as food stuffs and bolts of cotton.'

Leaving the town behind, they drove across flat countryside covered in tall, waving grass, the colour of ripening corn. The house that Mr Harvey had had built for his wife was a single-storey building made of the local stone. A wide verandah with a shallow flight of steps leading up from the driveway stretched across the entire front. The steps were polished a high glossy red as was the stone floor of the verandah, looking cool and inviting from where Lavinia sat in the roasting heat of the carriage.

Small tables and brightly cushioned chairs were arranged in inviting groups. Used to the more refined residences of Cape Town, Lavinia supposed it had a certain rough charm.

Evan, surprised by her arrival, hadn't welcomed her with the kind of enthusiasm she had expected. In fact, there were times when he irritated her greatly, spending so much time at his desk when he should be with her. The cultured social gatherings she was used to were a far cry from the distractions of this rough frontier-type town, although she enjoyed the sun-downers Mr Harvey gave of an evening, especially when Evan was able to be present. They would watch the huge red ball of the sun sink beyond an horizon flushed with gold and apricot and Lavinia would long for Evan to take her hand and sit with her in the cool stillness, with the sound of the crickets from the garden almost drowning the light conversation of the other guests.

Evan never did and Lavinia would feel like stamping her foot and screaming for everyone to go away and leave them alone.

Somehow, she had to convince Evan this was no place for him, that all the endless book-keeping he so assiduously pursued could be carried out equally well by somebody else. Goodness knows there were enough staff in the rapidly growing Jenkins empire. And she was sure that position in her father's firm was still open . . .

She played her hand one day by bribing the stable boy to procure a pair of horses. 'Something clean and controllable,' she warned him. It hadn't occurred to her to wonder where he would find such a luxury in this town. Most of the livestock were mules or wagon oxen, and riding horses were reserved for the favoured few. Even Mr Harvey's pair of carriage horses were unreliable and she wouldn't have gone near them for anything. Daddy wouldn't have given them bed or board but most likely had them shot and the carcasses sold for cat meat.

'I've come to kidnap you,' she told Evan, striding into his office early that morning. 'I want you to ride with me to the diggings. I've got two horses ready and saddled, waiting for us at the stables.'

Evan looked slightly aggrieved. 'Lavinia, I can't

just take time off like that! I'm busy this morning.'

She pouted. 'You're busy every morning. I don't know why I bothered to travel all this way up on that wretched train. I've hardly seen you since I arrived.'

'My father expects me to show an example. If I started taking days off, what would the other men think? In no time at all, they'd be doing it too.'

Lavinia's eyelashes fluttered and she gazed down to where the toe of her elegant riding boot made patterns in the dust. 'I don't think I like you very much any more,' she said in her little-girl voice. 'You've been perfectly horrid since I came. It's not at all what I expected after all those lovely evenings we spent together on the boat and then in Cape Town.'

Recognising defeat when it crept up on him, nevertheless Evan tried to explain. 'The ride would be very dusty, Lavinia, you know how you hate dust, and the flies would be relentless.'

'I don't care,' she smiled, knowing that as usual she was about to get her way. 'I want to see where they find the gold. Or perhaps a diamond. Wouldn't it be exciting if we found a diamond?'

In spite of himself, Evan laughed. 'I don't think it's quite that easy!' He sighed. He could not resist her when she gazed so appealingly into his eyes, her cheeks flushed with the sun, her own eyes sparkling.

They rode across the wide expanse of golden country-side, the grass so tall it brushed their boots, and Evan warned her to watch out for the ticks that lived in the grass, waiting for someone or something to brush by in order to transfer themselves to their new host. For all her years in Africa, Lavinia possessed a sweet ignorance of the very basic precautions known to the very tiniest of black children.

In the fields, known as the 'diggings', innumerable fires blazed everywhere and the noise was indescribable – hundreds of men laughing and shouting, dogs barking, a surging vitality that left her breathless. The men worked under the pitiless sun, shoulder to shoulder, bearded, dirty, intent only on the fortune that lay hidden under the red earth. Dust floated everywhere, a great cloud of it, drifting up from the horses' feet to be breathed in with the air, making eyes red-rimmed and sore.

The men's clothes were impregnated with dust, their broad-brimmed felt hats stiff with sweat, perched at a jaunty angle on their heads. Water was precious and the smell of unwashed bodies turned Lavinia's stomach.

Cape Town seemed another world. She thought longingly of the green slopes of the mountain, her comfortable bedroom with its wrought-iron balcony and cool sea breezes blowing in from the ocean. She hoped Evan Jenkins would prove worthy of her sacrifice.

'I don't think I want to ride any further,' she told him, and pointed with her riding crop across the golden veldt, shimmering in the heat haze, to where an isolated hillock rose, crowned by the spreading branches of a jacaranda tree whose blossoms merged with the blue of the sky. 'Look, we can sit in the shade and talk.'

Evan grunted and urged his horse into a canter, following Lavinia whose own mount flew fast as the wind before him.

Once Lavinia got her teeth into something, she wasn't going to give up easily.

Chapter Fourteen

The rain had ceased and a thin, wintery sun struggled to break through the banks of cloud far over the sea. The cottage felt lonely with its empty, echoing rooms and scant fire. Alys had debated whether it was worth buying another bag of coal to warm the place, then decided it wasn't. Instead she'd bought a rabbit and some vegetables, for there was nothing in the house, and made a stew.

Marcus, guessing Alys's predicament, had handed her a handful of coins, insisting, 'Call it a loan, or an advance on your wages if you prefer,' adding that she was to go out and buy herself something nourishing to eat. He couldn't abide skinny women. His cool gaze had raked her body and she felt like squirming when he added, without rancour, 'And God knows you're skinny enough already.'

Rabbits were one shilling each and came complete with their fur. She remembered her mother skinning a rabbit as easily as peeling a glove from her hand, cleaning it and then sewing it up with a needle and cotton. For all Mam's ladylike ways, very little had disconcerted her. Alys had never found it that easy.

The thick stew acted like a tonic, for she hadn't eaten

properly for days, and when she heard Mary's voice outside the front door Alys ran to hug her so fiercely the Irish girl looked surprised.

'Hold on, don't strangle me! Me mam wouldn't like it.'

'I'm just so pleased to see you,' Alys told her. 'Walk with me to the cemetery, I want to visit Mam's grave. And I've got something to tell you.'

Mary nodded and waited for her to fetch her shawl. With the few pennies she had left, Alys bought flowers from the old woman who sat with her basket under the memorial to the Boer War. It was rumoured that she had been selling her flowers at that spot since time immemorial.

Alys began to talk about Marcus's proposition, expecting Mary to express shock. When she didn't, but nodded knowingly, Alys gave her a sideways look. They walked past the old church and on impulse ducked their heads into the doorway. Neither girl wore a hat but a shawl would do. They touched their fingers into the font of Holy water at the door and crossed themselves.

Alys kept a wary eye out for Father Goodhew, for one never knew when to expect the old priest and she was reminded uneasily of his visit to the hospital and his imprecation for her to come soon to confession.

'So you're really going?' Speaking in a whisper, Mary sat back on the shiny pew, polished to a high gloss by the backsides of generations of worshippers.

Alys settled beside her. 'I am. I've decided I can't stay here. There's nothing left for me, Mary, not even a roof over my head, for with only the cockles for a living, how could I ever afford to pay for my food and clothing, never mind rent?'

'You could always change your mind about coming into service,' Mary reminded her softly, understanding all too clearly the dilemma her friend was going through, yet dismayed at the thought of losing her. What would she do without Alys's cheerful presence, her warm support in all the little crises of Mary's young life, of being able to confide in her about Jackie?

She saw how Alys's mouth twisted at the mention of service. 'I'd rather starve than work for someone like that old devil, Thomas Jenkins.'

'I wouldn't expect you to. It doesn't have to be the Jenkins's house, anyway. There are other places. Mrs Dean has lots of friends who work in big houses across the valleys. I could ask her if she knows of any vacancies . . .

But Alys was shaking her head. 'I don't think so, Mary. It's never attracted me, that sort of life. I would have to watch my tongue every minute of the day, especially if I got in with some old bitch who nagged like some of them do. Thanks anyway, but I think I'll stick to my guns and give the bright lights of London a go. If I don't like it, I can always come back. And, you never know, I might find it suits me very nicely.'

Still Mary looked doubtful. 'I'll miss you. Nothing will ever be the same again if you're not here. Who am I going to go to the church hall dances with, or wait for after Mass on Sundays to tell the latest bit of gossip to?'

Alys patted her hand. 'You've got Jackie.'

'Have I? I'm not so sure of that.'

Alys gave her a sharp look. 'Is there anything wrong between you and Jackie? You don't seem to have seen much of him lately.'

Mary felt for the blue rosary she always carried in the pocket of her skirt, slim fingers caressing the glass beads as though to gain comfort. She didn't want to burden Alys with her troubles, although she had always confided in her before. Goodness knows, these days Alys had enough of her own without bothering her with more. Mary thought of Jackie and how they seemed to be growing apart. She told herself that he was a grown man, that if she tried to hang on to him too tightly she might lose him, and that after his stubborn interest in Miss Netta had dissipated he would come back to her. Still, every instinct cried out to her to hold on, to tell him that she loved him, wanted only him. But she shouldn't have to tell him, she thought perversely. Surely he knew? She gave Alys a shaky smile. Alys took her hand and squeezed gently.

Softly Mary said, 'Be careful. Even though you've made love with a man and conceived his baby, you're still an innocent, Alys. You mustn't go trusting everyone you meet. People will hurt you.'

'What a terrible world this would be if we went around constantly mistrusting other people!'

Mary sighed. 'You see – innocent! You'll never be any different. But I liked that Mr Dillon. There's something about him that's very reassuring, I suppose because he's an older man.'

And Alys surprised herself by saying defensively, 'He's not old! It's only his beard that makes him seem older.'

'Yes, well, my girl, you be careful. Someone like you, let loose in a place like London! Cardiff was bad enough for me, and I imagine that place is a hundred times worse.' She gave Alys an austere look. 'Promise me you won't speak to any strange men. You never know who or what they might be.' Her voice lowered mysteriously and, amused, Alys thought of the terrible stories that abounded of girls being injected with drugs and then disappearing, never to be seen again. Someone sitting behind them shushed them crossly, and remembering where they were, the two friends bent their heads in prayer.

Later, towards evening, walking down to where she used to buy her shellfish from the returning fishermen, Alys felt a stab of nostalgia for the past, a feeling that, could she have it all over again, no amount of cajoling would have tempted her to leave for London. She belonged here in this wild, beautiful land of mountains where sometimes even in spring the peaks were covered in snow, where rivers boasted the finest fishing, and where vast hollows of green valleys sheltered the coal-workers' cottages. Even if, on the other side of the coin, industry flourished, with its constantly turning pit wheels and ugly slag heaps, it was still beautiful. In the dim misty haze of twilight she could just make out the stretch of sand where she gathered the cockles.

She thought of all this, weighing it against the life she would be going to, gazing out across Craven Bay where her father's boat had gone down with all hands. She must not let emotion cloud her judgement. She had to be sensible and face facts. If she stayed what would her life be like? The other women's animosity had been only too clear. They would never allow her to forget her past sin.

Telling herself she had made a wise decision, she stood for long, silent moments, gazing out at the grey-blue waters. A silent prayer that her father would understand filled her heart. She thought of all she had lost then with a sigh of resignation turned her face towards the future.

Mrs Dean did her employer proud on Sundays. Lunch was hearty, no matter what the weather; blazing sun or landscape covered in snow, there was always roast beef and Yorkshire pudding and vegetables, followed by a boiled sponge pudding covered in hot custard sauce. Thomas Jenkins heaved a deep satisfied sigh and sat down to enjoy it.

Netta, on the other hand, wasn't enjoying it at all. She pushed the food around on her plate and left half of it uneaten. She made an effort to reply to her father's small talk but was so obviously distracted and tense that he finally asked her what was troubling her.

She wondered what he'd have said if she answered his question truthfully. That she was thinking of the Co-op delivery man, with his engaging smile and clear, guileless eyes. That lately, her every waking thought had been of him. Her father, if he knew, would probably act as he had over Evan and dispatch her to somewhere on the other side of the world. All he was interested in was seeing that his children made advantageous marriages and gave him the grandchildren he longed for. Power and money, that was Daddy's creed. Generous enough, he refused her little but he made it clear that it was he who wielded the big stick and no one was to stand up to him. Evan had tried but it hadn't made the slightest impression on their father. He understood only power and production, not people, not even himself. She'd had no mother, no real home life, and a father who was always too busy with his various corporations to concern himself with her.

Without waiting for his permission, she pushed back her chair and rose to her feet. Her father looked up, dabbing his mouth with an immaculate damask napkin. 'Well, what are your plans for this afternoon, my dear? The weather has held and there seems to be no sign of rain.'

Netta picked up her own napkin, folding it into a precise square. The velvet-curtained windows behind her outlined the beautiful garden, still ablaze with flowers. She thought of Jackie, waiting beyond Jenkins land. Patient and composed, tucked away in a crafty hollow where no one would find them, he would wait no matter how late she came to him.

A shiver of anticipation ran through her. When her father reminded her she hadn't answered his question, it took her all her time to recall what it had been. 'Oh, I haven't decided. Probably go for a walk.'

Thomas Jenkins nodded. 'Might as well make the most of the nice weather. Winter'll soon be upon us.' He reached for the impressive gold watch at the end of his chain, flipped it open and studied its face as though it told the seasons of the year instead of the hours. Netta hated winter, with its cold winds and snow. It always reminded her of the passing years and how her youth was slipping away. Most of the girls with whom she had attended school were married by now, with a family of their own.

Daddy had been giving out on the subject just the other night, pacing up and down in front of the fireplace like one of those new mechanical toys that trundled around when you wound them up. She thought of a life with the sort of man her father had in mind. Dull, boring, filled with children and servants. Oh, why hadn't she been born a man to whom everything was possible? It wasn't fair! But before she did marry, she would know a little of another kind of love, one she chose for herself . . .

Escaping through the front door, she was glad Mary wasn't there to see her go. The girl's grandmother had taken a turn for the worse and Thomas Jenkins had let her go home to help her mother. Lately, Netta had found the Irish girl's eyes a constant irritation, always upon her, probing, calculating, like a spider waiting to pounce. Netta gave a secret little smile. Let her watch! Fat lot of good it would do her. Netta was sure of her domination. Jackie was like putty in her hands, eager to do anything she wanted.

The sun was warm on her shoulders as she ran the rest of the way, following the barely discernible path that led through the long grass and scrubby bushes. Jackie didn't hear her. He lay, stretched full-length on his back, his hands clasped behind his head, eyes closed against the brightness of the sun. Netta plucked a long blade of grass and, tiptoeing forward, lightly touched the tip of his nose with its feathery end. He grunted and brushed a hand across his face. Netta laughed and his eyes snapped open, seeing her silhouetted against the sun-filled day and blue sky.

'Netta!' He gazed at her like a man in a dream. He was never sure she would turn up for their prearranged meetings, never sure of her real feelings towards him. They had met like this several times over the past few weeks, and each time he became more daring, less hesitant, surprising her, and himself, by the depth of his feeling. The nearness of her was like a drug, blinding him to all else.

For herself, Netta loved the way he tried to overcome his feelings of inferiority while looking as intriguingly shy as ever.

Her breath came fast. When he made no move but continued to gaze at her as though he could never get enough, she said poutingly, 'Well, aren't you going to kiss me?' He did so, clumsily, and taking pity on his confusion she laughed and leaned over to glide her fingers through his hair, cupping his head and keeping the pressure of his lips against her mouth.

'I can't stay long,' he told her. 'I had to make up an excuse to miss the rugby, saying I'd got a bad cold. They might come to the house, asking how I am after the game . . .'

'Mmmmm.' It was a conciliatory sound, made while she nuzzled his smooth cheek. 'It would be awful if they came and found you had gone off somewhere without asking their permission,' she added.

Jackie knew he was being mocked. When she leaned away from him, he was still, uncertain what her next move would be. She was like quicksilver, swinging from one mood to another so swiftly he was never quite sure of anything.

A lazy smile barely touched the corners of her mouth and Jackie had the impression of a stalking cat, all sleek and purring with power. 'On the other hand, now that you are here, it would be a pity not to make the most of such a pleasant day,' she suggested huskily.

He felt his heart begin a slow, heavy thudding. 'A shame,' he agreed, and felt her talon-like fingers again in his hair and Jackie learned the wanton ways of loving and the excitement that kisses could bring. On their previous meetings he had found her bold and assertive, sure of what she wanted. Now, as their bodies strained together in a passionate embrace, it escaped Jackie that it would take a rare man not to be intimidated by her aggression.

He had never dreamt such feelings existed. None of the sly innuendoes of his fellow workers as they stole away to the shop basement for a quick drag on a Woodbine had prepared him for what had just transpired between him and Netta.

Later she sighed, lying back on the grass. 'You're such an innocent,' she told him. 'I think that's what attracts me so much. You're different to any other man I've ever known. The men of my class are all such bores, talking of nothing but business and making money. While you, darling Jackie,' and she lifted a languid hand to fondle his cheek, her eyes lazily half closed, 'don't talk at all. Just love me.'

'I don't know much,' he admitted, misunderstanding her meaning. 'Except maybe rugby and how to keep motor car engines running sweet.'

Stimulated by her way of looking at him, he tried to pull her into his arms again but to his surprise she pushed him away. 'No,' she said, her voice firm. 'Not yet. You're a real glutton for punishment, aren't you?' Her laughter was shrill. 'I really ought to be going.'

'Sorry.' He was almost afraid to meet her eyes. 'When – when can we meet again?' he asked after a brief pause.

'I don't know.' She shrugged, slowly doing up the tiny pearl buttons on the front of her blouse, knowing how well she could torment him by refusing to commit herself.

It rankled him that she could appear so calm after their recent passion and a flash of temper made him frown. 'But I must see you!'

'I'm at no man's beck and call,' she chided, tossing her hair back from her face, her mood swiftly changing. 'You can't command me like one of those fisher girls you're so pally with.'

Jackie was taken aback by her words. 'I'm sorry,' he said again, stiffly and awkwardly.

Netta immediately relented. She lifted one hand and trailed her fingers across his cheek. 'Don't be. I'm not promising anything, mind, but . . .' She allowed the sentence to die away. Jackie's cheeks flushed.

'What would you like me to do? Tell me, Netta. I'll do anything – anything to make you happy.'

She twisted a long curl about her fingers, her eyes downcast, not meeting his pleading look. 'Well, boys – men – usually give me some little something, a gift, after we've . . .' Again she let the sentence die away, looking at him from under long lashes.

Jackie drew a deep breath. A gift! Where was he to get the sort of gift a girl like Netta would appreciate? His wages didn't run to items that were good enough for her. He squared his shoulders and looked so worried that she laughed, relenting. She loved teasing him. It gave her a deep sense of satisfaction, a sort of perverse pleasure that was almost as good as his clumsy passion.

'A ring would be nice,' she decided, 'and then I could

wear it when we were together, and about my neck on a
ribbon when we're not. Close to my breast.' Looking
into his flushed face she felt an unexpected twinge of
conscience; she should really have told him she was
teasing him, but it would have been a shame to spoil her
little victory.

Chapter Fifteen

Looking back on them a long time afterwards, the days that followed seemed the strangest and most contradictory of Jackie's whole life. He should have been happy. Miss Netta had proved that she loved him. Well, hadn't she? How could he believe anything else after those ecstatic hours spent with her on that Sunday afternoon? Every day should have been happy, just counting the hours until he could see her again. The trouble was the gift she had demanded: the ring.

How could he, Jackie Rees, afford the sort of ring Netta would find acceptable? He became pale and inattentive at work, jumping when spoken to as though dragging his thoughts back from the place where they had been. And Mr Kimble had the impression that he wasn't listening anyway, for the errors he made in his deliveries were becoming increasingly more absurd.

For instance, yesterday he had delivered to Jones the farmer's wife an assortment of baby clothes – and her a woman well past child-bearing age. 'And,' stormed a red-faced Mr Kimble, 'this morning you left a parcel of boiled ham at the Cohens, and they of the Jewish faith! It won't do, young Rees. Indeed, it won't do at all. You pull your socks up, mind, or it's the Labour Exchange for you, boyo.' His eyes softened. The boy looked so forlorn. 'What ails you, son? Are you not feeling well? Got a touch of that old influenza they're talking about coming on?'

Jackie turned abruptly on his heel. 'I'm all right, Mr Kimble,' he mumbled. 'Don't worry about me, I'm fine.'

The thought of the ring caused him sleepless nights and it wasn't until one day when he was passing old Jakob's pawn shop and paused to look in the window that it came to him. His bit of savings wouldn't run to a new ring, but then Netta hadn't stressed a *new* ring, just a ring. Old Jakob had some very nice ones displayed in his window, embedded in a tray of blue velvet. One in particular, a gold band with a half circle of diamonds and rubies, caught his eye. He could just picture it on Netta's slim white hand.

The bell above the door jangled loudly as, rather nervously, he entered the shop. He was nervous because he was never very good at dealing with the people he secretly thought of as 'the bosses', and it was clear that Jakob Rozenberg, although bent and shabbily dressed, had once belonged to that elite class. Jackie felt he might be about to make a fool of himself. The ring, although old, was obviously valuable and he must be weak-minded to imagine it might be within his means. If it should prove too much for him, he would feel as if somehow he had belittled Netta, offering her second best, for then he would have to consider a cheaper one.

The old Jew had an animal instinct for fear. God knows he had encountered it enough times during his life; had lived with it more years than he cared to remember. The young man who entered his shop and stood before him now was fearful of something. Jakob thought of the young boys who came into his premises, a crowd of them at a time, milling about and pushing each other until he took the cricket bat he kept under the counter and chased them out. They fled, calling him names over their shoulders: names like 'Yid' and 'Old Ikey'. As long as they left empty-handed he didn't mind. Over the years there had been enough pilfering of the precious stock that was his lifeblood, and as long as he had strength he would prevent it from happening again.

His gnarled fingers touched the handle of the bat, reassured to find it within easy reach. The young man turned and then pointed towards the window. 'That ring, the one in the tray with the others, the one with rubies, how much are you asking for it?' It came out all in one long breath.

What had the young fool to be nervous about? pondered Jakob.

Jackie drew another, steadying breath and tried again. 'Can I see it, please?'

Oh, well, business was business! The English – Welsh, he corrected himself – were a crazy people. Perhaps the young man really was a genuine customer. He joined Jackie at the window, leaning into its cluttered depths and lifting out the blue velvet tray. Carrying it to the counter, he set it down. Looking Jackie in the eye he named a price.

'It's antique,' he explained, plucking the ring from its nest of velvet. 'Very rare design.' The untruths came easily to his lips. He had served a long apprenticeship in half-truths. 'It was left to me by a Baroness who had lost all her belongings in the Balkan uprisings.'

Even Jackie wasn't gullible enough to believe that. True, the ring was lovely, but it didn't look as though it had come from the family jewels of a European aristocrat. The bell above the door jangled again, capturing the old pawnbroker's attention. The impulse was irresistible. Jackie slipped the ring into his pocket.

There was the sound of children's laughter and then the door closed again with a jolt that sent the bell suspended above it jumping madly. Jakob shook his head. 'Boys!'

He turned back to Jackie who, averting his face, was pushing past him, muttering something about having to hurry.

'Wait, young man. Wait!' Surprisingly agile for someone his age, Jakob intercepted him, making a grab for his arm. 'What for you have changed your mind? We can bargain as to price . . .'

'Let go!' Struggling against the old man's hold, Jackie's expression became a grimace of fear. 'I've changed my mind. I don't want your stupid ring.'

'Why not?' Old Jakob was genuinely puzzled. 'Why you change your mind like so?' He broke off, taking in at last the space where the ruby ring had rested.

Panic-filled, Jackie stammered. 'I don't want it, I tell you. I've got to . . .'

'Young man.' The pawnbroker tugged at his arm. 'Something is wrong, yes? Where is my ring?' The hold on Jackie's arm tightened.

Terrified, he shouted, 'I told you, I have to go.' As the words left his mouth he swung upwards with his right hand, not caring where the blow landed as long as it freed him from the talon-like grasp.

The hard edge of his hand caught Jakob on the side of the head, sending him staggering. He made no sound apart from the first harsh cry the blow drew from him.

Jackie saw him fall back, striking the edge of the counter, and crumple to his knees. The hurt astonishment in the old man's eyes would haunt Jackie for the rest of his life. He backed away, sick with sudden self-loathing, then as the old man began to push himself up, bracing his hands on the counter, his voice rising on a string of foreign-sounding oaths, Jackie ran into the street, self-disgust and the shame of his action snarling like twin devils at his heels.

The man was not from Craven Bay. He'd come from further up the valley, Cilybebyll way, looking for work. So far his luck had been out and the parcel of food his wife had given him was almost finished. He'd spent the last two nights in the open and thought back with longing to his warm bed with Molly, his plump little wife, snug beside him. But although it was heartbreaking, leaving home, work had to be found somewhere and there was surely none up his way.

He bit into the last piece of bread and cheese, savouring it, making it last as long as he could. He screwed the paper up into a tight ball and thrust it into his coat pocket. If only he could obtain shelter for the night he could feel that things were looking up, but without a penny piece on him that was out of the question. He'd have to continue walking until he found an empty barn or, like that first night, the ruins of a cottage. He'd huddled up in the comparative shelter of what once had been the ingle-nook, his coat collar turned up, his arms wrapped about his drawn-up knees, and tried to sleep. He knew it would have been impossible if he wasn't so exhausted.

Keeping a watchful eye open for a likely spot, he came to a narrow cobbled street where the gas lamps were dim, with long distances between them. Even though it was so dark he could still see the outline of the shop door, wide open, with a dim light shining from somewhere within. It was a pawn shop; he recognised the three gilded balls that hung above the door. The pawn shop had, of necessity, become a way of life with him and Molly in these last few lean months. He approached the open door with a stealth that had been quickly acquired on his travels, dodging farmers and gamekeepers. He might be able to kip inside the doorway. At least there would be limited shelter.

Edging his way inside, ears and eyes alert for the slightest movement or sound, he gave a startled sob as a dark figure materialised before him, scrawny fingers with sharp nails clawing for his throat. It seemed to rise from nowhere. Terrified, he grabbed the first thing that came to hand, a tall brass candlestick that happened to be on the counter.

Frightened at the ferocity of his unseen assailant's attack, the blow he gave with the candlestick was probably harder than he intended for the figure gave a groan and collapsed on to the floor.

The man from the valley did not wait to see if it moved or not. He was away like a fox running before the hounds and didn't stop running until he reached the other side of the village.

A neighbour bringing his daily pint of milk found old

Jakob early the next morning, slumped against the counter. A tray of rings had been upset close to his out-stretched hand, suggesting that there had been an attempt at robbery which Jakob had interrupted.

The constable who came at the neighbour's frantic call was puzzled. Not once in his long career as a policeman in this peaceful community had there been a robbery with violence. And why here? In this dingy little shop with its pathetic collection of second-hand goods, none of which were valuable enough for anyone to go to such lengths.

Marcus lived in an elegant Georgian house in a quiet, tree-lined square. Although it was in the centre of London, thought Alys, you would never have known it. The front door with its handsome bronze knocker and narrow slit of a letter-box opened straight out on to the pavement and there were black iron railings with wicked-looking spikes along the top and steep steps that led downwards, probably to the kitchen quarters. A white open-top car was parked by the gutter.

Marcus opened the door with his key then stood aside and waited for her to precede him. The cab driver fol-lowed, carrying their few items of luggage, for Alys had little and Marcus obviously believed in travelling light. His paintings, canvas and easel and various other things were to be sent by goods train and would arrive in a day or two.

The interior of the house was at first only a blurred impression to Alys, tired after the long train journey, although she was aware of a small square entrance hall with a staircase rising out of it. Marcus explained that his housekeeper, one Mrs Mimms, would be back the following morning as he'd told her to take a few days off while he was away.

Thinking of them being alone together, Alys experienced a moment of near panic, then asked herself how silly could she get? That Marcus, with his aloof, almost negligent, way of treating her, whether he was aware of it or not, would make anything that she could remotely interpret as a pass, was laughable.

She opened her eyes the next morning to the sound of a passing delivery boy whistling 'Daisy, Daisy' in the street below as he cycled past the house. She lay blinking at the ceiling above her head, weighing up her thoughts. Was she really in London? Had the long train journey across England really happened? Surely she had to be dreaming?

Throwing the bed covers aside, she ran to the window, looking down on a scene that assured her she wasn't. That and the memory of the makeshift dinner Marcus had gathered from the various cupboards in the kitchen. It had tasted remarkably appetising. 'Eat up,' he'd commanded, laying the white dinner plate before her at the table. 'I'm no chef but I think you'll find it to your satisfaction. Can't send you to bed like a naughty child, can we, all forlorn and hungry?'

Alys had got used to his teasing and smiled and said nothing where once she would have answered sharply with an observation of her own. Now, peering down at the small green square across the road, guarded by tall iron railings, she saw that it was already filled with children and stiffly starched nannies who sat and gossiped on wooden benches while their small charges made the most of their brief period of freedom.

The boys wheeled huge iron hoops in front of them while the little girls, more sedate, pushed dolls' prams with high wheels at the back and smaller ones at the front, and white porcelain handles. They all looked so well dressed – and fed – that Alys could not help comparing them with the children of her valley.

She had slept late and the small clock on her bedside table told her it was nine-thirty. Hastily she dressed, choosing a plum-coloured skirt and a white blouse with a high lace-trimmed neckline and sleeves that ended in lace points on the backs of her hands. A wide black patent leather belt cinched her trim waist.

Before leaving Craven Bay, Marcus had insisted she visit the Co-op Stores and purchase a couple of outfits. She'd been glad to, swallowing her pride when he said she could always repay him out of her earnings as a model.

The task of unpacking could wait until later. She realised she was starving, and from somewhere downstairs floated the tantalising smell of fresh coffee. She'd hardly ever tasted coffee but she thought it would be easy to get used to.

She had a quick wash in the china basin on the wash-stand, pouring water from the matching jug. On her way down the steep, narrow staircase she thought of Marcus, wondering if he would be wanting to start the new painting straight away.

In the kitchen she found an elderly woman with grey hair swept into a tidy bun. She was slicing a large loaf of bread, holding it to her chest and using a long, black-handled knife. The action reminded Alys so much of her mother, she liked the woman right away.

'Good mornin', my dear. Mr Marcus said I was to let you sleep so I purposely didn't disturb you. Now, sit down and I'll get you some breakfast.'

Alys smiled shyly and pulled out a chair from the dark oak table. 'Thank you. You're Mrs Mimms, aren't you?' Marcus had said that a Mrs Mimms worked for him, keeping the studio clean – 'Although I imagine she finds it a losing battle,' he'd grinned. The housekeeper also cooked meals for him when he was in residence.

'That's right,' Mrs Mimms replied to Alys's question. 'I've bin with Mr Marcus for years, ever since he bought this house to use as his studio.' She shook her head, placing the thick slices of bread on a plate by Alys's elbow. 'What a man! Paint everywhere! Sometimes I don't hardly know how I'll get those white shirts of his clean again.' She smiled to show there was no malice intended. 'You drink coffee, do you, miss?'

Alys accepted a cup and sipped it appreciatively. Mrs Mimms next busied herself with cooking bacon and egg, then holding the plate with a white cloth and a warning, 'Mind, 'cause it's 'ot,' she deposited it in front of Alys.

She couldn't help comparing this with the squares of bread and hot milk sprinkled with sugar that had been her breakfast for years. Mam had been a great believer in bread and milk. 'Set you up for the day,' she said. Mam hadn't held with the mug of tea that a lot of people now took for breakfast. Alys's lips twitched. How Mam would have endorsed this!

While she ate, Mrs Mimms ran a damp cloth over the top of the large grey mottled gas stove, talking all the time.

'I'm glad Mr Marcus has decided to start work again,

234

and with such a pretty model,' giving Alys a sly smile. 'He's bin a perfect misery lately, couldn't settle on anything. I know 'is mother, poor dear, was weary listening to 'im, although she's a very calm and collected lady and wouldn't for the life of 'er say anything to 'urt 'im. But I could see she was worried. She likes 'er son to be 'appy, you know.'

She gave Alys a woman-to-woman smile. 'Don't we all? There's only one way you can live wi' a man, I say, and that's to keep 'im well fed and busy. Miss Joanna tried but it didn't work. Miss Joanna – that's Joanna Ambrey, her father's the Earl of Ambrey and she's really a Lady but she gets cross if she hears anyone call her by her title – *she* tried to involve him in her concerns but Mr Marcus wouldn't 'ave nothin' to do wi' 'em. She's one of them suffragettes. *You* know!'

Alys didn't know but smiled anyway, mildly wondering what a suffragette was when it was at home. Mrs Mimms, pausing only to draw breath, went on, 'What was I saying? Oh, yes, Miss Joanna is a lovely lady and Mr Marcus is very fond of her. We're all waiting for the engagement to be announced – and then Saint Margaret's Westminster better be ready for the wedding of the year.'

Alys finished her breakfast to the sound of Mrs Mimms gushing over the wedding, wondering why she should feel alarm at the idea. The thought of Marcus and another woman had never entered her head. Although why it should surprise her, she couldn't understand. Marcus Dillon was a good-looking man, entertaining in an enigmatic kind of way. And, after all, what did she know of his life outside Craven Bay?

She asked where Marcus was and if Mrs Mimms knew of his plans for the morning, already half over.

'Oh, Mr Marcus isn't here, love. He left quite early, think he wanted to see someone. But he did say he wouldn't be wanting you today so you was just to relax and find your way about.'

Alys pushed back her chair, wiping her mouth on the starched serviette at the side of her plate. 'I'll do that, Mrs Mimms. The small park across the way looks nice and peaceful.'

Mrs Mimms rolled her eyes expressively. 'If you could call it that wi' all them little 'orrors running around screaming somethin' terrible and their nannies not takin' a blind bit o' notice. Wouldn't 'ave done in my day, I can tell you. Children were brought up to be seen and not 'eard then.'

Solemnly agreeing with her, Alys made her escape. The morning sun was unexpectedly warm and pleasant and she wouldn't need a coat. She crossed the road and made her way across the grass, stopping to examine the last of the summer roses. The bushes were tall, grown straggly in their beds, the remaining petals needing only the barest breath of wind to dislodge them. Soon the small park would lose all its greenness, the trees become bleak and bare, the wind too chill for anyone to linger.

As she passed before the wrought-iron gates, flung wide open now but closed and securely locked at sunset, Alys saw a man standing watching her. Not Marcus. This man was fair and slight, not dark and arrogant.

'Good morning!' the laughing voice greeted her. 'You must be Miss Alys Hughes.'

She hadn't lingered to do her hair properly and now

lifted her arms to push it away from her face, quite unaware of the picture she made, standing there in her full, dark-red skirt and white blouse, her tiny waist emphasised by the tight black belt. Her pansy eyes sparkled with the exhilaration of new sights and new surroundings.

'And what if I am?' she asked tartly. 'How do you know my name?'

'I saw you come from number twenty-nine, and knowing Mrs Mimms doesn't have any relatives who remotely resemble you, I drew my own conclusions.'

'That still doesn't explain *how* you knew,' she pointed out.

He shrugged. 'Oh, come now, you can't be that ingenuous! Surely you know that all Marcus's friends have spent the last week discussing the identity of the young woman it was rumoured he was bringing back with him from Wales?'

Alys didn't know whether to be angry or flattered or just plain tickled pink. The young man's smile was so warm and friendly, and it obviously wasn't just in the mean streets of Craven Bay where gossip flourished. She said, 'Well, there's a thing! I didn't know myself that I was coming to London until the other day. Mr Dillon must have been very sure of himself.'

The young man grinned. 'That's Marcus! Now, come and sit with me,' nodding towards an empty seat, 'and you can tell me all about yourself. And after that I think I would like to take you to see the sights, before anyone else gets hold of you.' He cocked an eyebrow, leading her to the empty bench. 'You're not doing anything else I take it?'

'No, and I'd love to see the sights. But perhaps not today. I don't quite know what Mr Dillon's plans are. I'd better sort that out with him first.'

He made a slight bow, making her laugh. 'I shall await your answer with bated breath.' They talked until, pulling his watch from his waistcoat pocket and glancing down at it, he said he had to go. 'You might not believe it,' he told her, 'but I really should be working right at this moment.'

'Well, you had better get on with it, hadn't you?' she smiled, enjoying his bright and breezy manner.

'I will. But don't forget that you promised to let me show you London. I'll keep you to that.'

Mrs Mimms had cooked lunch which they shared sitting opposite at the heavy oak table and talking. Alys didn't mention the young man, who had introduced himself as Simon Rayne. Mrs Mimms, without sounding too nosy, was obviously interested in her background and they talked about that and how she and Marcus had met. Mrs Mimms nodded her head, murmuring, 'Aye, that's the sort of thing Mr Marcus would do. Unconventional, that's what folk say about Mr Marcus. Doesn't give a damn for nobody and worries less about what they think.'

Alys's eyes twinkled. 'So he makes a habit of going round picking up girls he feels he wants to paint, does he?'

'No, miss. First time *that's* happened. But 'e 'as got plenty interested enough to come and see where he does 'is painting, and by that time they're lost. I can't remember anyone ever refusing to sit when he's asked them.'

She gazed at Alys, her eyes thoughtful. 'You were in

that one everyone's talking about, weren't you? The one wi' the donkey.'

Alys had to admit she was, and her thoughts went winging back to her home. Poor Drogo! She wondered how he was getting on. Already it seemed an age since she'd last gossiped with Mary. How homesick might she be after a month or more?

After lunch, Mrs Mimms went home to 'see to her own man', as she put it. 'Lazy bugger,' she told Alys, 'won't lift a finger to 'elp 'imself. Be sitting there wi' the fire 'alf out and not a knob o' coal in the scuttle, moaning that 'e's not yet 'ad 'is dinner.'

She shook her head. 'Why do we bother wi' 'em, miss? Thought Mother Nature would 'ave come up wi' something better after all these years, wouldn't you?'

Still mumbling to herself she left the house, going out the back way and walking down a flagged garden path that led through an archway in the red brick wall that in turn gave on to a narrow back street used by tradesmen.

Alone, Alys roamed the house, discovering there were three storeys. The front door opened on to a square hallway, the kitchen to one side and at the back a large airy room with bay windows that looked out on to the garden. Obviously used as a sitting room, it contained a comfortable-looking sofa and two large chairs. The French windows opened on to a shallow flight of steps leading down to a small lawn. Lovely in summer, Alys thought, imagining tea set out on a white-covered table and wicker chairs made comfortable with flowered chintzy cusions.

Alys smiled, imagining Mary's face could she see her now and know what she was thinking. Climbing the staircase, she opened a door on the wide landing to find a studio painted all in white and reeking of oil paint, linseed oil and turpentine. The skylight was large and slanted, and the sunlight streamed in. Everything in the large cluttered room seemed rimed by the late burst of autumn sunshine.

Canvasses were stacked against the walls, face inwards so she couldn't see the subjects. Intensely curious, Alys bent and turned a number over, examining them with a suddenly critical eye. With her naturally quick mind she had learned quite a bit about the technique of painting, for on his more loquacious mornings in the cottage on the headlands, Marcus had explained as he painted, almost as though he were a lecturer at a college and Alys his pupil. There were portraits of women, young and old, gazing sombrely at the viewer, so real you almost expected them to move, and a number of seascapes Alys recognised as the coast near Craven Bay. She put them back where she had found them. The canvas on the easel was a new one, waiting for the first brush stroke. She wondered what sort of a pose and costume he wanted of her this time. She'd love to be depicted in a garden, perhaps seated on a marble bench with the moon shining through the trees and a nightingale singing above.

There's silly she was, she told herself sternly, letting her imagination run away with her like this! Continuing her tour, she tried the other two doors on the landing. The first was a large bedroom with a single bed made up. A pair of silver-backed hair brushes were on the dresser and a silk dressing gown, the colour of mulberries, thrown carelessly across a chair.

The second room made her eyes widen with pleasure.

It was lined completely with books, leatherbound, in such rich colours: crimson, tobacco brown, rust, a deep blue, and the green of beryl, most of them with title and author's name tooled in gold. They seemed to fill the room with a warmth that was almost tangible.

Alys promised herself that on days when Marcus didn't need her, she would spend time in this room, for here surely must be the gateway to another world.

As a child she had read whatever she could get her hands on, and once she and Mary had bet each other they could read right through the entire library that was housed in the Town Hall. Alys had got to the letter F before admitting defeat. That was about the time her father's ship had gone down. Mary had given up long before that. After the arrival of Dan in her life, there had been no time for Alys to sit quietly any more, with a book open on her lap.

The steep, much narrower, second staircase led to the third floor and her own room. There were carpets everywhere, even up here, and she thought she was really seeing how the other half lived now.

In her own room she unpacked a few things, slipping the yellow silk dress bought with Marcus's first guinea on to a hanger. She closed her eyes, pressing the cool silk to her cheek, trying to see Evan as they whirled round the room to the music of that ridiculous trio. She still hadn't heard where he had gone; no one at the big house would speak of it and Mary was as much in the dark as the other servants.

Sighing, she hung the frock in the heavy mahogany wardrobe, next to the green silk she had worn the day they sought shelter in the cave. There was another, purchased from the Co-op Stores along with the red skirt and blouse, a frock Marcus had had a hand in choosing, telling her quite abruptly that she would need something suitable for evenings. His tone had been half teasing, half ominous. Alys hadn't spoken. She was learning to control her temper and not retaliate every time he taunted her.

This was a gown the like of which she had never seen before. Not even a gown, really, more like an evening wrap draped like a Japanese kimono, in a deep plum colour with a design of pale pink. She'd thought it very daring for the slit at the front actually showed a glimpse of her knee and was surprised that anything so stylish should be found in a Craven Bay store.

The last thing she hung in the wardrobe was the peasant-type skirt and the fine cotton blouse she had worn in her street hawking days. If the grandeur of her new life started to take over and she found herself affecting the talk and manners of London society, this outfit would serve to remind her of her roots as nothing else would.

Chapter Sixteen

That resolution was quickly forgotten when Mrs Mimms returned and laid tea out on the square of lawn, just as Alys had imagined it. 'I'm expecting Mr Marcus, and 'e likes 'is tea 'ere. And as the sun's still out I thought you might like it 'ere, too, miss.'

Alys flushed with pleasure. 'Thank you so much, Mrs Mimms. But please don't call me "miss". My name's Alys.'

'Alys!' Mrs Mimms repeated it slowly, rolling it round on her tongue, not sure of the feel of it. Her face brightened. 'I only saw it written down before and it seemed right outlandish to me, but when you say it, why, it's just like our Alice!'

Alys laughed. 'Nothing outlandish about me, I'm afraid.' As she spoke, there was a faint 'Miaow!' and a large ginger cat leaped gracefully from a low branch of the oak tree and rubbed itself against Alys's ankles. She was enchanted. Bending, she fondled his ears. 'He's beautiful! I love cats.'

'His name's Rufus and it's cupboard love, ducks. He knows it's tea time. Come on, you,' she said, picking up the cat with a grunt and tucking it under one arm, 'into the kitchen with you, away from everyone's feet.'

Alys helped Mrs Mimms to cut bread, thin, wafer-like slices this time for the cucumber sandwiches and the egg and cress, and carried out the heavy crystal glass and silver cake stand with its three tiers of cakes, all different; a jam sponge cake covered in powdered sugar, scones thick with yellow butter, and Mrs Mimm's home-made Dundee cake, the top shiny and glistening with browned almonds.

The arrival of Marcus brought the beautiful marmalade cat out again, purring a welcome. It rubbed itself against the man's legs, twisting its sleek body round and round until Marcus laughed and, bending swiftly, scooped the animal up into his arms. Mrs Mimms followed him across the lawn, carrying the tea pot in its Irish linen embroidered cosy. Watching, Alys wondered idly whose hand had been responsible for the delicate pattern of coloured silks; scarlet poppies and ears of yellow corn intertwined with small white daisies. She had noticed cushion covers in similar designs plumped up on armchairs and sofas. Would Mrs Mimms have the time, or the inclination for such time-consuming work? She thought not.

Marcus came and sat near her at the tea table, his slender, long-fingered hands fondling the cat's pricked ears. Rufus's purring sounded like an old steam engine left running. 'You're an old fusspot, aren't you?' Marcus grinned and the cat looked up at him adoringly.

Mrs Mimms brushed away a non-existent crumb with the palm of her hand, and tutted. 'That imp of Satan's here again, is he? I thought I'd shut him in the scullery. Here, Mister Marcus, let me take 'im from you. Getting all those loose hairs all over your fine trousers.'

'No, it's all right, Mrs Mimms. Apart from you, he's usually the only one to greet me when I come home.' His fingers caressed the sleek ginger coat, and the cat stretched its neck high, enjoying the sensation, its sharp little chin raised invitingly.

Alys was mesmerised, sitting there in the bright sunlight, watching those hands that worked such magic with a square of canvas and paint achieve an even louder purring. Unheralded came the thought: imagine those hands gliding over her skin in that fashion . . . She shivered.

If she were a cat, she'd probably be purring too!

She saw that he was watching her and avoiding his eyes, feeling suddenly foolish, she leaned across the table to wave away a wasp that was demonstrating an interest in the Victoria jam sponge. 'Tea?' she asked brightly, reaching to lift the tea-cosy.

'Please.' He lifted his cup and saucer, passing them to her. 'Settled in all right?'

Alys nodded, busy pouring tea. 'Yes, thank you.'

'Good. I think you'll find your room very comfortable, and if there's anything you need, you only have to ask Mrs Mimms. She's my treasure. I wouldn't, to use one of her own expressions, swap her for a jar of tadpoles.'

Alys laughed and the cat turned its head and gazed at her, its amber eyes blinking sleepily in the bright sunlight. Then, its brief span of attention wandering, it jumped down from Marcus's knee, attracted by a rustling in a nearby azalea bush. Relieved of his burden, Marcus leant back, cup and saucer in his hands, and lazily examined the girl sitting opposite.

'So what did you do with yourself today? I must

apologise for not being here. There was someone I had to see. I hope you weren't bored.'

'Not in the least.' What made him think she would be bored just because he wasn't around? she wondered. 'After breakfast I went for a walk. Just across to the park. It's lovely, isn't it? So peaceful. I think it's important to have places like that in the middle of a city. Otherwise you could forget that nature *is* so beautiful.'

'At least we share some things. Thoughts on conservation, for instance.'

He lifted the cup to his lips and after a moment's silence Alys went on, 'I met a man in the park. He introduced himself as Simon Rayne. He said he knew you.'

Marcus nodded, but remained silent. 'He said he wanted to show me the sights,' she went on. 'I hope it's all right?' Suddenly she sounded doubtful, a frown marring her brow. 'I know I'm supposed to be working but I thought, sometimes, I might be able to have a few hours off . . . ?'

'By "sights", I wonder what he means?' Marcus sounded sceptical.

She shrugged. 'The usual things visitors to London see, I imagine. You did say it would be easy for me to get around, that there would be buses and taxi cabs, and you mentioned cafés . . .'

He gave a gruff laugh. 'I get the point! But Simon's idea of sights might not be yours. I think, if there's any sightseeing to be done, I'll see to that myself.'

Meekness was alien to Alys's nature. She lifted her chin, her eyes defiant. 'I'm not a child! And I don't think I want to be told who I may or may not see. Mr Rayne seems a perfectly respectable person, and this morning I felt quite at ease with him. So . . .'

'Why is it that we can never be together for more than five minutes without fighting? Can it be that really we're attracted to each other and refuse to admit it?' His gaze ran over her face, taking in the delicate features, the flushed rose of the cheeks. Mrs Mimms broke the sudden tension by appearing across the lawn, calling, 'Tea all right, sir? I've got water boiling if you need a top-up.'

'Quite all right, thank you, Mrs Mimms,' answered Marcus smoothly. When the woman had vanished once more into the house, he went on as though there had been no break in the conversation, 'Well? Cat got your tongue?'

With an unnatural display of cowardice, Alys got up to go and Marcus murmured, in a completely different voice, 'Don't.'

'I've still got things to do in my room,' she told him stiffly. She had the feeling that she had handled this situation badly, allowing him to get the upper hand. And what he'd said about their fighting had been so true. As she walked away, she could feel his gaze burning intently into her back.

Later, as brisk as ever, Marcus told her, 'I have to go out for the evening but I want to start work early in the morning, so be a good girl and get an early night. I'll try not to disturb you when I come in. Good night, Alys. Sweet dreams.'

Not sure whether she should be pleased or disappointed that he was deserting her for the evening, she watched from the window as he climbed into the waiting hansom, then with a sigh that she didn't quite understand, climbed the stairs to her lonely, if pretty, room. Earlier she had returned to the library and chosen an armful of books at random. She'd asked Mrs Mimms if she thought this was all right, hoping Marcus wouldn't mind.

'Well, ducks, it's like this. Some of them books are valuable, first editions and such-like, and some are very old religious books. Not that I'd want to read any of 'em, give me *Peg's Paper* any old time. But I'm sure if you was careful, and I know you will be, there'd be no 'arm in borrowing a few.'

'I'll be very careful,' Alys assured her.

'I know you will, ducks. Now, before I go to me own 'ome, I'll show you where the bathroom is.' Alys followed her down a long passage, past the toilet to a small room where a good half of the space was taken up by a large white bath with claw feet. It was the first fitted bath Alys had ever seen and she eyed it with an air of misgiving. Mrs Mimms proceeded to turn on the silver taps and a stream of hot water poured into the bath. 'We got all the modern things 'ere,' she told Alys smugly. 'Mr Marcus insists on it. This 'ere's the latest indoor water system you can get. No dragging out tin baths and carrying up pails of 'ot water for 'im. You just turns on the tap and out comes 'ot water. Magic, ain't it?'

Thinking of her own primitive bathing arrangements, how she would have to boil up kettle after kettle in order to enjoy a hot bath, Alys had to agree that it was indeed magic. Still she looked doubtfully at the steaming water. 'It looks awfully hot,' she ventured hesitantly. 'I'll boil like a lobster.'

'Turn the cold tap on until you've got it to your liking. There,' suiting the action to the words. 'Turn it orf when it's right. Now.' Mrs Mimms reached up to the white marble shelf above the bath and produced a cake of pale violet soap. 'Mr Marcus told me I was to get whatever I thought a young lady would need, and this lavender-scented soap was recommended to me by the young woman in the shop. Said you'd step out the bath smelling like roses. Well,' with a giggle that surprised Alys, 'lavender, anyway.' She gave a last, professional glance about the room. 'Got everything you need, ducks? There's plenty of towels in the cupboard there, and when you've finished you just pull this plug out and the water'll drain away itself.'

Like a cat basking in front of a roaring fire, Alys luxuriated in her first real bath. Drying herself afterwards, she was glad Mrs Mimms had reminded her to bring her nightgown and dressing gown from her bedroom, although it wasn't strictly a dressing gown but her shawl. She would have to make do with it until she could afford to buy the real thing.

While the fine weather continued afternoon tea in the garden became a sort of ritual. Alys thought she could accustom herself to this style of living quite nicely, thank you. Mam always used to say that you might not be born a lady, but there was no reason why you couldn't behave like one. This was going to be the easiest transition of Alys's life.

She was grateful, too, to Mrs Mimms for not making sly references about her role in Marcus's house. There were women, she knew, who would have had a field day over the situation, with suggestive nudges and winks.

Mrs Mimms was making her feel completely at home and treating her like a lady.

'Mind you,' she had told Alys, 'it's not everyone I'd do that with. Some of the models,' she paused heavily on the word, 'were pretty enough, but none o' them were in your class, dear.'

It was autumn and although not cold you could feel the chill fingers of winter already drawing nigh. The trees were clothed in their finery of golds and russets, and where the weak sunlight touched them leaves glistened like gold chains.

Jackie sat in the small Craven Bay jail that had only ever held one other prisoner, if you didn't count the drunks on a Saturday night. It had been back in 1902, when a returning soldier from the Boer War had got drunk and smashed up the corner tavern so badly the police had to be called.

Word had got around about the robbery and assault on old Jakob, and someone had come forward and reported seeing Jackie Rees running from the shop as though in a panic. Jackie, confronted by the constable, broke down completely and without a word had handed over the ring he had pocketed, glad to see the back of it. He'd felt a vast sense of relief – until word came that old Jakob had died in hospital. Jackie was taken to the jail in chains, there to be charged with the unlawful killing of Jakob Rozenberg.

The elderly constable, more used to clipping boys like Jackie around the ear for riding their bicycles without lights, ponderously filled in all the forms. Jackie was transferred to Cardiff to answer the charges there. The murder of the old pawnbroker was the talk of the taverns as well as the streets, people taking sides but most shaking their heads and saying they just didn't believe it. Not of the young Rees boy.

Evan thought again of the letter he had just received from his sister. After the usual tittle-tattle and inquiries as to his health, one paragraph stood out. Netta had written:

> You remember that girl you were seeing, the one who sold cockles? Well, it seems she's gone off to London with Marcus Dillon. Claims he wants to paint her again, but then he would say that, wouldn't he? Never did think much of that girl's morals.
>
> Oh, by the way, Jackie Rees, the Co-op van driver, has been arrested and languishes in jail, accused, would you believe, of murder! It seems he attacked old Jakob, the pawnbroker, during a robbery in his shop and the old man died a couple of days later. The doctors called it a brain haemorrhage, but of course the whole town is speculating on the real cause.

Evan was shocked. Jackie Rees! He couldn't believe it. Jackie had always seemed such a pleasant lad, aggressive only in his game of rugby. Off the pitch, he wouldn't say boo to a goose. He could never bring himself to believe that Jackie would resort to robbery with violence. There had to be some mistake. Whatever was boring, sedate little Craven Bay coming to, murder and robbery and young girls running off to London with older men?

The truth was he had never thought of Alys belonging to anyone but him. The words of the letter mocked that belief. He saw Alys's eyes, heavy with passion as they clung to each other that night in her kitchen, terrified that at any moment the door would open and an avenging stepfather burst in. Although he had tried to put her out of his mind, his heart still lifted when he thought of the way she had so innocently offered herself to him. And suddenly, jealousy burned inside him.

Beside Lavinia on the stone balcony, the French windows behind them open to the warm night, soft lamplight throwing shadows across the garden, Evan stared into the girl's face and wondered at the way emotions turned feelings into a battle ground. This girl, with her fine silk gown and necklace of pearls with its diamond clasp, would never know the trials or hardships Alys had experienced. Would lose no sleep if she did know. Although Lavinia radiated joy and gaiety, and every day was like a holiday with her, he knew she could never compensate him for the loss of Alys.

There were voices behind them and Lavinia said pettishly, 'Oh, bother! Just when I thought I had you alone. Why don't we walk in the garden? This place is becoming too crowded for comfort.'

They were attending a dance given by Mrs Harvey for her husband's birthday. The night was very warm and the men perspired in their dark evening clothes. Escaping on to the balcony had seemed the smart thing to do. Now, it seemed, everyone had the same idea.

Evan followed her down the shallow flight of steps. The lush green of the lawns, maintained at great effort and cost in this harsh, dusty climate, was soft under their feet. Watered at sundown by a team of gardeners with hosepipes, the lawn's moisture soon soaked into Lavinia's thin dancing slippers. But it didn't matter. At last she was alone with Evan, away from the watchful eye of Mrs Harvey.

She clung to his arm, full of her plans for tomorrow when they were due to ride out on a picnic to the wide river to the north. She'd heard it was spectacular and was looking forward to it.

Now it seemed Evan was displaying a definite lack of interest, and she wondered if he was even listening to what she was saying.

'What's the matter?' she demanded, coming to a stop and lifting her face to his. 'There's something, isn't there? Have you changed your mind about going on the picnic tomorrow? It would be just typical of you to do that.' Her mouth twisted down at the corners. 'I never know what you're thinking, and it upsets me.'

Evan searched for the right words. She deserved better than a man who was in love with someone else. With her background and the opportunities offered by her father's business to a bright son-in-law, she could expect more than second best.

'I have reservations about leaving the office at this time,' he told her, trying to sound convincing. 'There are men going round the work force intent on making trouble and I feel I should be there.'

'Oh, poof!' She made a dismissive gesture with one hand. 'There are always people making trouble. I'm sure there are others who can deal with a little thing like that. They don't need *you* there all the time.'

He sighed heavily. Why must he be so indecisive? Why couldn't he just say what he meant and clear the air one way or the other? 'I suppose you're right,' he admitted, 'but I have to keep reminding myself that I didn't come all this way to enjoy myself. My father relies on me . . .'

'And *I* rely on you to help me forget the kind of life I've given up to follow you up here to this God-awful place.' She pressed herself close, smelling of flowers, her eyes bright and shining as they devoured his face.

'Lavinia,' he began, 'don't expect too much. I . . .'

She didn't let him finish the sentence, but rose on tip-toe to kiss him full on the mouth.

'There, you've said enough. Let's enjoy the night. I know of a quiet little arbour beside a bush of flowering gardenias. You'll think you've gone to heaven.'

As she promised, it was indeed like heaven, the creamy, sweet-scented blossoms perfuming the night air. Lavinia snuggled up beside him on the wide stone bench. With the scarcity of suitable young men in the Colony, Daddy had a way of reminding her that she should not be too tardy in seeking a husband. She had a horror of being urged into a marriage she didn't want, which she knew Daddy would do if the fancy took him, telling her not to be silly and that she shouldn't confuse love with wedded bliss. Her father dreamed of a dynasty stretching down over the years. This new country had unlimited possibilities and he was clear-headed enough to join Mr Rhodes and the other Empire builders in their search for power and wealth.

In Evan Jenkins she had seen all those things, or rather the prospect of them once the right woman took him in hand. At the moment he was too much under his father's thumb but she guessed – hoped! – he was young and gullible enough for her to do something about that. Remodelled by her skilful hands, Evan Jenkins would do very well as a husband.

Being her father's daughter, Lavinia Dolman had no intention of being left on the shelf.

The weather remained good and Alys was able to enjoy her sightseeing outings with Simon Rayne. Perversely, ignoring Marcus's frowns when she told him where she was going, she determined to enjoy herself. To her, it was the beginning of a new kind of relationship. Simon took her under his wing, as he put it, and began to show her the treasures of London. He seemed free to escort her whenever she had spare time, helping her to appreciate the galleries and museums of the city with his sagacious and witty comments.

He bought her hot roasted chestnuts from the street braziers; made her laugh when he insisted on giving her china ornaments from the market stalls – ugly cats and dogs, and exotic necklaces and bracelets of beaten silver. For those who had money, Alys decided, life in London was full and exciting. For those without, a never-ending struggle to earn food and shelter, never mind money for warm clothing.

Simon took her one evening to see the mass of humanity who slept 'under the arches'. Huddled in sheets of old newspaper, coughing and moaning, men and women drained the dregs from bottles of cheap gin, then, before her startled eyes, vomited in the gutter. Even old Lilith, in all her shoddy glory, had not shocked Alys as this scene did.

With the spell of fine weather, the ideal conditions that Marcus needed for his painting soon put a stop to her outings with Simon. She strongly suspected that Marcus took secret delight when such an outing had to be cancelled as a perfect morning dawned and she was summoned to the studio for her sitting. As the portrait progressed, he seemed to relax his attitude somewhat, bringing in fresh flowers which Alys arranged about the studio, and amusing her with his reminiscences of his student days in Paris.

They were interrupted one morning by the arrival of a young woman. Alys was at last to meet Joanna Ambrey. Lady Joanna, she reminded herself, remembering what Mrs Mimms had said about using her title. The newcomer wore a red silk square tied about her head, low over the brow, the casually knotted ends hanging over one ear. A matching silk top hung loosely over a pleated white skirt; her stockings were pale, a shiny silk. She looked very modern and sophisticated and her smile as she gazed at Alys was friendly. Alys took to her at once. Her eyes were a rich, deep blue and glowed in a strongly featured but classically beautiful face.

Joanna, the only child of the Earl of Ambrey and his wife, Sarah, had been comfortably reared in their lovely home in Sussex. She had received a better education than most girls in that late Victorian era. A lively and precocious girl, her father had sent her to finish her studies in Paris, where she acquired a taste for romantic revolutionary heroes and toyed with the idea of communism. On her return to England her father clearly expected her to marry and settle down, the fate, he explained to an impatient Joanna, of every woman.

Joanna had ideas of her own, scorning the idea of marriage, although she declared, if she ever *did* marry, it would be to her childhood hero, Marcus Dillon. He had painted her portrait when she was a young girl and it hung over the drawing-room fireplace in her father's home, a constant reminder of the tender feelings created in the seventeen-year-old Joanna by the artist's dark good looks. As she'd grown older, the feelings had changed to warm friendship on her part and good-humoured teasing on his. Each time her father brought up the subject of her marriage, she would smile and say Marcus held her heart and had not asked her yet, receiving a sour look for what her father called her 'irreverent attitude' to something so important.

She became involved with the Women's Suffrage Party and soon earned herself the reputation of a fire-brand, much to her parents' dismay. Despite all this, she possessed a grace and charm which endeared her to society and made her a favourite at most social events. Hostesses thought she was most alarmingly daring and her presence at any gathering always caused a stir.

Marcus turned as she entered the studio, eyebrows raised in surprise. He had not seen or heard from her in months. 'So, what fragrant breeze blows you in our direction, Joanna?'

'Does there have to be a reason?' She smiled artlessly at the two men for Simon, as usual, was hanging around. She crossed the room and planted a kiss on Marcus's cheek. 'I just thought I'd like to see how your new pro-ject was getting on.' She stood back, scrutinising the canvas with a critical eye, and then nodded her approval. 'Good, Marcus. Very good. I can see now why you

257

insisted on bringing your model back with you . . .' Even
away from her usual haunts, Joanna kept up with society
gossip. She made a little moue, then turning her head
lazily to smile at Alys, said, 'Forgive me, I made you
sound like a package mailed through the post. I didn't
mean to. You're a very lovely young woman and I can
only admire your stamina and patience, posing all day
under Marcus's forbidding eye. I've experienced it
myself. It's not much fun.'

Marcus knew she was teasing, for she'd once told him
that every minute spent in his company while his brush
flew over the canvas had been ecstasy. He remembered
how he had smiled at her ridiculous claims, aware of her
fidgety impatience.

'Depends what you mean by fun,' Simon broke in,
giving Alys a sideways look. 'We've been having our share
of fun these last few days, wouldn't you say, Alys?'

Marcus grunted, and said quite rudely, 'Haven't you
anything to do, Simon, besides making facetious remarks
that aren't even remotely funny?'

Simon turned to pull poor Rufus's tail, causing him to
lash out with an irritated yowl. Marcus thought he knew
exactly how the cat felt. Until then it had been lying in the
sunlit window, surveying the scene outside with half-
closed sleepy eyes. Its extended claws just caught Simon
on the knuckles and a spot of bright blood appeared,
causing him to frown. He held the back of his hand to his
mouth and glared at Rufus over it. 'Well, I guess I get the
hint. A bad-tempered cat is one thing, a bad-tempered
artist at work is another.' Turning to Joanna, he waggled
his fingers in a farewell gesture. 'Toodle-oo, old thing.
See you soon.'

When he'd gone, Marcus apologised for his rudeness, adding, 'The boy has such talent, it's a pity he's wasting it this way.'

'He doesn't seem to do much,' admitted Alys, hoping she did not sound too critical. 'Is he any good, then?'

'Very, when he can be bothered. He had one or two earlier successes and the fame's gone to his head. His father is well off so he doesn't have to worry about earning a living, a fatal situation for anyone in the arts.'

'Your father's well off, too,' pointed out Alys in a mild tone. 'But you work.'

He didn't tell her that he also had his moments but that with her there in the studio with him, it was almost impossible for him *not* to work. She was his inspiration, his Circe, and he wondered how he would cope if – when she decided she'd had enough of foggy old London – she desired to get back to the green fields and valleys of her homeland again.

He was aware that something in their relationship had altered, so subtly that she probably wasn't even conscious of it yet. But he was. Since coming home, being with her under the same roof, seeing her every day, he knew without a doubt that his feelings had changed and was a little frightened, refusing to acknowledge to himself what it might mean. The knowledge made him more brusque than ever, endeavouring to hide the sensations that rose in him whenever she was near. He wondered if she guessed. The world would be a disappointingly empty place if she went away. He dreaded the time when he might come down to breakfast and find only Mrs Mimms and Rufus to greet him . . .

Suddenly impatient, he was saying, 'Unless you have

come to tell me something important, Joanna, I suggest you follow Simon and play your little games elsewhere.'

'Oh, well, if you're going to be like that!' With a shrug of her silk-clad shoulders Joanna retreated to the doorway, throwing back over her shoulder, 'I'll come back later, Marcus, when you're in a better mood.' To Alys she said in a light, clear voice, 'I glimpse in you a kindred spirit. Are you interested in women's suffrage, by any chance? Women as a group can be a powerful influence.'

Alys looked at Marcus, her eyes seeking his doubtfully. 'I shouldn't think she's ever heard of it,' he grinned. 'But, knowing you, I have no doubt you will soon remedy that.' He turned back to his painting with a curt gesture to Alys to resume her pose. 'On your way now, Joanna, and allow me to get on with my work.'

'Whatever Your Lordship commands,' she replied in a flippant tone. 'Don't let him work you too hard, Alys. He will, given half a chance. Stick up for yourself, as all we women are going to have to do once we're strong enough.'

'What did she mean by women's suffrage?' Alys asked as soon as they were alone. 'I've never heard of it before.'

Marcus grinned, one eye half closed as he studied the angle of her jaw. 'Lift your head a little. It's not quite right . . .' He made a few brush strokes, gazing at her critically. Then he said, 'You probably *haven't* heard of it. I shouldn't think the women of the valleys would be interested in it, anyway.'

Alys felt her cheeks flush with swift anger. 'Why not? Why shouldn't they be interested in it?' His whole attitude had been derisive, as though the 'women of the valleys' were a breed apart, to be left to get on with their lives as nature intended, accepting the poor conditions without complaint.

She heard his sigh, as though she were a trying child asking foolish questions. 'Well, consider this. It's a movement that wants the Government to give equal rights to women with men under the law. To be admitted freely to universities, and especially to the practice of law, where prejudice has always held them back. Even today, few universities will take females and there are not nearly enough places to go round. Branches of the legal profession are still closed to women, as are, more often than not, positions as doctors. And, of course, there's the vote.' He gave her a quizzical look. 'Now do you see what I mean by the women of your valleys not being interested? Can you imagine the men accepting those conditions from their wives? The right to vote, to have a say in the country's future?'

Alys gave him a hard look, slightly piqued. 'You make them sound like simpletons.' But these ideas were so novel to her that she listened to him elaborate further on the scheme, wide-eyed and incredulous, feeling a quiver of excitement stir in her as she pondered on the way her own thoughts had often run over the subjugation of women by men like her stepfather.

'Joanna has opened an office in the East End,' Marcus continued as he wiped his brushes, his eyes thoughtful as they examined the way the portrait of Alys was beginning to take shape. Why could he never go wrong with this girl? He was sure that even if he worked blindfold he would still capture the beauty of that face and form, for there wasn't a moment of the day or night when she wasn't in his thoughts. But that must remain a secret between him and his conscience. He thought of the man who had been the father of her baby, something he had never discussed with her and never would, and imagined her scornful laughter if he should ever reveal his true feelings.

Unconsciously, he squared his shoulders, as though about to take on an adversary, aware of Alys's inquiring regard. 'And . . . ?' she prompted.

He smiled. 'A place where women can go and talk to her. It may do some good.' He shrugged. 'Only time will tell.'

'I take it you don't think so?'

'Oh, no, you're not getting me with that! You asked me and I've told you. Whether I agree with it or not is my own affair. I just don't want you getting mixed up in it, that's all. Joanna was lucky not to have been thrown into prison after that last march on Parliament, like a number of her followers.'

Alys gasped. 'Prison!'

'Yes, prison, and to add to their indignities, force fed when they went on hunger strike. Not a pleasant thought, you must admit. Something you most certainly should stay clear of.'

Being thrown into prison for your beliefs – what a romantic sound that had! thought Alys. And she very much resented his dictatorial attitude. 'And what if I do decide to become interested in it?' She lifted her chin as she looked at him.

'Then you can expect no help from me if the police become involved,' he replied stiffly. Female suffrage was manifestly a red rag to a bull as far as he was concerned. A fact that couldn't help surprising her, knowing as she did his liberal views on most things. Her chin tilted higher. She met his eyes squarely. She would not allow him to intimidate her, she would not! All the old feelings of resentment surged back.

When, a few days later, Joanna called again, Alys was to put those feelings into words that told Joanna that here was a new conscript. One after her own heart.

Chapter Seventeen

It was late afternoon and Marcus was out. Joanna explained that she was on her way to a rally, surprising Alys for the other woman was dressed in a white muslin dress whose one note of colour was the broad band of purple, white and green stripes across one shoulder. Her dark hair was uncovered and her cheeks flushed with excitement as she explained to Alys what she and her ladies were about.

'We're going to demand to see Mr Asquith and we are quite determined that if he refuses to see us there is going to be trouble.' She was so pale and dainty that it was difficult for Alys to think of her as one of those 'raging suffragettes' described by the newspapers. Since their first meeting Alys had been doing quite a bit of research, even picking Mrs Mimms's brains on the subject, although the older woman clearly had no time for all 'that nonsense', as she put it.

Joanna grasped Alys's hands in her own, crying, 'Oh, you must come with us, Alys! It is every woman's duty to stand up and make her feelings over men's injustices known.'

Mrs Mimms, standing at the sink scrubbing the pots from the day's lunch, grunted in a disparaging way and gave Alys a warning glance over her shoulder. The girl was getting entirely too involved with Miss Joanna's antics. Mr Marcus wouldn't be pleased. Although, she thought, with a husband like *she* had to suffer, pity she wasn't a few years younger and she might join 'em herself.

The thought of Marcus's disapproval spurred Alys on. In a firm voice, she said, 'What a wonderful idea! Of course I'll come. Thank you for thinking of me, Lady Joanna.'

Joanna waved an admonitory finger under her nose. 'Please! I scorn all titles and if you call me by mine I shall refuse to answer. Joanna, plain and simple.'

In the smart car she had waiting in the street, she settled Alys beside her in the back seat and motioned to the uniformed chauffeur to move off. They drove to Downing Street where a small crowd of women were waiting. The crowd surged forward as the car approached. Passers-by stared and red buses sounded their horns in disapproval; trams clanged their bells, the drivers glaring down at the women from their high seats.

Men in bowler hats with carefully furled umbrellas paused in their homeward rush and stared with distaste at the sudden furore in the usually quiet street. 'Votes for women!' the cry went up, and as one the women swelled in a wave of silken banners up the narrow street, coming to rest at number ten. Joanna stepped forward and lifted the highly polished brass knocker on the front door, letting it fall with a resounding thud.

Obviously warned beforehand of the women's arrival, a couple of hefty-looking detectives opened the door and stood glaring at Joanna.

Alys, in front of the small crowd, heard them order her away, and Joanna's reply that she would leave only after she had seen the Prime Minister. Before she had finished talking they had closed the door in her face.

Alys watched, barely daring to breathe as, undeterred, Joanna knocked again. This time the door was thrown open by the two men who grabbed her arms and thrust her back into the street, so roughly that she fell. The door was slammed shut again and a murmur went up from the crowd. Joanna cried in a loud, clear voice, 'If the Prime Minister will not listen to our grievances then we will have to get our message across by whatever means we can.'

On her feet again, her white dress torn at one shoulder, the skirt stained from the mud on the pavement, she jumped into a car parked nearby at the curb and, balanced precariously on the back seat, began to make a speech. Immediately, a small contingent of policemen, followed by police on horseback, appeared from the bottom of the street and charged forward.

Pulled roughly from the car, Joanna was promptly arrested and the women scattered. Alys knew she would never forget the brutality of those men as they seized the women by the scruff of the neck and pushed them along at arm's length, thumping them on the back as they went. A long-drawn-out wail of fear and outrage rose above the crowd and was drowned among the shrilling of police whistles. The very air smelled of danger and fear, but all Alys could feel was a growing anger that made her want to pull the policemen from their horses, as some of the women were trying without much success to do, and beat at their smug faces with closed fists.

She remembered the old constable at Craven Bay, how kind he'd been to her after Dan's death, and was awed at the strength of her own feelings.

The few women who took refuge in doorways were dragged down the steps and hurled in front of the horses, beaten all the while by the men.

A number of them retaliated by throwing stones which they took from their handbags and they also were arrested. The last Alys saw of Joanna was a white face peering through the barred window of a Black Maria.

For what seemed like hours, Mary had been waiting in the cold, dim corridor that connected with the cells. The stuffy darkness was depressing, the lamplight not reaching this far into the corridor. She had been led between high, forbidding walls, through doors opened and shut behind her by heavy-set warders with great jangling keys hanging at their waists.

Commanded to sit there and wait until she was called, Mary listened to the far-off cries, the curses and obscene language, that echoed out of the darkness as prisoners in the cells argued the rights and wrongs of their cases. Mary listened to them with pity and a kind of shrinking feeling as, unutterably weary from the long journey to Cardiff, she sat shivering in the cold air.

The scene with Miss Netta when she'd requested time off for the visit hadn't helped. She had listened with scorn to Mary's plea.

'Are you telling me that you want to go all that way to visit a murderer?' she'd breathed.

Mary, quick to anger, managed to control the sudden flash of temper at the girl's disparaging tone. 'Yes, I am, miss, and he's not a murderer. Nothing's been proved yet. I'd have asked your father if he was here, but seeing he isn't I'm asking you.'

'It makes no difference that my father is away. He would have given you the same short shrift as I intend to do.'

Mary stared at her, pale-faced but determined. 'I shall go,' she said firmly. 'I didn't have to ask, Miss Netta, I could just as easily have gone without your being any the wiser. But being underhand is not in my nature and so I'm asking your permission.'

Her eyes, large and a clear blue, seemed to send out a plea for understanding. 'I need only a few days. With luck I can be there and back and see Jackie in that time.'

Netta's smooth brow wrinkled. She got to her feet, her skirt rustling as she moved. Today she was dressed all in white and looked young and winsome with her soft fair hair and blue eyes. Mary wasn't fooled by that look. As she stood just inside the door of Netta's charming sitting room, hands clasped meekly in front of her, hidden in her white apron, Mary had a chill feeling of apprehension. Something terrible was about to happen, she felt it in her bones. And yet what could be more terrible than the fact that Jackie was in prison, accused of murder?

For all her brave words, she wondered what she would do if Netta really did refuse her request. Mary was suddenly aware that here was a crisis, that she must finally make a stand against this young woman.

Standing by the window, Netta didn't even bother to turn her head as she said, 'I'm sorry, but I still have to say no.'

Mary gazed down at the floor, her fingers grasped so

tightly together that the knuckles showed white. 'Then I'm afraid there is nothing left to say, Miss Netta.'

Recognising the defiance in her voice, the other girl drew in a rasping breath. 'You mean to disobey me?'

There was a short silence while it dawned on Netta that here was someone who was actually answering her back. She turned and her small, closed fist came down on the top of the bookcase with a thud. 'You stupid, ignorant girl! What makes you think Jackie will even want to see you, anyway?' She had not meant to say that, but couldn't help herself. The question had come rushing out, willy-nilly. 'If he wants to see anyone at all, it will be *me*. And as soon as I can arrange it I shall visit him, so you may as well not waste your time, my girl.'

She glared at the maid as though she would like to do her bodily harm, her face flushed an unbecoming crimson as Mary murmured, 'I don't believe you. You're lying.'

'All right, to prove my point, go. See what his reaction will be when he realises it's you who has come to visit him, not me.' She gave a harsh laugh. 'Just remember that you will not be welcomed back to this house. From this moment, you are dismissed. Get your things now, this minute, and go. And don't let me set eyes on you again, you little strumpet, for I swear I won't be responsible for my actions.'

Head held high, Mary left the room. It had been like a blow in the stomach, the other girl's claims that Jackie would prefer to see her and not Mary. Her worst fears had been put into words. How was she to cope with the jumbled emotions that seethed through her? Then her loyal spirit stiffened. She'd made up her mind, and nothing was going to stop her making that journey to poor, incarcerated Jackie. Besides which, she decided, she had put up with Miss Netta's spitefulness and ill-temper long enough. She'd be only too glad to be away from the young madam's eternal fault-finding.

'I'm so sorry, *cariad*!' Mrs Dean looked stricken as Mary related the scene that had taken place upstairs. 'I shall miss you, and I hate breaking in a new servant.' She sighed, her plump bosom heaving with the effort. 'But I did warn you. Lately Miss Netta has been more jumpy than ever. I took it as just being that the master was away and she with all the worries of the house on her shoulders.' She gave Mary a sharp look. 'What will your poor mam do with you out of work and another mouth to feed at home?'

Mary gave a wry smile. 'I'll soon find another job, don't you worry. Now I've got experience, it shouldn't be difficult.'

Mrs Dean pursed her lips. 'Without a reference?'

The thought hadn't occurred to Mary. She frowned. 'Yes, I suppose that would be too much, asking that madam to give me a reference now . . .'

A clatter of footsteps roused her from her reverie and she looked up to see a warder approaching. He beckoned with one hand, as though she were an animal and unable to understand her own language. She wondered, if they could make her feel so degraded and inferior, what must it be like for Jackie?

Their footsteps echoed down the long corridors as she followed the man, and then he was unlocking a heavy wooden door and indicating that she should enter. The room was tiny, with a stone floor and a little barred window, not designed to open, set high up near the ceiling. A flickering gas jet was set in an opening in the wall, shielded by a thick, semi-opaque pane of glass.

There was a wooden table with a rough bench on either side and she was bidden curtly to sit down. A moment later the door opened again and Jackie was ushered in. She heard his breath catch sharply as he saw who it was, and heard her name breathed in a low, harsh whisper. 'Mary!'

Although her heart thudded so much she was sure he could hear it, she tried to make her voice sound natural. 'How are you, boyo? It's a treat to see you again.'

Looking into his drawn face and red-rimmed eyes, she wanted to take his hand and run with him from this awful place of confinement, out into the fresh air and sunshine, away from the hard-faced man who sat on a chair behind them, observing their every movement. If it were possible to swop places with Jackie, she would have, and gladly, for she guessed her own resources were superior to his. It would be the end of him if he was forced to stay in this terrible place for any length of time.

The only words he seemed capable of uttering were a strangled mixture of her name, and pleas for her to go and not see him like this.

'I had to come,' she told him, leaning over the table until the warder told her in a rough voice to sit back. 'I had to see how you were, didn't I?'

'I'm not worth your concern, Mary. Not now, not any more.'

'Don't you dare say that, Jackie Rees,' she flared at him. 'No one is going to stop me seeing you. *No one.*' She wondered if Netta Jenkins really did think enough of him to visit, then pushed the thought away in irritation. She'd cross that bridge when she came to it.

He asked her about her family, then about his Aunt Ellen, and Mary told him all the news. Tears came to his eyes and Jackie felt as if his heart was breaking, locked up with no way out. Not for a good, long time anyway. 'How is my aunt managing on her own?' he wanted to know. 'Oh, Mary, I would do anything to put the clock back to the time before . . .' He didn't think he had the courage to say the words aloud. 'I've made a right fool of myself, haven't I?' was all he could manage.

And she, with no beating about the bush, answered, 'Yes, you have.' Ignoring the warder whose attention for the moment was distracted by the rattle of rain on the tiny window, she took Jackie's two hands in hers and, gazing into his eyes, said gently, 'You haven't told me why you did such a foolhardy thing, stealing from that old Jew boy. I still think it must have been two other people, not the Jackie Rees I know.' And she smiled at her little attempt to find humour in the situation. The warder, his attention returning once more to his charge, said gruffly, 'Enough of that. No touching.'

'All right, keep your hair on,' she said flippantly. Through the side of her mouth she whispered, 'Thinks I'm slipping you a file, does he, to help you saw your way out of this hole?'

'And no whispering,' snapped the warder.

'Whist, someone got out of bed the wrong side this morning,' answered Mary unbowed.

Seeing her courage, Jackie wondered why he should be so lucky as to have a girl like her so steadfastly loyal to him. He didn't deserve it. Not after the way he'd played fast and loose with her affections. He'd known it was wrong and yet still delighted in the reeling of his senses whenever Miss Netta was near, his traitorous body yearning for her. She'd been like a drug, blinding him to all else, urging him to behave in a manner entirely foreign to his nature.

Mary's heart went out to him as she gazed at his stricken face. She loved him so much! Although the memory of that summer when she'd thought she had lost him would always torment her, there was not a thing in her loyal make-up that would have him any different. He was young and vigorous, a good-looking man, and she'd been the envy of her friends when he had taken her arm, walking out with her. She would rather belong to Jackie Rees, with all his faults and weaknesses, than any other man she knew. And she wasn't about to let a strumpet like Netta Jenkins spoil it all . . .

Her thumb gently rubbed the back of his hand to express her understanding. His gaze dropped from hers as he went on in a strangled voice, 'I was sorry the moment I did it, Mary. So ashamed that I ran off and left the old man like that. But I didn't have the nerve to stay and risk being caught. I meant to give the ring back – I wouldn't have kept it . . .'

She knew his thoughts were back in that ill-lit shop, with the old pawnbroker peering at him over his spectacles. She remembered the time she and Alys had gone there to inquire about Alys's mam's wedding ring and how scary the whole experience had been. How they had fled back into the sunshine, clutching each other in fright.

His voice had trailed away into nothing and Mary

longed to put her arms about him, to hold him close, but with the sharp eyes of the warder upon them she knew this wasn't possible. She couldn't risk Jackie getting into trouble as she knew the warders would take their displeasure out on him.

Her thoughts spinning in dismay, she reached for the words to convey how she felt. But all she could say was, 'It's all right, my love, all right.'

'I felt so humiliated, I couldn't bear it. I ran away in a blind panic . . .' He raised his head to look at her, his eyes beseeching. 'But I didn't kill him, Mary. I didn't hurt him as they say I did. He was still on his feet and cursing me when I left.' And then it came pouring out, the thing he would never have admitted to Mary under any other circumstances. 'She wanted a ring. I only went in to ask the price of the ring . . .'

The warder rose from his seat behind them. 'That's enough,' he said, unfeelingly. 'The visit's over.'

Mary reached out blindly. 'I'll come again. I will, Jackie. Nothing will keep me away.'

He reached for her awkwardly then turned away quickly and plunged through the door, closely followed by the warder. Mary stood in that cheerless room, shaken by soundless sobs, until she heard the door behind her open again and a voice tell her she might go. And as she walked back along the endless corridors, head held high, she couldn't help thinking that what she would dearly love the most was to get hold of that bloody ring and shove it down Miss Netta's throat. Aye, and watch the bitch choke on her own greed.

Chapter Eighteen

Dry winds blew flurries of red dust across the wide, flat veldt; whirling dust-devils that had the horses skittering with unease. Lavinia's gloved hands tightened on the reins. The small picnic party ranged ahead, voices and laughter strangely magnified in the dry air. Lavinia and Evan paced their horses sedately, enjoying the solitude this leisurely ride afforded. Particularly Lavinia.

At least she had Evan to herself. She was determined to make the most of this outing, and the overnight stop it would necessitate.

In the distance she could see the river, a wide, tumbling mass of green water, foaming white where large boulders lay partly submerged. She wondered how anyone dared to try and cross to the far lands in the north, and remembered the tales told by Mr Harvey of how the canvas-covered wagons were floated across with the team of oxen swimming before them. She shivered. Not for her the life of a pioneer! This well-planned picnic was the nearest she would ever want to come to it.

Choosing a place where a stand of wild mimosa cast welcome shadows on the grass beneath, the servants spread blankets and rugs, laying out an assortment of wines and bread, cold ham and roast suckling pig, and the apricots, peaches, mangoes and other delicious fruits native to the country.

It was proposed, very daringly and to the shrieks of the ladies in the party, suitably shocked, that they should sleep in the open, the weather being sufficiently tranquil. Lavinia looked pleased and excited. Evan fretted, wondering why he had allowed himself to be tempted into coming on this childish expedition.

But by the time the swift African dusk had set in and one of the young beaus was playing songs on a concertina to which the small party sang along, Evan's feelings had undergone a change. When Lavinia took his hand and drew him away from the fire, the moonlight and music and the slight hint of lurking danger seemed to go to his head. He followed submissively.

It was sheer magic there by the fast-flowing river, the sky a dark purple velvet and the stars so bright and enormous it seemed as though one could reach up and touch them.

'I like it here,' he said, stretching out on the lush grass, his hands behind his head. 'I didn't think I would, but I do.'

'Do you?' Lavinia's voice purred. 'You're not sorry you came?'

He opened his eyes and smiled. 'Does it matter now? We're here together, aren't we? Isn't that what you wanted?' Tentatively she put her hands on his chest, sliding them across his shirt, one slipping slyly to the gap between the buttons. He felt it warm on his skin, the fingers trembling slightly. His heart began beating heavily and he was conscious of a desire that was almost alarming. He ought to get up and walk back to the others, to the safety of the firelight and the singing group of young people. His limbs refused to move, his throat felt dry.

'God, you're lovely!' he muttered. Her face was close above him, shutting out the moon. He felt the soft yielding of her breast as she leaned against him and pulled her head down so that her mouth rested on his, giving himself up rapturously to the kiss.

He felt shivers run through her and her hands slid further under his shirt. He could feel the heavy beating of her heart joining with his own and their kiss deepened, her lips parting under the urgency of his.

'It's not fair,' he said at last, pushing her away with his hands on her shoulders. 'Starting something you can't finish.'

'Who says I can't finish it?' The sounds of music and laughter drifted to them from out of the darkness. 'We're sleeping under the stars, aren't we? And you know what the stars do to me . . .'

Mrs Mimms's guess had been correct. Marcus was furious at the news of Joanna's arrest and Alys's involvement in the demonstration. Ignoring her plea that she wanted to go with him to court the following morning, he stormed out of the house, calling on the heavens to damn all women and their stubborn resistance to the established order.

Joanna had been charged with trespassing and causing a disturbance of the peace. She was released with a caution that she was to behave herself and cause no further disturbance.

Her father came up to London and whisked her away

to their country manor, exchanging grim looks with Marcus. Later he faced a belligerent Alys. 'Have you any idea what the newspapers will make of this?' he shouted.

Alys sighed. 'No, but I'm sure you're going to tell me.'

'Can you take nothing seriously, girl? Didn't I explain about the threat of prison, the truly awful conditions you would be facing there? Are you too dumb to understand what I say?'

'Joanna did none of the things she was accused of,' replied Alys indignantly. 'She merely knocked on the Prime Minister's door and asked to speak to him. Where was the harm in that? In fact, it was the police who were in the wrong. I'll never forget the brutality they used towards those poor, defenceless women.'

'Defenceless, huh!' Marcus snorted contemptuously. 'With stones already in their handbags, ready to throw at anyone who tried to stop them? Premeditated violence, that's what it was. Joanna was lucky to come before a sympathetic magistrate. She could have fared much worse.'

They stared at each other in silence, and his eyes searched hers as though he could read every thought in her mind. Well, do him good if he could, she thought peevishly! She lifted her chin and for a moment his expression softened, his lips twisting into a smile. He turned away, as though washing his hands of the whole thing. 'Please, just heed my warning and stay clear of Joanna's crazy little schemes. It's a fad that I hope will pass, as all her others have.'

Alys felt her eyes fill with tears. 'They were so full of hate, those men, as though the women were beasts of the field, not wives and mothers.'

'It's the way they have to be. And don't cry, for God's sake! Please don't cry, Alys.'

'I'm not crying.'

'It was a gallant gesture. Joanna will remember it proudly, not with tears. I'm sorry you were there to see it. She should have had more sense than to ask you along.'

Alys shook her head. 'She didn't have to twist my arm. I wanted to go.'

'Well, now you've seen what can happen, perhaps in the future you'll not let emotion sway your judgement.'

For an instant she saw Evan Jenkins's smile and felt the stirring of an old emotion in her heart. A blush stained her cheeks as she wondered if it was her relationship with Evan to which he was alluding. 'I am inclined to do that, aren't I?' she said ruefully.

He gave her a searching look then turned away, speaking over his shoulder as he stood before the easel. 'And if you could arrange to hold that blush, I would be much obliged. It is worthy of Renoir.'

It was very civilised, reclining in one of the comfortable chairs before the log fire, wonderful not to feel crowded and hemmed in. Here there was room to breathe. They had heard no more of Joanna, and Marcus said she had gone abroad, to Paris, at her parents' urging.

When Marcus was out, Alys wandered alone through the garden at the back of the house or browsed to her heart's content in the library. When he was at home but busy, she didn't disturb him, seeming to know instinctively that he needed peace and quiet. After a time she knew he would come looking for her and they would sit and talk or perhaps just stroll in the garden. At times it seemed as though there was no one else in the world but the two of them; the whistling of the delivery boys as they rode their bicycles in the street outside, the horses and carriages passing, the laughter and shrill voices of the children in the small park opposite, all receding into the background. Sometimes he would take her for short drives in the white car.

Unconsciously she engraved certain scenes in her mind so that they would stay with her forever. There were late roses in the garden, yellow and pink and white, fragrant in the cool air. Marcus would pause in their stroll to pluck one, handing it to her with a small, mocking bow. And yet, not the same kind of mockery he had shown her when they first met. Rufus would come padding after them, purring softly, and she would bend and cradle him in her arms, holding him against her, feeling him kneading at her chest with soft, strong paws, the claws only slightly extended. Together they would laugh and fuss over him.

Alys had to face the fact that she was beginning to enjoy Marcus's company. When he had been away, visiting his parents, she would look forward to his return, watching from behind the lace curtains in the front room for his car to draw up and park by the curb.

She looked forward to his homecoming with an excitement that was disturbing. When he entered the room and smiled his hello, she had to lower her gaze in case her eyes gave her away. She avoided his touch, that casual way he had of grasping her by the elbow to guide her through a doorway or pulling her by the hand into the garden, eager to show her something. She knew that he would feel her tremble. When their eyes met, her breath caught in her throat and the tightness in her chest was painful.

As for Marcus, he had no thoughts, no eyes, for anything but her beauty. He remembered how she had knelt before the fire in her shabby kitchen that chill night when he had caught her washing her hair; the way she had turned her head to greet him from the back of the small donkey – haughty, proud, rejecting his proposals with withering scorn.

She had lived in his house for a while and at first he had tried to deny the feelings her presence aroused in him. Now he acknowledged to himself for the first time that she had bewitched him and he was actually enjoying it.

The days on which they did not work passed in a delightful haze of wanderings in which they discovered parts of the city which Simon had neglected to show her. And when Marcus was busy, when she walked alone, his face was always before her, imprinted on her mind's eye. She walked by the Thames, running her fingers along the top of the smooth, grey stones of the Embankment wall. Gulls cried above the shining, pewter-coloured water, rising and falling in their constant search for food, reminding her so much of Craven Bay that for a moment she experienced deep pangs of homesickness. And then she thought again of Marcus, his mouth so firm and well shaped, body strong and muscular and was glad that she was here.

She did not dare think of what might happen when the portrait was finally finished. He had made no reference to his future plans and she had not questioned him. Would he ask her to stay, to pose for yet another picture?

She had heard of artists who used the same model over and over again but it was usually a wife or mistress who filled that fortunate role. And she was neither . . .

She blushed for even considering such an eventuality. Marcus had always been the perfect gentleman, never once bringing up her past transgression with Evan. What would her reaction be if he should ever suggest such a thing? she wondered. And could she trust her heart to let her do the right thing?

She accepted Mrs Mimms's offer to trim her hair into a neater style, content to let the older woman brush the vibrant mass into shining waves and then weave them into a soft chignon low on the nape of her neck, allowing soft curls to escape about her cheeks, softening the severity of the style. She took out and studied the new dresses she had purchased from the Co-op Stores before leaving Craven Bay, slipping them on and posing before the bedroom mirror, admiring herself and hoping Marcus would also. For suddenly, it seemed very important that she should please him.

To distract herself – for she had been told that the best form of therapy for mental distraction was physical toil – she was sweeping the drifts of fallen leaves from the paved path in the garden one morning when Marcus appeared behind her. She heard his footsteps and turned, pink and slightly tousled by the wind. They both laughed as Rufus, never far away from her these days, made a sudden dart and buried himself amidst the leaves. 'Idiot cat!' said Marcus amiably, and Alys laughed again and shooed the sleek ginger cat away with her broom.

'He thinks I'm doing it for his benefit,' she said, watching as the cat scampered away through the bushes.

'Why are you doing it at all?' he wanted to know. 'The man will be here tomorrow. There's no need for you to worry your head about fallen leaves. Anyway, I've just received a letter from my mother, inviting us down to the country for the weekend.' She stared at him, surprised. 'So you can start thinking of what you will need to pack,' he finished, taking her acceptance for granted.

She scooped up the leaves in an untidy pile and carried them to the wheelbarrow at the end of the lawn. The small task gave her time to ponder his words. Releasing the leaves, she watched them settle on the pile already there. Some of them blew away and Rufus emerged from hiding and chased after them, enjoying himself immensely. She laughed again. 'I hate to say it, but you really *do* have an idiot cat.'

He grinned. 'At least there's one thing we agree on.' He turned to go and then said over his shoulder, 'And pack that evening dress, the Japanese kimono thing. There'll probably be a dance in the evening.'

Pushing aside her doubts about the future, Alys set off determined to enjoy herself, only slightly worried about what Marcus's parents would think of her. She found the drive in Marcus's car a truly thrilling experience. Seated on the leather seat beside him, she felt as if she were riding the wind. The road stretched ahead of them. Fields and farmland lay on either side, bounded by hedges or walls constructed of pale stones piled in intricate patterns, one on top of the other.

Marcus told her that some of these walls had stood for over a hundred years in spite of their fragile appearance and Alys didn't scoff, as she would once have done, saying airily that she knew that. The sky was a pale blue, washed on the horizon by purple clouds, the colour of the blackberries that she had seen ripening in the hedgerows as they passed. It was very quiet with only the wind nudging at the car and the cry of the rooks attracted by the sight of the harrowed but uncultivated fields. Beside her, Marcus was quiet, but for the odd reference to the countryside. He pointed out the land that belonged to his family when they came to it, and Alys saw the tenant farms dotting the vast estate at irregular intervals as they approached the main house along the narrow, winding road.

It stood in pastoral beauty with a wide, shining river sparkling in the background. The nineteenth-century mansion, consisting of a wide central section with two curved wings half circling a courtyard, enchanted Alys. Only in picture books had she seen anything like it and could hardly believe that she, Alys Hughes, the little cockleshell girl from Craven Bay, could actually be attending a function in this magnificent place.

Marcus's parents' were charming, coming out to greet them with outstretched hands and welcoming smiles. His father, a tall, elderly man with white hair carefully brushed to conceal its sparsity, smiled and held her hand and said how pleased he was to meet her after all this time as his son had talked about her so much. About to say flippantly: 'All good things, I hope?' Alys stopped herself in time, and with a dignity that had Marcus grinning bowed her head and said demurely how pleased she was to meet them, too.

Marcus's mother, a faded ash-blonde who was still beautiful, gazed at her thoughtfully but said very little after the first greeting. Alys wondered what was going through her mind, for surely of the many girls Marcus must have brought down here, she must be unique. She followed the rest of the family into a wide hallway and then into a drawing room filled with the scent of late roses. Mr Dillon gave her a chance to settle herself on a flower-patterned settee before offering her a drink. She accepted gratefully, taking the long-stemmed glass of pale sherry and sipping it slowly. Other guests joined them, some young, some obviously friends of his father and mother. They stared at her, the smiles on their faces studiedly polite, allowing her to interpret them as she pleased.

She wondered if Joanna Ambrey would appear and turned her head quickly when she heard the other girl's name mentioned. Someone remarked it was a pity she couldn't come as she always made a party. Joanna, it seemed, was still languishing abroad, licking her wounds after her tussle with the law.

Later, Alys came down from the pretty room she had been given, very self-conscious in her new evening frock. With it she wore the string of amber beads left to her by her mother. Their weight gave her comfort and confidence, two things she badly needed on this occasion. She stopped at the window halfway down the staircase, gazing out at a landscape that strengthened her feeling that all this must be a dream. A full moon pierced the darkness, and there were Chinese lanterns of many colours artfully placed among the sparse foliage of the trees. The house itself was ablaze with lights and dec orated with fresh flowers. Champagne flowed freely and fluted crystal glasses were filled and refilled. To her relief and gratitude, Marcus stayed by her side for the first part of the evening, as though to guide her through the unfamiliar territory of the English Society World. Aware of the curious glances directed at her, when he asked her to dance she was overcome with bashfulness. Marcus's hand on her elbow urged her forward.

As his arms enclosed her and they took to the floor, her colour was high. She had never felt so conspicuous and disconcerted in all her life. Marcus seemed to sense this. For a moment his arms tightened and he said, 'Relax, girl. You're supposed to be enjoying yourself.' He grinned affably. 'You are, aren't you?'

'I'm sorry. Of course I'm enjoying myself. Who wouldn't in this lovely house? It's just that . . .'

'What?'

How was she to answer? She was among people whom Mary would call her 'betters', while for him this was an everyday occurrence. It brought home all the differences between them. Who did she think she was, dancing with the heir to all this opulence, having attention shown to her by servants who were probably better educated than herself? Although everyone behaved impeccably, she was sure there were sly looks and whispers being cast in their direction. As they circled the floor she wondered how many of the couples present took it for granted that she was Marcus's mistress.

Then the music ended and he excused himself, saying he had to speak to some old friends but would see her later. 'Have fun,' he cautioned, and then vanished in the direction of a group of people standing on the periphery watching the dancers.

To her delight, she saw Simon Rayne. Or rather

caught a brief glimpse of him as he appeared to have arrived late and seemed intent on seeking out friends.

A number of young men asked her to dance and she enjoyed their company so much she began to chide herself for her earlier misgivings.

It was later in the evening, when she was passing through the throng of guests, intent on getting some fresh air for the room had become smoky and over-heated, that she heard snatches of a conversation that stopped her in her tracks.

Screened by a large, potted palm, two people were talking. She heard the woman's voice, soft and cultured. 'Don't you realise you are jeopardising the girl's good name? What do you intend to do with her once the painting is done? You surely cannot expect her to go back to the valleys of Wales after she's served your purposes.'

Spoken by Martha Dillon, the words were like a dash of cold water in Alys's face.

'Mother!' Marcus sounded annoyed. 'I hold no sway over Alys. She is a free agent and at perfect liberty to return to Craven Bay or stay in London. I certainly would not stand in her way, whichever path she chose.'

'And what on earth would she do in London? A girl like that, on her own.'

'From listening to fellow artists, I should think she'd have no difficulty making her way. She'd be inundated with offers of work that would keep her in comfort for years to come.'

As she stood rooted to the spot, something seemed to die within Alys, leaving a cold, empty pit of sickness and despair. Marcus had sounded so devoid of interest, so *bored*, as though what might become of her was not even worth considering. Her shoulders slumped; feeling as though her bright new world had suddenly come to an end, she hurried to the open French doors and walked straight into the arms of Simon Rayne.

'Whoa there, where's the fire?' He grinned down into her face. 'Slow down, old girl, or you're likely to end up in the lily pond.'

Angrily she dashed away the incipient tears. Of anger or disappointment? She wasn't sure. There was an element of both in the way Marcus's words had affected her. Her smile was rueful as she said, 'The way I'm feeling at the moment, I'd probably welcome it.'

'And spoil that very becoming dress!' His gaze took in the kimono-style gown with its daring wrapover skirt revealing her knees when she walked, the deep plum colour contrasting beautifully with her dark hair and pale skin. 'I won't hear of it. Come on,' taking her elbow in a firm grasp, 'let's seek out some more of our host's excellent champagne. You look as though you could do with a drink.'

Replenishing their glasses, he led her to a seat on the wide stone balcony with a view of the river shining under a full moon. He settled her with great care.

'This is marvellous,' he murmured, sipping his drink. 'I have to admit I wasn't exactly looking forward to this party. Sometimes Marcus's parents, although sweet, can be a bit of a bore, but finding you here has really made my evening. And that dress . . . wow!' His look was so expressive she had to laugh in spite of herself.

He settled back in his seat, stretching his legs before him. 'Now, you've never told me the story of your life. Don't you think, as we're such good friends, I ought to know who I've been escorting about London?'

It was the very last thing Alys intended to do. 'You wouldn't be interested. Tell me yours instead.'

He sighed. 'Very boring, but if you insist – born twenty-two years ago, grandfather made the family fortune in stocks and shares, went to the usual schools, got into the usual scrapes, met Marcus through my older sister, Ruth, who had a thing about him at one time. Didn't last long, Marcus tires easily. Funny bloke! Or maybe he's never met the one girl he considers right for him.'

Alys took a sip of her champagne. 'What about Joanna? I understood they . . .' She hated herself for bringing up the subject of Joanna – she hoped he wouldn't think she was prying – yet somehow the question slipped out.

'Joanna?' He looked blank.

'Yes, aren't they supposed to be getting engaged or married or something, quite soon?' Mrs Mimms's words came back to her: 'We've been waiting for the engagement to be announced, and then St Margaret's Westminster had better get ready for the wedding of the year.'

He pulled a clown's face. 'Believe that and you'll believe anything! Joanna's got her sights set on higher things.'

Another sip of the golden liquid had Alys giggling. 'You can't marry the Women's Suffragette Movement! You'd find it a pretty cold bed-fellow on a cold winter's night.'

Her cheeks flamed, seeing Simon's disbelieving look. Women – nicely brought up young women – did not discuss things like that in front of men, she reminded herself. She wasn't with Mary now, gossiping freely about subjects that would have had her own mother paling.

'You're quite a gal, aren't you, Alys Hughes?' he said. His gaze fell to her almost empty glass. 'Let me get you another drink.'

She held her glass to her chest, covering it with one hand. 'Oh no, I'd better not. I'm not used to this stuff.'

'You might get squiffy! So?' He slid her a questioning glance. 'What's so wrong about that? You only live once.'

But Alys was not to be drawn on the subject. She leaned her head back against the ivy-covered wall and looked up at the moon-washed sky. 'Isn't this a lovely night?'

Out of the corner of her eye, she saw his rueful grimace. 'What shall we do, then? Do you want to dance?'

She shook her head. She didn't want to go back into that room, perhaps seeing Marcus holding another girl in his arms while they danced to the music of the small band playing in its flower-filled alcove under the wide, curving staircase. Didn't want to see the way he would smile down into the girl's eyes, his lips only inches from her cheek . . .

'I'm quite happy here, aren't you?' She turned her head to smile at him lazily, the moonlight making pools of purple mystery of her eyes, her lips full and tempting . . .

Unable to help himself, Simon bent his head and placed his own mouth over hers, holding the kiss for a long, sweet moment. He could feel her trembling and longed to pull her roughly towards him, keep her in his embrace for the rest of the evening . . .

And then she was pushing at his shoulders, twisting her head. 'Simon!'

He drew back, hunching his shoulders as though warding off a blow. 'You know how to keep a fellow in his place, don't you? Just when I was beginning to enjoy myself, too.' He rose to his feet. 'I'll get another drink. For myself, at least, if you're sure you don't want one.'

He looked so dejected, she relented. 'All right. Just half a glass then.'

She sat there, eyes half closed, listening to the drift of music, humming the refrain: 'A sweet little nest, out there in the west, and let the rest of the world go by . . .' Feeling deliciously drowsy, she gazed at the river mist tinted amber by the diffusion of light from the full moon which hung suspended within it like a round yellow balloon.

'On an evening such as this, your friend Mary would no doubt swear to seeing fairies dancing over the garden.'

The words were so in tune with her own mood that she jumped. She opened her eyes fully and turned her head to see Marcus, an enigmatic smile playing about his mouth, staring down at her. Her stomach contracted and she cursed herself for allowing him to have this effect on her. 'Oh, hello,' she said feebly. 'I thought you were busy elsewhere.'

'Meaning I've been neglecting you?' He came closer and sat down beside her on the bench. She saw he carried a black wrap in his hands. 'I saw you running out and brought you this.' He gazed pointedly down at her dress.

'You must be frozen in that thing, although I have to admit that it's very becoming.'

'I'm all right.'

'Don't argue. Here, put this about your shoulders.' He handed her the black velvet wrap with its collar of white fur, watching as she took it and snuggled into its warmth, burying her chin in the soft luxurious fur. She hadn't realised it was cold but suddenly her bare arms were cold and covered in goose pimples, the pale skin exposed by the low neck of the icy gown.

'Thanks,' she mumbled, and he leaned over and tugged in a slightly proprietorial way at the long wrap so that it covered her exposed knee. He shrugged. 'It's one of my mother's.' Then, in a sharper voice: 'Why are you sitting out here on your own? Doesn't the music appeal to you?'

'I wasn't alone. I was with Simon. He's just gone in to get us another drink.' The way she said it, followed by a low laugh, set his mouth into a hard, straight line and she felt a thrill of triumph that he should read in her voice the fact that she wasn't averse to Simon's company.

'Sorry, I thought perhaps you needed rescuing.'

She turned wide eyes on him. 'Rescuing? Of course not. Why on earth should you think that? I find Simon very good company.'

'It's one of my more endearing traits. When I see a pretty young girl sitting alone in the moonlight, I always want to rescue her.' His tone was heavily sarcastic.

Alys wrinkled her nose. 'You're incorrigible!'

'I also help little old ladies across the road.'

She laughed again and he said, 'Well, I'll leave you in Simon's good hands.' The young man had come rushing back, carrying two glasses. 'Oh – hello, Marcus!'

He towered above the younger man. In his dark well-cut evening clothes he looked very impressive indeed. Beside him, Simon looked ordinary, with his longish fair hair and pink cheeks and boyish grin. Alys felt almost motherly towards him.

'Hello, Simon.' Marcus greeted him pleasantly. 'So you made it?'

'A bit late, but better late than never, what?' Simon laughed.

The other man's eyes fell on the brimming glasses he carried. 'Don't ply Alys with too much of that stuff, will you? She's not used to it.'

'Like many things in my new life,' she said blithely, holding out her hand for the glass, 'I believe it is something I could get used to very easily.'

To prove her point, she took too large a gulp of the champagne, feeling the bubbles go up her nose. She laughed again.

Simon grinned widely. He glanced at Marcus as though judging his reaction. Alys could feel the other man's eyes on her as she settled back once more in her seat, the champagne working its magic, making her feel warm and cosy and so light she wondered why she didn't float away, up into that midnight-blue sky to join the lovely yellow moon and the icily twinkling stars.

She heard Marcus say: 'As long as you know what you're doing.'

She smiled, closing her eyes again. 'I know exactly what I'm doing.'

Chapter Nineteen

The death of Jakob Rozenberg was still very much a topic of conversation in Craven Bay. Nobody could recall anything like it happening before and the small town was divided, with different ideas and opinions bandied about. Most were on the side of the accused young man, for Jackie Rees had been well liked in the town.

'Wouldn't hurt a fly, wouldn't Jackie,' declared David Davis, watching the barman fill his tankard with foaming ale. 'Only time I saw 'im lose 'is rag was when someone started to taunt Mary O'Malley about her Irish ancestry.'

There was a general laugh from the men crowding the bar. 'Aye, and that girl can look out for herself, all right, wi'out Jackie sticking up for 'er,' replied one of the men standing next to him at the bar.

'Right,' said David staunchly, 'so I can see no way that Jackie would do such a thing. Why should he want to rob old Jakob's shop, anyway? Naught but a lot of other people's old rubbish in there, as far as I can see.'

Silence fell on the company; loyalty to a mate was paramount in this close-knit community. Something that didn't always apply to their womenfolk, as Alys had found to her cost.

The figures of the two boys were silhouetted against the pale blue of the sea, their voices occasionally reaching Netta as she walked her horse along the path on the cliff top.

Last night in bed, she had finally made up her mind. It was as though everything had come to a watershed, made suddenly clear to her. Her father would be delighted with her decision. For the last couple of years he had been hinting heavily about marriage plans; how, when she finally decided, they would go to Paris where she would choose the finest silk and have it made up into a wedding dress by France's leading couturier. The Honiton lace veil worn by her mother was safely packed away in tissue paper but could be brought out at a moment's notice.

She knew now she had no choice but to go forward. There were of her acquaintance half a dozen young men who would jump at the chance of marrying into the Jenkins family, with its rapidly expanding empire of coal mines in Britain and the gold-mining venture in the new lands of Africa.

Most of them, she knew, had been in love with her for years. Or so they professed. The idea of tying herself to one man for the rest of her life was intolerable but she had left herself no other option.

She had known almost at once, as soon as she missed her monthly period, that she was pregnant with Jackie's child. Fool that she was, she should be furious at her own stupidity. She, who had always been so sure that she alone was in control of her destiny! Now she knew she wasn't. Outside influences intruded and all you could do was to accept the changes as gracefully as you knew how.

Perhaps, in a way, this was for the best, for who knows what terrible mistake she might have made if Jackie had not been taken out of the picture.

Below her on the beach, almost drowned by the shriek of the seagulls, the childish voices of the two boys sent a flock of the noisy birds swirling from their nests on the rocky ledges of the cliffs. The rubber sling on Kenny's catapult made a slight twanging sound as another well-aimed pebble sent them soaring again from where they had been quarrelling noisily over a dead crab at the water's edge.

'Got 'em!' yelled Dennis in admiration of his brother's prowess.

Kenny gave him a warning glance. 'Shhh,' he warned with a jerk of his head towards the cliff top. 'Don't want 'er to 'ear, do we?'

The little boys were playing truant, enjoying themselves immensely away from the watchful eye of the old soldier who ran the village school with army-style severity.

They knew if they were caught they would face a sound thrashing but that didn't usually stop them from enjoying their stolen moments of freedom. Dennis had always followed his older brother. They were as close as twins in spirit and only ten months apart in age but Kenny had always been the leader in all things.

Soon they were daring each other as to the height and length of their sling-shots. 'Bet you couldn't hit that bush up there,' said Dennis, pointing to where three-quarters of the way up the cliff side a shrubby bush covered in yellow flowers grew within a cleft of the rock.

Kenny's mouth twisted with derision. ' 'Course I can,' he boasted, fitting a large white pebble into the catapult. 'Nothin' to it.'

'Go on, then, let me see you do it.' His brother watched as Kenny let fly at the precise moment Netta approached the very edge of the cliff and peered over.

'*Duw*!' The boys turned and ran, scattering sand as they flew, the shrieks of the gulls all about them. 'She's the one who's got it in for our Mary,' breathed Dennis. 'That posh one from up by the big house. We oughtta do somethin' about the way she's been treatin' our Mary.'

Kenny, the instigator of any trouble, said thought-fully, 'We could make a plan. Perhaps lure her to the beach one night and then . . .' He made a gesture with the side of his hand, followed by a thumb slice across the throat. Seeing his brother's alarmed frown, he added indulgently, 'We wouldn't really have to cut her throat . . . well, maybe just a little bit.'

Dennis inwardly digested the suggestion then nodded and said, 'Good idea. Show 'er she can't treat us O'Malleys like that and get away with it.'

Once she had made up her mind, Netta was not one to dawdle. Time was of the essence, she couldn't afford to wait. Her father had no sooner returned from his busi-ness trip, jubilant and full of rhetoric about his successes in the city, than she was seeking his permission to visit Clarissa once again in Cardiff.

Thomas Jenkins looked perplexed. 'Again! It's not long since you were there. And, if I remember rightly, you didn't stay the full time but came home early, claiming you were bored.'

Netta dropped her eyes in a docile manner, knowing it was expected of her. 'I realise that, dear Papa, and it was extremely ill-mannered of me, you might say. That is why I want to make it up to Clarissa now.'

Thomas sighed. He had thought Evan puzzling. His daughter, it seemed, could be equally so. 'Very well. You may take Mary with you.' Netta's own maid had left after a disagreement about the time she had spent recovering from her illness.

'I can't take Mary, Papa. She is no longer with us.'

Thomas raised his eyebrows. 'Not with us? She's not ill, is she? Seems there's too much of that around lately.'

Netta shook her head, the golden curls dancing on her shoulders. 'No, Papa. But she has left our employ.'

Thomas grunted, staring at his daughter with sudden suspicion. 'It was rather sudden, wasn't it? Left us in the lurch, did she?'

Netta stifled a yawn with one white hand. 'Who knows what these working girls think? She didn't come in for days and then sent a message saying she wasn't coming back, so I got Mrs Dean to have a word with her and pay her off.'

The lies came smoothly to her lips. Netta had already had words with the housekeeper, reminding her to keep her mouth shut if questioned by her father or else she would go the same way as Mary O'Malley. Having decided long ago when she had first entered service that the man who pays the piper calls the tune, Mrs Dean did not argue, although the desire to wipe the smirk off that young madam's face was strong.

Netta decided that should her father by any chance run into Mary in the village – well, whose word was he likely to take? That of his own daughter or a servant girl's?

'I don't need a maid, Papa,' she went on artlessly. 'I can share Clarissa's.' A maid saw and heard too much, was too nosy by far. Clarissa's girl would do what was required and then leave her alone.

And so Netta arrived at the station in Cardiff to be greeted by an ecstatic Clarissa, waving a newly beringed hand and babbling about her engagement. 'It is to Idris – you know, Idris Dixon,' she told Netta as the carriage drove them through the outskirts of the town.

Netta tried to sound pleased. 'It's very sudden, isn't it?' she said slowly. 'There's no – problem, is there?' She gave her cousin an old-fashioned look that had the other girl blushing furiously.

'Of course not, Netta! As if Idris would . . .' She bit her lip, then smiled. 'I was going to write and tell you, but now that you are here it's so much more exciting to talk about it.'

Listening to her cousin prattle on in a thoroughly sickening manner, Netta's eyes rested on the ring on the girl's finger. It wasn't even new, she decided, but an old-fashioned cluster design of diamonds set on a thick gold band. Clarissa, seeing her interest, waggled her fingers, the stones catching the light from the street lamps. 'Isn't it beautiful! It belonged to Idris's grandmother.'

Netta's lips curled. 'Beautiful,' she agreed wryly. She thought back to that sunny afternoon on the headlands, with Jackie being so sweet – so passionate – and so bloody fertile! She thought of the ring she had asked him to give her and his foolhardy way of going about it. She felt a warm, self-satisfied glow, just thinking of the lengths to which he had gone to please her. So what if the village gossips, their chit-chat passed on to her by the talkative Mrs Dean, were saying the police had made a mistake, that Jackie Rees didn't have it in him to hurt anyone? Was that really any concern of hers?

She realised that Clarissa was still chattering and was forced to pretend a show of interest in what the girl was saying. Her talk was solely of incidents in which Idris Dixon featured. Netta remembered him that summer when she was sixteen and he had declared his undying love for her, popping up whenever he could catch her alone and, in Netta's opinion, being a thorough bore. And yet, there had been something about him that had always appealed to her. His devil-may-care attitude to most things other young men took seriously. Work and a career and making your way in the world, those things were of no consequence to Idris. His father was wealthy and it was a fact of life that Idris would go into the business when his education was completed. Netta had no time for the staid young men who were overcome with scruples and so able to withstand her guiles. She had thought it might be fun to be the wife of someone like Idris Dixon. At least they were of a kind, and she would at last escape the boring environs of Craven Bay.

She had not let him see how she felt, of course. That was against all the rules. So she flirted with him, along with half a dozen other young men, and enjoyed the stolen kisses freely given whenever they had a chance to be alone, ignoring Clarissa's forlorn expression and sulky pout and moans about how they were neglecting her.

On her last visit, such a short time ago, she had seen the flame, still hot in Idris's eyes when he looked at her. And so Clarissa's engagement had been something of a shock. Later that evening, in her cousin's bedroom, she forced herself to listen to the other girl's catalogue of complaints. Clarissa lay on her bed, swathed from chin to ankle in a long blue flannel nightgown, her earlier excitement vanished.

'I know there are things, certain things, that you must share with your husband, Netta, but I don't know what they are and it scares me. Mama refuses to talk about it, saying I will understand when the time comes.' She looked away, avoiding Netta's eyes, pleating the edge of the white sheet with nervous fingers. 'Idris has told me that he adores me, and I love him, and know our families would like nothing better than for us to marry. But although I am grateful at his choosing me, I dread not being able to – to adjust!'

There was a soft tap at the door and it opened to reveal a middle-aged woman whom Netta knew to be Nancy, her cousin's maid. They would be sharing her. Netta smiled. Indeed, that might not be all they would be sharing . . .

She shrugged, roused momentarily from her fit of ennui by Clarissa's confidences, a plan swiftly forming in her mind. She smiled again and said consolingly, patting the other girl's hand, 'Don't worry. Things have a way of coming right. And,' she pursed her lips, 'Idris seems to me an experienced man so at least you won't have to put up with a fumbling, raw lad who'll put you off marriage right from the start.' She'd carefully considered her words before she said them and now watched the effect they had on Clarissa, the blood leaving her plump cheeks, hand going to her mouth to stifle a soft moan.

'Oh, Netta!'

She smiled again and watched as the maid bustled forward, giving her a forbidding look as she brushed past. 'Now, Miss Netta, don't you be frightening our young lady. She has enough to worry about as it is, with plans for a summer wedding, without you putting all kinds of alarming thoughts in her head.' She bent over the trembling girl, brushing the hair back from her forehead as she had done since Clarissa was a child. 'It'll be all right, my love. Nancy will be with you and will see that no harm comes to you.' She smiled down at the girl. 'Why don't you tell Miss Netta about the ball your dear mama and papa are giving in honour of your engagement, and the new gown you will have?'

At the mention of clothes, Clarissa's face brightened. 'Oh, Netta, wait till I tell you! Mama has chosen the style but I was allowed to choose the material. It's a pale blue satin with a raised pattern of ivy leaves, outlined in tiny seed pearls. You'll be green with envy when you see it, I swear.'

Netta smiled and thought of her own dress, bought for such an occasion, made by the admirable Mrs Powys from the valley whose skills were reserved now only for Netta. It was of pale lilac chiffon with floating panels of a deeper shade falling to points below the hem of the skirt. The deep, far from modest, neckline would have her dear aunt reaching for her smelling salts, she thought maliciously.

It was the very essence of sophistication and would

make Clarissa look like a pantomine Cinderella got up for the ball. Make some of those stuffed shirts who had poked fun at her as Clarissa's country cousin, sit up and take notice too.

The longed-for evening arrived and Netta greeted Idris Dixon as he stood in the hall, handing his hat, gloves and cloak to the maid. He caught her eye and blinked, her appearance startling him. He hadn't expected her to be back visiting so soon after the last time. Before he could speak, someone claimed her for a dance, and with a grimace he went to seek out his fiancée.

Lilting waltz music floated through the house, the sounds of voices and laughter seeming to permeate even to the gardens. Dancing in her partner's arms, Netta was momentarily dazzled by the finery of the other guests and the many candelabra which lit the large room.

Her gaze grew speculative as she watched her cousin float by in the arms of her fiancé. Clarissa looked like a little girl dressed in her mother's clothes. Netta thought of the rainy afternoons she and Clarissa had idled away, dragging out armfuls of dresses and petticoats from wardrobes in unused bedrooms and parading around in them, tripping over the long skirts, helpless with laughter. Clarissa hadn't really grown away from that giggly, slightly nervous girl, Netta thought. She doubted that she ever would.

Although they had shared a closeness usually reserved for sisters, which neither of them were lucky enough to possess, that was not going to discourage Netta from the plan that was forming in her head, secure in the knowledge that Clarissa was no competition.

Later she was able to get Idris alone in a quiet corner of

the hall. He held two brimming glasses of champagne and deftly Netta removed one and held it to her lips, ignoring Idris's half-hearted protest that it was meant for Clarissa.

'She won't mind,' she said. 'You can get her another. Besides, I haven't had a chance to talk to you yet.' Pensively she gazed at him. 'So you really are going to marry my cousin?'

Idris straightened his shoulders and looked important. 'Yes, I am. We shall be very happy. Our parents are pleased, they say we are well suited.'

'Your parents say?' Netta smiled over the rim of her glass. 'And what do *you* say?' She leaned closer, affording him a glance down the deep V of her neckline. 'I always thought you liked me better than Clarissa. You used to say you did.'

Idris's already ruddy complexion flushed an even deeper shade and he looked about them uncomfortably. The other guests, concentrating on enjoying themselves and sampling Aunt Lucy's fine repast and champagne, nodded as they strolled by but otherwise ignored them.

'Yes, well, that was a long time ago. We weren't much more than children.' His chin stuck out aggressively. 'You told me I was nothing but a pest, remember?'

Netta stirred her champagne with one long finger, watching the golden bubbles swirl in the glass. She placed the finger across his mouth, lingering for a long moment.

'I wouldn't say that now.'

Idris's flush deepened to a dull crimson. 'Netta . . . ?' His voice held a warning. Again he glanced about them and she laughed. 'I can see that the thought affects you as much as it does me,' she told him softly. 'Oh, Idris, if you had only waited . . .' She allowed the sentence to trail away into nothingness, then with a slow smile walked away, leaving him gazing after her with open mouth, like a fish out of water. Which, he thought later, was exactly how he felt.

It was understood that the party would be late finishing and some guests might want to stay. Bedrooms had been prepared, fires lit in the grates and beds aired.

Idris bade a sweet but chaste goodnight to his fiancée and retired for what was left of the night. Sleep was hovering over him when a broad band of light cut into the room. Startled, he sat up.

There was a suggestion of movement, of bare feet padding across the floor, the sweet, heavy scent of roses, and outlined against the open doorway with the lamp on the landing shining behind her, Idris could see Netta. She was dressed in a long, white peignoir of some filmy material. Even as he watched she placed one finger to her lips and closed the door behind her, securely turning the key.

'Shhh,' she breathed. 'It's only me.'

'Netta!' His throat almost closed up in panic so his voice came out in a croak. 'Are you mad! You can't . . .'

'I have never listened to "can't" in my whole life,' she told him, not in the least disconcerted by his show of alarm, 'and I don't intend to start now.'

Then she was beside the bed, her voice a low, husky whisper. 'How can you know how the news of Clarissa's and your engagement has wounded me?' she breathed. 'All I ask is that you leave me one sweet memory for when I am old and all alone. Remember what we once meant to each other. How can you ignore what was once so sweet.'

Idris tried to remember but all his memory retained was an image of Netta sniping at him for being in the way, calling him names that hurt. He laughed, amazed that he was able to. 'Alone! Not you, Netta. Never alone. There'll always be men attracted to you like bees around a honey pot.'

'Am I so attractive then?' The long lashes were lowered demurely as she peered into his face from under half-closed eyelids.

'Next to Clarissa, the most attractive woman in Cardiff.'

The eyelashes fluttered, the full lips he had once so ardently desired pouted. Slim white fingers plucked at the full skirt of her gown, transparent and more than hinting at the pearly flesh beneath.

His heart raced, his mouth went dry, and when she said, her voice a near whisper, 'Show me, then. Are we to part without experiencing one last stolen moment of the love we could have shared had fortune favoured me instead of my cousin?' He thought it the most romantically phrased invitation he'd ever been given. He grinned, realising suddenly the enormity of what she was offering. And yet, here in the house of his future in-laws, with Clarissa only doors away, it held the kind of excitement that he craved. And if he refused, would she scream, plead, lash out at him in anger and frustration . . . ?

While he hesitated, she did none of these things. Feminine wiles were to Netta far more effective weapons than resorting to anger. She raised her arms above her head, stretching catlike, slowly, sensuously. Her back arched and somehow, he was never quite sure how, the loose peignoir was slipping from her shoulders, revealing the handsome breasts, the handspan of a waist, and opulent hips.

His arms reached out, enclosing the naked body, and she allowed him to bring her close to him, her leg going between his, her thigh pressed tight against his body. 'Forgive me, my darling,' she was murmuring, 'for being so bold. I know a well-brought-up young lady is not supposed to show her feelings, but we both know what we feel about today's hypocrisy. You must know I was sick with jealousy when I thought of my cousin, fond of her as I am, sharing your love – your bed. I do not mean to be cruel, my dearest, but I am only flesh and blood and so cannot help saying I am afraid you will find Clarissa a cold fish, full of fears and inhibitions.'

She would have made a wonderful actress, she told herself. Sarah Bernhardt would have had to look to her laurels . . .

She leaned forward so that he could feel the heaviness of her breasts against his chest. 'Whereas I . . .' and she allowed the words to trail away, full of promise. 'Surely you would not be so beggarly as to refuse me one last kiss?'

Swept along by his feelings – for what man could resist a woman as persistent as Netta when she had made up her mind not to be resisted – he pulled her down on top of him and began to kiss her. All thought of resistance had left him and he made love to her with an urgent passion that, rather than subduing her, urged her into a rage of lust that equalled then overtook his own. Afterwards, he fell into a deep, exhausted sleep and when he awoke some time later was delighted to find her still beside him. There had been a moment when he reflected on the consequences of his actions, about to slip out of bed without waking her. At that moment, she sighed and her eyes opened and he was lost. He roused her with soft kisses and they made love again that this time was long and leisurely.

Chapter Twenty

The gallery in Mayfair to which Marcus insisted on taking Alys was, not counting his parents' magnificent home, the most breathtaking place she had ever entered. Gilt and marble were everywhere and she was almost afraid to walk on the white marble floor in case she left footprints.

Marcus had laughed when she admitted to feeling awed and somewhat out of place in the company of so many wonderful paintings.

'Drogo looks nice, though, doesn't he?' she said, head on one side. 'So lifelike you'd think he was going to step right out of the picture, giving these fine people here heart attacks.'

Marcus grinned. 'Dear old Drogo! But you look pretty good yourself, don't you think?'

'Of course. You have a great talent, Marcus. If it wasn't for you I would still be in Craven Bay selling cockles, and never knowing that in some parts of the country people live differently. I'll always be grateful to you for introducing me to so many new and wonderful things.'

'You're not in any hurry to get back, then?' He leaned forward, covering her hand with his. At his touch her heart gave a crazy lurch and the blood rushed through her body, burning into her cheeks. His face was so close she could see the tiny wrinkles beside his eyes, the way his thick coppery hair grew back at the temples. As though sensing her withdrawal he gave her hand a pat and released it. 'I thought by now you would be missing your old life with the little O'Malley and the people you grew up with.' His speculative gaze rested on her face.

When she didn't answer, he went on, 'The new portrait needs only a few touches and it will be finished. Had you given any thought to what you might do then?'

She tucked a strand of hair behind one ear, avoiding his eyes, her thoughts flying to the fragment of conversation overheard between him and his mother that evening at the party. 'Simon has asked me to sit for him,' she said at last.

He thought back to that evening he had found Simon joining her in the garden; her words, 'I know exactly what I'm doing.'

He grunted. 'Good idea, providing you can get him to pick up a brush and actually start. He's got it in him. With the appropriate encouragement he could equal, if not improve on, his earlier successes. Who knows, maybe another version of "The Cockleshell Girl". '

A number of visitors in the gallery had stopped and were studying the portrait of Alys in her guise of fisher-girl, at the edge of the sea, a basket tucked under one arm, her hair and skirts streaming behind her like banners in the wind. One woman remarked loudly on the freshness of the colours and the way the artist had caught the melting warmth of the little donkey's eyes. 'I could swear that at any moment it's going to blink,' she told her husband, a stout businessman in a dark suit who appeared bored, obviously not sharing his wife's enthusiasm for art.

Some of the other visitors were casting rather pointed looks at Alys and she felt Marcus take her arm, urging her gently towards the high domed entrance of the large building. 'God,' he said, 'I hate being recognised!'

She wondered why he should object so strongly. Was he ashamed of being seen with her? Could it be that gossip still percolated through London society about the girl who had come up from the wilds of Wales to live with him at his house under the pretext of being his model?

In the weeks that slipped by, edging the late Indian summer into autumn, it became too chilly to take tea in the garden and on some days too wet and unpleasant to set out on the long walks Alys had come to enjoy. Marcus seemed busy with outside interests and she saw less and less of him. When she did, he hardly spoke. She almost dreaded the time when the painting would be finished for without even that employment Alys felt she would be left in a void. Apart from that dreadful time after her abortion, she wasn't used to waking in the morning wondering how to occupy her day. The thought of her poor little unborn baby still chilled her, bringing paroxysms of pain and distress. She had to keep busy or her thoughts would be too much to bear.

She spent a good part of her time in the kitchen with Mrs Mimms, shelling peas or peeling apples, listening with amusement to that good woman's tirades against her husband. Mrs Mimms seemed the only person who took a genuine interest in her, so it was with delight that

Alys greeted Joanna Ambrey one morning when she called unexpectedly at the studio. As luck would have it, Marcus was out and so they were able to talk freely and about the things that had become a way of life with Joanna and which Alys found so intriguing.

She agreed wholeheartedly with everything Joanna said and began to talk about Craven Bay. Especially the people who lived in Craven Bay. The hard and the soft ones. The women whose husbands drank and those who didn't. 'Although,' Alys admitted ruefully, 'there are more of the first kind than the second.'

Joanna laughed. 'That's how it is in most communities, and why we must all stand together and remedy things.' Her eyes lit up. She took Alys's hands in hers. 'Tomorrow we're going to paint all the benches in Hyde Park with our slogan, "Votes for Women". Some of the ladies, the more daring ones, will carry fish in their handbags and at the first sign of harassment from the police or anyone else, we shall pelt them all with dead fish.'

In spite of her smile, Alys felt a cold finger of alarm touch her spine. 'Oh dear, do you think that's wise? I mean, from what I saw the last time, the police *will* interfere, and if they have no intention of treating you like ladies . . .'

'We don't expect to be treated like ladies. If we did we should all be at home looking after our children and making jam. We relish every bit of brutality these men hand out. It only makes us more determined to follow our chosen path.' Her hands squeezed Alys's. 'Oh, do say you'll come! It will be very exciting.'

Trying not to think of Marcus's reaction, Alys agreed.

*　　*　　*

Mary watched the warder walk across the cobbled yard towards her, his huge bunch of keys dangling from a hook at his hip. With a face completely devoid of expression, he crooked a finger, beckoning her to follow him. Unlocking the heavy wooden door, he entered the prison. Mary followed. As always the lack of daylight blinded her, and the smell of wet stone floors and unwashed human bodies assailed her nostrils.

Silently she walked the corridors then seated herself at the rough wooden table. A moment later Jackie was shown in.

Mary caught her breath sharply, her heart beginning its slow, heavy thudding at the sight of Jackie's drawn, white face. Gone was the fresh ruddy complexion, the sturdy well-set-up figure. In their place was a stooped man, with hunched shoulders and a wild thatch of black hair that badly needed washing.

Determined not to let Jackie see how much his appearance upset her, Mary smiled and settled herself placidly at the wooden table. 'How are you?' she asked softly.

For a brief, unguarded moment, unmanly tears appeared in his eyes. He blinked rapidly, willing them away. 'I'm all right. How are you?'

'Never mind me, boyo. Are you getting enough to eat? Sleeping well?'

He thought of the pig swill they called food in this place, the watery soup and the chunk of dark bread that by the time the prisoners got it was already days old, the oaths and curses that rang out through the night, keeping him awake. He thought of his aunt, and his warm cosy bedroom in her clean, comfortable cottage, and again tears made him blink.

He looked down at his clasped hands on the table before him, a young man sick with self-loathing, bewildered by events that he couldn't understand. He'd had more than enough time to think and knew he must have been half-witted to have allowed himself to be manipulated like that by Miss Netta. What did she really want from him? It certainly couldn't have been just the stolen kisses or the one afternoon of passion in that secret hollow on the headlands.

He admitted to himself that he had never stopped feeling inferior when he was with her, always wanting to please her, to keep her interested in him. Her interest had for a while seemed all-important . . .

'*Are* you?' Mary probed insistently. He had to think back to her question.

'Oh, yes, I suppose so.'

Mary's own throat ached with tears she must not shed. She forced another smile. 'Your aunty sends her love, as well as Mam. Have you heard anything? Have they said what's going to happen?'

Jackie shook his head. 'No. No one but you has been near.'

She reached out to touch his cheek then drew back sharply at a harsh warning from the attentive warden. 'No touching! Keep your hands on the top of the table.'

Mary felt her temper stir. The colour bright in her cheeks, she rose to her feet and said, brogue suddenly very noticeable, 'Sure, and what do you suppose I was about to do, you misbegotten heathen, you? Smuggle him something to enable him to escape from this stinking hole of poor wretched divils whose luck has run out? Why, you . . .'

'Mary!' Jackie's voice held a warning as the warder rose to his feet, fist raised in a threatening gesture. Biting her lip, she sat down again. Losing her temper wasn't going to help Jackie. He still had to face the man after she was gone.

Fate took a hand. There was a shout from somewhere outside in the corridor, a scuffle and a cry for help. The warder hesitated, clearly torn between the desire to help one of his mates and his duty to keep guard over his prisoner.

With a muttered warning he ran from the cell, slamming the door behind him. Suddenly tears were pouring down Jackie's cheeks. 'Mary, I'm so ashamed.' Unused to thinking deeply, his tongue tripping over the words, he groaned. 'Why does everything have to be so complicated? I would give anything for things to be as they were when we were happy together.'

She reached out and brushed his hair back from his forehead. 'All you have to do is put your arms around me. That's all that really matters.' She marvelled at the change her words wrought in him. In a moment she was held closely to his breast, his lips on her hair as he murmured her name over and over again. 'Mary, my love, you'll wait for me, won't you? I couldn't bear it if you didn't wait.'

She pulled his head down to her breast and let it rest there. For a moment she felt as if he were her child. And maybe that was the way it was supposed to be. 'Daft ha'porth!' she said gently. 'Of course I'll wait.'

Their brief moment of joy was ended a moment later when the cell door burst open and the warder returned. 'All right,' he barked, dragging them rudely apart.

'That's enough of that. Visit's over. And you, young woman,' glaring at Mary with a forbidding expression, 'after this carry on it might just be the last one you're allowed. I've had more than enough of your abusive manner.'

It took every bit of Mary's self-control to make her clamp her lips together and return no answer. She doubted that he had the authority to deny her any further visits. Dear Holy Mother, she hoped so! For how could she exist with the thought of not seeing Jackie again? Perhaps for years. Perhaps, a tiny voice inside her murmured, forever. For didn't they hang people for murder, and wasn't that just what they were all saying he had done? Murder!

Squaring her shoulders, she walked quickly through the prison gates. She would face that horror if – and when – she came to it.

With this fervent hope in her heart, Mary soldiered on. But her cross seemed increasingly heavy to bear, and even with her usual energy and her faith she was inclined to stumble. Only her faith in Jackie's innocence kept her going.

Worried half out of her mind by her daughter's unusual quietness and pallor, Mam spoke to her one afternoon, coming out with things she would never have dared to mention before. 'So, you're still prepared to forgive him, then?'

'You know I am, Mam. I love him with all my heart. He's my whole life and always has been, even if I was slow to show it. A man needs to be shown, I've realised that, Mam, and if only we could live that part of our lives over again, I wouldn't be so – so stand-offish.'

Her pretty face was drawn and pale and Mam, her own face creased by emotion, put her arms about her. 'Oh, my little love! I'm so deeply sorry but I pray each night to the Blessed Virgin that things will come right and the dear boy will soon be back with us.'

Mary's small brothers listened and observed from the corner of the kitchen that was recognised as their space. Kenny caught his brother's eye, jerking his head towards the back door. Dennis nodded, and silently they rose and went out of the house. In the privacy of the piece of wasteland at the back where the remains of an old cart made an ideal hiding place, Kenny settled himself down and looked at his brother. 'Well, are you still wanting to help me get our own back on that woman?'

Dennis nodded, quite ready to cooperate but still a little uncomfortable at his brother's daring. 'You know I am.'

'All right, let's think up a plan.' They put their heads together and were soon deep in discussion. Back at the house, the sympathy shown by her mother became too much for Mary. Suddenly she had to get out, away by herself. She said she was going for a walk and Mam agreed with an alacrity that made her smile. She left the house and walked towards the beach, the sky so low she felt she could have stood on tiptoe and plunged her hand into the purple clouds. She noticed for the first time the glory of the trees clad in their raiment of autumn colours and wondered where the time had gone. It seemed only yesterday that it was full summer.

Hearing footsteps, she looked back, her mouth falling open with astonishment when she saw they belonged to Netta Jenkins. Dressed in the height of fashion, she looked a picture of maidenly propriety as she paused before Mary. 'Well,' she said, 'if it isn't the little O'Malley girl! Still hanging around to pick up the crumbs, I see.'

Mary bristled at the implied insult. 'What are you doing here, Netta Jenkins? You're a bit off your beat, aren't you?' At the moment and in her present mood, Netta was the last person on earth she wanted to see. And the girl's snide remark about picking up the crumbs enraged her so that her cheeks flushed a dull red. She regarded her former mistress with contempt and loathing as Netta said, 'My goodness, we are sharp this afternoon, aren't we? I imagine I am doing the same as you, in all innocence enjoying the last spell of good weather before the winter sets in.'

Mary snorted. 'Nothing you do is innocent, Netta Jenkins. You're nothing but a crafty, scheming little bitch and I'd thank you to keep to your own part of town and not come trespassing this way. Everything you touch, you pollute. We don't need the likes of you around here.'

Mary paused as she caught the cold venom in the other girl's blue eyes. She was shocked at the hatred she saw there as Netta replied, 'Don't you talk to me like that, or I'm going to get very angry . . .'

Placing her hands firmly on her hips, Mary leaned forward so that her face was only inches from the other girl's. 'Well, you'd better get a move on, then, 'cause I'm beating you to it.'

Netta's voice took on a blustering tone. 'How would you like me to tell my father what you've just said? The chief constable of this county is a personal friend of his, you know. He might be interested in your feeble attempts at defamation of character . . .'

'And how would you like your backside kicked from here to the other side of the street?' retorted Mary belligerently. 'For me boot's sure itching to get on with it.'

Drawing a deep breath, Netta tilted her chin and walked on, pausing half a dozen steps away to turn and shout back, 'Poor losers have no place in this world, and no one to blame but themselves. Why don't you face it? You're livid because Jackie preferred me to you.' Netta might no longer want Jackie Rees, but she was not going to give Mary the satisfaction of knowing it. Suddenly, tired of the whole thing, she tossed her head and walked on, feeling the eyes of the other girl boring into her back as she went. If looks could kill, Netta would have been a dead duck.

Her purpose in coming this way was to post a letter to Idris Dixon at his home in Cardiff. Let her get that out of the way, and she felt she could relax. The right or wrongs of the affair did not worry her. She was pregnant and after that night in Cardiff, when she had gone to his bedroom with the express purpose of seducing him, Idris would think it his child and be bound in all honour to marry her. How it would affect poor Clarissa, she did not even stop to think. And seven-month births were quite common; trust her to think up some good excuse . . .

The walk down to the sea shore lost all appeal for Mary and she almost broke into a run to get back to the house. Entering by the back door, she slammed it so hard that Mam looked up from her ironing to say mildly, 'Mary, lass, that door's only got so many slams in it and you've used most of them up already.'

'Sorry, Mam, only I'm just so *mad*. I've just seen that

Netta Jenkins and she . . .' She bit her lip, bending to pick up the big basket of clean washing and set it on a chair. 'Oh, never mind. Why should we depress ourselves with the likes of Lady Sourpuss? Here, I'll help you damp the washing.'

Busily, she began sprinkling water from a basin on to the freshly washed sheets and pillow cases, rolling them up into tight sausage-like rolls ready for Mam to iron. Her mother watched her. She wished the job that the girl had been promised would materialise for Mary these days had too much time on her hands and Mam worried about her. The job was serving behind the counter of a small, family-run grocery store on the corner, and Mr Morgan had promised that as soon as the Christmas trade looked like picking up, Mary would be sent for. It couldn't be too soon for Mam.

The early dusk of winter had set in, making the stretch of headlands a ghostly place. The two boys crept across the rough, dried-out carpet of once purple heather. In their imaginations they were Red Indians, creeping up on an isolated farmstead, just as they had seen the other day at the pictures in that cowboy film.

They had stared wide-eyed at the flickering screen; the old upright piano played by Gladys Williams thumped out its warning notes of danger, and the germ of an idea began to form in Kenny's fertile imagination.

Catapults stuffed in their trousers pockets, out of sight, they seethed with the mixture of emotions which their sister's melancholy had instilled in them. They couldn't have explained these feelings to anyone; all they knew was that the Jenkins woman had been the cause first of Mary losing her job and still not being able to find another, and then of her bewildering changes of mood that left them feeling as though the family had suffered a bereavement.

In some mysterious way they knew, too, that Jackie Rees was involved and that he now languished in prison. Although their father kept a wary eye open for the slightest sign of misbehaviour or swearing, fighting or answering back to their mother, they still experienced quite a bit of freedom. The black leather belt prominently displayed hanging from a nail on the back of the kitchen door was seldom used, Mr O'Malley being the kindest and gentlest of men. It was a deterrent and the boys respected it. But there were times when even the threat of the strap wasn't enough. Such as now.

Colour was already fading from the landscape, the bright greens and yellows dimming, turning to shades of grey. It would be dark early tonight. Thomas Jenkins drove his newly purchased car along the dusty white road. He had been away on one of his periodic business trips and was looking forward to reaching home.

Getting too old for this lark, he told himself. Should be taking it easy at your age. Now, if Evan was still here, if he hadn't been forced to send him halfway across the world, things might have been different. Evan would have been carrying out these tiresome journeys, giving him a well-earned rest. Thomas's aptitude for work had given him prosperity but little freedom. It was difficult to escape from all those business interests or the affairs of the many branches of mining ventures which he controlled. Of course, this new automobile he had bought and learned to drive was a blessing, relieving him of the long, irksome train journeys of the past. He could do the journey in half the time and actually enjoyed passing through the many small communities that dotted the valleys, causing horses to shy in alarm at the four-wheeled monster, geese and hens to squawk and scatter to the safety of the hedgerows.

He always looked forward to returning home to his lovely Netta who remained the light of his life. He often wished the roles of his daughter and son could have been reversed. But in time, with a bit of luck, Netta would provide him with a healthy grandson. Lately she had been hinting at marriage and he knew on her visits to her cousin in Cardiff that she had been seeing a lot of that young Dixon boy. With Idris's engagement to Clarissa, though, that hope had been nipped in the bud. Still, likely there was someone else she was interested in, for on her return from the last visit she had been in high spirits, and with the bloom on her cheeks and her blue eyes sparkling, Thomas thought she had never looked better.

Busy with his thoughts, he did not see the horse and its rider until they were alongside him. Alarmed at the fool-hardy recklessness with which she rode, the way she tackled most things, Thomas called aloud for his daughter to slow down. The light was bad and she really should be more careful on a stretch of road like this . . .

He heard her laugh scornfully in the gathering dusk and twisted his steering wheel sharply as with a kind of horror he glimpsed the two small figures rising as if from nowhere, dancing and gesticulating like banshees. Netta's mount whinnied and reared and although normally she would have been able to handle him, she found it difficult now, for the sudden appearance of the two figures had startled the horse and with a terrified snort its front legs crashed down on the bonnet of the car. The next thing Thomas Jenkins knew was an agonising pain as the vehicle slammed into one of the large boulders that lined the road.

Chapter Twenty-One

Lavinia rode regularly through the outskirts of the small town, always with a haughty manner. Sometimes she ventured as far as the diggings and the men would pause in their eternal pursuit of the buried gold and watch with red-rimmed eyes as she rode gracefully by, unsuspecting of the rush of emotions she aroused in them. They noted how she controlled her sweating horse with great skill, her slim and shapely figure under the well-cut riding habit, and their imaginations ran wild.

Often Evan was busy and caused Lavinia to lose her temper by refusing to join her on her ride. Then she would sweep out of the office, striking impatiently at her leg with her whip, two angry red spots high on her cheeks.

'Very well,' she would say, 'I shall go on my own.'

'I'd rather you didn't, Lavinia,' he would plead. 'You know it isn't safe.'

'Poof! No one would dare lay a finger on me.'

Evan sighed. Bandying words with this girl got him nowhere for she would win every time. All part of the sexual attraction he felt for her, for she was a very exciting young lady and used to getting her own way. At the moment, she wanted Evan and made no effort to hide it. Over the months, with changing conditions and a different way of living, more open and unrestricted than that of Craven Bay, the visions of Alys had faded into water-coloured reminiscences of a lovely girl with whom he had spent an enjoyable time in the summer. He would remember her with delight, her beauty and the natural charm that had captivated the boy straight down from university. She had been a taste of a very different life from the one he would have to get used to, certainly from the one he was living now. He watched with misgivings as Lavinia mounted the horse held by a young African boy outside on the dusty street. The small cloud of red dust caused by the prancing hoofs dissolved into the hot, humid air and the rider and the horse vanished into the shimmer of heat that seemed to vibrate over the hard-packed earth.

The large man stood on top of the small hillock, waiting for her to appear. There she was at last! She came towards him, riding all alone. The watcher crouched down in the shadows of the thick bush as she urged the horse into a canter, and squinting his eyes against the sun's brightness the man wondered what such a lovely and privileged woman could be thinking about to cause a frown like that!

Still smarting at Evan's refusal to join her, at his insulting preference for working in the stuffy old office to riding with her, Lavinia thought back to the day of the river picnic. She had hoped that by allowing him to compromise her that night under the stars she would be wearing his ring by now. They had clung together, there in the deep, purple-black shadows of the trees, kissing with rising ardour, the shrill sounds of the cicadas mingling with the laughter and murmur of voices from the rest of the party on the far side of the wood fire. Sweat had risen on his brow and he called her a she devil, while her eyes, dark and twinkling, veiled by thick lashes, looked steadily up at him, seeming to possess a snake-like fascination.

Now, as Lavinia passed, so intent on her thoughts that she wasn't even aware of another presence, the waiting man sprang from the shadows, grabbing her horse's bridle. With a scream, Lavinia tried to beat him off with her riding crop, but he hung on tenaciously as the horse reared in panic.

Grabbing her legs he unseated her and pulled her to the ground while her horse cantered away, snorting with fright. For a long breathless moment she lay on the grass while the earth seemed to revolve around her, the fierce rays of the sun making her eyes water. Then she scrambled to her feet, her face scarlet with rage. 'I'll see you hanged for this, you bloody maniac,' she screamed. 'What do you think you're doing? Do you know who I am?'

The miner stood in front of her, then grabbing hold of a fistful of her jacket pushed her against the rough trunk of a tree. His hands reached out again to tear at the buttons that fastened the tight-fitting jacket, scattering them everywhere. Her pale skin gleamed in the dusky shadows and she could feel the rough dry bark of the tree scrape the delicate skin on her back as the thin white cambric blouse was ripped from her and tossed aside.

Screaming, she tried to fight him, biting him when he tried to stifle her cries with the calloused palm of a

331

sweaty hand. She could taste the acrid moisture on her lips, salty and disgusting. It made her want to vomit. She sank her teeth again into the soft part of his palm and he caught at her hair and tugged savagely. 'Stop that, you bitch, or I'll slit your throat right here and now.' And he held a knife to her white throat. 'I'm goin' to teach you a lesson, so I am, ridin' past here every afternoon, your nose in the air, lookin' on us as if we was bits of dirt under your boot. Ain't got nothin' like you in camp, that we ain't, so I intend to enjoy it while I can.'

'My father will kill you for this,' she said through gritted teeth. 'You'd better let me go if you know what's good for you.'

He laughed and began to tear at her riding skirt while she tried desperately to push him away. 'For God's sake!' she pleaded.

But he was past hearing. One thing alone was on his mind as he threw himself on her. But his eagerness was such that it was ended before it started and he collapsed in a powerless heap, his breath coming raggedly.

Lavinia gave a violent push and escaped to where her mount waited, reins dangling loosely around its neck, patiently cropping at the grass.

The outrage in that frontier town when she finished telling her story had never been equalled, even in the early days of the Zulu raids and the blood letting that followed. There was talk of forays into the diggings by the authorities and employees of both her father's and the Jenkins mines. Evan was deeply upset, blaming himself for not accompanying her.

There were whispers from some, however, that she

had been asking for it, that any well-brought-up young lady should know better than to flaunt herself before the hordes of hard-working, beer-swilling diggers the way Lavinia had been doing. The police wanted her to ride out with them to try and identify the man who had attacked her but with a shudder she refused.

She never wanted to go near that place again or smell those hot, unwashed bodies. The thought of the man, lying across her although in the end he'd been unable to do anything, the remembered smell of the dried sweat clogging her nostrils, sickened her. She said that the very idea of looking into those faces again, all with lustful eyes, would give her nightmares for the rest of her life.

Seeing that no actual harm had been done, save to her dignity and a ruined riding habit, they fell in with her wishes and Lavinia wrote immediately to her father in Cape Town, informing him of her change of heart. She'd seen enough of the frontier life, she wrote, the heat and the dust. And even though Mrs Harvey and her husband had been very kind, she longed for the green slopes of the mountain and the white sandy bays where the cheerful Malay fishermen hauled in their nets.

She added, as a postscript, that Evan would be coming back with her and that dearest Papa was to prepare himself for some good news. After what *she* had been through, how could he refuse her now?

But Evan had ideas of his own.

'I can't leave just like that,' he said. They were walking in the Harveys' garden in the cool of the evening, in that brief period between the sun setting and the emergence of the mosquitoes and other flying insects. 'I'm not my own boss, Lavinia, no matter how much it pleases you to think I am.'

She sniffed. 'You could have been, had you taken the position Papa offered.'

He made an impatient gesture. 'If things had been different, I probably would. But they are not, so it's no use wishing for something that can never be.'

She lowered her eyelashes, her mouth petulant. 'You didn't say that on the river that night. That night you were so sweet and understanding. You're like one of those dust-devils that spins across the veldt, twisting and turning in all directions.'

'Yes, well . . .' Confused, Evan hardly knew how to answer, wondering if he was destined to go through life disclaiming one woman after another. Was there some flaw in his character that prevented him from committing himself freely?

'Well, will you come with me?' Hardly giving him time to speak she went on scornfully, 'You don't have to think up an answer, Evan. I can see it in your face.'

He swallowed with difficulty. 'It would be kind of you to listen, you're not being fair.'

'Fair? You've hardly been fair to me! You've done nothing but put on an act since we first met.' She had been so sure, this time, that she had found a man who would marry her.

Evan took both her hands in his, pulling her towards him in the darkness. Tilting her chin with one finger so that he could look into her eyes, the look she gave him made his senses stir. There had never been anything but the lightest of entanglements in his life; even the affair with Alys, looking back on it, was more like a dream than reality. All this talk of him going back to Cape Town with Lavinia, of accepting a position in her father's business, was wishful thinking on her part. The imagining of a young, badly spoiled girl. His father would never forgive him if he tied himself down at such an early age. And to the daughter of one of his rivals, too! For every gold-mining camp that thrived about here was a bitter enemy to the rest, competing for the African labour without which the mines would be inoperable.

'Perhaps,' he said, 'I didn't play fair with you, Lavinia, and I'm truly sorry if I hurt you. But I was sent out here to do a job. I can't just pack up and leave and traipse off with you to the other end of Africa.' He could not suppress a grin, thinking of the lovely house on the mountainside and the wonderfully pleasant life it offered. 'Much as I'd like to.'

She turned away, plucking an hibiscus blossom from a nearby bush, shredding the delicate scarlet petals with angry fingers. There was a tense silence, then: 'You had better go in, hadn't you?' she said and there was a sneering note in her voice. 'Or they'll be sending out a search party for you!'

'Lavinia!'

'If you say one more word I shall scream.' She turned to look at him, her lips curling with scorn. 'They've really trained you well, haven't they? Your beloved father and his business friends.'

He tried to pull her close but she tugged away impatiently. 'To think I let you make love to me, that night under the stars! I must have been mad.' Her voice was full of contempt. 'I thought you loved me.'

'I never once told you that,' he said defensively. 'It

335

was a warm night, the moon was full – and we'd both had more than our fair share of wine. You were as eager as I, Lavinia, or have you forgotten so soon?'

Curling her hands into clenched fists, she said 'I've forgotten nothing, Evan. But I think you have.'

He sighed. 'How can I make you understand?'

She gazed at him in the purple dusk, an enigmatic look in her eyes. 'So what happens now?'

'We made a mistake, Lavinia. We didn't take into account the new sights and sounds that would be all around us, the lure of this land . . .'

She lifted her chin. '*I've* lived here for the last six years. *I* knew what I was doing even if you say you did not.'

He shifted uncomfortably, wishing he was anywhere but in this lovely garden, facing this girl's accusations. Feebly, he repeated, 'I have a job to do for my father. I can't let him down.'

She laughed. 'And how can I possibly compete with your father?' As she walked away, she turned once to say, 'You should have been on the stage. Everything you say is so melodramatic, it's almost comic. No one should believe a word of it.'

It was almost a relief to wave goodbye as the train pulled out of the station. Lavinia leaned out of the window, waving a languid hand, as with great gusts of steam and ear-piercing shrieks the green and gold engine pulled slowly away. The station was crowded with people coming and going, carrying boxes on their backs; the sound of many voices, in many tongues, all shouting at once.

Yes, Evan definitely felt lighter of heart as the train finally vanished round a bend in the tracks and he turned to make his way back to his horse. It was tethered outside the main entrance. The heat was fierce at this time of the year, and what with that and the strain of parting from Lavinia, excessively demanding as she had been of late, he was glad to enter the comparatively cool interior of a hotel and make his way to the bar.

Lavinia had been a pleasant diversion and he supposed he had grown fond of her over the months. But not enough to fall tamely in with her plans. He sipped the drink the waiter brought him, a long, cool, freshly squeezed lime juice and seltzer water, for it wouldn't do for his colleagues in the office to smell strong drink on his breath, not at this time of day. He carried it out to the small tables and chairs set in groups on the deeply shaded veranda. Gazing lazily along its cool length, he caught the eye of a couple of young girls taking the air with an older woman. A dark-haired girl, reminding him of Alys, smiled then lowered her eyes shyly – but not before Evan had caught her blatant wink.

His interest was aroused. Lifting his glass, with the elderly woman's attention elsewhere at that moment, he silently toasted her, his smile widening engagingly.

Lavinia had only been gone a few days when a telegram arrived from Netta. It read: 'Come home at once. Something terrible has happened to Father.'

Chapter Twenty-Two

There were headlines in the papers, the strident voices of the newsboys shouting: 'Read orl about it! Suffragettes cause 'avoc outside the 'ouses of Parliament.'

Londoners paused from their homeward flight at the end of a long day to select a penny from a handful of change, and then with the newspaper folded under one arm hurry on their way. The police had apprehended a number of women who had been daubing paint on the benches in Hyde Park. The slogan 'Votes for Women!' was everywhere.

Gas lamps had been broken and flower beds trampled underfoot.

When the police intervened a cry went up from the women, causing couples out for their daily walk to call their children and dogs to their side and head in the opposite direction. The women lost no time in opening their handbags and aiming dead fish and rotten tomatoes at the oncoming police.

Helmets were sent flying and a cheer went up from the protesters as they dodged the uniformed constables between the ancient oak trees.

Alys was to learn of all this later. She had accompanied Joanna to the House of Commons where her friend promptly lay down in the entrance and declared that she would not move until either death took her or the Prime Minister agreed to receive a deputation of her ladies.

Other women soon joined her and within minutes the entrance to Parliament was blocked by the prostrate bodies of a dozen of Joanna's followers. Alys watched from the shadows, wide-eyed and with a thudding heart. There was something stirring in the brave defiance of the suffragettes, and she thought of the treatment she had sometimes suffered at the hands of her stepfather, and the knavish way Evan had treated her, and without another moment's hesitation joined in.

They kept up the cries of 'Votes for Women!' and towards early afternoon a manservant, very stiff and disapproving, came out to say that Mr Asquith had relented and would see them the following day. A barely audible sigh of relief went up from the women. As they prepared to depart, brushing dust from their skirts, their voices rising in triumph as they gathered about Joanna, the doors were darkened by a mass of figures and uni-formed police burst in.

Onlookers watched as the women, herded like cattle, were pushed roughly into the waiting Black Marias and driven away. Coldly defiant, Joanna put her arms around one of the younger women who was in floods of tears and held her close, whispering words of comfort while Alys tried to soothe a white-haired grandmother who unbelievably had to be in her eighties and whose chief concern was what her grandchildren would say.

Even so, there was a ring of pride in her voice and Alys, although she in turn speculated over what Marcus would say, experienced the same thrill of achievement. Joanna would have her interview with Mr Asquith on the morrow and surely that was the object of the whole exercise.

They were driven to Holloway prison for women and held there overnight. They were allowed to see no one, being informed by a hard-eyed wardress that they would appear in front of a magistrate in the morning. Separated from Joanna, in a cell with two women she did not know, not even suffragettes but loud and common street walkers who suggested things that made her cringe, using words she had never heard before, Alys felt nauseated. She thought of Lilith and how she had condemned her, refusing the money the prostitute had offered. Looking back on it, Lilith seemed like an angel compared to these two.

She could hear the wardress sniggering in the corridor outside the cell and knew the arrangement had been deliberate. The authorities were determined to break the suffragettes' spirit and were prepared to use whatever means were at their disposal.

That night she was told stories by the two prostitutes of the forced feeding carried out by the staff and supervised by a prison doctor. 'Force a rubber tube down your throat, so they do,' said one woman, gloatingly, pushing her face into Alys's. 'Scrapes all the skin orf yer insides, but they don't care. If you won't eat, that's what yer gets, no messing about.'

Alys felt a sense of unreality. She went to the tiny barred window and stood gazing out, trying to blot from her mind the presence of the two fierce women and their revolting anecdotes. She slept little that night and appeared in court heavy-eyed and bedraggled, her face dirty and her hair a mess. Her whole body felt sore, every single bone, even her feet.

But then, she decided, gazing about her at the crowded courtroom, in that she was no different from Joanna or the other women, some of whom looked in even worse condition than Alys, with scratched faces and torn gowns.

Joanna stood cold and proud with her chin held high while the charges were read out. Intimidation and unlawful assembly. They were each fined large sums that made Alys gasp, with the injunction that those who refused to pay would receive a prison sentence.

Alys's eyes darted about the court, wanting to give Joanna an encouraging smile. Instead they came to rest on Marcus Dillon who sat with the small crowd of working men in their cloth caps and scarves, gloating over the women's misfortune. Marcus, however, looked white-faced with anger, his own gaze never once leaving the magistrate.

He must be frantic with worry, Alys thought, seeing Joanna like this.

The magistrate spent the next five minutes lecturing the women on their duties as wives and mothers and the bad example they were giving their children. 'And,' turning his grey head to gaze steadily at Joanna, 'you in particular, Lady Joanna, should know better. I believe you led these women into this unsavoury manifestation of bad manners. I must warn you that should you appear before me once more, I shall have no alternative but to send you to prison.' His frown was forbidding. 'And you can look upon that, madam, as a firm promise.'

When Alys glanced across again Marcus was gone from his place on the public benches. She learned later that he was paying the fine for Joanna and herself. Walking between them, a firm grip on the arm of each girl, he escorted them from the court house.

'What about the other women?' Alys queried, feeling as though she was deserting them.

'Their husbands and fathers are being informed and will do what is necessary. Although,' he said, his fingers tightening painfully on their arms as he hurried them towards the waiting hackney cab, 'if their feelings are anything like mine at the present moment, they would be better advised to leave their womenfolk to stew in their own juice.'

'Marcus!' Joanna turned her head to look at him, outraged. 'How can you say that?'

Preferring the anonymity of a cab at a time like this, he propelled Alys to the waiting vehicle and none too gently thrust her inside. He turned to face Joanna, eyes narrowed and glittering.

'Very easily, my dear. For two pins I would have done the same with you both. Now, come on, let's get you back home. You look such a pair of ragamuffins, I can't say that I'd be thrilled at anyone seeing you with me right now.'

Joanna drew herself up and looked at him steadily. 'I'm not going to your home, Marcus. I must go and give comfort to the other women in the East End office. If you will call another cab I shall relieve you of my company, since it seems to bother you so much.'

She leaned forward into the cab to peer at Alys. 'You'll be all right, dear. For all his bear-like ways,

Marcus is really quite harmless. But you must know that by now. Thank you for giving us your strength and courage. You won't be forgotten.'

A moment later she was driven away and disappeared in the morning traffic. Leaning back on the leather seat, Alys suddenly felt cold and clammy. Oh God, she thought, how on earth did I allow myself to get into such a position! Locked up for the night in a prison cell with those disgusting women, and then facing a grim-faced magistrate the next morning. She shivered violently, the shock really only hitting her now. She heard Marcus mutter something but it didn't seem to make sense to her frayed nerves. The enormity of her actions finally sank in and she wondered where it was all going to end.

The hackney cab drew up outside Marcus's house. Waving aside the cabby's assistance, Marcus placed an arm about Alys's shoulders and led her inside. Mrs Mimms was waiting in the hall, eyes wavering anxiously from Alys's face to Marcus's as he all but dragged the girl in with him.

'Oh, sir! Miss Alys . . .' She hurried forward to help Alys up the stairs but Marcus waved her away. 'It's all right, Mrs Mimms, I'll see to it. Would you be good enough to go out and pay the cabby and then make us a nice cup of tea.'

As though exasperated by Alys's stumbling steps, he lifted her in his arms and carried her to the top of the stairs and across the landing to her room.

Dumping her on the bed he stepped back and stood looking down at her. 'Well,' he began tersely, 'don't you think you owe me an explanation?'

She struggled to sit up. 'Marcus – I'm truly sorry . . .'

Why was she using that word? She wasn't sorry at all. Dismayed over the outcome, yes, apprehensive as to what might still happen, but still exhilarated by the show of defiance in which she had taken part.

'I can't believe you could have been so infantile.' He glared down at her furiously. 'Actually to throw yourself down in the entrance of the House of Commons and defy everyone to move you! Don't you recall what I said that last time – that you were to stay well clear of Joanna's little battles? Why can't you just do as you're told?'

That was what was enraging him, then. Not that she had joined in the protest – that she had actually spent the night in prison – but that she had disobeyed his orders!

It wasn't easy to remain dignified, sprawled on her bed like that while he stood glaring down at her, but she did her best as he went on, 'What *did* you think you were accomplishing, you little idiot?'

'Well, if you must know, all that I could think about was that my feet were killing me.'

She heard his mumbled curse and could feel the sudden tension in the small room as he stood there, motionless. Then, abruptly, he went out and closed the door behind him with a sharp click.

The craving for a hot bath was overwhelming. Later, after a good, long soak, she felt better, both physically and mentally. By the time she had dressed in her plum-coloured skirt and white blouse with the wide black patent leather belt circling her waist, and had brushed her hair so vigorously that it crackled, falling across her shoulders in burnished waves, the effects of her ordeal had left Alys and she felt ready to face Marcus again.

She marched downstairs, her head held high, and found him in the kitchen. There was no sign of Mrs Mimms and he told Alys he had given the housekeeper the rest of the day off.

He handed her a cup of hot, sweet tea. It was too sweet but his expression was so black that it seemed safer not to argue but to drink it. She went to the window and stood looking out, sipping her tea. She heard him come up behind her, and his voice, soft and almost tender: 'What *are* we going to do with you?'

Suddenly she thought of all he *had* done, coming back into her life at the very moment she most needed him, paying her fine that morning in court; she'd be back in that cell with those two squalid women if it hadn't been for his intervention. She was only too aware of that. Joanna would be able to reimburse him, but to Alys the sum asked had seemed immense and she doubted if she ever could. Things had been going so well between them too until now. Though he seemed more than usually preoccupied and was absent for long hours, Alys had come to savour his company when he was at home.

She knew now she'd been a fool to risk his condemnation.

The way he stood so close to her was having a disturbing effect on her breathing. If she leaned backwards, just briefly, her body would touch his. If she turned her head, her lips would brush his shoulder.

And then? The blood coursed wildly through her veins as his nearness evoked sensations she had thought she would never experience again. Not after the way Evan had so cravenly abandoned her.

He stood very still behind her, as though waiting for

her to make the first move. And the thought of Evan brought sanity rushing back. With a small ironic smile she turned and neatly side-stepped him, going to rinse her cup.

'What are you going to do with me? Now that the painting is almost finished, you mean?' Repeating his words, she looked him directly in the eye, waiting for his answer. She didn't know what she hoped to hear; that he'd changed his mind about wanting her to go away, that he would clear the way with Simon to paint her portrait so they at least could see each other sometimes?

But all he did was glance at his watch and say briskly, 'I must be off. I promised my parents I'd drive down. My mother hasn't been very well. I'm not sure what time I'll be back but I'll try not to disturb you.'

At the door he stopped and looked back at her. 'Now just try and behave. You'll be all right on your own?'

She smiled sweetly. 'I've never minded being on my own, thank you. Sometimes I prefer it.'

He frowned and then was gone. In spite of her brave words she wished Mrs Mimms was still here, and then was glad she wasn't for the older woman would want to hear all the juicy bits, as she would call them, about being in prison and what the judge had said. It was annoying to be told by Marcus what she should do, but on the other hand she would appreciate a bit of peace and quiet after the recent tumultuous events.

In the sitting room overlooking the back garden a cheerful fire blazed. She decided she'd make another pot of tea and just relax, immersed in a good book. There was a novel of Thomas Hardy's she had been promising herself she would read, *Tess of the d'Urbervilles*. Placing the tray with the tea things on the table beside her, she curled up in the large easy chair, immediately happily enthralled in the adventures of Hardy's heroine.

There was a 'Miaow!' and an orange shape landed in her lap. Alys smiled. 'Oh, all right, pest! Feeling lonely, are you? Mrs Mimms not here to spoil you?'

Rufus purred loudly, kneading her lap with soft, furry paws as he settled himself comfortably.

Time ceased to register and she was surprised to notice the early winter evening setting in and the gas lights beaming their golden circles through the dusk. Fog insinuated itself in twists and curls across the garden, playing hide-and-seek in the evergreen bushes and the bare branches of the trees.

She thought of the summer, and sitting out there with Marcus, pouring tea from the silver pot just as if she was a lady, born and bred.

She sighed and reached for the bookmark on the table to keep her place. She would never forget folding down a corner of a page and Marcus's reprimand. Now she used the bookmark, made by herself from a long narrow strip of Irish linen and embroidered with purple and yellow pansies.

It was not right that they should be quarrelling. Marcus had taught her so much. Alys watched the fog gathering until the garden was quite dark, until the sound of a car drawing up outside in the street made her sit up. The front door opened and a moment later Marcus came striding into the room, shattering the peace.

'You're a great one for sitting alone in the dark, aren't you?' He eyed the closed book in her lap. 'Thomas Hardy. You don't find him a bit long-winded?'

'Not at all. I find him very true to life.' One hand caressed the silky ears of the sleepy cat. 'And as you see, Rufus has been keeping me company.' She looked up at him questioningly. 'I thought you were visiting your family?'

He shrugged. 'Yes. I decided not to stay. My mother was much better and I didn't like the idea of your being here all alone, and getting up to goodness knows what mischief again.'

If he had phrased it differently, if he had said, 'I didn't like the idea of you being on your own and lonely,' she would have been overcome with joy. She tucked the novel under her arm, and brushing Rufus from her lap made to leave the room. 'You've probably got an engagement for the evening and I wouldn't want to take up your time. You'll want to bathe and change.'

'I didn't drive back all that way to want to go straight out again. I thought we might have a quiet supper at home. How would you like that?'

She stood still, wondering what he would say if she gave him a blank refusal. But it was his house and she was still, in a way, his guest, still in his employ. She inclined her head. 'If you think you can stand my cooking.'

'I can hardly wait.' His hair was tousled from the drive in the open Hispano Suiza, his skin fresh and glowing. He was wearing a pale grey suit and a crisp white shirt and looked devastatingly handsome and debonair – and disgustingly self-satisfied.

She found all the ingredients for a meal in Mrs Mimms's well-stocked larder. Watching disconcertingly closely from his place at the kitchen table, Marcus drawled, 'Before I forget, my mother requested that we visit them again for the weekend. I did not like to accept for you but said I was sure you would enjoy it. She felt she didn't really have the chance to get to know you before. There were too many people about.'

Before she could reply, he went on, 'Towards Christmas is always a busy time for Mother. It's as if she really comes alive then and won't rest until the house is full of family.' He smiled as Alys turned from the stove to stare at him.

Dan hadn't been much of a one for Christmas, she thought, preferring to spend the day time carousing with his friends. It would make a nice change to spend a holiday in a civilised way for once. She had not done that since childhood.

She lifted the lid on the pan of tiny new potatoes – first prize to Mrs Mimms, obtaining them at this time of the year! – and peered in, the steam making her cheeks flush. Boiling nicely. She'd put on the chops now, and the other vegetables. None of them should take long. Hunger pangs rumbled in her stomach and she remembered with some surprise that she had eaten nothing today but the bowl of disgustingly thin gruel that had been thrust into her cell by a hard-eyed wardress early that morning.

She sprinkled black pepper over the chops and put them in the frying pan. Mrs Mimms's gas stove was such a delight! Mam would have thought she'd gone to heaven, indeed she would, cooking on this instead of the old kitchen range that needed constant black-leading to keep it looking nice.

Satisfied with the preparations Alys went and sat

opposite Marcus at the table, propping her elbows on the scrubbed wooden top and resting her chin on her hands. In that position, thought Marcus, she looked about twelve years old, her face still flushed from the heat of the stove, her sleeves rolled up to the elbow, showing the fine sprinkling of freckles on her arms.

'Do they really want me?' she asked. 'Or are they just being polite? You don't have to feel you're obliged to take me everywhere you go. As I've said before, I don't mind being on my own. I'm used to it.'

'Not at Christmas! And my father would never forgive me if I didn't bring you. I think he took quite a shine to you.'

'I liked your father,' she admitted. 'Your mother, too, of course. But your father seemed to have that same sort of sparkle in his eye that my dad did. As though inside him he was always happy, always laughing.' Looking across at him quickly, she added, 'Not that I'm saying anything against your mother.'

He reached across the table for one of the slices of bread she had cut and arranged on a plate. He tore it in half impatiently. 'I'm starving,' he confessed, catching her eye.

'Won't be long,' she assured him and went to peer at the chops.

'Mother takes a little more understanding.' he said, as though their conversation had not been interrupted, 'If she likes you, you'll know it. If she doesn't – well, you'll know that, too.'

'I don't think she did like me,' answered Alys ruefully. 'And she's not going to like reading about me and Joanna spending the night in prison, either.'

'Don't talk rubbish!' In a detached sort of voice he went on, 'Mother especially emphasised that you should be invited, so that's all there is to it. Besides, I don't want Simon hanging around here while you're on your own. I wish you'd stop encouraging him. That young man doesn't usually need any encouragement.'

Alys's cheeks flamed. '*I* don't encourage him! He's your friend, not mine.'

'Well, let's say you don't seem to be trying very hard to *dis*courage him!' Before she could answer, he sighed and said briskly, 'Now, how's that supper coming on?'

There had been a fall of snow during the night, enough to turn the park opposite into a wonderland of white. A weak sun shone through the windows of the elegant house in the square, but although it warmed Alys's shoulders it brought no lifting of her spirits. Spread on the table before her was Mary's latest letter, telling of the soul-destroying visit to Jackie in prison. The carefully formed print ran neatly along ruled lines, slanting near the bottom of the page in spite of them, as though the agitation Mary felt extended right down to her finger tips. Her answers to Alys's own queries had been desultory, the sentences rambling, exactly the way she talked. Alys could almost see her, sitting at the kitchen table, the tip of her tongue protruding slightly as she concentrated on the words and the spelling. Letters from Mary usually brought a smile to Alys's lips. The last few, however, had been heartbreaking.

They told of the attack on the old pawnbroker and Jackie's apprehension for the crime. Alys was struck with disbelief as she read. Like most other people who knew Jackie Rees, she could not imagine why he should do such a thing. Mary was hiding something from her, she suspected. She knew things had cooled somewhat between Jackie and the Irish girl but this was one time when Mary had not confided in her.

Mrs Mimms appeared beside her and Alys looked up as the woman said, 'I 'eard all about the things that doddering old judge said to you ladies in the court that morning. They say 'e scolded Lady Joanna something chronic. Still, take more'n that to bother Lady Joanna. Tough as old boots, she is. It'll go in one ear and out t'other.' She gave Alys a smile. ''ear you're goin' down to the country again for the weekend!' she went on. Although her words were meant to cheer Alys up they were having the opposite effect. She caught the shadow in the girl's eyes and was immediately all concern.

'The drive'll do you good, I expect. All that fresh air.'

Alys gathered the scattered pages together and folded them slowly. 'Yes, I expect it will.' She rose to her feet, pushing back the kitchen chair with its old-fashioned ladder back. 'You'll want to set the table, won't you? I'll get out of your way.'

Sometimes, when Marcus was away, she would eat in the kitchen with the housekeeper. In fact, often when he was there, he would suggest they eat at the kitchen table, scorning Mrs Mimms's proposal that she lay the table in the dining room. 'Don't worry, ducks,' Mrs Mimms smiled at Alys, 'I can do it in a minute or two, while the eggs are cooking.' She bustled over to the stove, reaching up for one of the copper pans that hung decoratively about the bright room. 'Boiled eggs do you this morning? Master Marcus said he only wanted a light breakfast. He intends to take you for a long walk, brush some of the cobwebs away, he said.' And also, she thought to herself, bring back the smile to that woeful little face of yours, me girl! I don't know what it does to the Master, but it surely doesn't help my disposition any.

Over breakfast Marcus put the suggestion to Alys himself, and she said she thought a walk would do her good. Watched by an approving Mrs Mimms, they left the house and walked, hopping on to the occasional tram that passed going their way. As it was so near Christmas, the streets nearer the centre of town were crowded, the shops an Aladdin's cave display of all the things those lucky enough to have money could buy. Alys thought of the East End where Joanna had her office, of the white-faced street urchins she had seen hanging about, and compared them to the gentlemen and their ladies who walked slowly past on the crowded pavements, dressed warmly and with money in their pockets.

Detesting crowds, Marcus soon took her arm and propelled her towards Westminster Bridge. The river gleamed under a pale sky, fingers of the feeble sun catching and highlighting the Houses of Parliament, and Alys was reminded of the day she lay down with Joanna and the other women and tried to disrupt the very heart of the nation.

It had gained them nothing. But other women, she knew, would come along to resume the fray and although it might take years, in the end they would get the things they fought for.

They walked in St James's Park, beneath trees that were sere and bare, black branches against a pewter sky. The fall of snow during the night had been just enough to cover the grass and the ducks on the lake waddled from the water, burying their bright orange beaks beneath the snow, seeking titbits hidden there. The cold brought a bright flush to Alys's cheeks and her eyes glowed, exactly the colour of wild violets. For a moment, she was her old self again, the news in Mary's latest letter something to be faced later, not now. To his amusement, Marcus watched her do a little dance, flinging her arms wide and crying. 'Oh, how beautiful and quiet everything is here! I love the snow, don't you? It makes me feel like a child again.'

Marcus grimaced. 'At your advanced age, you should be showing more decorum, instead of prancing around like a wild New Forest pony.'

She knew he was teasing and pulled a rude face at him, then deliberately dropped back while he marched on ahead. She bent and gathered a handful of snow in her gloved hands, shaping it into a hard ball, hearing the squeak of the compressed snow as she pressed it between her palms. Then, standing poised and ready, she called his name and he turned to receive the snowball in his left eye.

She had aimed for his nose so it wasn't a bad shot. He gave a shout of mock outrage and bent to gather ammunition of his own, working more quickly than her so he was able to let fly first, pelting her so swiftly that she was forced to take shelter behind the thick trunk of a giant oak. Poking her head out, she shouted, 'That wasn't fair! You didn't give me a chance.'

The artist that was forever at work in him immediately visualised this scene on canvas; Alys with cheeks flushed wild rose by the cold, with ruby lips and a cheeky tilt to her head in its white fur cap. It matched the long, heavy woollen cloak with its deep collar of the same fur pulled up against her face.

She had protested, but not too forcibly, when he had suggested they buy the cloak and hat, and he'd pretended to agree to her offer to pay him back. She had already paid him for the other outfits he insisted she had and so her conscience was clear. Getting ready to aim again, he called back to her, 'All's fair in love and war. Besides, you started it. Now take your medicine. I thought that all you suffragettes were supposed to be tough.'

'All right, be like that,' she shouted back, and emerged from behind the tree to stand in full view and receive a half dozen snowballs which landed with deadly accuracy all about her person. She was able to get in a few shots of her own and passing couples, walking arm in arm, all wrapped up to the nines against the inclement weather, raised their eyebrows then smiled as they strolled by. Needled by his mention of the suffragettes – spoken in that dismissive tone all men used when referring to them; hadn't she seen it with the judges at that travesty in the court room – Alys kept up the battle as long as he did and it was Marcus who finally called an armistice.

'What do you promise if I accept your offer of surrender?' she called, holding back the last of her ammunition.

'A meat and potato pie and a hot drink,' he called back. 'Taken at a place I know nearby.'

Now she had ceased the frantic dodging of his snowballs and the constant bending to fashion her own, she could feel the chill creeping into her. Her woollen gloves were soaking, her fingers numb with cold. Still she felt exhilarated, as though she had drunk too much pink champagne and it had gone to her head. The truce was agreed upon. He approached her cautiously and took her arm, staring down at the silken strands of hair that had escaped the close-fitting fur cap. 'You look like a street urchin,' he told her. 'One of those adorably innocent young ladies who appear in those film melodramas.'

'The ones who usually live in the gutter?' she queried, pulling a comical face.

A shiver went through her and it was not entirely the cold that caused it. A sudden vision of Lilith and the rest of the 'ladies of the night' came to Alys's mind. Caused, no doubt, by her own reference to the gutter. After the comfortable life she was leading here, would she ever be content with the ways of the Welsh valleys again?

She longed to see Mary and her small family but, sadly, she no longer felt the same about Craven Bay. Marcus bent over her, concern on his face as he noticed she was shivering. His hand came up and brushed traces of snow from her cap and the cloak. Then, tucking her right hand into his coat pocket, his fingers curled protectively about hers, they walked across the snow-covered grass.

The small tea room, not long opened to the public, looked out upon the lake and he chose a table near the window so that they could enjoy the antics of the ducks and other wild birds that in winter made the lake their home. The deliciously hot pie and the tall white mugs of hot tea warmed them gratifyingly.

They walked back across the Park and joined the groups of people in the Mall who, when Marcus asked them, said they were waiting for the King and Queen to drive out. The heavy ornamental gates of the Palace swung open and a carriage drawn by four beautiful horses appeared. Standing on tiptoe, Alys was able to catch her very first glimpse of Queen Mary and her King. The Queen sat ramrod stiff and inclined her head and hand gracefully, acknowledging the cheering crowds.

King George smiled and nodded from the other side of the carriage and the people cheered and cheered, calling out 'Good luck,' and 'God bless your Majesties.' And Alys felt tears fill her eyes and the lump in her throat stopped her from answering Marcus's question was she all right.

Suddenly, it seemed all wrong that she should be so happy when poor Mary – and Jackie – were suffering . . .

Chapter Twenty-Three

For yet another night Alys heard the distant church bells strike three and still she turned restlessly on her pillow. She did not like what was happening, she told herself fiercely. She should get away now, while she was safe. No good could come of a relationship between such as her and Marcus. No good at all.

And Mary's latest letter had troubled her deeply, making her feel she should be there beside her friend, helping her overcome this tragedy. She had stuck loyally to Alys in her own troubles, despite her disapproval and distress, so it was only right that Alys should reciprocate now.

She thought of the other half of the return train ticket which she had insisted on, feeling safer in her heart if she knew there was a way to get back to the valleys any time she wanted. There was money saved from the fees Marcus had paid her for posing, so she would be all right until something else turned up. Then she thought of Mary without a job and her words: 'The train fares to Cardiff to see Jackie are not cheap and I'm still not working, although Mr Morgan from down the street has promised me a job working in his shop come Christmas. But whenever Mam tackles him about it, he just makes excuses . . .'

As though to strengthen her own resolution, she remembered Marcus's mother saying on the night of the dance: 'Don't you realise you are jeopardising the girl's good name?' And his reply, 'I hold no sway over Alys. She is at perfect liberty to return to Craven Bay or stay in London. I certainly would not stand in her way, whichever path she chooses.'

She thought of the fun he had been that morning in the park, the growing change in their relationship, and knew that if she did not get away from him soon, it would be too late. She had sworn, after Evan, that she would never again allow herself to be hurt by a man.

She thumped her pillow restlessly. It was no good. Sleep refused to woo her and eventually she threw back the bed covers and swung her feet to the floor. The sound of a loose shutter banging in the wind had her crossing to the window, drawing aside the curtains and peering out.

The moon slid across a sky filled with clouds, shedding a cold, wintry light on the snow-covered skeletons of the trees in the small park across the way. Alys shivered and made to snuggle back into her warm bed. But the loose shutter was making too much noise and she knew she'd just continue to be disturbed if she ignored it. Slipping a warm woollen shawl over the long flannelette nightgown she wore, unable to find her slippers in the dark and so doing without, she opened her bedroom door and crept down the stairs. The old boards protested, creaking loudly. Draughts snatched icily at her ankles. The comfortable sitting room at the back of the house where she spent the afternoons reading with only Rufus for company was the only room with shutters: long, narrow ones painted green, folded back on the inside during the day.

They could not have been secured properly, she thought. She reached the lower landing where Marcus had his bedroom, noting that the door was ajar. Unaccountably holding her breath – there's silly she was! – she hurried across to the dark opening at the top of the stairs. In her haste, her foot became entangled in the hem of her loose nightgown and she gave a small cry as she felt herself pitch forward and begin to fall.

She let herself go limp and tumbled the rest of the way, seeing stars at one point when her head came into contact with the banister. Lying in a huddle at the bottom of the staircase, feeling the cold marble of the hall floor biting through the nightgown, chilling her body and making her shiver uncontrollably, she tried to pull herself up by the banister rail, then cried out again as a shadow, darker than the rest in the hall, moved beside her.

An arm went under her knees, another round her back, and she was lifted effortlessly and carried through the open door of the sitting room. The unlatched shutter swung open, allowing enough of the moonlight in for her to see Marcus's face bending above hers. His voice, strangely gruff, asked, 'Are you all right? Nothing broken, I hope?'

She shook her head, realised he couldn't see and said, 'No, at least I don't think so. Just shaken.' She gave an embarrassed laugh. 'What a silly thing to do, falling downstairs at my age! Did I startle you?'

'That would be putting it mildly!' He sounded amused. 'I came down to investigate the banging shutter. It had kept me awake long enough and you know what a bear I can be if I don't get my sleep. I'd just reached the bottom step when, like a thunder clap – and a very bewitching one, too, I might add – you landed almost on top of me.'

Alys couldn't resist a giggle. 'I could have hurt you. I'm sorry. I had the same idea, to fix that blessed shutter. I couldn't sleep, either.'

'It must mean something that it should affect us both the same way.' His voice was soft. She realised she still rested in his arms and the urge to lean her head back against his shoulder and just stay there, safe and warm and sheltered from all the things that had been bothering her, was almost irresistible.

The sheer, sensual impact of his nearness, his large hands as they tightened seeming to hold her more closely still, caused a shudder to run through her from head to toe. She closed her eyes, waiting helplessly for his mouth to come down on hers. For she knew that in the natural course of events he would kiss her and she was powerless to stop him. She didn't *want* to stop him. Her body reacted with a will of its own and her hands went up to his shoulders, her fingers locking behind his head, tangling in the chestnut hair that grew low on his collar. He was in no hurry and when at last she felt his lips close over her own, a long, gratified sigh was wrenched from deep inside her.

She felt his mouth move against hers, hard and demanding, heard him moan, 'Alys!' She moved her hands so that her palms were against his cheeks, holding his head still as his mouth ravished hers. Small purring sounds came from her throat and she felt him moving, carrying her to the large chair beside the now grey ashes of the fire and lowering himself into it. He cradled her on his knees, his mouth never once leaving hers.

His hands were warm through the nightgown, burning her flesh. She was aware that the full skirt was rucked up, exposing her legs. Had she never before experienced a man's love, she knew she would have been shocked, even frightened by the sudden passion Marcus was displaying.

She felt his beard under her palms, silky and soft, and drawing her head back tried to gain a moment's breathing space. She said provocatively, 'I've never kissed a man with a beard before.'

He grunted. 'How many men *have* you kissed?'

She pursed her lips, pretending to frown, 'Oh, I've lost count. But never anyone with a beard.' She put her head to one side, gazing at him thoughtfully. 'Did I ever tell you it was very dashing and distinguished – very aristocratic?'

'But you don't like it?'

'I don't know. It's – different.' She pressed her finger tips to it, feeling the strong line of his jaw beneath. 'Why do you wear it?'

'Because I happen to like it.'

Alys laughed. 'Well, each to their own taste, as the old woman said when she kissed the goat.'

He grasped her hands and held them behind his back. 'Enough of my beard. Concentrate on *me*, you little vixen.'

The warm, hazy stupor of his kisses returned. One hand found its way through the buttoned opening of her nightgown and closed over her breast. Flames of desire raced through her and she clung to him almost desperately, giving back kiss for kiss as she strove to press her body yet closer to his.

'You know what's happening to us, don't you?' he murmured between kisses.

'Yes, I know.'

'You feel it, too?'

'I feel something,' she admitted slowly. 'But it's wrong, Marcus.'

'Why is it?' His arms tightened and he bent his head once more to claim her lips. She struggled and tried to sit up, her heart beating so swiftly she was sure he must feel it under his caressing hand. 'It's too sweet a feeling to be wrong,' he said softly. He kissed her throat, his lips burning her skin. And then, just when it seemed that nothing mattered but the warmth of his arms about her, his mouth moving against hers, when her body cried for blessed release, in the hall something fell with a loud crash. She gave a little cry and jerked upright in his arms, her eyes opening wide in alarm. 'What was that?'

Marcus muttered an oath beneath his breath. He stood up and pushed her back down into the big easy chair. 'Stay there. I'll take a look.'

There was enough light to see the shattered fragments of the large china vase lying on the floor. It had stood on the oval walnut table in the centre of the hall and Mrs Mimms had enjoyed using it for displaying chrysanthemums and the large-headed dahlias of autumn. Alys had often stood and admired the delicate pattern of thin-legged storks and water lilies, painted in pastel shades on an ivory-coloured background.

Now, as Marcus emerged into the hall, a sinuous shape appeared from the shadows and wound itself about his pyjama-clad ankles. 'Rufus!' He bent to scoop up the purring cat in his arms. 'You wretch, you! How are we going to explain this to Mrs Mimms when she arrives in the morning, eh?'

Rufus's purring became louder. Dozing in his warm basket in the kitchen, he must have heard voices and, his never-failing curiosity aroused, had wandered out to investigate. Holding the cat firmly, Marcus turned as Alys joined him in the hall. He grinned ruefully and murmured, 'With his penchant for leaping up on to tables and mantelpieces, over the years this cat has cost me a small fortune.' Looking into Alys's white face as she stood in the open doorway, the woollen shawl wrapped tightly about her, he thought that maybe the cat's intervention had been a blessing, for God knows how he could have faced Alys in the morning if events had been allowed to reach their natural conclusion.

He was angry with himself. It was not often that he let his emotions get out of control. And to think that with this lovely girl he'd almost . . .

His mouth tightened. Although he seethed inside, his voice was gentle when he said, 'You must still be feeling the effects of your night in a prison cell, which couldn't have been comfortable. Followed by that long walk. You must be exhausted.'

She knew he was trying to gloss over what had almost happened. She could not decide whether she was glad or angry. Seeing the way he was looking at her, that silly cat still nestling in his arms, she felt all shivery, her stomach tied up in knots. How could she have let this happen after the mistake she had made with Evan and all its ghastly consequences? Tonight, all her good intentions had faded like mist in the morning sun. She had almost made another mistake that would have haunted her for the rest of her life.

'Yes, you're right,' she said. 'I ought to be in bed. Good night, Marcus.' She walked away from him, up the stairs and along the landing to her own room. The sheets were icy cold and she lay on her side, curled up into a ball, and tried to capture the sleep which had earlier eluded her. She felt tears start in her eyes and it was only later when she felt a soft thud land against her feet and heard the familiar purring that she relaxed.

Sleepily, she murmured, 'You certainly know how to save a girl's bacon! Thanks, you old softie,' and fell asleep with the comforting weight of the ginger cat on her feet.

She crept down to the kitchen the following morning, perking up a little at the sight of Mrs Mimms. The woman took one look at her and clicked her tongue reproachfully. 'You look washed-out this mornin'! Still affected by the night you spent in that terrible place, are you?' Mrs Mimms could never bring herself to actually say the word 'prison'. She went close to Alys and swept the girl into her arms. 'Much as I admire Mister Marcus I know sometimes 'e can be very 'ard. Don't suppose 'e means to be, but there it is. There, there, my gel,' one podgy hand patted Alys on the back, 'don't upset yourself, now. That's not like you. I thought all you Welsh gels were tough!' she stepped back, holding Alys at arm's length, smiling into her eyes.

'I'm all right, Mrs Mimms, really.' She wiped the back of her hand under her nose, remembered her handkerchief and felt in her pocket for the small square of lace-edged cambric. Mrs Mimms turned to the stove and lifted the heavy frying pan on to the front ring. 'A good breakfast and you'll soon forget all that. Mister Marcus 'ad 'is a while ago.' She busied herself with lifting slices of bacon from the white wrapping paper, placing them side by side in the pan. 'That dratted cat! Did you see what 'e did to me favourite vase? In pieces all over the floor it was, when I walked through this mornin'.'

There had been no sign of the broken vase when Alys came down that morning so she supposed the housekeeper must have tidied it up right away. She gave a noncommittal smile. She was glad when a little while later Marcus came into the kitchen. Immediately, the room felt different, more alive for his presence. 'Aren't you ready yet?' he asked Alys.

It was as though the events of the night before had never happened. He might never have held her so sweetly in his arms, murmuring endearments that had turned all her good resolutions to naught.

Mrs Mimms gave him a withering look. 'Now, sir, we won't 'ave no more bullying, if you don't mind. You don't want Miss Alys arriving at your mum and dad's looking as though she's lost a shilling and found a farthing, do you?'

'Indeed I don't, Mrs Mimms.' The scowl on Marcus's face lightened. He gave Alys a deep, mocking bow and said, 'When you are ready, my dear.' He smiled down at her and saw her hesitate, obviously still uncertain whether to accept his mother's offer or not.

He hadn't really asked her, she thought, but told her she was to go. She didn't like being told she had to do something. All ready to argue, she gazed up into his eyes and was lost.

Marcus saw how the lovely colour flooded her cheeks

and was reminded of the large, roomy chair in that dark room, with her in his arms, the sweetness of her lips beneath his. Of all the women he had known, none had affected him as had this slip of a girl from the world of his childhood. The thought of what would happen when the painting was finished disturbed him deeply. She would vanish from his life, whether back to the valleys or some other place it did not matter, she would not be with him. What could he do to remedy that? he wondered. The idea that he might be contemplating marriage to this girl filled him with astonishment.

He remembered Evan Jenkins and experienced a stab of jealousy quite alien to his nature. How far would she have allowed him to go if he had ignored her pleas and continued with his lovemaking? Would it have been the whole way, as she had with the Jenkins boy? Was he looking no deeper than the beauty he had captured on canvas?

If later Alys flinched because his grip on her arm was tighter than usual as he escorted her to the waiting car, she made no comment.

Chapter Twenty-Four

Alys tried to ignore the tension between them and concentrate on the scenery. The fields had lost their green lustre, muted by winter, their boundaries marked by fringes of darker green where the snow had melted.

Marcus drove into the wide courtyard of the lovely house and Alys wondered why there were no other cars or carriages parked there. When she commented that they must be the first to arrive, he answered casually, 'Oh, didn't I tell you? We are to be the only guests.'

Two spaniels, mother and son, hearing Marcus's voice, came skidding out to greet them, long silky ears flopping against their shoulders. Alys thought, at least somebody is pleased to see me, and then chastised herself for her hypersensitivity.

The maid took Alys's coat and fur hat, and escorted her and Marcus into the large drawing room where flames leaped and crackled in the huge fireplace and a large fir tree covered in crystal ornaments and streams of silver tinsel glittered in a corner near the French windows. Plump cushions with embroidered covers sat on the sofa and chairs, and Alys recognised the designs and colours as similar to those on the tea cosy and other things at Marcus's house in London. Funny that she had not noticed them on her last visit, she thought. Smoothing her hand over one cushion as she seated herself on the sofa, she murmured, 'Beautiful!' Catching Martha Dillon's eye, she added, 'Did you do them?'

'Yes. One of my little hobbies.' Martha smiled. 'Are you keen on embroidery, Alys?'

'I've never really had the time. Although I admire any-one who can do it. Creating those beautiful things must be very rewarding.'

Martha nodded. 'Also time consuming. But then, I have plenty of that, these days.' Her eyes, set deep beneath gently arching brows, were of a piercing bright blue and suddenly Alys was wondering why she ever imagined this woman did not like her. Before she could say anything further, Marcus's father claimed her, saying, 'So you made it, I see!'

'Didn't you think we would?' Alys couldn't help the teasing note in her voice.

Gerard Dillon chuckled. 'The way my son drives, I'm always in doubt that he'll ever arrive in one piece. The good Lord never meant man to travel faster than a horse can gallop.'

Although she had liked him on sight, there had been little time or opportunity to talk with Marcus's father the last time Alys had visited, but now he more than made up for that. Under Marcus's amused eye, Gerard settled himself beside Alys while his wife talked to their son. 'Did you really throw dead fish at the police at that last suffragette gathering?' he wanted to know.

Alys laughed. 'Not me. But I threw myself down on the floor in the entrance to the House of Commons, along with a lot of other women, and they had to move us by force.'

'Joanna organised all that, I bet.' His eyes sparkled. 'How I wish I had been there! I bet that knocked some of the starch out of those old stuffed shirts.'

Remembering the choleric muttering of the dark-suited men, their faces red with fury, she laughed again. 'I gather they weren't very pleased. I reckon if the police hadn't arrived, they would have had a go at moving us themselves.'

He grinned. 'Easier said than done, I bet.'

Alys's nose wrinkled. 'You could say that, sir.'

He raised one hand in protest at her use of the word. 'Oh, please, my dear, not sir. My friends call me Gerard.'

Alys lowered her eyes in a gesture so demure it enchanted the elderly man. It was only recently that she had taken to calling Marcus by his first name. 'I don't think I could do that, Mr Dillon. I'm really just an employee of Marcus's. Just like her,' nodding towards a young woman dressed in neat black with a lacy cap perched on her head and a matching minuscule apron. She carried a silver tray in both hands which she offered to Marcus and his mother with their choice of drinks. Sherry for Martha, whisky and water for Marcus. 'We both give our services for a wage. Perhaps on a different level, but it boils down to the same in the end.'

'It's a sad day when a lovely young woman is so over-awed by class distinctions that she refuses the hand of friendship I so gallantly offer.'

Alys didn't know what to say. She had found him a genuinely nice man and would have loved to have been able to call him friend. Perhaps in time . . . Then she reminded herself that she wouldn't be around long enough to strike up any kind of friendship with Marcus's father or mother. In the cold light of day, reliving the events of the night had disturbed her deeply. What must he have thought of her? The wild, wanton woman she had become in his arms! She couldn't blame him, for it takes two to indulge in a love scene and she had relished every touch of his lips; on her mouth, her throat, the gentle fondling of the long artist's fingers on her breast. She wondered again how it would have ended had not Rufus jumped on to the hall table, sending the vase flying – and shattering a very dangerous mood.

She didn't want to think about it. Marcus had known of her past transgression with Evan. Had he hoped that she might yield to his demands without demur? That was not the Marcus she had come to know. But then, two people in the dead of night, both newly risen from bed and dressed to return . . . The whole scenario was powerfully charged.

Later, when they were still talking, Gerard predictably dominating the conversation, claiming all her attention, Marcus looked across at her and delighted Alys with a knowing wink. He seemed to be saying: 'There, you've clicked!'

The weekend passed quietly and pleasantly. They took walks with the dogs scampering before them, sniffing busily at all manner of enticing scents, their breath misty in the cold air. Very little of the snow remained and they were able to enjoy the countryside to their heart's content. Alys caught an enigmatic glance in their direction from his mother when Marcus buttoned her coat, carefully tucking in the stray curls of hair that escaped from the white fur cap. There was speculation there, and – could it be? – amusement.

Assisting her over the trunk of a fallen tree that blocked their path, Marcus allowed his hand to remain around hers and she kept silent, enjoying the warm, firm grasp of his fingers.

Neither had mentioned the night-time incident, each loath to bring it into the open for fear of distressing the other, although a certain tension surfaced between them from time to time.

They sat in a clearing and watched the dogs investigate a rabbit hole, laughing at their excitement. Then Marcus gazed up at the lowering sun and said, 'Better get back. Mother will be expecting us for lunch.'

Unwilling to leave the peace and solitude of the woods, Alys hung back. He leaned over to take her hands and pull her almost roughly to her feet. 'Come on, slowcoach! I'm starving even if you're not.' He held on to her even though she made an effort to pull away. She wouldn't meet his eyes, keeping her own lowered to the rough grass beneath them. Then he was pulling her even closer, his arms going about her body, holding her close. Turning her face away, she felt his breath warm on her cheek; heard his voice, whispering in her ear, 'Don't fight it, Alys?'

'What?' She spoke sullenly, not wanting him to see how much his nearness affected her.

'The chemistry.'

'I don't even know what that is.'

'It's this . . .' One hand went up to pull the fur cap from her head, throwing it haphazardly towards the low branch of a nearby tree. His fingers crept into her hair, tangling themselves in its silky softness, holding her head still so that when she finally turned to look at him his lips were just above hers. His kiss was long and intense, as though he drew her very soul from her body. A feeling of dizziness overcame her and she was forced to cling to him to steady herself, knowing she would fall if he suddenly let her go. 'See what I mean?' she heard his murmur. 'It's something no one can ignore.'

He spoke with such calm assurance that Alys felt anger stir in her. Suddenly she was pushing him away with all her might, saying tersely, 'Well, it just happens to be something *I* can ignore.'

'You could have fooled me,' he replied, the self-satisfied look on his face making her even more angry.

'How long before the painting is finished?' she asked, turning her back on him so that he could not see her face. 'How many more days?'

His reply had her turning with clenched fists, looking as though she would like to strike him. 'I put the last touches to it a couple of days ago.'

'And you let me go on thinking it would be a while yet?'

'I had to keep you here somehow.'

'It's nice to know you're so concerned for my welfare.' Her words were filled with scorn. She went over to snatch her hat from the tree where he'd tossed it, and pulled it on so violently that she heard him laugh. Then, without another word, she started back to the house, hearing his footsteps behind her, his whistle to call the dogs to heel.

After lunch, with a determined glint in her eye, Alys tossed a bombshell into their cosy little world. Marcus and his father were sprawling in easy chairs, one each side of the fireplace with its roaring log fire. Pages of the

Sunday newspapers were spread across their out-stretched legs and scattered on the carpet.

Civil war was brewing in Ireland and there were reports of trouble in the Balkans with claims of Germany rearming at a furious pace. The word 'Suffragette' featured prominently in the headlines and Alys wondered what Martha Dillon must think of it all. She already knew Gerard's views on women's suffrage. Alys could see that he was on the point of dozing off and so she went to stand beside Martha, admiring the splendid display of prize blooms she was arranging in a deep blue porcelain vase. Alys picked up one of the bronze chrysanthemums, inhaling its damp, slightly acrid scent. For some reason she could not explain, she said, 'I heard from a friend the other day, and I've decided to go home.' She wanted to add: 'Now that Marcus doesn't need me any more' but didn't.

He glanced up from his study of the scarlet heart of the fire, and frowned. 'What exactly do you mean by that?' His voice grated.

Alys turned her head to look at him coolly. 'Just what I say.'

'Oh!' He frowned. 'It's the first I've heard of it.' And something in his voice made her say, more sharply than she had intended, 'I didn't realise I had to ask your permission. You say the painting is finished, so you don't need me any more – and Mary does.'

'Of all the ungrateful, contrary women! And what do you suppose I shall do?'

'Oh, no doubt you'll survive.'

'You can't just walk out on me!' Rising to his feet he threw down the newspaper in disgust and strode across the room, grasping her roughly by the arm. 'I think we should talk about it, don't you?'

Alys said calmly, 'Talking won't help. I've made up my mind. I consider I've given you enough of my time. Now someone else needs my help. I shall leave just as soon as I can make arrangements.'

His mouth twisted. 'Just like that? Even a condemned man is allowed a few words in mitigation.'

Martha stood looking from one to the other, an expression of bewilderment on her face. 'Oh, that's too bad, Alys. I was hoping you would be able to join us for the Christmas celebrations.'

Alys smiled. 'I would have liked that, Mrs Dillon. But I really must go. My friend Mary needs me. Things have been happening at home that you wouldn't believe.'

'Women!' With a disgusted snort Marcus left the room, calling to the dogs and slamming the door behind him. Alys stood and rubbed the place where his fingers had dug into her arm. She would be bruised later, she thought.

A soft snore from the direction of the fireplace had Martha glancing at Alys with a smile. 'Do we really want to stay indoors with a sleepy old man and a grumpy young one? The sun's out, if only for a little while. Why don't we take advantage of it while it lasts? I'll show you my chrysanthemums. They won first prize this year at the autumn show.'

Slipping warm coats about their shoulders, they walked slowly round the lovely gardens. Although the vast banks of rhododendrons were brown and sere, the flower beds lacking their glorious show of summer colours, Alys felt strangely at peace and wondered what it must be like to live here, to be able to call this lovely place your home.

Still, she was glad she had finally made the decision to return to Wales, a decision that would probably affect the rest of her life. Wasn't it better to face up to something that you knew to be inevitable rather than vacillate as she had been doing lately? Deep in her own thoughts, she was still aware of her hostess's own introspection.

Dead-heading a thick clump of chrysanthemums, Martha said without turning to look at Alys, 'I really was hoping you would be able to join us for Christmas. Joanna Ambrey will be here. I know Marcus will be looking forward to seeing her. You know Lady Joanna, I believe? So full of spirit, so vivacious!'

'Oh, yes, I know Lady Joanna.' Alys wondered if this elegant woman knew the real story behind the reports of the suffragettes. The papers had mocked them, calling them interfering busybodies who should be home looking after their husbands and children instead of creating havoc. So she was surprised when Martha said, straightening up, both hands pressed to the small of her back, 'Were I a few years younger, my dear, I should be in their ranks.' She shook her head. 'But now we have Christmas to think about. It's a tiring time, I find, but very worthwhile.'

Alys smiled. 'Yes, Christmas is a grand time to spend with family and friends.'

'Oh, very little family, dear,' Martha told her. 'There's only myself and my husband, and of course Marcus.' It seemed sad, somehow, for her to admit that and just as they were about to go back into the house, for already early darkness was beginning to set in, Alys plucked up courage to say, 'Before we join the others, wouldn't you like to tell me what is bothering you?'

The other woman's brows rose in amusement. 'Remarkable girl! As a matter of fact, I've been trying to find the right words to thank you, words that didn't sound too condescending.'

Alys looked surprised. 'Thank me? For what?'

'The things you said to my son. It's some time since anyone was as straightforward as that.'

Alys's lips quirked. 'A bit *too* straightforward, was I?'

'Not at all. You were delightful. You know, Alys, he's a very nice man, if at times infuriatingly smug. But, of course, that's only a fond mother's opinion.'

'I wouldn't presume to argue with you there, Mrs Dillon.'

'Thank you. Also a brilliant man. The only thing he has never learned is how to relax and enjoy himself. But, you know, when you spoke to him like that, there was a look in his eyes that I've never seen before. It was like a baby's expression on learning to walk.'

Alys nodded. 'But he still resents being spoken to like that.'

'Of course. But if I know my son he will follow you to wherever you go to see you again and you won't be able to do a thing about it.'

A look came over the girl's face that had the older woman's eyes softening. 'I don't think I'd mind that at all,' murmured Alys.

Mrs Dillon laughed aloud. 'Now let's go indoors and persuade someone to make us a cup of tea.'

*   *   *

Learning that Alys was leaving London, Joanna made a surprise visit to the studio, clearly perturbed by the news. Secretly, she blamed herself for Alys's unexpected decision, for the merciless attitude of the police and then a night in prison must have been horrific for a young woman brought up in the country.

She hugged Alys to her, saying, 'Oh, my dear, I would have given anything to have shielded you from that ghastly experience! You'll return to your lovely valley thinking the very worst of us, and with good reason. And yet,' she smiled, 'you were such a brave little thing. I'll always hold the memory of you kicking that red-faced policeman on the shin when he tried to lift you into the police van. His expression – and the language! It was an education.'

'It certainly was,' agreed Alys wryly.

'Are you sure you won't change your mind? We are badly in need of an organising secretary for our branch in the East End. We would pay you £2 a week. Not much, but think of the satisfaction you would get in doing such a job.'

'Thank you, Joanna, for your faith in my abilities, but I really have made up my mind. I can't go back on it now.'

Joanna clicked her tongue in exasperation. 'Marcus said you were a stubborn little wench! Still, I respect your decision. Only promise that you will come back to see us sometime, won't you?' She smiled. 'Even if you have to visit me in prison, for I and my ladies are determined to carry on the battle.'

'If ever I get the chance, I will. I promise,' said Alys softly. But that was most unlikely, she thought. When would she ever have the money to pay for a train ticket to take her all the way back to London to see Joanna – or anyone else? Once back in the valleys, who knew what her future would be?

Marcus refused even to try to understand. 'Have you thought what you are going back to? What sort of future awaits you?' he barked. 'Don't expect me to feel sorry for you if things don't work out.'

Determined not to let her anger get the better of her and so end up exchanging bitter words with him, she said lightly, 'I could very well end up a little waif on the streets. Would you feel sorry for me then? You could buy a box of matches off me at the very least. You always did accuse me of looking like a street urchin.'

'Stop acting the fool and tell me why you are going away. The truth,' he said tightly. 'Why you want to leave me. Haven't you been happy here? Haven't we done everything for your comfort?'

She hung her head. 'Yes, and I'm grateful for it. Mrs Mimms has been like a second mother to me – and Rufus always made me welcome.' Rufus knew when I was around, she thought, came and told me in his own way that he enjoyed my company. Not like some I could mention . . .

'Then what idiotic notion has got into that silly little head of yours to make you want to go back to a place where you know you'll be unhappy?'

'I don't know that!' The shocked denial came out before she could stop it, and her eyes looked at him so beseechingly that it took all his self-control not to drag her to him, carry her bodily upstairs and make violent love to her, thus ensuring that she would stay with him forever. Then the hard shell snapped back into place to cover his vulnerability and he turned away and walked from the room. 'Let Mrs Mimms know when you are ready to leave,' he said, without turning his head. 'And I'll see that a taxi cab is here to take you to the station.'

Chapter Twenty-Five

A few days later Alys was back in the valleys. The station was deserted. Except for the few passengers and some workmen who were loading produce in the rear of the station, she seemed the only person about.

Holding her ticket tightly, she was beset by conflicting emotions as she crossed the wooden platform and emerged into the lane that led to the small town. Nothing had changed. But then, nothing ever did change in Craven Bay. A few people recognised her and smiled uncertainly, unsure of her in her new and elegant outfit of soft beige wool.

Settled in a first-class seat by Marcus who brushed aside her protestations that really third class was fine, she had given him a last wave and then leaned her cheek against the cool window pane and watched the smoky suburbs of London gradually vanish and the lovely countryside take its place.

Mary had insisted that she come to them, at least until she found her feet. 'Mam will be offended if you refuse, and *I'll* never speak to you again,' she wrote.

It would be a tight squeeze in the small house, with Mary's three brothers and father, but a small thing like that had never bothered the hospitable O'Malleys.

She would help with the boys, and between them she and Mary should be able to give Mrs O'Malley a well-earned rest. And it'll do *you* good, she told herself. A bit of honest housework after all that spoiling Mrs Mimms dished out.

The housekeeper had fretted and fussed and adjured Alys not to speak to any strange men who might seek to make her acquaintance on the long train journey. Alys had smiled, thinking of Mary and her dire warnings about white-slave traders. The housekeeper zealously assured Alys that she would be sure to tell Mr Simon goodbye and that Alys was sorry she hadn't seen him before she left.

'And once you're gorn,' Mrs Mimms muttered, thumping the bread dough she kneaded on the kitchen table, 'I suppose 'e'll be like a bear wi' a sore 'ead again, no livin' wi' 'im. Oh, Alys, are you sure you know what you're doin'?'

'He?' Alys queried. 'Mr Simon?'

Mrs Mimms grunted, giving the dough an extra threatening thump as if it alone was the origin of her displeasure. 'Not Mr Simon. Mr Marcus.'

Alys could see in the woman's eyes that she guessed her reason for running away, and disapproved. For that was what she was doing, wasn't it? Running away from Marcus and her own feelings?

But from the moment Mary opened the front door of the little house to her, there was no more time to think. The warmth and generosity of the O'Malleys chased all other thoughts from her mind. Even little Billy joined in the welcome, winding fat little arms around her neck, his open-mouthed kiss sloppy against her cheek as she bent to cuddle him. It was so good to hear the familiar lilting voices, to bite into a still warm Welsh cake with its spicy aroma filling the small kitchen, to sip the fragrant tea from the thick cup that Mrs O'Malley offered so smilingly. The two other boys, Dennis and Kenny, put in an appearance to gulp their tea and receive a clip round the ear from their mother for snatching at a second piece of cake without first asking permission.

They stared at Alys, awed by the well-cut costume of fine wool, the small hat with its eye-veil skimming her eyebrows, the coils of shining hair, and couldn't for the life of them associate her with the girl in the faded pink skirt and blouse who once sold cockles from the back of old Drogo and whispered about boys with their sister, their giggles filling the house.

'You've changed,' Mary told her later when Mr O'Malley had come in and then gone out again, the few shillings he had won on that afternoon's races burning a hole in his pocket. 'You're quite the lady now, aren't you?'

'I don't think I have much. Changed, I mean. It's been a while, you know, and people *do* change. Even you have. But it's not going to make any difference between us, is it? You're still my best friend.'

Mary smiled and nodded, and Alys went on, 'Tell me about Jackie. I was shocked when I read your letters. I just can't believe it.'

Mrs O'Malley had followed her husband's example and left the two girls to talk, saying she was visiting the woman across the road who had been ill, to see if there was anything she could do for the poor soul. She took Billy with her and directed a warning glance to the older boys, cautioning them to behave themselves. As soon as they were alone, Mary began talking. 'I've never admitted this to anyone, Alys, not even Mam. I've always put a brave face on it, and I know people think I'm hard. It's just that if I once let myself go, I know I wouldn't be any use either to Jackie or myself. But I have dreadful nightmares about him and that place where they're holding him. You don't know how bad it is, how soul destroying. I think if he has to stay there much longer he'll crack. The warders treat you like dirt. When you visit you're just a faceless body being allowed to see another faceless body, and yet you're made to feel as though you should be grovelling in gratitude.'

Tears welled in her eyes and ran down her cheeks. Alys put her arms about her and held her while the two elder boys watched silently. Thinking back to all that had happened since she left Craven Bay with Marcus, Alys said, softly, 'You still love him then?'

Mary gave her a scornful look through the tears. 'Of course! What else? Haven't I always loved the silly bugger?' Not waiting for Alys's answer, she went on, 'I suppose I always will. We women are fools, aren't we? Put up with all kinds of treatment from a man if we love him.'

Silently, Alys had to agree with her.

The two boys exchanged glances. The shared memory of that afternoon when they had frightened Miss Netta's horse into rearing directly in front of her father's car on the headlands, causing the accident, concerned them not in the least. In their eyes, the Jenkins family *had* to suffer, *was* suffering, so as to pay back some of the misery caused to their sister.

Alys thought of her own night spent in jail and how terrible it had been. But, instinctively, somehow she had known Marcus would soon be there to help. How much more terrible must it be for Jackie, with no prospect of release?

Mary was wiping her eyes on the corner of her apron, saying, 'I've been thinking, Alys. I might try to find work in Cardiff. I'd be closer to Jackie and able to see him more often. As it is now, the train journey's expensive. I can't expect Mam to fork out the fare every time I want to go, and I'm never sure when I do get there if they are going to let me see him.' Fresh tears threatened.

'That sounds a good idea,' agreed Alys quickly, although she did not like to point out that Jackie's stay in prison might be a lengthy one, and would Mary really want to live and work in a strange town for who knows how many years?

If something very much worse wasn't to be Jackie's fate . . .

She pushed the terrifying thought away, praying that Mary wouldn't read her mind, although the possibility must have occurred to her at some time. Murder was the ultimate crime. And murder, if that was what they declared Jackie guilty of, was punishable by hanging . . .

'Mr Morgan from down the road promised he'd let me help in his store as soon as the Christmas rush started, but this year things have been so bad it doesn't look as though there's going to be any Christmas rush. I've tried everywhere else and the answer is always the same – a pitying look and a shake of the head.'

She raised her eyes to look at Alys, a pleading look in their blue depths. 'I feel, with you here, at least I'd be leaving Mam in safe hands. You wouldn't mind, would you, Alys? Perhaps when I'm settled you could come to Cardiff for a visit, and bring her? She's never been out of Craven Bay in her life.'

A thought struck her and she frowned. 'But there's selfish I am! If *I* can't get work here, how are you going to?'

Alys patted her hand. 'I've used hardly any of the money Marcus paid me for posing for him. Nothing I wanted to spend it on, see. I got my food and board, and there was a young man called Simon who was very good to me . . . But never mind that. I'm all right for money for a bit, and I can always keep my eyes and ears open for any work that's going. I don't mind what I do, as long as I can remain independent and beholden to no one.'

The association of ideas caused her to ask, 'How's Drogo? Do you ever see old Lear who minds the stables?'

'The two boys are always hanging around there – cheeky they are! They earn the odd penny for sweeping out the stalls. Drogo must be all right or we'd have heard.' She reached out and squeezed Alys's hand. 'Always one for worrying about other people and things, weren't you? Even smelly old donkeys.'

'Drogo might be old but he isn't smelly!'

Mary laughed and bent forward to poke the fire, thrusting the long black poker into the very heart of the coals, causing a welcome flare of orange flames. 'I don't know how you're going to take this, Alys, or if I should even be telling you, but you'll find it out sooner or later. Evan Jenkins is on his way home. I was speaking to the woman from the post office the other day and she said Miss Netta had been in to send a telegram to Evan, telling him about his father's accident and saying he must come home.'

To her own exasperation, Alys blushed and said bluntly, 'So? Why on earth should you imagine a little item like Evan Jenkins coming home would interest me now? I'm much more interested in Drogo's welfare than something like that.' She suppressed a deep sigh then asked, 'What accident anyway?'

'His father had a terrible smash in his new car and they thought he wouldn't live. Mrs Dean told me it was touch and go for a few days. Even so, they say he'll never walk again.'

'Oh dear, I'm sorry!' For a moment she was, but memories of the heartless old man came crowding in, diluting the pity.

She gazed at her friend compassionately. 'You've all had a bad time, haven't you, while I've been off gallivanting in London? Poor Mary!'

The Irish girl's lips firmed and her blue eyes glittered. 'I'll bounce back,' she said with an air of determination. 'I always do. And I'll be all the better for it, you see if I'm not.'

Mrs O'Malley returned from her mission of mercy and Alys couldn't help wondering what they had talked about, Mrs O'Malley and her sick neighbour. Would it be her return to Craven Bay and the whys and wherefores of it all? she wondered. Mrs O'Malley was no plaster saint, and warmed by the kitchen fire, a cup of tea on the table and a sympathetic ear, the gossip would fly. Providing her listener didn't probe too deeply or ask too many questions, for Alys was a favourite of hers and she would not dream of hurting her intentionally.

The older woman stood by the kitchen sink, filling the kettle, her gaze thoughtful as she looked at the two girls. She noted her daughter's flushed cheeks and elated manner. After the recent months of gloom and despondency, it was good to hear the soft laughter of the two friends again. For, faith, wasn't laughter the singing of the angels?

Christmas came and went. At church on Christmas morning Father Goodhew greeted Alys warmly; a strayed lamb safely back in the fold.

She received a card from Marcus and Mrs Mimms, one from Marcus's parents, and one from Joanna. Marcus asked politely after her health and sent regards to Mary and her family. Apart from that, he made no mention of personal matters. A scribble on the back of the card said he was very busy with a new model and the portrait was proving to be fascinating.

Pangs of jealousy twisted painfully inside her when she read the words. She wanted to catch the first train and go rushing back with her recriminations. How childish and stupid that would appear! Just what he was hoping to achieve, she thought bitterly, so that he could accuse her of more childish behaviour.

But that didn't stop her from thinking about him.

Visions of Marcus came to mind at the oddest times and in the most unexpected places. While she stood at the kitchen sink peeling potatoes for Mrs O'Malley or sewing a button on one of the boys' jackets, her hands would slow and she would lift her eyes to the window and gaze unseeingly at the small garden outside. The pictures of him lasted no more than a brief second but were so disturbingly real they left her breathless, distracted from the task in hand.

Marcus solemnly mixing paints on the palette, his face a study in concentration; Marcus scooping up Rufus in his arms and scratching the long fur between his ears, the contented purring of the cat loud in the room; Marcus red-faced and cursing under his breath as he tried to turn the starting handle of the white Hispano Suiza which coughed and sputtered but refused to start.

There were times when she became so swept up in these imaginings that tears would shimmer in her eyes, but she was determined to remain strong and aloof.

If only there wasn't such a heavy price to be paid for independence.

Mary had departed for Cardiff, tight-lipped and pale, clearly plagued by second thoughts. Swallowing her pride, she had been to see Mrs Dean at the house on the headlands, choosing an afternoon when she knew Netta would be out and conscious of the fact that old Thomas was still in hospital.

Mrs O'Malley flatly refused to allow her daughter to depart for foreign parts, as she thought of Cardiff or anywhere else that wasn't Craven Bay, without the address of respectable lodgings in her handbag. Mrs Dean was Mary's only hope, and for all of their differences in the past, she and the old cook had remained on speaking terms.

Gossip flew thick and fast as Mary sat drinking tea beside that familiar fireplace. Mrs Dean had clearly missed the company of the Irish girl, for she vowed the new maid who had replaced her was a dolt and good for nothing. 'So you're thinking of going off to Cardiff to find work, are you?' Her gaze was shrewd as she peered at Mary. 'Well, as it happens, I do know of a family who are always on the look-out for new staff. Their cook is a friend of mind. At school together, so we was, and kept in touch ever since. I don't see 'er as much as I'd like to, mind, but she's been in that position for a long time and seems 'appy enough.'

Just as shrewdly, Mary asked why in that case they were always short of other staff. Mrs Dean shrugged. 'Gels of today don't want to stay long anywhere, do they?' She reached across the table for a pencil and the pad she used for her grocery list. 'I'll write the address down for you, dear. I won't say it'll 'elp for definite but at least it's a start. And I'll add the address of a boarding 'ouse I've stayed at the few times I've bin to Cardiff. Cheap, it is, nothing fancy, but clean and comfortable. Just in case you're a while getting fixed up, like.'

She folded the piece of paper in half and handed it to Mary. The girl smiled her thanks and thought about going; darkness was already setting in and the wind across the headlands would be icy. But it seemed discourteous to leave too abruptly and so she accepted another cup of tea and listened politely to the latest developments in the Jenkins family saga.

'How is Mr Thomas now?' she asked after Mrs Dean had finished detailing the treatment the old man was receiving, with a fair amount of relish.

'They say he'll be away for a while yet. But Mr Evan will be 'ome soon and 'e can take over.' She shot Mary a cunning glance from under her eyelashes. 'Did you 'ear about Miss Netta getting engaged?'

Mary looked surprised. 'No. That was rather sudden, wasn't it?'

'Yes, it's to some man she's known for years, met when she was staying with her cousin, Miss Clarissa, on those visits to Cardiff. Of course, it's just like Miss Netta to make up 'er mind when 'er father is so poorly, but she says it'll be an excuse for a quiet wedding which is what she wants.'

Mary's lips twitched. Somehow that didn't ring true. A quiet wedding for Netta Jenkins! Still, with her father indisposed and liable to be so for some time, she supposed it was for the best.

Mary speculated on the suddenness of the union and wondered how Jackie would take the news. Did he still have some feelings for the girl who had led him such a merry dance? And was she, Mary O'Malley, a complete idiot to go traipsing off to a strange city which she didn't know and had hated on her one and only visit there, in order to be closer to a man who . . . ?

She pushed that thought away, smiling at Mrs Dean.

'When's the wedding, then?'

'As soon as Mr Evan arrives. 'e's to give 'er away.'

On her first free day from her new job, Mary set out on the long tram ride to see Jackie. Without the slightest hesitation she had been taken on by the woman whose address Mrs Dean had supplied, and although she worked long days, with her new mistress proving to be a hard and meticulous task-master, over-particular about the tiniest detail, Mary savoured the ease with which she could now visit Jackie.

In the prison corridor, terrified that her request would

be refused, she sat nervously pleating her handkerchief, her knuckles white with tension. Churlishly, they had made her wait for what seemed like hours and the precious time was slipping away, for she had to be back at her job in time to serve supper. The other women, mothers and wives, were ushered in to see their menfolk. They shared a joke with the warders, some of the younger ones actually flirting. When at last they called Mary's name – O'Malley, not even the dignity of Miss – she rose and followed the uniformed guard to the tiny cold room where Jackie waited.

Although his face brightened when he saw her, today he was uncommunicative; sullen and morose. Mary hated to see him like this. Ignoring the warder's fierce glance, she caught his hand. 'Cheer up, love. Now that I'm working in Cardiff I can see you more often. I'll come whenever I can.'

She gave him a bright smile as he looked at her from under a tangle of thick black lashes. 'Here, let me tell you about the new lady I'm working for. She's got an awful habit of letting off wind! Can't help it, poor soul, but she chooses the worst possible places and times. There was the other night, when the vicar and his wife came to supper . . .'

The short time allowed was soon over, but even so she thought Jackie looked a little more light-hearted as she said goodbye.

She had told him about Alys's return to Craven Bay and how she was staying with Mary's family until she got herself sorted out. She didn't tell him about Netta or her forthcoming marriage. Mary's gentle nature was such that if Jackie still felt anything at all for Netta Jenkins, then she didn't want to be the one to cause him further pain by passing on the news.

She was walking through the outside courtyard, the joyous manner she had deliberately adopted in front of Jackie already evaporating, when there was a sudden commotion in the main entrance. A man's voice called out, loudly, 'I've got to see him, I tell you. It's important. A matter of life and death.'

Curiously she stared at the youngish man as two warders grappled with him. You couldn't just walk in here and demand to see the prison governor, they told him. 'But you don't understand! It's played on my mind for so long I won't rest until I've told somebody.'

The bright colour of an approaching tram gleaming through the thin fog had Mary running to the stop, the man's words already forgotten.

Despite Mary's dislike of the prison warder, there must have been a spark of compassion still in him for the following day he approached Jackie in the high-walled yard where the prisoners were allowed brief periods of exercise. He said gruffly, 'Got somethin' to tell you, Rees. There was a bloke in 'ere yesterday, talking to the Governor. Seems as though he's confessing to a part in old Rozenberg's death.'

Jackie stared, sudden hope flaring in his breast. 'And?' he prompted.

The warder shrugged. 'Just talk, mind. Don't know if there's any truth in it. 'spect you'll soon know if there is.' And with that, Jackie had to be content.

Chapter Twenty-Six

For the first time that he could remember, Marcus felt at a loose end. It had been bad enough before he had brought Alys back to London with him to begin the new painting. This was far worse. He wandered about his quiet house, depressed and restless, irritably refusing Mrs Mimms's offers of cups of tea and freshly baked scones. For all his brave words in the letter to Alys, about finding the new model fascinating, it wasn't wholly true. He realised now that no one could take her place. Mrs Mimms understood her employer far better than he believed she did and often felt like shaking the young man until some sense penetrated that thick skull.

He shouted at the new model, apologising a moment later then shouting again. His feelings for the new work he had started were negative. Only Alys could inspire him.

The model left in haughty silence and he turned the empty canvas to the wall and tried to forget it. He haunted the bleak, bare garden, the grass squelching under his boots after the intermittent rain they had been having, Rufus following glumly, leaving small, muddy paw prints behind on Mrs Mimms's newly scrubbed kitchen floor.

Everywhere he looked, Alys was there. He heard her laughter echoing through the cold misty air, her voice as she teased Rufus and then in the next breath fussed over him. He, who had always told himself he could live without a woman hanging on to his shirt tails, was missing her so badly it was like an actual physical ache.

He heard the housekeeper calling from the room Alys had used, 'Do you want me to put these books away, Mister Marcus?'

He climbed the stairs, coming to stand where Mrs Mimms hovered in the open doorway of the pretty bedroom. The bed was neatly made, with fresh sheets and pillowcases, as though at any moment Alys might step back into it. The pale coffee-coloured silk dressing gown he had insisted on buying her after she had admired it in the window of the big store in Knightbridge was draped in graceful folds over the back of the pink velvet-upholstered chair.

Alys had loved that dressing gown – peignoir, really, with its wide edging of deeper coloured lace at the neck and hem – and had ached with indecision over whether to pack it or leave it behind. Finally she left it where it was. Craven Bay and the O'Malley household was hardly the setting for a silk dressing gown.

Marcus gazed at the small pile of books Mrs Mimms indicated, standing beside the lamp on the bedside table. 'No, Mrs Mimms, leave them. I'll see to them.'

'Very good, sir.' She held out the string of amber beads she had found coiled on the dressing table. 'Careless young lady, sir. She left these behind.'

She gave him a fond look as he took them from her. With one last glance around the room, she went out, quietly closing the door behind her.

Dropping the beads into his pocket, Marcus went over to the bed. He picked up the top book from the pile, flicking its pages, noticing where she had left the linen bookmark. The novel was Hardy's *Tess of the D'Urbervilles*. There was a volume of poetry by Keats, and a heavy tome on philosophy. The last made him smile. Under the window, standing side by side, so neat and prim, were a small pair of mud-stained boots half concealed by the long velvet curtains. Apparently they had gone unnoticed by the usually scrupulous Mrs Mimms.

He bent and cradled them to his chest, heedless of the mud.

Would he ever understand women? Alys had seemed so happy here. Well, if not ecstatically so, at least contented. She had only to ask for something and it was hers. He'd spoiled her as one would a beloved child.

She had left him, seemingly on a whim, giving the impression that she couldn't bear to be close to him one minute longer. Ungrateful hussy! He could not deny the sexual attraction he had felt for the girl, right from the start. But love . . . ? Really, old man, you're losing your marbles, he told himself. Go out and have a drink. Better still, get drunk, and get everything back into perspective again.

And yet she was not a child nor a hussy, but a lovely young woman who one day would make an excellent and loving wife. His mother would have understood the expression that suddenly appeared on his face. Alys was interfering in his work, his whole life. It made him furious yet nothing seemed worthwhile without her nod of approval. Her 'Yes, I like that.'

Carefully, almost tenderly, he replaced the boots where he had found them and went downstairs. Passing the kitchen door, he called out, 'I'm just going out, Mrs Mimms. I won't be long.'

'Where shall I say you've gone, sir, if anyone inquires?'

'Oh, I have a few calls to make and then I'm going to my barber's.'

'Very good, sir.'

That evening, when he went to his club, the remarks made by his friends were caustic. 'Talk about Samson cutting off his hair! I can only assume it was a woman, old man, for who else would insist that you shaved off your beard.'

Marcus ignored them all. He didn't give a damn about their taunting remarks, merely smiled his cool smile and strode briskly through the high-ceilinged rooms and corridors until he found the quiet spot that he sought. He sat in a large leather chair, the brooding expression on his face warning others not to approach him. When an ancient club servant who had worked there most of his life gave a courtly little bow and inquired, 'Can I get you anything, sir?' Marcus grunted. Glancing at the empty glasses on the silver tray the man carried, he said, 'Can you drown trouble in one of those?'

The man gave a polite cough. 'I can boil trouble down into two classifications, sir.'

Marcus's lips quirked. 'And what are they?'

'Women and their mothers, sir.'

'Not her mother.'

'Well, then, sir, is the lady blonde or brunette?'

'Oh, brunette, and very beautiful.'

'Very well, sir, I will see what the bartender suggests.'

And Marcus, in spite of himself, had to smile when a few minutes later the man servant came back with a double whisky. As he placed it before Marcus, he said in a discreet manner, 'Hoping you won't take it the wrong way, sir, but the barman says to remember that it's always darkest before the dawn.'

Marcus downed the drink and then another, by that time agreeing that the barman was probably right.

February was usually a dismal month and this February was the worst she could remember. Alys felt the wintry cold nip her cheeks and ears as she walked along the street, felt the awful depression settle in her all over again. After the card at Christmas she'd not heard from Marcus again. Too busy with his *fascinating* new model to drop her a line, she thought resentfully. Her life was so empty and there seemed no hope for the future. And she was so damned lonely now that Mary had gone. How she missed her, missed the fun and secrets they had shared, the evenings before she had met Evan spent together at dances in the church hall.

She was grateful to, and would never, ever, be able to repay Mrs O'Malley for all the things she had done, offering Alys a home and the comfort of a warm and loving family. Something she could hardly remember. But, she was coming to discover, it wasn't enough. Her life lacked cohesion; the feeling of really belonging was not there.

Lost in her thoughts, her eyes cast down, she wandered absent-mindedly towards the headlands, deep in her memories of yesterday. So when a familiar voice called from behind her: 'Alys! Hey, Alys!' she was stunned into immobility.

Turning slowly, her breath coming fast, she saw Evan hurrying towards her along the path, a wide grin on his face. The deep suntan made him even more breathtakingly handsome, his fair hair seeming more golden in contrast.

He couldn't have chosen a more opportune moment to appear. Although Alys didn't know that at first . . .

She should be pleased to see him, should be over the moon that he was back and so obviously pleased to see her. But she wasn't. She felt anger stir within her, felt her face flame with hot resentment. As he came to a halt before her, reaching out to take her hands in his, his grin growing wider, she evaded his touch. Raising her own hands, now curled into fists, she struck out fiercely.

'You bastard, you! You're the very last person I expected to meet. Or wanted to. I suppose you've come to gloat, is that it? Well, let me tell you . . .'

He was shaking his head in bewilderment, his own hands raised almost playfully, warding off her blows. 'Hey, steady on, old girl! I haven't come to gloat. Of course I haven't. I wasn't to know you'd be walking this way. But I can't think of anything more auspicious, can you? Oh, Alys!' as a particularly hefty blow handed on his shoulder. 'Be reasonable. I want to talk.'

'Well, *I* don't!'

'Come on! We've got so much to talk about, don't let's waste time arguing.'

She snorted with derision. 'Oh, we've got something to talk about, all right. You went off and didn't tell me that you were going or for how long you'd be away. If you had thought anything at all of me, you could at least have told me that.'

'But I didn't know I was going, or for how long,' he argued. 'It all came as a shock. My father doesn't waste time once his mind is made up. There was nothing I could do.'

She shook her head disbelievingly. 'There was nothing you *wanted* to do. You didn't care. And that's God's own truth.'

'No,' he said, 'I'm sorry, but you've got it all wrong. Please, Alys, I swear I didn't know . . .'

'You can swear all you bloody well like,' she yelled, turning away so that he couldn't see her face or the hurt there. 'It won't make a scrap of difference.'

He stood back a step, shaking his head, genuine puzzlement on his face. 'I'll see you again when you've calmed down. We can talk then, I certainly hadn't imagined our first meeting after so long would be like this.' A smile twisted his lips.

The small chin tilted disdainfully. 'You can come back if you want to. I don't have to see you. As far as I'm concerned, you can go to hell and be damned.'

'Oh, Alys!' Again he shook his head. 'I can't believe you've changed so much. Before I went you were so sweet and soft and . . .'

'Aye.' She nodded her head. 'Soft's the word, all right. But a lot has happened since then and I've had to grow up quickly.' She stared into his face, remembering the day they met, the sunlit garden with the dogs straining at the leash. Remembered the time when first they'd kissed, the kitchen where they had made love. A hard knot of pain lay like a stone within her.

She could never tell him about the child and prayed he would never find out from anyone else. He moved forward and placed his hands on her shoulders. She tried to push him away but then she was in his arms and he was kissing her as though he would never stop.

'Alys, my sweet, sweet Alys! Why did I leave you? How could I have been so blind and stupid?'

His hands moved across her back, feeling the softness of her body under her coat. He had told her once he would never feel this way about anyone again, believing then that he meant it. When he had known he would have to return home because of his father's accident, he had reflected on his feelings about seeing Alys again. At the thought, trepidation mingled with excitement. Such was his arrogance it did not even occur to him that she might not want to see him. That she would have viewed his leaving her as desertion.

Still, he thought he knew her well enough to get round any ill feeling that might still be rankling with her . . .

And now here she was, safe in his arms, and despite Lavinia, despite everything, his feelings towards her were still strong. The things she had said about him not wanting, not caring, were untrue.

Suddenly she was pushing at his chest, her hands still bunched into tight fists. 'This isn't what I meant to happen,' she said brokenly. 'It's all wrong, Evan.'

'No, it's not. It's all *right*.' He tightened his grip, kissing her eyelids and her neck just below the ear, delighting in the tremor that went through her and which she couldn't hide. 'You love me, you know you do. How could there be anyone else for you, feeling the way you do?'

'I don't know. You're making me dizzy. Please go, Evan.' She took a deep, steadying breath and gazed at him pleadingly.

'Very well, if it means that much to you, I will. But make no mistake, I'll be back. And next time I won't take no for an answer.'

Idris Dixon wondered what was happening to him. One day he had been engaged to Clarissa, the next to Netta, with Clarissa sobbing and having hysterics all over the place. What was there about Netta that made him want to jump to her commands, like a great, pet poodle, hating it and yet at the same time unable to resist?'

'I'll die!' Clarissa had screamed, flinging herself on to the couch in her bedroom. She flung one white arm across her eyes in a dramatic gesture. 'I want to die! How can I face my friends and our relations after this? Oh, Mama,' beseechingly to the distressed woman who leaned over her, 'let me die.'

'My darling,' replied her mother, her voice barely audible above the sobbing, 'all these histrionics! They're in the worst possible taste, Clarissa, so please do try and pull yourself together.' The girl was taking this very badly, as well she might, but better she should find out the perfidious nature of the man she had been going to marry before the wedding than after it when the knowledge would have come too late.

'I hate her! I hate her!' Clarissa wailed, her hands tangling in her long hair as though in her anguish she would tear it out by the roots. 'She's spoiled everything. Idris and I were going to be so happy, and now *she's* taken him and I'm going to be an old maid . . .' And she threw out her arms as though in supplication to the embarrassed young man who stood by the door. To give Idris his due, he had broken the news himself to his unfortunate fiancée, and was now wishing he hadn't. He'd stood there, red-faced, fully aware of the distress his words had caused but unable to do anything about it. He mumbled things like 'better for everyone . . .' and 'a mistake – should never have asked you in the first place . . .' and 'seeing Netta again made me realise that I was still in love with her . . .' and 'I'd only have made you unhappy, Clarissa, and that I wouldn't want for the world . . .'

He finally escaped from the agonising scene with the vivid memory of a white-faced girl weeping copiously all over a pink velvet settee. Clarissa had shown no signs of taking her mother's advice and 'pulling herself together'. He wondered if he was lucky to have escaped from a wife prone to such violent hysterics.

Mrs Dean had advised postponing the ceremony until Mr Thomas was home from hospital and more himself again, but Netta would have none of it. 'My father can be taken to the church quite comfortably in a wheel-chair,' she declared firmly. 'And as I intend the wedding to be a quiet affair, with as little fuss as possible, it will not put too great a strain on him.'

Mrs Dean tried not to allow her feelings to show on her face. But, as Mary had been before her, she was obviously perplexed by the latest developments. Hesitantly, she tried again. 'Why don't you wait a while, Miss Netta? Until spring, say? May is a lovely month for weddings. Or June. You could be a June bride.'

Netta's own eyes very carefully hid what she was thinking which was: a very noticeably pregnant June bride if I am forced to wait that long! She gestured impatiently. 'My mind is made up, Mrs Dean. My brother has this morning instructed the vicar to commence calling the bans.'

Her mouth settled into a hard, straight line as spitefully she went on, 'Of course, Mrs Dean, if you feel that you are not up to organising such an event, I am sure other and more experienced staff can be found, even if we have to recruit from Swansea or even Cardiff. Perhaps,' and her gaze settled on the older woman speculatively, 'you feel you are getting too old for the job? After all, you have been with my father for a long time, haven't you? Maybe it would be better if we started to look elsewhere and you retired to that little place I've heard you talk about up north.'

Bitch! The word, outrageous as it was, sprang to the old cook's mind. Lowering her eyes submissively, she said, 'Very good, Miss Netta. You know you can rely on me. I'll see that everything goes smoothly. You won't have to worry about a thing.'

Beneath her breath, she muttered, 'And may the Good Lord have mercy on young Mr Idris, for no one else will.'

With the departure of Alys, something seemed to have gone from Mrs Mimms's life. As depressed as her master, Marcus caught her giving him belligerent looks, clearly blaming him for the girl's decision.

Excellent servant that she was, she would never say a word in recrimination although she muttered many a one under her breath. Mrs Mimms had been with him for a long time. Had, in fact, been a parlour maid at his parents' home until her marriage to Albert Mimms when she had followed her husband to London and then gladly accepted Marcus's offer of work in his house in the quiet London square.

She had expected that by now he would have married that nice Lady Joanna and settled down to a proper life with a wife and children, as befitted a man in his position. Until Alys had come along . . .

She sighed. For all the lazy, sometimes good-for-nothing ways of her Albert, she could read him like a book. Nothing he did surprised her. She sighed again. Maybe, in the long run, that was the best kind of man to have.

At times Marcus read in the paper about Joanna's exploits, smiling at the descriptions of the chaining of women to the railings outside number ten Downing Street, and the commotion when the police arrived to cut them loose. He hadn't seen Joanna since Alys went away, had been too preoccupied with his own thoughts. Too busy feeling sorry for himself, he chided himself. It was time he did something constructive, like persuading that model to come back so that he could start on a new portrait. She had walked out in a huff, but she would be over that by now and ready to earn a bit of money again.

It didn't work. He found himself comparing the scene he had chosen to the sands at Craven Bay, remembering the headlands yellow with gorse blossom and the wide golden beaches over which a girl with long black hair and eyes the colour of spring violets ran barefoot, shedding adulthood with her shoes and stockings.

With a muttered curse, and telling the girl she could have the rest of the day off, he strode from the house, calling impatiently for a hackney. Where he was going, the immaculate Hispano Suiza would cause too much speculation. Giving the driver an address in the East End, he sat back and tried to sort out what he would say to Joanna. He was no longer the young man who had painted the seventeen-year-old girl all those years ago, in love with the thought of love and not its realities.

The squalid streets through which they drove depressed Marcus even further, reminding him vividly of his own childhood in Craven Bay, watching with his father the marches of hungry children and unemployed miners. Here, in this city that was the centre of a great Empire, he saw again the filthy choked gutters, the pubs that seemed to stay forever open, small children sitting on the doorsteps, knees drawn up to their chins, waiting with a patience beyond their years for their parents to finish drinking and take them home.

In this part of London, people slept in deep doorways at night, huddled in newspapers or sacks to protect themselves from the weather. But in spite of the poverty, the public houses were open all day and did a roaring trade, for men would always find money to cheer themselves with a drink.

If the children were lucky and there was a penny to spare, a bottle of fizzy drink would be passed out to them. It would have to last them for as long as they sat there, until the darkness descended and the gas lamps threw their alarming shadows across the cracked pavements.

Lady Joanna Ambrey, it seemed, had deliberately chosen the very worst neighbourhood of the East End for her office. Her 'ladies' not only worked for the advancement of women's rights, but helped in any way they could the poor children of the district. Marcus had been there only once before, when Joanna had asked him to go with her to look at some empty property and give his opinion as to its suitability.

He had taken one look at the building and given an emphatic no. In his opinion it was entirely *unsuitable*.

'Do you walk around with your eyes closed?' he'd challenged harshly. 'Have you not noticed the kind of streets that surround this place? You'd be attacked or robbed or even worse, in no time. No, Joanna, I will not permit you to be so criminally reckless. And I'm quite sure your father will take the same view.'

She had pursed her lips, looked at him, then shrugged and gone blithely on with her own plans. 'I'm sorry, Marcus,' she had said, 'but this is something I simply must do. It's not a bit of good your telling me to stop and think again, not a bit of good running to Daddy, either. I intend to sign the lease just as soon as I can, and get my ladies organised.'

Smothering a strong desire to drag her bodily across the pavement and away from these mean streets, he knew it was futile to argue further. Joanna, once her mind was made up, was a force to be reckoned with. Instinctively she knew she had won the argument. Throwing her arms about his neck, she had given him a resounding kiss.

'Dear, *dear* Marcus! Remind me one day to tell you how much I love you.'

He hadn't been back to the office since that day, although he had seen blurry black and white photographs of it in the newspapers, the caption underneath invariably speculating derisively about the meetings that took place behind those dingy windows.

Joanna dismissed the newspaper stories with derision.

'Men always vilify things they don't understand,' she said. 'The women of the East End require more help than most of their sisters in the rest of the country, and where else should they come but here, right in the heart of their community? Would they rather we asked them to make the journey all the way up to Westminster, to consult us in the comfort of some grand hotel?'

Alighting from the hackney cab while still quite a distance from his destination, Marcus requested the driver to wait, saying he'd walk the rest of the way. Cabbies were loath to take their vehicles further into these narrow streets. The crowds frightened the horses and you had to have eyes in the back of your head in order to watch what those heathen scallywags of children were up to.

Joanna, although up to her eyes in work, as she put it, was pleased to see Marcus. One of those new contraptions, a typewriter, heavy and cumbersome, took pride of place on her large bare desk. She was struggling valiantly to change the ribbon, with the few ladies who were on duty blushing and giggling over her use of choice words and phrases normally heard only in a stable yard.

Lifting her eyes to look at Marcus as he entered, the first thing she said was: 'You don't know how to change one of these bloody things, I suppose?'

Marcus admitted ruefully that he didn't. 'Damn and blast!' she said in exasperation, running inky fingers through her hair. 'I give up. Somebody else is going to have to take on the monster.'

The next thing she said was: 'You've shaved your beard!'

Self-consciously he raised a hand to his cheek, his fingers tracing the pale line of the scar.

'It's an improvement,' she decided. 'Makes you look younger. And that scar is quite dashing. A pirate on the Spanish Main!'

There was a murmur of agreement from the other women in the room and one said, 'Why haven't we seen *him* before, Joanna? Trust you to keep hidden a handsome devil like that.'

'Ladies, ladies, you're making my gentleman caller blush!'

They laughed as she took Marcus's arm, urging him into a tiny room off the main office. 'We don't get many men visiting us here,' she explained teasingly. 'All this womanly activity without a fainting fit in sight goes to their heads, poor dears. Come on, let me make you a cup of coffee.'

With the kettle resting on the old gas ring, she asked, 'How is Alys? Why didn't you bring her along with you?'

'Alys is not here. She suddenly had some foolish notion that she was needed in Craven Bay.'

Joanna turned to give him a shrewd glance, recalling Alys's words about returning to the valleys. 'So she really did go! You must miss her.'

'The house is certainly quieter.' His mouth twisted sardonically. 'Even Simon doesn't come to visit any more. But that I can live with.'

Joanna came closer, standing on tiptoe to kiss his cheek. 'You poor thing!' A man as vital as Marcus wasn't meant to be lonely. Handing him a thick mug of coffee, she said, 'Why don't you take a trip down to see her? Give her my love and say we all miss her.'

Consulting the tiny gold watch that was pinned to her

tucked woollen blouse, she continued, 'Heavens, is it that time already? I'm going to have to be very rude and run, I'm afraid. After all this time, we've finally got the Prime Minister to agree to a meeting. Isn't is exciting? Everyone warns me that it will do no good, that I'm wasting my time, but I still have to do it. It is work I shall devote my life to.' She lifted a hand and her cool fingers pressed his cheek. 'There can never be anything quite so important, can there, as the compulsion that drives you on?'

Marcus's lips twisted. He knew about compulsion all right! The compulsion to paint the same girl over and over again, never tiring of looking at that pure, flower-like face, the cloud of midnight hair and those incredible eyes.

'Joanna, we must talk,' he began, and at that moment the door from the street opened and a young woman and a tall man came into the office. Joanna turned to greet them, a radiant smile on her face.

'Oh, it's Doris and her brother! Come on, Marcus,' tugging at his coat sleeve, 'I want you to meet them. Such genuine people. Doris is our new organising secretary and John helps with all kinds of things we poor weak women can't do for ourselves.' Catching his grin, she admitted, 'Oh, yes, there are some things we cannot do. Such as lifting heavy furniture and crates of secondhand clothing we collect for the children. Although they've only been with us for a short time, already they have proved invaluable, especially John. He also escorts our ladies through the street when it's dark and they've been working late. We all agree it is a great relief. Some of us have had some very distasteful experiences.'

Doris Lindsey was an exuberant young woman in her early twenties, with fluffy brown hair and piquant looks. She fluttered her eyelashes at Marcus and laughed a lot. John Lindsey, however, was just the opposite, with a calm demeanour and steady blue eyes that gazed at Marcus as though summing him up before deciding he would do. Marcus liked his firm handshake, and the genuine warmth in his eyes when he said hello.

He learned later that the Lindseys were a banking family, and very wealthy owing to a legacy left them by their grandmother.

He couldn't, he thought, have found a better man for Joanna if he had knitted him himself – one of Mrs Mimms's favourite sayings – for John looked strong and competent. Marcus was aware of the looks that passed between him and Joanna, and the way she edged closer to him as they talked.

Following Marcus on to the pavement where he excused himself, Joanna said on a hesitant note, her eyes lowered, 'Don't say anything if you *don't* like him, Marcus, but please, please *do* like him! I need your approval on this. It means so much to me.'

He smiled, seeing the flush suffuse her cheeks. 'You have it, you little imbecile! Believe me, I'm happy for you. He'll look after you.'

She opened her mouth and he stopped her with a raised hand. 'And don't tell me you don't need looking after. We all do, it's nature's way. Goodbye, my dear, and be happy.'

Chapter Twenty-Seven

'No.' Mary shook her head decisively. 'I'm sorry, but I won't admit to that.'

Her eyes, large and blue and very direct, met the angry ones of the man on the opposite side of the room, and for a moment she almost felt sorry for him as his face slowly turned beet red and the sparse fair brows drew together over pale eyes that seemed to dart shafts of pure malice.

In all his twenty years nobody but his mother had ever dared say no to Eric Doughty. Even his father side-stepped whenever an argument threatened with his son and heir. Nobody but this impertinent new trollop of a maidservant who had been in his mother's employ for barely five minutes.

'Won't!' he said in what was supposed to be an intimidating roar but ended up sounding more like a squeak. 'What do you mean, you won't do it? Of course you will. You'll do exactly as I tell you or you'll find yourself in such hot water you won't know how to get out of it. When my mother comes in you will explain how you fancied a drink, and finding the brandy left out on the table, and you chilled to the bone from shopping so early at the market for Cook, you helped yourself to a glass and ended up taking more than you meant to.'

'But I didn't . . .' began Mary.

He went on as if she hadn't spoken. 'You can say once you started you couldn't stop. Everyone knows how the Irish like their drink.' The pale eyes roamed Mary's face with its fluffed-out curls over her forehead, fair hair smooth in a neat chignon at the back of her head and on top a demure white muslin cap, crisply starched, with two long lace streamers floating down her back. They had never had a prettier maid or one who was so stubborn. 'Mother will believe you,' he added blandly. 'With that butter wouldn't melt in your mouth look, anyone would.'

Mary's cheeks flamed as he came forward, one hand going up to fondle her cheek. 'If you play your cards right, you'll be forgiven. And then perhaps, sharing one secret, we can begin sharing another . . .'

Mary stepped back smartly, avoiding his touch. She was so angry she was trembling. She was aware of the danger of the situation, but she was in the right and they both knew it. Why should she confess to something she hadn't done, just so he could remain the apple of his mother's eye?

More than once she had caught him helping himself from the cut-glass decanter of brandy in the study.

Jaysus! thought Mary. Why the blazes should she allow this lumbering youth to get away with it? And then, adding insult to injury, have to endure his doltish attempts at seduction?

Her smooth brow wrinkled. 'I think you've said enough, Mr Eric. I'd better get on with my work, if you don't mind. There's still plenty to do.'

She made to push past him and he heaved a gusty sigh.

'Acting like someone straight from a Sunday school meeting won't wash with me either,' he exclaimed. 'I know all about you. About your young man in prison. Robbery with violence, wasn't it? Well, you can bet *he* won't be among us for quite some time, if ever, ready to snuggle with you in some quiet dark corner.'

His voice changed, became placating, slightly cajoling. 'You want to get on in the world, don't you, Mary? The first time I saw you I thought to myself, now there goes an ambitious girl! Well, here's your chance. You just do as I say and I'll see you don't lose by it. I've got connections – important ones, through my father. You won't be sorry you tossed your future in with mine.'

She gave him the most brilliant smile she could manage and he, hearing victory bells ringing, moved closer to her, one greedy hand fumbling at the buttons of her bodice. At the same time Mary brought her knee up sharply, catching him between the legs, and as he gagged, doubling over, chopped down at the back of his neck with the straight palm of her hand, a form of defence her little brothers had delighted in teaching her.

She left him trying to scramble to his knees from the carpet, pulling himself up by the arm of the chair. Although her own knees were like rubber and her palms clammy with sweat, Mary felt a thrill of achievement. She had, she decided, put up with the Doughty family's blustering and uncertain temperament long enough, especially the young man's lies and continual attempts to catch her in a dark passageway. She had even made excuses for him! He was at an age when the blood runs high, and the girls of his own class were so strictly cloistered it was impossible even to talk to them on their own without dear Mama being present . . . But no more.

She ran up to the small bedroom high under the eaves which she shared with Nancy, the other parlour maid, and stood, palms pressed against her cheeks, gazing at herself in the spotted mirror on the dresser top. Mam had always said her temper would lead to her undoing one day.

Oh, well, it wasn't the end of the world! There must be plenty of jobs available in this large town. A different proposition to Craven Bay with its high unemployment. As long as she could stay close to Jackie, remain able to visit him for those precious few moments, anything would do.

She sighed, pulling open the drawers of the shabby dresser and lifting out her neatly folded and ironed things. It had been an experience, working for someone other than the Jenkins family. She had enjoyed the challenge, trying to fit in with new colleagues. At first the attentions of Eric Doughty, unwelcome as they were, were merely an irritation, something to giggle over in bed at night as she and her room mate gossiped about their day. But she knew that after that scene in the study, Mrs Doughty would be after her blood.

Later, she preferred to forget the strident remarks made by her employer when at last Mary was sent for. Smoothing her apron with her palms, glancing quickly in the mirror to make sure her cap was straight, she made her way with calm dignity to where Mrs Doughty waited in her sitting room. There she listened to the woman's lecture on ingratitude and spitefulness and how poor, dear Eric was so upset he couldn't even bring himself to talk about the events leading up to Mary's quite unprovoked attack. Questioned indifferently by his father, Eric claimed he had found Mary helping herself to the brandy in the study and, when he had remonstrated with her, the girl had assaulted him.

Mary, listening, opened her mouth to argue, realised the futility of it all and closed it again with a snap. She accepted the pittance owed her in wages without a word.

Mrs Doughty's tight lips drew even tighter. Ungrateful hussy! Let her see that without a reference it would be almost impossible to get another job.

Mary went back to the boarding house where she had stayed until starting to work for the Doughtys. After that, it was walking the streets in the damp and the rain, continually seeking work. The only offer she received was work as a barmaid serving behind the counter at The Bull and Boar. It wasn't to her liking and she knew Mam would disapprove but beggars couldn't be choosers.

Walking home late one night, not long after she began there, a man jumped her from the mouth of a dark alley-way. Before she had time to cry out, he'd seized her about the waist, dragging her backwards into the alley, releasing her for a moment as he began to fumble at his trousers.

Mary went white with fear and backed against the wall; the alley was so narrow it gave her little room for manoeuvre. She tried the defence used against Eric Doughty, but this assailant was a different matter.

'Just you try that again,' he snarled and brought his fist down heavily on her breast. She felt a piercing sensation and looked down in sudden terror. Blood was welling from a small wound.

'Like the next one in yer face, would you?' He raised

his hand again. There was a glint of steel in the dim light from the gas lamp at the far corner of the alleyway. Her heart felt as though it would leap from her breast.

If he wounded her, who could she turn to for help? If he murdered her, who would know or care?

He was tearing at the buttons of her coat, pulling it open, lifting her skirt. Her bleeding chest rose and fell and she took great gulps of the cold air, trying to regain her composure. The hand holding the razor seemed to relax a little and as a great rush of outrage took over from panic, she managed to gasp, making her voice soft and inviting, 'Hold on a minute. What's the rush? Why don't we get a little more comfortable?'

'Hmmm.' He gave a grunt. 'Where?'

The blade moved closer despite the slight relaxation of his hand. She drew a deep breath. 'Come on then.' She gritted her teeth and sidled away from him until she was free of his grasp. Then, hearing his shout, she whipped round and ran up the alleyway towards the welcome circle of light from the gas lamp, to the street where people hurried on their way home.

In a few moments she was panting along the uneven pavements, sobbing under her breath, hearing footsteps behind her and knowing he followed.

When the expected letter arrived, Marcus read it before the roaring fire in the sitting room, Rufus curled at his feet, luxuriating in the warmth from the blaze. The curtains were already drawn on the long windows, shutting out the bare and desolate view of the garden. The sky above the small square was grey and overcast, with rain clouds threatening.

Spring, as the newspapers forecast, would be a little late this year. It matched his mood. However, reading the letter he felt some of his depression lighten, for the news of Jackie Rees was good.

Using the name and position of his father as a former M.P., Marcus had written to the prison authorities, inquiring about one Jack or John Rees, presently being held in Cardiff Prison. Marcus explained that he was a friend of Jackie's family.

Although it was not strictly true, Marcus found it impossible to sit back and do nothing. Besides, he ached to see Alys again.

The reply to his letter came quickly. It stated that a man had come forward, confessing to his part in the pawnbroker's death. The trial was to be held in two weeks. Thoughtfully Marcus noted the time and the place.

There was nothing to keep him in London. Why didn't he take Joanna's advice and travel down to see Alys? The idea was comforting. He smiled at Mrs Mimms when she brought in his tray of tea, placing it on the small oval table beside him. The smile encouraged her to say, one eye on the open letter on his lap, 'From Miss Alys, is it, sir? How's she doin'?'

'No, Mrs Mimms, not from Alys, although I hope to be seeing that young lady fairly soon.'

She straightened her back, easing the tired muscles. 'I'm pleased to hear it, sir.'

'Yes, so what would you say to a couple of weeks off, Mrs Mimms? Fuss over your old man. He'd enjoy that. You're always telling me how he complains that he hardly ever sees you.'

'Well, sir, we're not exactly newly-weds, like, who can't abide to be parted from each other.' Mrs Mimms was tempted to add: 'And a couple o' weeks wi' 'im under me feet would drive me barmy.' But she said aloud, 'It would be nice for a change, though. Pity the weather is not better. I could go orf to me sister in Margate. 'aven't bin down there for ages.'

'Then as soon as the weather clears up, you shall go,' Marcus promised solemnly. 'And take as long as you like.'

Accompanied by Rufus, for Marcus didn't know how long he would be away, Mrs Mimms departed very grandly in a hansom cab, the orange cat glaring balefully from the large wicker-work basket she held on her lap. Marcus locked up the house in the square, and, his car safely garaged, took another cab to Paddington Station.

Alys gazed through the window at a day that was almost springlike after the heavy overnight downpour. Everything was silent except for the drip-drip of rain from the trees, the gurgle of water as it flowed along the gutters and down the drainpipe. The barrel Mr O'Malley kept for catching the overflow, to be used on the garden when drought threatened, spilled over the sides and flooded the small area of moss-covered paving beneath the kitchen window. Young Billy was standing, enjoying the sight, heeding, for once, his mother's warning not to get wet.

In the silence she could hear someone whistling cheerfully: 'Daisy, Daisy, give me your answer do . . .' and a moment later there was a sharp knock on the front door.

Mrs O'Malley was upstairs making the beds so Alys

called, 'It's all right, I'll get it.' She opened the front door and the smile died on her face when she saw who it was. She didn't even have time to pull herself together. He looked wonderful. Her eyes drank him in, the lean body, thick chestnut hair and shining eyes, the strong jaw . . .

Unconsciously, she put one hand to her mouth, stifling her exclamation of wonder. Marcus's neat beard had been almost a disguise. Without it, she could see how very handsome and young he was. She could not take her eyes off his face and stood in the open doorway, motionless, gaping at him.

'Hello!' she said at last, foolishly. Then: 'What are you doing here?'

He remained silent, just looking at her. 'Have you driven all the way from London?' she asked. 'You must be tired out.'

He looked beyond her into the dimness of the hallway at the sound of Mrs O'Malley's footsteps descending the stairs. 'It's too far to drive.' He smiled and her heart turned over. 'I came by train.'

'Oh, that's good.' The words sounded foolish even in her own ears. She felt breathless, as though she'd received a sudden blow in the stomach. Behind her, Mrs O'Malley inquired, 'Alys? Who is it?'

She turned, colour flooding her face. 'It's Mr Dillon. He's come down from London.'

'Well, ask him in, girl. Where's your manners? Don't leave him standing on the doorstep.'

Alys stood back in the open doorway. 'I'm sorry. Won't you come in? I've just made some tea. I'm sure you'd like a cup.'

In the narrow, dark hallway they were almost touching. Before she knew it she felt his hands on her shoulders. 'I can think of other things I'd rather have,' he answered softly. His eyes roamed over her face, committing to memory every detail. As though he needed to! he thought. 'I've missed you, Alys. I've missed you so much it hurt.'

Her eyes pricked with tears. 'I've missed – London, too,' she said, not able to bring herself to admit that it was him she missed and not smoky, noisy old London.

'Why did you leave?' he demanded, his voice suddenly harsh. 'It wasn't just Mary, was it? How dare you run away when I need you so badly?'

If it hadn't been for Mrs O'Malley lurking in the background he would have taken her in his arms and that would have been the end of her wavering. As it was, he gazed at her with a kind of hunger. 'Come with me to my hotel,' he muttered thickly. 'I've booked a room, we could be alone . . .'

She could feel his heart beating against her. From a distance there was a clattering of cups, and Mrs O'Malley's voice calling: 'Alys? Is that young man still out there? Won't he come in?'

She gave him a little push, palms flat against his chest. 'We'd better,' she smiled. 'Else she's going to get all sorts of ideas.'

Seated at the kitchen table, she introduced Marcus to Mrs O'Malley. The older woman was quickly charmed by his manner, and beamed approvingly.

Clearly curious, she asked about 'The Cockleshell Girl'. 'You must feel ever so proud,' she said to Alys. Then, to Marcus, 'Fancy being able to put a picture on canvas so good that everyone can see who it is.'

'I think I did her justice,' he admitted quietly.

There was the thunder of running feet outside the back door and a moment later it burst open and in spilled the two older O'Malley boys. As usual, their faces were dirty, their spiky hair standing on end. Mrs O'Malley had long ago given up trying to figure out how they achieved such a transformation from the neatly dressed morning pair, with their scrubbed shining faces and combed hair, to the young ragamuffins who stood before them now. Young Billy followed, unsteadily climbing over the high back-door step.

Her sons froze into an unnatural silence on seeing the stranger seated at the table taking tea with their mother and Alys, and Billy toddled to his mother to stand leaning against her knees. The boys stared at him, eyes narrowed suspiciously. But after Marcus's friendly smile and comradely greeting, they relaxed a little, though they still watched the way his eyes lingered on Alys.

They had come across her and Evan just the other day and watched from behind a rock, nudging each other and stifling their laughter as Evan took her in his arms and kissed her. 'Perhaps she's goin' to marry him!' said Kenny thoughtfully. 'Perhaps,' agreed his brother. Although they liked Alys, for in a way she took the place of their sister, they would be glad when the house belonged just to the family again.

Their mother was asking, 'And what have you two been up to? Left the house like bats out of hell, so you did. Won't you ever learn to stay tidy?'

'We try, but it's not easy.' Ten-year-old Dennis smiled at Alys. Then, out of the blue, he asked: 'Which one do you like best, Alys? This one or the one you were kissing the other day? That Evan Jenkins?'

Alys's cheeks flamed. At the same moment Mrs O'Malley gave a shocked exclamation and sprang to her feet, pushing both boys through the door and into the hall. Alys could hear a clatter of boots as they scampered before her upstairs, Dennis's voice raised in shrill protest. 'Well, it's true! We *did* see her and they *were* kissing . . .'

Silence closed over the warm kitchen. Marcus sat very still. The accusation in his eyes made Alys cringe inwardly.

'Well,' he said quietly, when she didn't speak. 'Is it true?'

'Is what true?' Alys stalled. She hardly knew how to answer. Marcus looked so forbidding that for the first time since she had met him she felt actual fear. He leaned over the table, taking her hands in a tight grip. 'You know bloody well what I mean. Have you been seeing that man again?'

She tilted her chin, stung by his tone. 'What if I have? It's none of your business. You don't own me.'

'Well, then,' he said, and again that pang of fear went through her. 'We know where we stand, don't we? I thought you, of all people, had more sense than to go crawling back after the way he treated you.'

She shook her head. 'You don't understand . . . We met quite by accident and he . . .'

'The trouble is, my girl, I understand better than you think I do.' His lip curled. 'I was right about you that first time. You want to get away from all this . . .' his glance raked the shabby if spotless kitchen '. . . and

Evan Jenkins is the means that will enable you to do it. Was Simon Rayne too difficult to land? Better than you have tried and failed, I can tell you! So as soon as you return home and find young Jenkins back and available, you go right ahead with your plans to become a rich man's wife.'

Tears rolled down her cheeks at the unfairness of his accusations. She fumbled for her handkerchief. 'Marcus, it wasn't like that at all. Please listen for a minute . . . I can explain . . .'

'Oh, I'm sure you can. It comes easy to you, doesn't it, explaining? Well, I don't want to hear.'

Releasing her hands he flung them from him and rose from his chair just as Mrs O'Malley came back into the room. Full of apologies for the behaviour of her sons, she took one look at their two faces, one white with anger, the other flushed and tearful, and decided in this case retreat was the best policy.

Muttering excuses she went into the yard where Alys could hear her moving about in the wash house, then water running and the clatter of the wash tub.

After Marcus had gone, Alys stumbled upstairs and closed the door of the bedroom that had belonged to Mary, as though shutting out the ugliness of what had happened. She sat on the bed, arms folded about her, shivering. When the tears had ceased to flow she went to the china bowl on the dresser and poured water from the matching jug, bathing her face and eyes. There's silly she was! Letting herself go to pieces like that. Marcus would realise his mistake and come back to listen to her explanation. Of course he would. But then, her old resentful feelings surfaced, why should she have to grovel to

Marcus, or, for that matter, any other man? Hadn't she learned anything from her short association with Joanna and her women's movement?

If he came back, all well and good; if he didn't, that she could also deal with.

Jackie had gone through that period of numbness and self-pity that follows sudden disaster and was now beginning to see the way ahead. There had besides been the regular visits from Mary, always so cheerful and refusing to let anything get her down, although he worried when she didn't turn up on the latest visitor's day. His hopes rose when a suddenly solicitous warder announced there was someone to see him.

When Marcus Dillon entered the tiny cell Jackie looked puzzled. Marcus explained who he was and how he had come to be associated with the case. 'My father's firm of solicitors has agreed to act for you in court,' he told the bemused Jackie. 'They're very good. I don't think you could find anyone better.'

'I don't understand.' Jackie stared at him in bewilderment. 'I don't even know why you are doing this for me.'

Marcus smiled. 'Never question Lady Luck. Accept all she offers with good grace and be thankful. Let's just say I once met your Mary and would like to help her. Also that I believe in a fair hearing for every man, and reading the report on you I don't believe you are guilty of anything but a foolish aberration.'

He gazed at Jackie thoughtfully, noting the forest of thick lashes that veiled his eyes; that look alone would capture the heart of many a woman. Thinking back to the report, he said, 'What on earth made you take that ring in the first place? You don't strike me as being the type of man who would take another's property.'

'Miss Netta wanted a ring . . .' It was as though a breached dam had burst. The words poured out in a flood until Jackie felt drained, felt clean and whole again, the bitter guilt that had been eating away at his soul expurgated. He understood at last how Mary must have felt after she had been to confession, although his own sweet girl couldn't ever have to confess so heavy and vile a sin as his. But he'd make it up to her. He swore on his father's grave he would make it up to her. He wiped his eyes on the back of his hand and looked at Marcus.

For this visit the warder had given them privacy, although Jackie could hear his footsteps pacing outside the cell door. 'Is Mary all right?' he asked. 'She didn't come last visiting time, last Sunday.'

Marcus frowned. 'I have no idea. Where is she now?'

Jackie gave him the address of the boarding house. 'She left her job,' he said, 'I'm not sure what she's doing now.'

Like her mother, Mary knew Jackie would view her working behind a bar with abhorrence and so had kept it to herself.

Leaving the grim prison building, Marcus went straight to the address Jackie had given him. He was met with cold hostility from a slovenly old woman who grunted at his request to see Mary and led him upstairs.

The greasy, uncarpeted boards creaked as they climbed higher and higher, until the woman leaned against the banister rail, panting, and pointed with a none-too-clean finger to indicate the last flight.

'Up there, she is. Can't go no further, me 'eart won't

take it. You'll 'ave to go the rest of the way yerself. Sir,' she added grudgingly, realising that this was a gentleman and not one of the scruffs who usually visited her boarders.

Marcus thanked her gravely and climbed into the evil-smelling gloom. One door faced him on the tiny landing. He knocked gently, listening for Mary's answer.

When none came he grasped the door handle and turned it slowly. Mary, dozing on the bed, heard it open and sat up quickly, visions of another attack springing to mind. She wondered how long it had been since Mrs Dean had stayed here. She wouldn't find it so clean and comfortable now!

Her sudden movement sent a shaft of hot pain through her body as the wound on her chest tightened. Wide-eyed she gazed at the door, her breath held then released in a gusty sigh when she saw Marcus. Even without the beard she recognised him.

'Marcus – Mr Dillon!'

He frowned, coming closer to the bed. 'Good God, girl! What happened to you? Have you been in an accident?'

Mary lowered herself back on the solitary pillow. 'I suppose you could say that. A man attacked me.'

She looked up into a face tight with anger as she told her story. 'I managed to get back to my room, and the landlady sent for a doctor. In spite of her appearance, she's not a bad old stick.' Fresh tears welled in her eyes and slid down her cheeks. 'I haven't been able to pay him, though. I don't know that I can . . .' She gulped. 'How did you find me?'

.'That's not for you to worry about,' he told her gently.

'Explanations later. Our main concern is to get you comfortable and in a safe place.'

His gaze took in the dingy bedroom with its strip of threadbare carpet and faded curtains. It was the gentleness in his voice that was her undoing. Still weak from loss of blood, Mary clutched at his hand and sobbed her heart out. 'Take me home, Marcus,' she moaned brokenly. 'I want my mother.'

Cautiously he lowered himself on to the edge of the bed and folded her in his arms, careful not to cause her pain, for he could see where the white edges of the bandage showed at the neckline of the shabby cardigan she wore over her nightgown.

'Of course I'll take you home, *cariad*.' He smiled down into her tear-streaked face. 'And what I have to tell you will cheer you up no end.' The news of Jackie would be better than any tonic.

To Marcus's chagrin his conscience was bothering him. He'd told Jackie that every man deserved a fair hearing, and yet he'd turned away from Alys without even giving her the chance to explain. He'd spent the last two nights sleepless with worry. As soon as he'd arrived back in Craven Bay with a pale but blissful Mary in tow, he had waved down one of the horse-drawn cabs that frequented the station yard and ordered the cabby to take them to the O'Malley residence.

Seated on the worn leather seat, his arm around Mary to minimise the jolting and swaying of the ancient cab, he said, 'Your mother's going to get the surprise of her life.'

Mary's eyes sparkled. She was almost her old self

again. 'Jaysus, she is that! Especially if she sees us arrive like this with your arm around me.'

They watched the familiar sights of the High Street go by: the chippies, closed until dinner time and then open for the rest of the evening; the pub, also closed; the steeply cobbled alleyway that led down to the quay. Here, Dan Radloff had staggered arm in arm with Lilith the night he was drowned. As though her thoughts had conjured up the woman, Mary saw her cross the square, hawking faded blooms in place of the old flower seller. 'Would you look at that!' she exclaimed in disbelief, 'Selling flowers is it, now? Trade must be bad.'

Marcus smiled at her shocked voice, remembering other things; the marches of hungry and desperate miners, flying stones and shattered shop windows. Here in this very street it had happened, the long, straggling lines of men winding over the cobblestones, their worn-out boots offering little protection from the swilling gutters. His father, shame-faced, muttering angrily beneath his breath . . .

Their arrival at the house was almost an anti-climax, for to his disappointment he heard that Alys had just gone out. It was obvious that Mrs O'Malley had been busy in the back garden. She opened the front door to their knock still wiping her hands on her apron. Pale with anxiety, she fussed over Mary and her rescuer, urging her daughter to a chair by the fire, to put her feet up on the old black leather stool, to have some beef broth she had simmering on the stove. Vastly enjoying all the fuss, Mary did as she was bid, really relaxing for the first time since leaving home. Marcus listened to the women talk, for Mr O'Malley was out, as usual, and the two older boys, for a change, at school. Billy, seated on the hearth rug where he'd been hastily deposited when his mother had had to answer the door, played with his collection of wooden toys, pausing just long enough to smile at his sister and Marcus.

Marcus longed to ask where Alys had gone and waited for a break in the conversation to do so. Mrs O'Malley gave a vague wave of her hand. 'Over to the headlands somewhere, I think.' She turned to Mary. 'And how is Jackie? You were able to get to see him, weren't you?'

Mary nodded. 'Yes, Mam, but not since I had this accident. But Marcus went to visit him just the other day and . . .' She smiled widely. 'Why don't we let him tell you all about it himself?'

Chapter Twenty-Eight

Earlier that morning it had suddenly come to Alys: the decision that she must speak to Evan. She was standing in her bedroom – or rather Mary's bedroom – brushing her hair into some semblance of order. Her face in the mirror looked pale and drawn, but there was nothing she could do about her lack of colour. She went downstairs and sought out Mrs O'Malley who, incongruous in a pair of her husband's boots, was in the small back garden, turning over forkfuls of moist black soil. If she waited for *him* to do it, Mrs O'Malley had decided, she would wait forever.

Alys asked if there was anything she could do to help, at which Mrs O'Malley shook her head.

'No, love, not really.' She rested on her fork, noting the shawl about the girl's shoulders. 'Goin' for a walk, are you?'

'Thought I might. The headlands look very inviting today.'

It was the first real day of spring. There was warmth in the sun and on the flat expanse of headlands wild flowers bloomed. Alys smiled at the older woman, warning her not to work too hard, then dropped a kiss on the top of Billy's fair head.

Mary's family were wonderful, but smothering. Mrs O'Malley still treated her like the little girl who had once come to visit Mary, and the boys sometimes drove her crazy with their teasing. But they *were* only boys and she hadn't been able to resist their wide, penitent gazes when they had come to her, begging forgiveness for what they had said in front of Mr Dillon.

'It's already forgotten,' Alys had assured them. But it wasn't. She wondered for the umpteenth time how you handled a man with the sort of pride Marcus Dillon had.

The path she took zig-zagged over the heath. On one side of her was a view of the quay and the old harbour wall, on the other the sea, deep and still, purple over the rocks and jade green over the sand. Buffeted by the gentle wind, she wondered if she was being wise, seeking out Evan like this. Wouldn't he take it as a sort of capitulation on her part? She wondered what sort of a reception she would get from Mrs Dean but to her surprise the elderly woman actually smiled and asked her in a pleasant voice to wait while she saw if Master Evan was in or not.

Minutes later there were footsteps and Evan appeared, throwing the door wide open with a crash, his face beaming.

'Alys!' There was a world of pleasure in his voice. Aware of Mrs Dean's sidelong glances, he took her by the elbow and guided her outside in the direction of the seat where in the past she had sat and gossiped with Mary.

Seated like this in the open, the wind from the sea was cooler than she'd expected and she pulled the shawl more closely about her. Was she cold or was it an unconscious defence against Evan and his blandishments?

She said the words she had prepared in her mind on that long walk over the headlands, and felt sad when she saw how his face immediately changed, becoming obstinate, his mouth set sulkily. His eyes gleamed dangerously as he mumbled, 'What are you trying to tell me, Alys? That you've found another man to take my place?'

She closed her eyes, not wanting to see the peevish look on his face; a little boy denied something he'd regarded as his own. 'Yes, Evan, I'm in love with someone else. I've changed a lot since I last saw you.'

'I don't believe you!' Roughly he tried to take her in his arms.

Alys drew away. 'It's no use . . .'

'I'll decide that. *I* know what's good for you, if you don't. We must talk about this.'

She shook her head. 'I haven't anything else to say, Evan, except that I'm sorry. I truly am.

'The way we felt about each other wouldn't have lasted,' she said slowly. 'Our feelings – mine, anyway – were too intense to be real. Nobody can go on feeling that way, morning, noon and night. That's not *true* love, Evan. It's infatuation, a kind of obsession, blinding you to real life.' She gazed into his eyes, willing him to understand and not to condemn her. 'We built our love up into something that didn't exist.'

She remembered Mary's words after she had received Evan's farewell note. 'Forbidden fruit is always the sweetest . . .'

That's what it had been: forbidden fruit.

Her commonsense fell on deaf ears. Tersely, he said, 'You say you've changed. Well, *I* haven't. I still love you. Give me time, Alys, and I'll make every effort to prove it.' He took her hands in his, leaning forward on the bench so that he could look into her eyes.

She sighed. 'Please don't make it any more difficult than it already is.' The air around them was heavy with spring, with the perfume of newly cut grass and daffodils growing by the hundred in the flower beds beyond the opening in the hedge. 'I'm sure you would have tried, tried hard, but we're different people now. It's nobody's fault. Maybe when we were getting to know each other, we were playing a part. We can't go back. Too much has happened in between. We're too different.'

His face crimson, he said, 'You're right there! We *are* different, and I have better things to do with my life than spend it begging for your favours.'

He turned away and she made to grasp his arm but he shook her off. 'Please, Evan,' she pleaded, hurt by his bitter words. She hadn't wanted it to end this way.

He rose to his feet and stood glaring down at her. 'This is goodbye, Alys. I won't see you again. Just don't come begging to me if your latest lover decides he's had enough and leaves you with egg on your face.'

She had thought him a fine man. Now, as she studied the narrowed eyes, the weak, handsome mouth, the fair hair brushed so dandyishly, catching the glint of the bright sun, she saw him at last for what he was. Take away his youth and good looks, and Evan's was an empty, insignificant personality.

She watched while he disappeared around the corner of the house with not even a backward glance, then with a sigh she began the long walk home.

The silence of the headlands was all-enveloping. Above her hung soaring, screaming gulls, white wings outstretched against the blue. She could see by the quayside newly arrived fishing boats. The scene was exactly the same as she remembered it. It was only herself that had changed. Faintly, on the still air, she could hear the voices of the fishermen as they hurled the catch up the quayside in baskets while the traders and the fisher girls bartered for their wares. As she had once done when the stretches of sand had yielded an inadequate catch.

Her thoughts were miles away. She started violently when she heard her name called and through a tangle of tear-wet eyelashes, splintering the bright day, saw a figure striding towards her.

She waited, standing quite still, her mouth suddenly dry, her hands trembling as they held the shawl about her shoulders.

'Mrs O'Malley said I might find you here,' said Marcus. 'Although instinct would have guided me in any case.'

She must not let him see how disturbed she was. Battling for composure, she answered coolly, 'So you're back again.'

He grimaced. 'Yes, I wanted to apologise for the things I said the other day. I had no right. You must have thought me crazy.'

She forced a smile. 'You've probably been working too hard. All those fascinating new models you wrote to me about! You know what it does to you when you work too hard. You should listen to Mrs Mimms and take more care of yourself.'

'Careful! You nearly said something nice then.' He stood looking down at her and she saw how his eyes crinkled with warmth and affection. 'That's what I've been missing – I had nobody to boss me about or tell me what to do. Mrs Mimms, bless her heart, does her best as you know, but it's not the same.' He gave her a long, steady look that turned her heart completely over, sending a bright tide of crimson to her cheeks.

'Alys, despite everything I never stopped thinking about you, and do you know what's really crazy? I found myself thinking, I could get really sentimental about that pest. With very little trouble, too. You know how your mind runs away with you at times?'

Alys sniffed. 'Oh, yes, it happens to me all the time. You just ignore it. Although sometimes it can be fun.'

'But not exactly fun where I'm involved?'

She looked away, viewing the scene through a shimmering haze. Would he notice if she wiped the tears from her eyes? It was taking every ounce of self-control she possessed to stand here, swapping platitudes with him, when all she really wanted was to throw herself into his arms and plead with him to hold her and never let her go.

But if this kind of foolish talk gave him satisfaction, then she could keep it up as long as he could. She felt him move a step closer and draw a deep breath, letting it out slowly when he said, 'Alys, Alys! Don't you know I only come alive when I'm arguing with you?'

She noticed the pale scar on his cheek. Somehow it

made him seem more vulnerable and she felt herself weaken. 'I can't be held responsible for your shortcomings, Marcus Dillon,' she said primly.

He gave a grunt of frustration. 'I mean,' he said tightly, 'look at us! Two proud, stubborn, headstrong people. One of us *has* to give way.'

His arms reached out and she tried to push him away, her face tight and fearful. But his mouth was on hers, as sweet and reviving as dew, and a long, unsettling tremor coursed through her body. The fear that he was just playing with her affections began to fade. This was the man she loved. With him she felt safe. Irritated, certainly, sometimes to the point of wanting to throw things, but never threatened.

Extraordinary sensations were crowding in on her. How warm his body was and how perfectly it moulded against hers . . .

'I love you,' he said softly. 'I think I fell in love with you the first time I saw you.'

She lifted her hand, touching the pale scar. 'No one would ever have guessed, least of all me. You didn't make it easy for me.'

'You didn't make it too easy for me, either. You treated me as though I was a conniving braggart, on your high horse all the time, not even giving me a chance to be friendly.'

'Well, you know how I enjoy playing games.'

'Don't I just! But I want you to promise me you won't play any more.'

Alys laughed. 'I promise.'

'I want you to make another promise, too. I want you to promise that you'll marry me.'

'Marcus, of course I will.' She stood on tiptoe to plant a kiss at the corner of his mouth. 'I love you very much, in spite of everything.'

'Let's go back,' he said softly. 'Not to my hotel room but to Mary's. I've got a surprise waiting for you.'

She felt him slip his arm about her waist as they began to walk back. This was the man for her, a safe refuge. Evan was in the past. Marcus was her future.